BLOODY DOMINIONS

BLOODY DOMINIONS

THE CONQUEST TRILOGY: 1

NICK MACKLIN

Matador
9 Priory Business Park,
Wistow Road, Kibworth Beauchamp,
Leicestershire. LE8 0RX
Tel: 0116 279 2299
Email: books@troubador.co.uk
Web: www.troubador.co.uk/matador
Twitter: @matadorbooks

ISBN 978 1800463 080

British Library Cataloguing in Publication Data.
A catalogue record for this book is available from the British Library.

Printed and bound in Great Britain by 4edge Limited
Typeset in 11pt Cambria by Troubador Publishing Ltd, Leicester, UK

Matador is an imprint of Troubador Publishing Ltd

In memory of those whose lives feature in this novel:
in recognition of the writers, academics and museum curators
who inspired my desire to put pen to paper;
and, in thanks to all those who supported me to do so.

CHARACTER LIST

Atticus Volteius Capito – Legionary in the newly established XIIth Legion. Serves in the Second century of the First cohort.

Decimus Aemillius Crassus – Legionary and signifier (standard bearer) for the Second century, First cohort, XIIth Legion.

Fortuna* – Goddess of fortune and the personification of luck in Roman religion.

Gaius Julius Caesar* – Roman general and statesman. Commander of the Roman army during the Gallic Wars 58–51 BC.

Gaius Trebonius* – Legate. Legion commander under Caesar during the Gallic Wars.

Gaius Volteius Capito – Atticus' father. Resident of Verona. Respected estate owner.

Garmanos – Auxiliary scout from the Remi tribe, allies of Rome.

Julius Valerius Naso – Legionary in the XIIth Legion. Serves in the Second century of the First cohort. Atticus' best friend. Enlisted with Atticus and member of his tent party.

Jupiter* – Roman god of sky and thunder. King of the gods in ancient Roman mythology. Typically represented carrying a thunderbolt and/or eagle.

Lucius Minucius Aquila – Legate and commander of the XIIth Legion, under Caesar.

Marcus Volteius Capito – Atticus' grandfather. Father of Gaius, named after Gaius Marius,* with whom Marcus served in Africa and again during the battles with the Cimbri and Teutones in 102/101 BC. First spear of legate, Claudius Marcellus.*

Maximus Antonius Syrus – Legionary in the XIIth Legion. Serves in the Second century of the First cohort. Friend of Atticus and member of his tent party.

Publius Sextius Baculus* – Veteran centurion. First spear of the XIIth Legion. Senior centurion of the legion and advisor to the legate.

Lucius Cornelius Plautius – Veteran centurion. Commands the Second century, First cohort, XIIth Legion. Good friend of Publius Sextius Baculus.

Titus Cassius Victor – Legionary in the XIIth Legion. Serves in the Second century of the First cohort. Friend of Atticus and tent party member. Has previous military experience.

Tullius Fabius Rescius – Veteran legionary and optio, Second century, First cohort, XIIth Legion. Plautius' second-in-command.

Publius Licinius Crassus* – Young legion/cavalry commander, under Caesar.

*

Albiorix – Son of Cimbri King Boiorix.* Adopted by Brogimarax when his father is killed at Vercellae, 101 BC. Succeeds Brogimarax as King of the Aduatuci, descendants and survivors of the Cimbri defeated by Gaius Marius in 101 BC.

Allerix – Son of Albiorix. Warrior and chieftain of the Aduatuci.

Allia – Youngest daughter of Ariovistus,* King of the Suebi.

Ambilo – Warrior of the Aduatuci and member of the Royal Guard.

Ariovistus* – King of the Suebi and other allied Germanic peoples, who entered Gaul to assist the Arverni and Sequani to defeat their rivals, the Aedui, before electing to occupy the conquered lands themselves.

Boduogenus – Nervian prince and warrior. Son of Boduognatus.

Boduognatus* – King of the Nervii, one of the most powerful Belgic tribes of northern Gaul at the time of the Gallic Wars. Belligerent and insular tribe, who shunned foreign trade and forbade themselves the use of alcohol and other luxuries, which they believed undermined a warrior's spirit. Eschewed cavalry and known to trek long distances to take part in battle.

Brogimarax – Warrior and chieftain who led the remnants of the Cimbri army back to northern Gaul, where they and their descendants settled as the Aduatuci.

Cabrus – Warrior of the Aduatuci, member of Royal Guard and friend of Allerix.

Cernos – King of the Ambiani, a sea-faring tribe of northern Gaul, famed for their trading and capacity to mint coins.

Correus* – King of the Bellovaci, a tribe from northern Gaul, one of the most powerful and warlike nations at the time of the Gallic Wars.

Cottabus – Warrior of the Aduatuci and member of the Royal Guard.

Egus* – Son of Abducillus,* King of the Allobroge, a powerful tribe of south-western Gaul, allied to Rome at the time of the Gallic Wars. Warrior who rode with Caesar throughout his campaign in Gaul.

Epomedius – Sworn hand of King Albiorix. Fearsome warrior and head of the Royal Guard.

Epona – Warrior and princess of the Aduatuci. Orphaned

daughter of Queen Olluna's sister, adopted and raised by Albiorix and Olluna.

Galba* – King of the Suessiones, powerful tribe of north-eastern Gaul. Elected commander of the Belgic tribal alliance that stood against Caesar at the start of the Gallic Wars.

Iccius* – King of the Remi, one of the most prominent of the Belgic tribes, prospered on the back of agricultural production and trade. Allied with Caesar throughout the Gallic Wars.

Magnus – Slave trader, from the Turones, a tribe of western Gaul. Allied to Rome at the commencement of the Gallic Wars.

Olluna – Queen of the Aduatuci, wife of Albiorix.

Roucillus* – Son of Abducillus,* King of the Allobroge. Warrior who, like his brother, rode with Caesar throughout his campaign in Gaul.

Senila – Healer. Epomedius' wife.

Taranis* – In Celtic mythology, Taranis is the god of thunder, typically represented holding a thunderbolt and "sacred" wheel.

Tascus – Smith and warrior of the Aduatuci.

Valis – Experienced warrior, member of the Royal Guard. Allerix's most trusted lieutenant.

*denotes real character or contemporary deity

Roman Army Structure

Gaul, 58 BC

Caesar marched into Gaul with four legions and had two more (the XIth and XIIth) recruited shortly after his arrival. Each legion was commanded by a legate, who was supported by a number of staff officers or tribunes and a senior soldier, the camp prefect, who was responsible for the organisation of the legion, its buildings (or camp), equipment and legionary training. A legion was made up of ten cohorts, each comprising six centuries of eighty men. Each of the centuries was commanded by a centurion, supported by a second in command called an optio (literal translation, chosen man). The legion's most senior centurion, referred to as the primus pilus, or first spear commanded the First century of the First cohort.

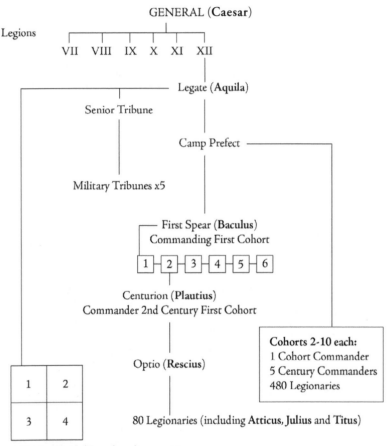

GENERAL (**Caesar**)

Legions

VII   VIII   IX   X   XI   XII

Legate (**Aquila**)

Senior Tribune

Camp Prefect

Military Tribunes x5

First Spear (**Baculus**)
Commanding First Cohort

| 1 | 2 | 3 | 4 | 5 | 6 |

Centurion (**Plautius**)
Commander 2nd Century First Cohort

Cohorts 2-10 each:
1 Cohort Commander
5 Century Commanders
480 Legionaries

Optio (**Rescius**)

| 1 | 2 |
| 3 | 4 |

80 Legionaries (including **Atticus, Julius** and **Titus**)

4 Cavalry Units (Squadrons) comprising:
1 Decurion (Squadron Leader)
30 Mounted Legionaries

1

Vosges Valley

Atticus was relieved to see the Germans retreating back across the plain as he made his way towards the wall. With their chance of taking the camp gone and losses mounting, it seemed that the enemy leaders had seen enough. The battle was over. He dragged his bloodied hand across his brow and stepped into the sun, still bathing the wall with light as it began to dip slowly below the horizon. Feeling cold and faint, he shivered and paused to allow the gentle warmth to wash over him. With a weary sigh, he rejoined his comrades, giving Allerix a smile as he slid into line beside him. The Gaul nodded and clapped Atticus on the back.

"It is good to see you, my friend. I don't think my men will ever grow accustomed to fighting on foot but they will have a tale to tell tonight."

"I should like to hear those," said Atticus, although he was beginning to feel a little unsteady on his feet. He put down the borrowed German shield and took hold of the palisade for support.

Allerix gave him a gentle nudge.

1

"I see you have adopted a less Roman look. We may make a Gaul of you yet."

"He will be staying in the legion!" said Plautius as the centurion joined them on the wall.

Vaguely aware of the two men talking, Atticus was finding it increasingly difficult to concentrate on what was being said. His head was swimming and his breathing suddenly felt very laboured. He grasped the palisade a little tighter as his legs began to weaken beneath him. Plautius flashed him a look of concern and took hold of his shoulder.

"You okay, lad? I'm trying to thank you for what you did today but you seem miles away."

Atticus looked plaintively at Plautius and down to the hand he had drawn across his wound. The blood felt warm as it trickled between his cold fingers. His legs buckled. He felt someone reach out to catch him and he could hear the concerned voices of Julius and Titus, but they seemed so very far away. His vision began to fade. Was this it? Was this how it ended? It couldn't be. He needed to see his father again, to discover the truth and right the wrongs of his departure. He fumbled for his pendant. For the second time that day, his world went dark.

*

2

SEVERAL DAYS LATER

SEPTEMBER, 58 BC

Sequani Territory

The orderly paused as he passed Atticus' bed. Reaching down to feel his forehead, he beckoned over his older comrade.

"The fever is taking hold. I'm not sure he's going to survive the journey back to Vesontio."

The second orderly shrugged.

"He's one of the younger and fitter ones. He might pull through, though I wouldn't bet on it."

"Are you sure? I hear fresh bottles of the Mulsum wine have arrived…"

The older man rolled his eyes.

"Go on then… I'll try and cool him down. You fetch the surgeon."

Atticus stirred as the orderly mopped his brow.

Why am I so hot and why can't I get up?
Everything hurts.
I feel so tired…

*

As the last of the stretchers was removed from the wagon and set down in the corner of the tent, the orderly sighed. It was going to be a busy night. The journey was nearly done; they would be back in Vesontio tomorrow night but it was taking its toll on the wounded. They'd lost several men during the course of the day and he doubted if some of the others would make it through the night. He snapped to attention as the camp surgeon ducked into the tent.

"Is this him?"

The orderly nodded.

"Yes. His fever has taken hold and we thought you'd want to look at the wound again."

The surgeon lifted the bandage beneath Atticus' arm and shook his head.

"That will need dressing again, and fetch me some willow. If the fever doesn't break, we're going to lose him. And soon."

Atticus tossed restlessly.

I feel so weak. Pain everywhere. Where am I?
Grandfather, is that you? It's me, Atticus.
He looks younger than I remember… and who is that sparring with him…? It's Maximus! Maximus, I'm sorry I couldn't save you.

The orderly took the old dressing from the surgeon and passed him the willow.

"Do you think he's reliving the battle?"

The surgeon shrugged.

"I've no idea but it looks like something is troubling him."

Is that home?
It is. That's the courtyard and those were the decorations for my birthday feast.
And there's Father. But he looks sad.
I'm sorry, Father. I never meant to hurt you. I was angry and scared.

The surgeon paused as he turned to leave.

"Give him some opium too. It might help him to sleep more peacefully."

Sleep. Yes… sleep…
No, stay awake. Fight it.
Can't focus. I'm so tired.
But I don't want to remember…

Atticus opened the door and greeted Julius with a smile.

His friend looked surprised.

"Don't you have servants for this kind of thing?"

"I just needed to get out of the house for a while. Let's walk."

Julius gave him a pained look.

"Okay, but not far from the path. Keeping this bloody toga clean on the way over was a nightmare. I know we're celebrating your birthday but honestly, white robes! What is it with you Equestrians?"

Atticus pulled up his own toga and quietly closed the door behind him.

"Well, I do appreciate the effort. It's good to have you here. And I've got to admit you've scrubbed up better than I thought, though I suspect that owes more to the presence of female company than it does to honouring me!"

Julius laughed.

"Knowing the types who attend your father's social gatherings, I suspect the presence of eligible woman will be distinctly limited. That pleasure will have to wait until later. Back at the tavern!"

Atticus gave his friend a gentle push.

"I assume you mean easy, not eligible?"

"I think all women weaken at the sight of soldiers from the legion, my friend."

Atticus shook his head.

"Well, that's as may be, though I prefer those that are slightly harder to get, myself. And in case you've forgotten, we haven't actually done any soldiering yet."

"True. But we march tomorrow and that's got to count for something. I suggest that tonight we make the most of any feelings of civic pride the ladies of Verona might have for their brave military. In the meantime, why are we out here, when there's food, wine and hopefully warmth to be had inside?"

Atticus turned to his friend with a frown.

"It's Father. I know these family occasions always make him think about Mother, but he was even more emotional than usual this morning when we made the sacrifice at the shrine. He's agitated and hardly seems able to look me in the eye. That's when he isn't hiding in his study. It's all very strange."

"Maybe he's just worried about your going away. It's all anybody can talk about in the tavern. That and the mayor's plan to regulate all the drinking establishments in town, of course. It's bound to affect him. You're his only family and here you are about to march off to war."

"Perhaps, but I thought he'd made peace with that when I enlisted, although I know he'd rather have seen me 'settle down' and follow him running the estate. Can you imagine?"

Julius laughed.

"No. Not really. I know you're smart enough, all those personal tutors, you bloody well should be. Even if you did have a habit of 'forgetting' when they were scheduled. I never knew you to miss a lesson with your grandfather or Severus, though. I always assumed you'd end up in the legions. I just didn't know I'd end up getting dragged along with you."

Atticus smiled.

"As I recall, you were quite happy to get away. What was her name? Flavia? Though I'm guessing it was her brother you really wanted to escape?"

Julius shuddered.

"Yes, Tertius. Big brute. He and his friends had a very different view about my suitability for his sister than she did."

"Do you regret it? Enlisting, I mean, not Flavia."

"No, although there were times when I wondered if I'd make it through training. Fuck, I still have aches in places I didn't know I had, though I think Tertius might be surprised if he tried it on again now."

He paused.

"I feel part of something too. Does that make any sense?"

Atticus nodded.

"It does. I feel it too. So did Grandfather. I had to pester him for tales about the battles. Camp life and camaraderie on the other hand… those he talked about endlessly. I still don't know why he left Rome and the legion to come to Verona when he did. He never wanted to talk much about that last campaign against the Cimbri and the Teutones. Or what happened afterwards. But I know he missed it, even after all those years. It was his stories that inspired me to sign up."

Julius smiled.

"His willingness to teach you how to fight didn't go amiss either."

"He didn't want to, not initially. Father didn't approve. But when I kept getting into trouble… Grandfather persuaded him it would be a good way to channel my 'restless spirit'. It worked too. I was never happier than when he and I were sparring."

Julius laughed.

"Or practising at my expense."

"It gave you a head start too, brother."

"That's true. Especially the tips from Severus. Nothing like training with an ex-legionary to set you up. Even better, one who's happy to share things you wouldn't find in the training manual."

"He earned his money. Grandfather made sure of that, especially after he realised I was determined to volunteer. Time may have been catching up with him, but he was always there to supervise and offer advice. And not just to me. Though Severus took it well…"

"Once a first spear, always a first spear, I suppose. I'm sure he would be very proud of you."

Atticus smiled.

"Thank you."

"I'm sure your father is too. Even if he is having trouble telling you for some reason. But we'll never know, wandering around out here in the damp, will we?"

"Okay, okay. Let's get inside."

As the two friends approached the house, Atticus tugged Julius' sleeve to slow his progress.

"Before we go in, I should probably warn you that the mayor and Flavia's father will be amongst the guests tonight."

Julius looked to the heavens.

"Of course, I should have guessed! And you think you've got problems."

*

Atticus took another sip of wine. It wasn't the Falerian; that was doubtless locked up somewhere for more intimate gatherings, but it was still good. Probably some of the local Rhaeticum sourced from Flavia's father, who would be especially pleased about how freely it had been flowing. It had certainly helped keep things convivial and all seemed to have gone well. Even Julius had managed to stay out of trouble and if it was true that an army marched on its stomach, he imagined his comrades in the XIIth could have travelled some distance on the volume of food available. Nicia and the others in the kitchen had done them proud. Now that the formal feast was over, however, guests were beginning to mingle around the courtyard, doubtless as grateful as he was to stretch their legs. Grateful too for the columned portico that surrounded the courtyard and helped keep the drizzle at bay. The torches lining the walls offered a degree of warmth and quickly became natural focal points around which the guests could cluster as they were entertained by the musicians and storytellers, now busy plying their trades. He watched with a wry smile. He was very grateful to his father, who had clearly put a considerable amount of time and money into the organisation of tonight's celebration. But formal social occasions had always made him feel uncomfortable and this was no exception. If anything, being the focus of attention only served to make matters worse. He had spent much of the evening edging as far to the periphery of events as etiquette would permit and if he hadn't been the host, he might have absented himself some time ago. As his father seemed to have done. He sighed. That was at least consistent with his behaviour over the last few days. Tonight, however, he would be missed, and this time Atticus was going to find him. He passed his drink to one of the servants and hurried across the courtyard. The surface of the pond seemed to dance as the drizzle fell lightly but relentlessly on the uncovered open space, and he was grateful to reach the other side of the house.

Picking his way through the steady flow of servants still heading in and out of the busy kitchen, he passed quickly by the domestic quarters and storerooms and headed for the atrium. Usually the focal point of the house, tonight it was quiet. Eerily so. A sense compounded by the shadows cast haphazardly about the walls by the flickering torches lighting the way. He paused as he approached the annexe housing the family shrine. He'd been very young when his mother died. Taken to the gods all too early by illness. With no siblings and his father throwing himself ever deeper into the management of the estate as he struggled to cope with her loss, his grandfather had been the one constant factor in his childhood. It had been almost two years since his death and he still missed him terribly. He wished he could have been there to see him return home after his training. A proud member of the new XIIth Legion. He reached inside the folds of his toga to find the pendant his father had given him earlier that night. It was an odd thing. Jupiter, he had always supposed, although he had never seen him presented in quite this way. It had apparently been his grandfather's dying wish that his father pass it to Atticus should he join the legions. Something about "gods on all sides"? He wasn't sure… His father hadn't explained and now he had disappeared. Again. Something was clearly troubling him. He had orchestrated the festivities well enough, observing all the necessary social niceties, but he had done so with little of the flair and enthusiasm with which he was usually associated. Even his toast had seemed subdued. His oratory missing the spark with which his father could normally be relied upon. He offered a silent prayer to the gods of the house and headed across the atrium to his father's study. A shaft of light stretched across the mosaic floor. The door was ajar. He reached for the handle.

"Well, Gaius, your father was adamant the boy should know once he reached eighteen."

Atticus froze. He recognised the voice. It was Quintus Tullis

Rufus, one of the town's magistrates and a long-time friend of his father. What was it that he was supposed to know and why was his father discussing it with Quintus? Should he go in? No. He didn't want to interrupt their conversation. Not now. He slid into the dark and pressed himself tightly against the wall.

"I know, Quintus, but Father didn't foresee him heading off to war the moment he reached eighteen. I can't tell him now."

"It might be more important now than ever. Don't you think?"

"That's easy for you to say. I fear when he discovers the truth it will change everything."

"It was a bigger issue for you, and you adjusted well enough."

Hardly daring to breathe, Atticus heard his father sigh.

"I had to and it wasn't easy. How could it be? I had been living a lie. My life was so very different than it might have been. But with time, I made peace with that. I accepted my changed destiny. My life has had its share of anguish, as you know, but have I not also been blessed? I have enjoyed a comfortable lifestyle, married the woman I loved and most of all have a son of whom I am very proud, although the gods know, with everything going on, I haven't been able to find a way to tell him. But he is young and he has no time. You hear the rumours. When he marches, it will be to war."

"Maybe he has the right to choose whether he marches at all."

"Perhaps. But it's all I've ever known him want to do, despite my best efforts to have him take an interest in running the estate. And you've seen him tonight. Joining the legion has been the making of him. It's exactly how Father said it would be. I fear this news will tarnish Atticus' fond memories of him and place doubt in his mind about the wisdom of joining up at all."

"Maybe that is for the best, my friend. Now that we know where the legions are headed. He is a fine young man, Gaius; he will make a good life outside of the army, if that is the path he must choose."

"Thank you, my friend. You are right, of course. I must tell him. But it can wait until morning. Then he must learn of our secret and make of it what he will."

Hands pressed ever tighter against the wall, Atticus was struggling to make sense of what he had heard. His father's words of pride had lifted his heart but his mind was reeling. What could possibly cause him to think less of the man he idolised? How could anything make him regret joining the legion? It was the first time he'd ever felt like he truly belonged. His heart was racing and feelings of anxiety and fear were threatening to overwhelm him. He didn't care what it was. He wouldn't let anything blemish the memories of his grandfather or threaten his place in the legion. He didn't want to know. He would leave. Now.

Atticus hurried back across the atrium. He had to find Julius. He had to get away. Wholly unconcerned with his role as dutiful host, he left a trail of startled guests in his wake as he waved away all attempts at conversation and pushed quickly through the courtyard. Pausing for a moment, he spotted his friend on the edge of the feasting room. Evidently, Julius had not yet satisfied his appetite for food or the company of the younger slave girls, one of whom was busy trying to clean up. Atticus hurried over. Julius looked surprised at his sudden arrival.

"What's up, brother? You look like you've seen a ghost."

"I'll explain later… right now I need to be somewhere else!"

"You want to leave your own party? And go where?"

"Anywhere but here. Preferably somewhere I can get a drink."

"Well, funnily enough, I know just the place. If you're sure?"

"I am. Let's go."

Julius put down his wine and stepped towards the atrium.

"No, not that way. We'll use the door at the back. It's quicker."

"You're not going to say goodbye?"

Atticus shook his head.

"No, I'm not."

Julius shrugged.

"Whatever you say, brother."

Atticus led Julius across the garden, cursing the seemingly endless drizzle which appeared destined to provide a fitting backdrop for this unsettling day. They ducked back under the portico, heading for the corner and a narrow, unlit passageway leading to the back of the house. They were about to disappear into the night when Atticus heard his father.

"Atticus. Wait, my son. Wait!"

He paused and glanced to his right. His father was hurrying towards him with as much dignity as he could muster in his ceremonial toga. He'd come this way precisely to try and escape without seeing his father. He had time; they could still make it. He sighed and his shoulders dropped as he waited for his father to arrive. He smiled hesitantly at Atticus as he approached.

"You're leaving?" he asked with a note of concern in his voice.

Atticus fought to control his anger and hurt.

"Yes," he replied curtly.

"Is something wrong? Where will you go?"

"I'm fine. I promised Julius' parents that I would get him home tonight so that he can spend some time with them before we leave."

He hoped his father hadn't seen the quizzical look that flashed across Julius' face.

"I see, I see. That does seem reasonable. Then you must go and do your duty to get him home. I will explain your absence. You will return later? I would like to speak with you in the morning."

Atticus clenched his fists behind his back. He'd heard enough and had absolutely no desire to hear whatever else it was that his father had to say. He wanted to tell him not to bother but at that moment, he just wanted to get away.

"Yes, I will return."

"Good. Then I won't detain you any longer. Enjoy the… offerings… at the tavern, and be careful."

He nodded to Julius.

"Give my regards to your parents. Goodnight, son."

Atticus turned away. He didn't want his father to see the tears beginning to well in his eyes.

"Goodbye, Father."

Dragging Julius by the arm, he marched off into the dark.

*

The orderly smiled as Atticus stirred and kicked off his blanket. He gave his friend a nudge.

"Well, he's still with us. The lad's a fighter if nothing else."

"Lucky too. But he's not out of the woods yet!"

"No. I'll get him some more opium. He needs to rest."

Rest. Yes, rest.
My head is so sore. I feel so weak.
And why is Julius wearing robes…?

Julius couldn't hide his surprise.

"You lied to your father?"

Atticus nodded, a look of grim determination on his face.

"Yes. I told you what I heard. I don't want to go back."

He hung his head.

"I can't go back. This is my life. I've made my choice. There is nothing left to say."

Julius filled the empty beakers in front of them with wine from the simple terracotta jug he'd collected as they arrived, and offered one to Atticus.

"If you're sure, brother?"

"I am."

"Then let's drink. To us and the Thunderbolt XIIth, '*et nobis legio duodecima fulminate*'!"

Atticus screwed up his face as the acidic tang of the wine hit the back of his throat.

Julius smiled.

"Something wrong, brother? Not quite the same vintage as earlier?"

Atticus laughed.

"Not quite but I suspect it grows on you."

Julius topped up his beaker.

"It does. If you drink enough. Which is always good for business."

And business was good, if tonight was anything to go by. The place was positively heaving. All of the small wooden tables dotted about the irregular-shaped room were occupied, and people clustered about the bar and the large open fireplace. The press of people made the servants' job of negotiating the journey from kitchen to table even more perilous than usual, in more ways than one. He smiled as one of the girls gave a sharp slap to a customer who had tried to get a little too familiar with her as she passed. His friends roared with laughter. The practised manner in which she landed the blow suggested she had seen it all before. He watched her weaving a path through the eclectic mix of people. Slaves, freedmen, ex-soldiers, traders and, judging by their attire, even one or two foreign visitors. They were all there. As were the other regular visitors, the local prostitutes. Busy negotiating the same journey as the servants but far less concerned about the clientele getting their hands on them, providing the price was right, of course. They would do well tonight – if any of the customers could be persuaded to venture away from the gaming tables. Despite the mayor's repeated, and seemingly wholly ineffective, attempts to ban such pursuits, gambling was very much alive and well here. As if pouring scorn on the mayor's failed attempts, the tavern even had a huge wall painting showing groups of people playing dice. Alongside a variety of other frescos, all depicting mythological scenes, considerably more graphic than he remembered from the stories he'd been told. And under the ever-watchful but unnoticed gaze of the painted characters, the motley and largely happy clientele went about their business.

"It's a different class of gathering altogether, isn't it?" said Julius with a smile.

Atticus nodded and raised his beaker.

"It is. But no less convivial for it."

Julius pulled a face and gestured to their robes.

"Of course, we might feel more relaxed if we weren't stuck out like a couple of vestals at a brothel."

Atticus had almost forgotten. He realised it was the first time that evening he'd actually felt comfortable, despite Julius' protestations about their attire. He liked it here, the informality a pleasant contrast to the more structured way of life at home. Julius' parents had always made him feel welcome, even if that sometimes meant being put to work in the kitchens, for which he knew they would be rewarded with food and drink of their own.

"What are you smiling at?" asked Julius.

"Just thinking about food," Atticus replied.

"Well, that's fortunate," said Julius, gesturing to the tray of stew, flatbread and olives that his mother was about to set down on the table.

"Although that's a whole different class of fare to what we had earlier too."

He ducked as his mother swung a slap in his direction.

"Cheeky beggar. Don't think just because you've gone and got yourself in the army that you're too big for a slap from your mother!"

Atticus smiled and helped himself to a piece of the flatbread, dunking it eagerly in the steaming bowl of stew.

Julius raised his eyebrows.

"You're surely not still hungry?"

Atticus took a big bite of the bread and savoured the warm and pleasant flavour. Rabbit. It was good.

"I'm famished, brother. I hardly ate a thing."

*

The surgeon raised his eyes as Atticus' stretcher was carried past.

"Well, he survived the journey. Which is more than I expected. Get him settled in the corner. I'll look him over again later."

Where am I? So many beds.
Hospital? Why am I in hospital?
Am I injured? Try to remember.
Can't keep awake…

*

The orderly clapped his friend on the back.

"Seems like our patient here is going to make it. Looks like I'll be collecting that wineskin after all…"

Are they talking to me?
What are they saying?

"He's trying to talk."

"What's that, lad? Okay? Yes, it looks like you're going to be okay. Home? No, you're not home. Unless you're Sequani. You're back in Vesontio. We brought the wounded back here after the battle with Ariovistus."

The battle. I remember. The Germans broke through.
Fighting to hold the camp.
Why do I feel so stiff? Stretch.
Argh… Fuck, what is that pain in my chest?
Is that a bandage?
I was… stabbed. Shit, that hurts.

The orderly mopped Atticus' brow and raised a beaker to his lips.
"Now stay still and drink this."
He gave Atticus a smile.
"I owe you a proper drink when you get out of here but for now you still need to rest."
Atticus swallowed the contents of the beaker and closed his eyes.

Rest…

*

Atticus rubbed his eyes and slowly hauled himself up onto his elbows. He gratefully took another drink from the orderly. He tried to look around but that made him feel dizzy and he slumped back onto the bed. Everything hurt, especially his chest. He stretched his head to look at the bandage. It looked clean, which was good. It didn't seem to smell either, which was more than could be said for the rest of him. He was in desperate need of a visit to the bathhouse, that much was clear, though he doubted anybody would notice amongst the heady mix of smells threatening to overwhelm his senses. He closed his eyes and tried to shut out some of the noise. He was exhausted and… hungry. No. He was ravenous. He had no idea why but right now he would kill for a bowl of rabbit stew.

*

Pulling up his legs to make room for Julius and Titus at the end of his bed, Atticus greeted his friends with a smile. It had been several days since his fever had broken and he was slowly beginning to feel brighter, though frustratingly not strong enough for the surgeon to consider letting him leave the hospital. He was bored and had been hoping his friends would be able to find some time to pay him a visit.

"It's good to see you."

Titus smiled.

"You too, brother."

Julius helped himself to some of the bread and cheese left on the plate Atticus had discarded as they arrived and made themselves comfortable.

"I was beginning to worry we wouldn't see you again this side of the Styx."

Atticus gave him a kick.

"And now you're confident enough to steal the food off my plate?"

"What? You don't need it. Living the life of luxury whilst we march for days and then have to build the biggest camp any of us have ever seen."

Atticus smiled.

"Then you won't be pleased to learn that I'll be on light duties and double rations for a while after I leave here."

"Lucky bastard," spluttered Titus.

"Lucky? He nearly died, you big ox," Julius replied, giving his comrade a shove.

Titus looked suitably chastised.

"You're okay now, though, yes?"

Atticus nodded.

"I'm still sore and the stitches smart like buggery whenever I move, but they say I'll get used to that."

"We thought we'd lost you… more than once," said Julius.

"According to the orderlies, you nearly did. Bastards were betting on whether I'd make it. But it seems I'm destined to be around a little longer. Until the next time, at any rate."

Julius sighed.

"Well, let's hope that isn't anytime soon. I think we've earned a break, don't you?"

Titus nodded.

"I'll say, brother. At least Ariovistus won't be bothering us again."

"How was it?" asked Atticus. "I only get to hear bits and pieces."

Julius quickly outlined how the battle had unfolded.

"And that was it. Their lines broke and we took the camp. I thought we were in for another bloodbath when it began. But we made it through and it could have been a lot worse."

Atticus nodded.

"And afterwards?"

Julius shrugged his shoulders.

"We only know what Plautius heard from Allerix before he left."

Atticus stopped his friend.

"Allerix has gone?"

Julius nodded.

"Aquila and the cavalry were tasked with chasing down enemy survivors. Trouble is, they didn't stop with the warriors. The women and children weren't spared. Allerix was horrified."

Atticus shook his head.

"Our legate hasn't become any less of a prick whilst I've been away, then?"

Julius laughed.

"No argument here, brother. According to Plautius, Allerix and Aquila almost came to blows about it. But you know Allerix can look after himself. I think he was more concerned about

Caesar's decision to have us stay here during the winter. Allerix thought it would provoke a war."

Atticus looked surprised.

"We're staying? Why?"

Julius smiled.

"Because Plautius told us we had to, brother. When do we ever know why we're doing something?"

"Do you think he's right? About war, I mean?"

Julius shook his head.

"No. We beat the Helvetii, and Allerix saw what happened to Ariovistus' army. Why would anybody stand against us after that?"

"Because we're here, lad," said Titus mournfully.

"But surely our presence here guarantees peace?" Julius protested.

Titus shook his head.

"In my experience, there's never a whole lot of peace in the vicinity of a Roman army."

A shadow fell across the bed as a burly orderly approached, clutching the tray from which he had been dispensing the nightly round of medications.

"Right, you lot. That's enough. You must have duties to attend to. If you don't, I can find some for you soon enough."

It wasn't meant in jest, and Atticus smiled as Titus and Julius scrambled to their feet and quickly said their goodbyes.

At the foot of the bed, Julius paused.

"Allerix came to see you, by the way, before he left. I just thought you'd want to know."

"Thank you, brother. Goodnight."

Atticus studied the foul-smelling draft he'd been given by the orderly. Familiarity had not made it any easier to take. He swallowed it quickly and tried not to retch. He swept up the remains of the food on his plate and washed them down with some of the fortified wine he'd also been given. That was altogether more agreeable. He was definitely looking forward to trying something a little stronger when he finally escaped the hospital. He set down his beaker and reached under the small pillow at the end of his bed. He fished out the dagger that had inflicted his wound and turned it over in his hand, as he had done on many occasions during the last few days. It certainly looked like Jupiter; well, the one Atticus wore anyway. But that didn't make any sense. Why would the German have a weapon depicting a Roman god? Unless his pendant owed more to the gods of the enemy than it did to those of Rome? Julius had joked about that often enough, although he'd still been happy to benefit from whatever assistance Atticus had been able to call upon. From whomever it came. They'd needed to seek the help of the gods on rather more occasions than he would have liked. And in such a short space of time. He was beginning to wonder if they were in danger of exhausting the gods' goodwill, such as it was. He had been spared but Maximus had fallen. As had so many others on both sides, all most likely with gods to whom they offered prayer. He had unexpectedly won acclaim and somehow fallen foul of his legate in the process, something for which he continued to pay. He'd lost friends but also made new ones from amongst the peoples in whose territories they were now settled. Individuals to whom they owed their lives but who it now seemed they were destined to fight. As the orderlies began to dim the lamps for the night, he tucked the dagger back under his pillow and stretched out on his cot. He sighed. Maybe he wasn't supposed to understand. Perhaps the gods had a plan and each of their fates was preordained, however randomly it appeared the patterns of life and death played out. It would explain a lot. There had certainly been nothing predictable about the last few months. Nothing predictable at all...

3

THREE MONTHS EARLIER

JUNE, 58 BC

Aduatuca, Ardennes Forest

Allerix tugged gently on Isarno's reins. Easing to a halt, he ran the back of his hand across his brow and took a welcome drink from the skin slung across his saddle. He was sure this was where the boar had gone to ground after crossing the stream and throwing the dogs off the scent. He'd split from the rest of the group some time ago and it didn't look as if anybody else was in the vicinity. With luck, it would be him and not his sister who claimed the prize. He nudged Isarno off the sun-drenched path and into the mottled shade beneath the trees. As they moved slowly forward, the boar broke cover, bolting from behind a fallen log. He'd been right. Smiling, he reached for his spear. Following the animal's progress as it crashed through the undergrowth, he picked up the pace, determined not to lose him again. The boar weaved skittishly through the trees, testing the agility and confidence of his pursuers, but, risking a quick glance ahead, Allerix could see the copse of trees was about to give way to a small clearing. This was his chance. Bursting into the sun, Allerix urged his mount into a breakneck gallop. Closing rapidly on his quarry, he hefted his spear into position. Just as he pulled back his arm to administer the final strike, there was an anguished squeal of pain and the boar disappeared from view. Allerix cursed and quickly wheeled Isarno around. He looked up as a small group of people emerged from the trees. His heart sank as he recognised the white-haired figure at the centre, bow nonchalantly slung across her back. Epona. A few yards away, the boar lay dead, an arrow embedded deep within its chest. Beaten by his sister, again. It was going to be a long ride home.

Allerix dismounted and took another welcome drink as he waited for the group to arrive. Flanked by a couple of warriors from his father's Royal Guard, each battling to restrain a hunting dog, Epona and Epomedius chatted happily as they crossed the clearing, horses in tow, Epona doubtless savouring the moment, her petite stature accentuated by the immense size of the man who had served as the sworn hand of King Brogimarax and now fulfilled the same role for Allerix's father. His greying hair and lined face a nod to his advancing years, belied by the sheer physicality of the man and the intensity of the weapons training for which he was renowned. He had earned a fearsome reputation on the battlefield and from an early age Allerix's father had pushed him to train with the warrior. Under Brogimarax, the Aduatuci had risen to become the dominant tribe in the region, respected for their military prowess. His father's reign had been largely peaceful as a result, which was perhaps just as well during the early days of Allerix's training. A natural and accomplished horseman he may have been, but he was not a born warrior. He smiled. His father had probably despaired in the early years; he knew Epomedius had. But he'd worked hard and had acquired a level of skill which satisfied, if not entirely impressed, his demanding tutor. Epona, on the other hand, had proven to be naturally gifted, almost from the moment that she had insisted on being permitted to train alongside her brother. Deceptively strong, she was also incredibly light on her feet. Many of the tribe's male warriors had found themselves flat on their backs before they knew what had hit them. Particularly skilled with the bow, she was an excellent warrior, one of the best, but perhaps her greatest gift was her ability to work with horses. Possessed of a fiery temperament that sometimes got the better of her when dealing with people, she seemed altogether calmer and more patient amidst the fields and stables. Her successes with the sick, injured or simply troublesome horses of the tribe had earned her an almost mystical reputation. He ruffled Isarno's mane. He was one of Epona's projects. A magnificent grey Andalusian stallion she had relieved from a passing trader as a foal, when it became clear that the man's approach to training bordered on the brutal. Allerix doubted the trader would even look at an animal the wrong way again after his encounter with Epona. She had taken the injured and skittish horse under her wing and devoted hours to his recovery and subsequent training. Though compact, he had a strength and presence about him that couldn't fail to catch the eye and it had come as quite some surprise when Epona had gifted Isarno to him. His mother had told him later that Epona believed fate had brought the horse to her and that it was somehow entwined with her and Allerix's destiny. He wasn't sure about that, but he'd been grateful nonetheless and had quickly formed a strong bond with the horse, who had proven to be both brave and intelligent. He nodded at his sister as she arrived, trying to ignore the big smile on her face.

"I would have got it, you know."

Epona laughed.

"Of course, brother, of course. Although I think that might have had more to do with Isarno than you."

Epomedius slapped Allerix on the back. "I think Isarno could probably carry a spear better too, Lord, but no faulting your tracking skills. Even better than the dogs."

Allerix acknowledged the compliment and watched as Epomedius went quickly about the business of skinning and dressing the boar. Whispering an incantation under his breath whilst he worked, Epomedius was careful to add a small slice of prime meat to the offal he would leave as an offering to Arduinna. Though the boar was destined for that night's feasting table, it was big enough to spare the flesh, and Arduinna's spirit was one that you definitely wanted looking out for you in the right way. It was the first time that Allerix had thought about the feast since they had left early that morning to begin the hunt. They had best get back. He knew that his father was troubled about the request he had made of Allerix and that he wanted them to talk again before the festivities started. In truth, Allerix wasn't sure if his imminent departure was something he wished to celebrate, but he couldn't let his father down. Helping Epomedius hoist the boar onto the back of his horse, Allerix quickly leapt aboard Isarno. Waiting until each of the party were all similarly mounted, he leant across to Epona.

"Race you back."

Without waiting for a response, Allerix spurred Isarno into a gallop and headed back towards the shade of the forest.

*

BIBRACTE

Atticus absent-mindedly ran his tongue across his parched lips. It was late morning and they had been standing in the warmth of the sun for hours. His tunic was already clinging uncomfortably to his body beneath his heavy armour and he longed for a drink. It would be worse for the men on the plain but at least they were involved in the fight, unlike him and his comrades in the newly formed XIth and XIIth Legions. They were stuck up here on the hill. Watching. After all that marching. They had pursued the Helvetii for fifteen long and arduous days. Footsore and growing increasingly frustrated, it had been a huge relief when the enemy were finally sighted and they were ordered to prepare for battle. Atticus' nervous excitement had quickly turned to dismay, however, when his centurion Lucius Cornelius Plautius had confirmed that the XIth and the XIIth would be guarding the baggage! Minding the possessions of the men fighting the battle he was being forced to watch unfold below.

He had still looked on in awe as the veteran legions took to the field and their general, Julius Caesar, dismounted his horse and took his place in the line. This was a man you would follow into battle. If you were given the chance. Those on the plain had quickly been engaged by the enemy and a huge roar had echoed around the hill as they had discharged their javelins, wreaking havoc in the front ranks of the advancing Barbarian army. There had been another, when the legions had taken advantage of the chaos and unexpectedly charged the enemy. But there had been no further headway and as the enemy regrouped, the battle had become a bloody and attritional stalemate, watched in almost total silence by the men of the two legions on the hill. Almost.

Atticus shook his head.

"We should be down there."

Julius looked quizzically at him from beneath his helmet. "I suspect most of them would rather be up here. Besides, I'm not sure we're ready for that, are you?"

Atticus frowned. "Well, we'll never know standing here, will we?"

Plautius had heard enough. "Quiet! Any more and I'll have you digging latrines for a week. Not a task I would fancy in the aftermath of our victory celebrations." A few laughs rippled through the crowded ranks.

"Enough," ordered Plautius.

Despite a kick from Julius, who knew what was coming, Atticus couldn't refrain from opening his mouth.

"We've spent the last fifteen days taking shit from the other legions about how we aren't real soldiers, sir. What's a little more?"

A few hesitant laughs followed before those responsible thought better of it and the century fell silent. Plautius shared the sentiment well enough. He wanted nothing more than to see his new command tested in battle, but he couldn't let the comment pass unpunished. "Legionary Capito, do you have any advice that you would like me to pass on to the legate?"

Resigned to what was coming, Atticus could already feel the glaring eyes on his back. He sighed and trotted out one of Plautius' own oft-stated remarks.

"No, sir. I serve at the general's pleasure, sir."

Concealing a smile, Plautius nodded to his optio, Tullius Fabius Rescius.

"Optio, please record Legionary Capito's kind offer to volunteer his tent party for latrine duty."

The groans were almost loud enough to drown out the ribald comments aimed in their direction by the rest of the century. This time, Julius' kick wasn't half so measured.

The century had barely settled down when a wave of noise rolled across the hill. Desperate to see what was happening, Julius tried to crane his neck above the helmets of the men in front. Atticus beat him to it, thrusting out his arm and pointing towards the fringe of the battle.

"Look! They're running."

He watched as individual warriors, then small groups and finally whole sections of the enemy line began to disengage and stream away from the fight. Those not doing so cautiously were ruthlessly cut down by the legion's front rank, freed from the rigours of the close order combat with which they had been engaged just moments before. Atticus grimaced as one or two of the legionaries advanced just a little too far, paying for their lack of discipline with their lives, as individual warriors looked to redeem their honour and cover their retreat. A buccina rang out across the battlefield and as order was quickly restored, the legions began to advance as one in pursuit of the fleeing enemy. Julius smiled.

"Quite a sight, though not for the Helvetii, admittedly."

Atticus nodded.

"No. And if we catch them before they can regroup on that higher ground, we might get off this bloody hill tonight."

Julius gave him a gentle shove.

"Just in time to start shovelling shit."

"And don't think we'll forget how that happened, lad," Titus added grumpily.

Another member of the tent party, Titus Cassius Victor was ten or so years older than Atticus and the others. He had re-enlisted after years of service with another legion and had assumed an unofficial leadership role, though not one that afforded him any particular respect.

Julius laughed.

"I thought that was what you spent your time doing in Hispania, Titus."

"No, it was the mules he 'looked after', wasn't it?" added Atticus, grateful to have attention temporarily diverted elsewhere.

Titus was about to respond when a second wave of noise put paid to the conversation. And this time the cries were ones of concern. The source of the anxiety quickly became clear as a huge influx of new warriors suddenly appeared to the left of the legions on the plain.

Rescius barked out an order above the noise.

"Settle down, ladies!"

A grizzled veteran, Rescius' scars bore testimony to the many battles he had seen, although Atticus wondered if at least some of them might have been inflicted in fights with his own side, after one of the drinking sessions or dice games of which he was so fond had turned sour. He was a good soldier, though, and whilst Atticus would never admit it, having received more than his fair share of punishment duties, a fair disciplinarian too. Rescius had formed an immediate bond with Plautius, another veteran and an experienced centurion, who had also been promoted when he joined the XIIth. Together they worked the century hard, very hard, but Atticus had never seen either of them fail to do their bit. He'd heard enough from the men of other cohorts to know that the Second century of the legion's First cohort had been lucky with its leaders. He shifted uneasily on the spot as the enemy's menacing advance continued. Leadership was what was required down there too. If somebody didn't do something soon, the enemy would fall on the legions unchallenged. He was beginning to think that the alarm would never be raised when he caught sight of a cavalry officer riding frantically along the Roman line. Prompted by his hurried instructions, men began to peel away from the pursuit of the Helvetii and position themselves to tackle the new threat, which was growing more real with every second that passed.

"Centurion."

Atticus recognised the unmistakeable voice of Publius Sextius Baculus, the legion's first spear, as he greeted Plautius. The two men had served together previously and were long-time friends. Baculus had a reputation for bravery and honour that afforded him something akin to legendary status within the fledgling legion. The two officers exchanged greetings and Atticus turned his head to try and overhear their conversation as Plautius pulled Baculus aside.

"I was beginning to wonder if anybody down there had noticed the danger."

"You and me both. That's Crassus, I think. He's only young but Caesar sees something in him. He gave him command of the cavalry today, much to Aquila's annoyance."

Plautius snorted.

"If our esteemed legate isn't content with guarding the baggage, he could always order us down in support. If that line doesn't hold, they'll be surrounded!"

Baculus sighed frustratedly.

"I know, brother. The trouble is, he's anxious not to do anything wrong, which I fear means being reluctant to do anything at all. I'm heading back to the command tent now, but don't hold your breath."

Atticus watched Baculus stalk away and, turning his attention back towards the plain, offered a silent prayer for his comrades below.

*

Atticus stole a quick look along the line. He felt decidedly uneasy and the feeling had been getting worse as the afternoon dragged on. Judging by the looks of his comrades, he wasn't alone. This had been the legion's first taste of combat, and their relative distance from the fierce fighting did little to dampen the sound of battle, nor lessen the smell of blood and gore wafting on the wind as each assault and counterassault played out. But it wasn't just that. Buoyed by the sudden change in fortune, the fleeing Helvetii had turned tail and rejoined the fight, leaving the legions hard-pressed on two fronts. And he and his friends had continued to stand idly by, watching. It felt wrong. Frustrated, he turned to Julius.

"Why is nobody doing anything?"

Rescius tapped him on the shoulder.

"Relax, lad. We can all see what's going on. You won't do them any favours forgetting your discipline and training."

He leant forward, edging closer to Atticus' ear.

"I'm as keen as you to be doing something, and Plautius has gone to see Baculus, but until they can persuade Aquila to take his head out of his arse, we're stuck up here. And you're already shovelling shit for a week, so I suggest you wait quietly."

Atticus nodded and let out a deep sigh. That was going to be easier said than done. The legions were holding their own but their defensive line was looking painfully thin and he hated seeing them struggle when help was so close to hand. To make matters worse, the enemy appeared to be brazenly using the elevation of the slope on which the waiting legions stood to coordinate their attacks against the Romans.

"Bastards are laughing at us," muttered Atticus.

The sharp look from Rescius suggested his observation hadn't been quite as far under his breath as he'd intended. Fortunately, Rescius' attention was drawn away as Baculus and Plautius returned. The discussion in which the two officers were engaged was a good deal more animated than their last, and Atticus could sense the frustration in Plautius' voice.

"He can see what's happening, can't he?"

"Of course, but his initial orders were not to engage the enemy, and he's sticking to those like a vestal sticks to her virtue."

Plautius threw up his hands.

"He does realise that the circumstances have changed, surely?"

Baculus let out an exasperated sigh.

"He does but he's a politician, not a soldier. You know these senatorial types. This is his first command and he doesn't want to rock the boat. If I push him one more time about getting down there, he's going to have me on a charge, first spear or not."

Plautius gave a resigned nod and seemed about to turn away when he raised his hand, clearly not yet ready to concede defeat. He gestured towards the small group of horsemen that had congregated below.

"If Aquila won't order the legion forward, what about something smaller? If we could just get after that group down there, it would be a start. You've got to admire their nerve but they're controlling everything from there."

Baculus nodded.

"I agree but the legate won't even authorise that. He's afraid he will be criticised if a unit gets caught out of position."

Plautius groaned.

"Gods above, there might not be anybody left to criticise him if he waits any longer. It won't change the course of the battle but it might help tip the balance. And they could do with all the help they can get right now."

Rescius stepped forward as the two officers continued their discussion.

"Sir, if I might? The legate won't release a unit, but how about one man? I've been watching that group for a while now and, from what I can see, the big bastard on the black horse is the one giving all the orders. If we could get to him, it might disrupt things, for a while at least."

Baculus looked at him incredulously.

"One man? Are you serious?"

Rescius nodded.

"Yes, sir. They aren't expecting any trouble from up here. I'm not sure they're even bothering to keep a check on us. A unit would catch their eye but one man might get close enough for a shot with a javelin."

Baculus pursed his lips and nodded his head as if weighing up the chances of success.

"I'm not sure if it's brave or foolhardy but I suppose it could be done. He'd have to have a bloody good arm, though, and be keen to get after the enemy." Plautius and Rescius exchanged a glance. Plautius smiled.

"I think we may have just the man."

*

Albiorix ducked through the wooden arch and stepped onto the settlement walls. He'd been coming up here ever since he was a child and never tired of the view. He acknowledged the greeting of the guard and strode to his favourite spot. Stretching in the sun, he gazed out across the plain. No more than 200 metres wide, it ran from the edge of the forest to the lofty stone and timber wall on which he now stood. It was the only means of access to the settlement that nestled in the natural citadel created by the steep and rocky cliffs that surrounded it on three sides. His ancestors had chosen the site well. As it often did when he found himself alone, his mind wandered to those who had ruled before him. He had precious few memories of his father; he'd fallen in battle when Albiorix was young but his character endured. He'd led the tribe over the Rhine and across Gaul, forging a fearsome reputation for their nation that had worried Rome herself. When that anxiety resulted in the nations clashing and his peoples suffering defeat, Brogimarax had become king. He'd taken Albiorix in and raised him as his own during the difficult and turbulent times that had followed until the Aduatuci had found peace and security in their current home. Both had been hard won and fiercely defended but the nation had slowly risen to prominence amongst the neighbouring tribes. That was Brogimarax's legacy. He sighed. It had been almost twelve years ago, on a day much like today, that the chieftain had called for Albiorix as he lay dying. Brogimarax had wanted to share the tales of their ancestors with him one final time. Albiorix had heard the stories so many times before but he'd listened warmly as one of the tribal elders recounted the tales, grateful for the opportunity to share the old man's company. In his younger days, he hadn't always appreciated the seemingly endless hours devoted to the stories, always itching to be somewhere else, playing with friends, or, when he was older, hunting and drinking. His appreciation of the stories had come as he grew older and began to understand how valuable they were in keeping the history of his people alive. An appreciation that had only grown stronger since he had become king. By rights, that should have been Atessorax, Brogimarax's son. Albiorix and Atessorax had grown up together and been as close as any natural brothers. They had shared many adventures and misadventures along the way and had been destined to serve together as members of the Royal Guard. That was until the fateful day Atessorax had been thrown from his horse and killed whilst out hunting. Albiorix had wept for the first time that day. Something he couldn't recall doing again until the night Brogimarax passed away. The night the chieftain had told him the Council of Elders had agreed to his succession. The night Brogimarax had passed him his sword and Albiorix had become king.

"You were thinking about him, weren't you?"

Olluna smiled as she eased in beside Albiorix and took his hand.

He looked at her quizzically and she gestured to the side of his face.

"You were touching your scar. It's that or the pendant whenever you are thinking about the past."

Albiorix squeezed her hand. She knew him so well.

"He took me in when other men might have killed me. I owe him everything. We owe him everything. How many men could have done what he did…? Could I?"

Olluna turned to look him in the eye.

"We have not maintained our position by chance, husband. We've had our share of challenges too, and yet here we stand. He saw something in you. So did the elders. You are a good leader."

Albiorix dropped his head.

"Am I? I swore an oath of vengeance against Rome after they killed my family and now I am about to send my son to fight with them. I fear the gods may not take kindly to such a betrayal." Olluna leant forward to kiss him gently on the forehead.

"If we can use these Romans to help rid us of a problem, will the gods not be amused? They know that you do what you must to protect our people."

Albiorix smiled. It wasn't necessary to be a god to know that he and Olluna didn't always see eye to eye. When things got heated, anybody with the misfortune to be within earshot would be painfully aware of that fact. But he had always valued her wise counsel, and he knew she made him a better man. They had enjoyed more years together than most, and he was eternally grateful that she had seen enough in him as a younger man to accept his proposal. If it had been up to her father, their union would almost certainly never have happened. Albiorix hoped he would be proud of the man that he had become, and his daughter's choice. He pulled back his shoulders, still keen to impress after all these years. He had been feeling his age of late, but Olluna remained as youthful-looking as ever. Aside from the intricate silver broach pinned to her shawl, a gift from Albiorix that accompanied her everywhere, she wore no adornments of status and favoured the simple tunic dress common to the women of the tribe. It didn't diminish her beauty or hide the figure that he had been so attracted to when they were young, that he was still attracted to. He was a lucky man. Perhaps later he may have the chance to prove that he wasn't as old as he felt. Olluna nudged him gently.

"What are you smiling about? It can't be tonight?" She poked him gently in the belly.

"You will enjoy the feast, I'm sure, but I know you are worried about Allerix and what lies ahead."

Albiorix gently turned his wife around and leant down to kiss her neck. He slid his hands onto her ample breasts and she reached up to stroke his head as he whispered into her ear.

"I was hoping the immediate aftermath of the feast might offer some distraction."

Olluna laughed and gently squeezed his hand.

"If you think you can handle it, Lord. Although if Epona and Allerix don't return soon, there will not be much of a feast."

Albiorix pointed towards the foot of the plain where a small group of riders had just emerged from the forest.

"Then it's just as well that I think I can see them now." Olluna laughed. "Are they racing?"

Albiorix nodded. "Do you even have to ask? Nothing changes."

Always competitive, the two were nonetheless very close. Albiorix sometimes wondered if they would have got on quite so well if they had been related by birth. He and Olluna had lost their first son to illness. He had been a sickly child and, although immensely painful, it had come as no surprise when he hadn't survived the winter of his second year.

The following spring, Olluna's brother had died in battle. When she had lost her sister-in-law during childbirth so shortly afterwards, their grief had only been eased by the arrival of Epona to raise as their own.

When Allerix was born two years later, strong and healthy, Albiorix had truly felt the gods were smiling on him and his family. "She will miss him whilst he is away." Olluna took his hand and gave him a knowing look. "I know we all will."

*

BIBRACTE

Atticus looked at Plautius in disbelief as he finished outlining his plan.

"You want me to do what?"

4

"Do you think you can do it? That's all I need to know. I won't send you out there if you don't think you can," asked Plautius impatiently.

Atticus thought for a moment. He knew he was one of the best in the legion with a javelin, and with the group's attention fixed on events unfolding before them, rather than on the stationary legions, there was every chance he could get close enough to launch it. The problem was going to be getting back.

As if reading his mind, Plautius placed a reassuring hand on his shoulder.

"You'll have the element of surprise and I'll have the boys ready to give a warm welcome to anybody chasing you, if you can just get close enough to our lines."

Atticus sighed. "Just." As he looked on, another rider galloped up to the group of enemy horsemen. Having engaged in a brief conversation, he set off in the direction from which he had arrived, presumably with fresh orders to impart. Orders doubtless destined to increase the misery being heaped upon his comrades on the plain. They had to do something to try and drive the horsemen away. Hadn't he spent most of the day frustratedly looking down on the action, desperate to get involved? Now he could, even if it wasn't quite what he'd expected.

He smiled at Plautius and cleared his throat, hoping his voice would convey a good deal more confidence than he was actually feeling.

"Yes, I can do it."

Plautius nodded.

"Good lad. I'll let Baculus know."

Atticus watched him stride purposefully away and then returned his gaze to the enemy horsemen, who suddenly seemed an awfully long way away.

Baculus waved away Atticus' salute as he returned with Plautius.

"Well done, soldier. Let's get you ready."

Atticus handed his sword to Rescius and with a little help from Plautius eased his armour over his head. It was lovely to be free of the weight but he suddenly felt very vulnerable. He reached to recover his sword but decided against it. The sheath would only inconvenience him, and having the blade would provide only symbolic protection. His fate rested with the audacity of the plan, his ability to deliver it and his comrades' skill with their javelins, which would offer a pointed deterrent to any would-be pursuers. Baculus gave him a nod.

"Good luck, lad. They'll be in your debt. Even if they never know whose act of bravery it was that helped them out."

Atticus swallowed nervously. He wasn't sure whether he should feel proud or alarmed that even Baculus thought this undertaking was brave.

The first spear gave Plautius a nod and gestured back across the hill.

"I'd best get back to the legate. I need to be there when he sees what's going on."

Plautius shot him an anxious glance.

"Do you think you'll be able to persuade him that it was right to act?"

Baculus shrugged.

"I'm honestly not sure. He seems more concerned with how things will look for him than he is about doing the right thing, but there's nobody else and we've got to try something. It's the least they'd expect down there. We can worry about the implications later. If the enemy break through that line, they'll sweep the entire bloody army away."

Plautius frowned.

"Except us, although I'd wager it won't take them long to try and rectify that, hill or no hill. And I wouldn't fancy our chances either."

Baculus nodded.

"Me neither, brother. Let's hope this little escapade helps spare us that fate."

Grasping forearms in lieu of a more formal salute, Baculus marched off, leaving Atticus with Plautius and Rescius. Looking at their anxious faces, he was beginning to wonder if it wasn't just his fate that depended on the outcome of the attack.

Atticus offered a silent prayer to Fortuna and kissed the small bronze pendant he wore alongside his legionary identification. Tucking both safely back inside his tunic, he made his way through the lines, pausing for a moment as he reached Julius.

"Make sure they aim high. I'd hate to make it back and be skewered by one of you."

His friend laughed.

"You'll be okay with me but as for the rest, I think it depends how many of them have money on you making it back alive."

Atticus smiled; he'd learnt early on in training that there were few things his comrades wouldn't hazard a wager upon. It was probably just as well he didn't know which outcome was favoured. Titus slapped him on the back.

"Don't worry, lad. You'll be okay. You look like a bloody Gaul. They'll think you're one of them."

Atticus shook his head. He'd been wondering when that would start. The comments about his appearance had begun almost as soon as he'd started training and had been a regular feature ever since. It didn't help that he seemed to bear more resemblance to the enemy than he did to most of his colleagues. But his grandfather had served in the legions, with distinction too, and his father was as Roman as they came, in manner and lifestyle if not in looks. Taking after his father and standing at least a head taller than most of the recruits, with a broad and muscular physique and a mop of blond hair, it was those looks that made Atticus stand out. It had been a relief to lose his unruly locks to the prescribed military haircut. One less thing to catch the eye of his comrades, or the training instructors, who needed no assistance identifying those responsible for even the smallest transgression.

However, he'd coped with the training better than most, enjoyed it even, and his size and natural athleticism had proved a huge advantage. He'd acquired a level of military prowess that was the envy of his friends; a fact he was all too happy to remind them of if the taunts about his appearance began. Of course, it was that military prowess that had brought him here. He sighed. That and his big mouth... Now he had to deliver.

Julius smiled as Atticus made his way forward.

"Good luck, brother. Pull this off and we might just escape latrine duty."

Shit! Shit, shit, shit! What had possessed him to say yes? The task had looked hard enough when he was safely tucked away with the rest of the legion, although he'd still thought he could do it despite all the risks. Alone in front of the line, Atticus felt a lot less sure. He took a deep breath and shifted the weight of the wrought iron javelin in his hand. It was too late now. He couldn't go back, and Plautius had urged him to make haste when he got out into the open. Muttering one final prayer, he set off, desperately trying to watch his footing on the uneven slope as he gathered pace. Risking a glance at the small group below, he cursed as he stumbled and almost lost his footing. Too fast. He had to measure his approach. Push on too quickly and he risked falling. Or being too spent to make it back. Too slow and he might lose the element of surprise. Achieving that balance would be a whole lot easier if every fibre of his being wasn't screaming at him to get this over with as quickly as possible. The problems of remaining upright weren't helped by the weight and ungainly nature of the javelin, which hadn't been designed for anything remotely like this. Something he might have reflected on before agreeing to venture beyond the lines. The gentle breeze did little to stop the sweat forming on his brow as he pushed on, his tunic sticking to his body as the physical effort began to take its toll. But he was almost there and nothing about the enemy horsemen's demeanour suggested they had been alerted to his presence. Atticus was close enough now to make out the features of the riders, to catch the distinctive smell of the horses on the wind. He was sure that he would have been able to hear the battle more clearly now too, if it hadn't been drowned out by the sound of his heart.

He began to slow his pace. Just a little further… As he began to believe he might actually make it into position unseen, a rider came galloping around the bend at the foot of the hill. Fuck! The horseman came to a halt in front of the mounted warriors. Focussed on conveying whatever news he had been tasked to deliver, it was only when he raised his head to await a response that the rider's cry of panic alerted the group to Atticus' presence. A little more than twenty metres away from the startled group, he felt very exposed. His only chance was to strike before the warriors could properly react. It was now or never.

Atticus planted his feet and quickly hefted the javelin onto his shoulder. With his eyes locked on the thickset warrior they had identified earlier, he took a couple of steps forward to build a little momentum. Reminding himself of the need for a lower and flatter trajectory than those of the endless throws he had made in practice, he drew back his arm and released the javelin. The effort sent him sprawling to the ground and he scrambled to his feet as the weapon flew towards its intended target. The riders had quickly wheeled their horses around but they were still tightly packed and the warning had given them precious little time to react. As if at last sensing the danger, the targeted warrior tried to heft his shield across his body but it was too late. The momentum of the strike drove him back in the saddle as the javelin tore into his chest and punched clear through his body. As the lifeless warrior slumped to one side, his startled horse reared up and threw him to the ground before galloping off towards the Roman lines. *Where he should be going.* He turned and set off back up the hill. Free of the need for any form of caution, he put down his head and ran as fast as he could, desperately fighting the urge to look back, knowing that to do so might prove fatal. He climbed higher, driven on by the unmistakeable sound of hooves gaining ground behind him. Pushing himself to the limit, Atticus could feel his breathing becoming ragged and his legs beginning to weaken beneath him. With the shouts of encouragement from his comrades ringing in his ears, he made one last desperate charge for the Roman lines. But it was no use; he wasn't going to make it. Unable to quicken his pace and struggling for breath, he threw himself to the ground. It was up to his comrades now. His whole body tensed as the hooves drew closer and he heard Plautius' bellowed command to release javelins. Time seemed to stand still and for a moment all he could hear was his laboured breathing as he desperately sought to refill his lungs. Then in a cacophony of noise, javelins thudded to the ground and several agonised cries, along with the pained whinnying of injured horses, pierced the air. Almost immediately, these were overtaken by the enthusiastic cheers and vociferous shouts of his rapturous comrades. Atticus cautiously raised his head to cast a glance behind him. A swathe of javelins decorated the hill. One or two had landed a lot closer to him than he would have liked but the barrage had worked. Twenty feet below him on the slope, his two closest pursuers lay dead. A third rider had managed to call off his pursuit a little further down the hill, sparing him the fate suffered by his comrades. The warrior gesticulated angrily at Atticus as he hauled himself slowly to his feet. His legs felt like lead and he was utterly exhausted. But he was alive. Thanks to his comrades and Fortuna and Jupiter. He felt for the pendant beneath his tunic and clutched it to his chest. Wiping the sweat from his brow, he watched the surviving warrior rejoin the two remaining horsemen at the foot of the hill. With some difficulty, they recovered the body of their leader and rode away, to another chorus of cheers. Atticus allowed the sound to wash over him, a sense of pride and relief coursing through his body. He turned and, with renewed vigour, completed the climb back to the safety of his waiting comrades.

*

ADUATUCA

Albiorix shuddered, grateful that he'd remembered to bring his cloak. Dusk was beginning to fall and the breeze, so comforting in the heat of the day, now offered the first hint of a chill. He and Allerix had covered some distance as they talked, and he was anxious not to go any further. It may have been Olluna's idea that they escape the settlement whilst arrangements for the feast were completed, but he knew that wouldn't save him from a dressing-down if they returned too late. And after their earlier conversation, he was very keen to remain on her good side. He tapped Allerix on the arm and gestured for him to stop.

"I think it's time we were heading back. Before we do, though, I want you to have this."

He reached beneath his tunic and slipped off his pendant. Taking one last look at the bronze figurine, he pressed it into his son's hand.

"Your mother would never forgive me if I let you go without it."

Allerix carefully turned the pendant around in his hand and studied the intricately crafted figure, Taranis, the Thunder God. Clutching his familiar chariot wheel in one hand, in the other he held a two-headed axe and not his customary thunderbolt. He hadn't noticed that before. Nor could he ever recall seeing one quite like it. His father smiled.

"Unusual, isn't it? My father had it made especially. It's one of a pair. The other belonged to my younger brother. The gods must have had other plans for him when they took him from us, but the pendant has always helped me tread the right path. I hope it will do the same for you."

He patted his son affectionately on the back. "Come, we should be going."

Allerix couldn't remember ever seeing his father without the pendant, and his decision to give it to him had come as something of a surprise. All the more so given its personal significance, something Allerix had been unaware of until now. His father must be more concerned than he was letting on.

"Do you believe blood must be spilled?"

His father grimaced.

"I wish it were not so but I fear bloodshed is unavoidable. Nothing has persuaded Ariovistus to relax his grip on the territories of the Sequani and the Arverni. Every year, he annexes additional land and more of his people cross the Rhine to settle. To take advantage of the weakness shown by our cousins. It will not be long before others feel emboldened to cross elsewhere, spilling into the lands of the Usipetes and Treveri. When that happens, our borders will be threatened and we will be forced to defend our territories on the battlefield once more. I cannot allow that to happen."

Allerix shook his head.

"I don't understand what possessed the Sequani and the Arverni to seek help from Ariovistus in the first place. Surely, they must have realised the risks of inviting such a powerful nation into their lands. What were they thinking?"

Albiorix threw up his hands in disgust.

"They weren't thinking. That's the problem. They saw only the chance to end their battle for supremacy with the Aedui once and for all. They were too blinded by thoughts of wealth and power to pay any heed to what might follow. Only a fool would invite a wolf to a hunt and think they could do it safely."

"And this Roman, Caesar, do you believe he can defeat Ariovistus?" Albiorix shrugged.

"Perhaps. He stands against the Helvetii, and that is not something you do without courage and a powerful army at your back. Seeking his assistance to move against the Germans has appeal. It's why the Tribal Council agreed to approach him and why the delegation travels immediately, to take advantage of his proximity should he defeat the Helvetii. But I am not so sure."

Allerix shot his father a quizzical look.

"You have concerns?"

"We know nothing of this man and little of Rome's intentions.

If the Roman is victorious, he will have proven himself a worthy ally but also a threat. We expose weakness by asking for his support, and I fear we may simply be replacing one wolf with another."

Allerix paused as his father came to a halt. He looked troubled.

"It is because of these concerns that I now place you in harm's way. I persuaded the Council that it would be prudent to have a trusted presence in the camp of this general and his legions. To learn what forces he may call upon and how he might intend to use them in the future. It made sense for that person to be you. If what we hear about the Roman cavalry is true, they will struggle to defeat Ariovistus' horsemen without our assistance. That's why I volunteered our cavalry to join the delegation and why I ask you to lead our warriors to ride in support of Caesar, if he is minded to confront Ariovistus."

Allerix reached for his father's arm.

"I wouldn't have it any other way. Our nations cannot seek refuge behind this Roman's battledress whilst he goes to war on our behalf. Honour dictates that we fight alongside him, and I would rather volunteer than wait to be asked. Caesar will be lucky to have our warriors riding by his side, and I am proud to lead them on your behalf. I won't let you down."

Albiorix wrapped his arm around Allerix's shoulder.

"I know, son. I have always known. I just never imagined the time would come when I had to ask such a thing of you without being there to stand by your side."

Allerix quickly slipped his father's pendant over his head.

"You will be there and, hopefully, so will the gods."

Albiorix smiled.

Come, that is enough of matters of state. We really must get home." He punched Allerix playfully on the arm. "Tonight, we eat, drink and, gods willing, plough."

*

BIBRACTE

Plautius shook his head as he paced beneath the earthworks one more time. The evening light had begun its doomed battle for supremacy with the coming dark of night, and he was ready for a drink and his cot. That was if they ever finished the marching camp. The centurion rolled his eyes and bellowed at one of the legionaries labouring to complete the palisade at the top of the rampart.

"Fabius! Put your fucking back into it, lad, or I'll come up there and use your head to get those stakes in."

It had been a long and frustrating day. The battle on the plain had continued for some time after Capito's attack, but the Gauls had finally been broken and forced to retreat. Pursued by the legions, the battle still raged somewhere to the west. In the meantime, he and Baculus had led the XIIth down the hill, not to join the pursuit but to oversee the escort of the baggage train and the construction of that night's camp. He knew his men were raw and untested but there was only one way to rectify that, and he thought it was a mistake that at least one of the new legions had not been thrown into action alongside the veteran units. Worse still, whilst Capito's attack and the loss of their leader genuinely did seem to have disrupted the enemy's capacity to counter the Roman attacks, Baculus had sent word that Aquila was angry. As Baculus had predicted, it seemed the legate was concerned about how their decision to act would reflect on him. For fuck's sake, didn't he realise his reputation was more likely to be tarnished by his indecision than by anything they'd done? Would he really have left men to die needlessly because he was uncomfortable about doing something that might expose him to even the slightest risk? That wasn't the kind of leader on whose behalf you wanted to be ordering men into battle. As it was, neither he nor Baculus believed that the attack was a challenge to Aquila's orders. It had been successful. What more did he want? Plautius sighed; such was the life of a centurion. As he began to retrace his steps, he saw Baculus approaching. He was a leader you could trust to do the right thing, regardless of risk. It had been the opportunity to serve again with his friend, rather than the promotion, that had tempted him to leave the VII when Baculus had come calling, although he might have thought twice if he'd known the XIIth's first legate was going to be Aquila. Baculus greeted him with a smile and nodded towards the ongoing construction activity.

"I'm grateful we are unlikely to need shelter from the weather tonight, my friend. Gods above, I hope they move faster in battle than they do when building."

He gestured towards Atticus, toiling at the corner of the rampart.

"Mind you, we know one of them can do a passable impression of a soldier. You weren't wrong about his ability. Got a good head on his shoulders too. It was the right thing to do. That's why the gods were on our side today."

Plautius frowned.

"Let's hope they are tomorrow. I still can't believe the legate intends to pursue this. He should be thanking the lad, not dragging him along with me to face an insubordination charge."

Baculus raised his hands.

"You'll get no argument from me. Do you think we should tell him?"

Plautius shook his head.

"Not now, let's give the lad tonight. It's the least we can do. I'll call for him in the morning. In the meantime, you and I had better get our stories straight. You'll join me for a drink when the camp is settled?"

"Of course, brother. I'm on my way to see an old friend and

deliver a message. Something I hope will be of help tomorrow. I'll look in when I return."

He slapped Plautius on the back and marched off into the dark, leaving the centurion alone with his thoughts.

*

ADUATUCA

Albiorix gave Allerix a smile as they emerged from the forest and the welcome lights of the settlement came into view. Hurrying up the gentle slope, the sounds of laughter and singing grew louder as they approached the gate. He had no desire to say goodbye to his son but there was no better place to do so than within the familiar and comforting surroundings of the Great Hall. In the company of family and friends, they would eat, laugh and drink to Allerix's return. All the while watched over by the spirits of their ancestors, who would surely raise their own drinking horns in support of his son, even if they didn't fully understand why Albiorix had tasked him to support a Roman general. They would know it wasn't a decision he had taken lightly; he'd sought their advice often enough in the days before the Tribal Council and many times since. As a younger man, he'd sworn to secure vengeance for the loss of his father and brother at the hands of Rome's legions. It was an oath taken by many of his people after the crushing defeat of their Cimbri ancestors. Time had gone some way towards mellowing that hatred, but now the spectre of Rome had returned and it was hard not to be suspicious of this new general and his intentions. Perhaps working as allies, however uneasily, might signal the start of a new relationship with Rome, but he would not take that on trust. And so, he would reluctantly say goodbye to his son. He waved Allerix through the gate, pausing for a moment as his son stopped to commiserate with the small group of warriors on guard duty. He smiled as Allerix promised to have some of the food and a little of the mead sent out to them. He had become quite the leader, thought Albiorix proudly. As they approached the Great Hall, the door swung open and Olluna, Epona and Epomedius emerged to greet them, presumably alerted to their arrival by one of the sentries. He was pleased to see the full jugs of mead in their hands. Equally reassuring was the warm look on Olluna's face, which suggested she had deemed the timing of their return to have fallen on the right side of acceptable.

5

JUNE, 58 BC
Bibracte

The summons from Plautius had taken Atticus by surprise. He was barely awake and feeling very much the worse for wear. It had been a long night. To his delight, Baculus and Plautius had credited his attack with helping to make a difference, as the tide of battle down on the plan turned favourably towards the legions. It had still taken a mighty effort to break the Gauls, and, as he descended from the hill, he hoped it might be to take up arms in the stead of his weary comrades from the plain. But they had not joined the pursuit. Instead, he had spent the evening manhandling baggage before being set to work on camp construction. It wasn't until first light that they had received news the enemy had been defeated, after battles lasting well into the night. By then, he was nursing the after-effects of a night spent enjoying the congratulations of his comrades and recounting the details of his story to anybody willing to listen, although Julius had been the only one with whom he'd shared just how scared he'd really been. Quite what Plautius wanted this early in the day was a mystery but he wouldn't find out here, and he knew better than to keep Plautius waiting. He quickly splashed his face with water and tried to tidy his uniform. Head still ringing, and hoping he looked at least a little better than he felt, he gingerly scooped up his helmet and set off for the tent Plautius shared with Rescius. He arrived just as the optio was exiting alongside Decimus Aemillius Crassus, the century's signifier. Rescius was by no means a small man but he was dwarfed by Crassus. Tall and rangy like Atticus, but much thicker set, he was the perfect choice to wield the cohort's standard in battle. The two exchanged a nod of greeting. Rescius rolled his eyes as he looked Atticus up and down.

"Go on in, Capito. He has Baculus with him."

Leaving the bright sunshine behind, he ducked into the cool and shady interior of the tent.

Sparsely furnished with military issue cots and a small table and chair, the space might have seemed austere, rather than functional, but for the concession of a small, ornate oil lamp and an ivory carving of Mercury. It was the perfect match for Plautius' professional demeanour. Atticus drew himself rigidly to attention and saluted the two officers. Plautius waved the salute away.

"At ease, lad."

He gestured for Atticus to take a seat on one of the cots.

Baculus nodded.

"You did well yesterday. Although I have to say there was a moment when I wasn't sure you were going to make it back."

Atticus laughed. He needed no reminding.

"Me neither."

Unable to resist a dig at his friend, Baculus gave Atticus a wink.

"Though some of the girls in your century might need a bit more work with the javelin, Centurion. One or two of them nearly did for the lad."

Atticus saw Plautius bristle slightly before he caught sight of the smile on Baculus' face.

"Well, the one that mattered did the trick, didn't it?"

"It did and it made a difference too. Unfortunately, as Plautius now knows, the legate isn't at all happy."

Atticus wasn't sure he understood. He hadn't expected to receive any acknowledgement for his endeavours, but he had assumed they would be regarded positively. How could the legate be displeased about something that had helped swing the tide of battle in their favour? Seeing the look of confusion on Atticus' face, Baculus repeated what he had outlined to Plautius just minutes before.

"The legate has heard nothing from Caesar and he's worried. I'm certain that the general will have been grateful for our intervention, but the legate wants to ensure he's covered if that's not the case. He is concerned about how it will look for his standing if he isn't seen to take some kind of disciplinary action. The two of you are therefore required to appear before him this afternoon. The charge… disobeying orders."

Aghast, Atticus leapt to his feet.

"The two of us? But you knew what we were doing."

Plautius put a hand on Atticus' shoulder.

"Of course he did, lad, and he doesn't like this any more than you or I, but it will play better for us if Baculus is advising the legate, rather than standing in front of him."

Baculus nodded.

"I have tried to call in a few favours and you know that I will speak on your behalf, but a word of warning. Lucius Minucius Aquila has a reputation for being quick to anger and for applying punishments with more relish than most. From what I've seen, it's a reputation well earned. Tread carefully."

*

"Remember what we said this morning," Plautius said gruffly to Atticus as they turned into the avenue leading to the legates' command tent. "Leave the explanations to me and say nothing unless addressed directly. Let's pray the gods look favourably on whatever it is that Baculus has set in motion."

Atticus felt nervously for his pendant. He wondered if he might be tempting fate asking Fortuna and the gods for help again quite so soon.

"Centurion Lucius Cornelius Plautius and Legionary Atticus Volteius Capito reporting as ordered," Plautius barked out in his best parade ground voice as he stopped and saluted the centurion in charge of the legates' security detail. If the tall and burly soldier knew Plautius, and Atticus was sure that he must, he was not giving anything away.

"Wait here," he instructed brusquely as he turned and made his way into the legates' tent.

After what seemed like an age, he reappeared at the entrance and beckoned them forward.

"The legate is ready for you."

Atticus followed Plautius into the tent. He knew that he shouldn't have been surprised, but with an array of furniture that wouldn't have been out of place in a country villa, the sheer opulence and grandeur of the scene that greeted him still caught his breath. No wonder the baggage train was so bloody large. Dominating one end of the tent was a large wooden desk behind which sat Aquila, deep in conversation with what Atticus assumed must be the legate's clerk. Baculus sat slightly to one side, his gaze focussed on the front of the tent, as if he had been expecting somebody other than Atticus and Plautius to present themselves. Aquila gave them a cursory glance and returned to his conversation. He was dressed simply enough in a plain white tunic, albeit one that Atticus could see immediately was far too high a quality to be military issue. It was augmented, of course, with the scarlet band of his office and, in what Atticus thought was an entirely unnecessary reminder of the respective positions of those present, his scarlet cloak draped ostentatiously about his shoulders. Apparently on the short side (if his stature in comparison to Baculus was any guide), he had oiled and coiffured hair and wore a short beard in the style currently favoured in Rome. The beard did nothing to mellow the sharp features of his face. Finally calling the two soldiers forward with a curt wave of his hand, Plautius and Atticus stepped up to the desk and saluted. Aquila half-heartedly returned the salute and leant back in his chair to appraise the two men before him.

"Well, gentlemen, you have presented me with quite a dilemma. I have finally received news from our illustrious general and it seems he is not displeased about the launching of our little venture yesterday. In fact, he believes that it was crucial to our victory and for that I am grateful. Anything that brings the legion to the attention of Caesar in a positive light can only be good news."

Aquila leant forward in his chair and allowed a slight smile to run across his face.

"Especially for me. I am sure you understand that, as legate, I must shoulder the responsibility for the plan when appraising Caesar of events."

Atticus couldn't believe it. Had Aquila even left his bloody tent? Now the slippery little bastard was going to try and take the credit. The only saving grace was that the nonsense of them having to answer charges would surely now be dropped, although if that was the case, Aquila was giving no indication that the meeting was about to end.

"My first spear tells me that he believes the opportunity to act might have been lost if you hadn't launched your little attack when you did."

If Plautius thought that was an invitation to respond, the dismissive wave of the legate's hand as he went to open his mouth was clear evidence that Aquila was not yet done.

"He also argues that your actions did not undermine my orders. Thankfully, as a result of your success, that is not an issue that I will have the misfortune to explore with Caesar. Unfortunately, my staff officers all know that I did not give the instruction to attack and yet you did. I'm sure that you of all people, Centurion, will appreciate that I cannot allow acts of insubordination that reflect badly on me to pass unaddressed."

Again, he waved his hand to confirm that the comment was very much rhetorical. Atticus couldn't see Plautius' face but he could see the clenched fists at his side well enough and wondered if they would ever have the opportunity to defend their actions.

Aquila leant forward.

"And I think we all know the fitting punishment for such a flagrant abuse of my orders."

Leaving that thought hangingly menacingly in the air the legate motioned for his clerk to stop writing.

"I will concede however that Capito's actions were courageous. Helpfully for you both, quite visibly so. My dilemma therefore is how to restore my reputation and punish Capito without drawing any more attention to him."

Atticus glanced anxiously at Plautius as Aquila beckoned Baculus closer and began a whispered conversation, presumably about how best to proceed. Atticus had begun to fear the worst and he shifted uncomfortably on the spot as he steeled himself for Aquila's verdict.

Before Baculus and Aquila could conclude their conversation, the flap of the tent suddenly burst open. Out of the corner of his eye, Atticus could see a tall figure marching towards them.

Aquila's startled expression and flustered demeanour was in marked contrast to the beaming smile that Atticus saw fleetingly flash across Baculus' face. The visitor strode up to the table and nodded towards Aquila.

"Lucius."

If not immaculately turned out, the blood-stained armour that sat atop his legate's uniform still clearly displaying the signs of the fighting with which he had evidently been engaged, he was still an imposing individual with the presence of one used to carrying authority. Aquila rose to greet his new arrival, though not at all warmly.

"Gaius. I was not expecting the pleasure of a visit from one of my fellow officers today."

The visitor shrugged.

"Julius intended to visit yesterday but as you know, some of us were unfortunately engaged elsewhere."

The barely disguised sleight was not lost on Atticus, nor it seemed on Aquila. Before he could reply, however, the visitor turned and addressed Atticus and Plautius directly.

"Forgive me, gentlemen, I am Gaius Trebonius, legate and commander of the VIIIth Legion. I assume, Lucius, that this is the individual to whom we owe a debt of thanks for his exploits yesterday?"

Aquila looked flustered.

"Yes, this is Legionary Capito and his centurion Plautius."

Trebonius smiled.

"Then it seems I have arrived just in time to add my thanks and those of the legions engaged yesterday to your own. That is, I assume, the purpose of this gathering?"

"W… w… why, of course," stammered Aquila. "I was just, erm… telling Capito how… grateful I was for the manner in which he had executed my plan."

If the wind had been taken out of his sails by Trebonius'

arrival, Aquila had recovered quickly. He really was every bit the politician Baculus had described.

"Excellent. You know how much Julius admires initiative, especially when it's exercised by those in the ranks."

"Indeed, Gaius, although in this case the initiative was mine."

"Of course, of course," replied Trebonius a little dismissively, "though you know that is the least expected of us, Lucius. Even if it is displayed a little later than those of us engaged in the fighting might have wished."

It was Aquila's turn to bristle.

"What are you suggesting, Trebonius?"

The switch to the formal term of address suggested Aquila was rather more rattled than he was letting on, thought Atticus, who was by now beginning to relax a little and enjoy the discomfort that Aquila was evidently experiencing. The same discomfort that just minutes before he and Plautius had been experiencing.

"Lucius, Lucius, I meant no offence," Trebonius replied calmly. "We have all seen failures of command and all experienced the types of delay that can occur in the communication of orders. You may rest assured that Julius is entirely clear which it was on this occasion."

Leaving that thought hanging and ignoring the look of anger on Aquila's face, Trebonius turned back to Plautius and Atticus.

"So how has Legate Aquila decided to reward you?"

From over Trebonius' shoulder, Baculus responded.

"The legate had not yet decided his approach, sir."

"Ah, Baculus, I had quite forgotten that you were there. It is good to see you again."

Baculus nodded a greeting in return, with what Atticus thought looked suspiciously like a look of satisfaction on his face, though he was quick to hide that as Aquila turned to face him.

"My first spear is correct, Gaius, and I am in no rush to conclude matters. I think my deliberations will wait until tomorrow."

"Nonsense," said Trebonius firmly. "My guess is that Julius will want us all on the march tomorrow if we are going to hunt down what's left of the rabble we saw off yesterday. Besides, you know him, always happy to take an opportunity to boost morale." Aquila, now clearly quite angry at the unexpected turn of events, had moved around his desk in an attempt to reassert control.

"Well, that's as maybe, but this is my legion, not yours, and you would do well to remember that."

Trebonius took a step forward, closing the gap between himself and Aquila in a deliberate move to emphasise his superior stature.

"And you would do well to remember whose army it is."

Atticus wondered if the two senior officers had quite forgotten that the three soldiers were still there.

"You speak for Caesar now?" enquired Aquila with an air of cynicism.

"No, my friend, but I believe I know what he would expect."

From outside the tent, a sudden flurry of activity and shouted commands accompanied the arrival of a number of horsemen.

Trebonius smiled.

"But no need to speculate. You can ask him yourself. I believe that might have been him and his escort just arriving."

A look of horror flashed across Aquila's face and he hurriedly fussed with his uniform before scurrying out to present himself to his visitor. Trebonius smiled and gestured Plautius forward.

"Centurion, I suggest that you go and round up as many of your men as you can and have them report here immediately in parade order."

"Yes, sir," Plautius replied, saluting swiftly.

"Oh, and, Centurion, have them try and look their best. It's not every day they will get to parade before their general."

Thinking about just how rough he had looked after the night before, Atticus could only imagine how difficult it was going to be getting the century into the kind of shape that Plautius would want. He knew he would, though, doubtless with a little help from his vine cane and the persuasive assistance of Rescius. Atticus watched as Trebonius and Baculus clasped forearms in greeting.

"Thank you, sir. You know that I will always do my duty come what may, but that man is not easy to serve."

Trebonius nodded.

"I can imagine, and this episode won't improve his demeanour any, I'm sure. He's wise enough to know that he'll need your counsel as first spear. It's not an accident he was assigned to your legion, but be careful."

Baculus nodded.

"It's Capito who is going to have to be careful, I suspect."

"Ah, yes, Legionary Capito," said Trebonius, placing an arm around Atticus' shoulder. "It may be best you keep something of a low profile after this, but first, are you ready to meet your general?"

Atticus wasn't ready. Not by any stretch of the imagination. He hadn't expected anything good to come from his appearance before the legate, and nothing could have prepared him for the events that had just occurred. But here he was being led forward to meet his general, Julius Caesar. Ducking out of the tent, Atticus shielded his eyes from the sun and surveyed the scene before him. Aquila was deep in conversation with someone whom Atticus assumed was Caesar, who was still holding the reins of the magnificent-looking white horse on which he had arrived. Milling around him, a number of staff officers similarly dismounted. A small crowd of intrigued headquarters staff and those legionaries who happened to be in the vicinity had begun to form. Finishing his conversation with Aquila, Caesar approached Trebonius and Atticus. He smiled at Trebonius and inclined his head slightly in greeting.

"Gaius. It seems that you have made your customary impression. Is this the subject of our visit?"

"Yes, Julius."

Trebonius nudged Atticus to offer his own introduction. Looking older than he had expected, his head topped with a grey, slightly receding hairline, Caesar had the face of a scholar rather than a soldier. His piercing gaze commanded attention, though, and he had a presence about him that demanded respect. Stepping forward, Atticus saluted.

"Legionary Atticus Volteius Capito, Second cohort, First century, XIIth Legion, sir."

"At ease, soldier," said Caesar, mulling on the name for a moment. "Are you by any chance related to Marcus Volteius Capito?"

Atticus was stunned that Caesar knew of his family.

"Yes, sir, he was my grandfather."

Caesar turned to address those present.

"Gentlemen, it seems it's true that the apple doesn't fall far from the tree. Legionary Capito's grandfather served my uncle with distinction at Aquae Sextiae and Vercellae."

Atticus wasn't sure that anybody else had caught the look of surprise and consternation on Aquila's face, but he had.

Gesturing to those who had accompanied him to remount their horses, Caesar spoke quickly with Aquila.

"Lucius, we are guests of your legion. You will do me the honour of making the necessary introductions, I trust."

It was more of a command than a question, with Caesar heading back to his horse before any response was forthcoming. Trebonius beckoned Atticus forward.

"Time to rejoin your century, lad, and be quick about it."

As he jogged across the square, he could see his century hurriedly forming up, Plautius and Rescius moving between them, cajoling the men into position. In the front row, Crassus looked resplendent in his bearskin, century standard held proudly aloft. Julius handed Atticus his shield as he arrived, still scarcely able to believe what was happening.

"So, not going to be strung up then? I did wonder what we would find when we got here."

"Sorry to disappoint you, brother," Atticus replied with a smile, positioning himself in line just as Aquila led Caesar and his entourage forward to address the waiting century.

"Soldiers of the XIIth Legion," Aquila bellowed, "you parade today to honour one of your own and you do so in the presence of our esteemed general, Gaius Julius Caesar."

Nodding to Aquila, Caesar trotted his horse forward, acknowledging the cheers.

"Soldiers, you will know by now of Rome's victory over the Barbarian hordes. You will know that once again, the bravery, discipline and skills of the legions have triumphed in battle. I am proud to lead an army such as this."

More cheers from the crowd, which was growing all the time.

"It is not the destiny of every man to fight in every battle, but those that are assigned other tasks, as you were yesterday, must always be ready to display the same levels of courage. Sometimes, that duty may go beyond entering the melee of battle and offer instead an opportunity to display courage of the highest order. Yesterday, Legionary Capito volunteered for such a task, placing himself in harm's way, to engage in an act of combat that was instrumental to our success. His valour does honour to his family, to his century and to your legion."

A wave of sound echoed around the natural amphitheatre that had been formed by the watching crowd, and Atticus realised his comrades were banging their shields on the ground, adding to the cacophony of noise.

Allowing the clamour to reach a natural crescendo, Caesar held up his hand to elicit quiet, which was immediately forthcoming.

"Legionary Capito, step forward."

Atticus took a deep breath and walked stiffly towards Caesar, who acknowledged his salute before addressing the crowd again.

"It is customary in situations such as these for an individual to receive the Hasta Pura, a fine honour, it is true. But the award of a decorative and purely ceremonial spear did not seem very apt, given the nature of his courageous act."

He paused to draw his sword.

"Besides, the only weapons we need to concern ourselves with during this campaign are those of the cold, hard Roman steel that won us such a great victory yesterday."

Again, Caesar let the huge cheer that followed play out before raising his hand to indicate his wish to continue.

"Instead, I present Legionary Capito with a bronze phalera to wear with honour so that all might know of his bravery."

Caesar leant down from his horse and handed Atticus the small bronze disc.

"Your actions do you credit, Legionary. I'm sure your grandfather would be proud."

Caesar focussed his attention on the crowd once more.

"Tomorrow, we march in pursuit of the Barbarians who ran from us yesterday, the remnants of a huge army who thought they could defy Rome and her legions. Thought they could defy legionaries like Capito, legionaries like you. They were wrong and we go forth tomorrow to ensure that is a lesson they do not forget."

With that, he spurred his horse forward and, followed by his escort, galloped back towards his camp, leaving Atticus standing in the centre of the square with Aquila and Baculus.

Aquila fixed Atticus with a cold glare.

"Well, Capito, it seems that you have established quite the reputation. I will have to ensure that I never have an opportunity to provide you with the chance to live up to it."

He turned and stomped back towards his tent. Atticus wasn't sure he liked the sound of that; he'd had all the opportunity he wanted for now. Baculus tapped him encouragingly on the shoulder before turning to greet Plautius, who, having dismissed the century, had hurried over to join them.

"Best help the lad keep his head down, my friend, for a while at least. I'm not sure the legate wishes Capito here quite the good fortune that Caesar does."

Plautius nodded.

"I assumed he would be unimpressed by how things have turned out, although I'm guessing you knew events might take a different turn?"

"I wasn't expecting a visit from the general himself, but Trebonius, that was my doing. You know his first spear, Tullius Fabius Cotta, I believe."

"I do," said Plautius.

"Well, Tullius and I go back a long way. I served with him long before either of us achieved any rank of distinction. We've pulled each other out of more taverns and brothels than I expect either of us would care to admit or even remember," laughed Baculus. "I've shared a drink or two with him and Trebonius in the past. He's a good man, though not always the model of command that we witnessed today. I knew if I could get a message to Tullius, I could trust him to have Trebonius do the right thing."

Plautius nodded.

"Then we owe you our thanks."

"Yes," Atticus added, still clutching his phalera. "Thank you."

"That's okay, lad. You were only following orders after all and we were right to do what we did. Aquila knows it too. His desire for punishment was prompted by dented pride and concerns about protecting his position. It wasn't right. I couldn't stand by and allow that to happen. Now, with Plautius' permission, I suggest that you rejoin your tent party and enjoy the evening."

Plautius smiled.

"Go on, lad, but make sure you report to Rescius en route."

Atticus turned and walked back across the now deserted camp square, his mind reeling as he reflected on what had been quite an extraordinary day.

"What's that about?" Baculus asked.

Plautius smiled.

"The legate was right about one thing, brother, the need for discipline. Capito may be a hero but Rescius will be reminding him that he and his tent party still owe me one week's latrine duty, starting tonight."

6

AUGUST, 58 BC

Vosges Valley

Atticus darted between the tents as he made for the centre of the camp. Finally, he might get the chance to do something other than march. He didn't know how many miles they had covered since Bibracte, but he had blisters on his blisters and was thoroughly pissed off chasing the enemy back and forth across the countryside. The pursuit of the Helvetii, he understood. Caesar had promised to finish that job and they had surrendered when it became clear they weren't going to be allowed to slip quietly away. Now, though, they were pursuing the king of some German tribe who had settled in Gaul and the marching had just been relentless. He didn't know who this Ariovistus was or why Caesar had been in such a hurry to catch up with him, but they had marched day and night, forcing the pace for mile after mile until they reached Vesontio. They had been able to enjoy some respite from the marching there but the journey had left its mark. And not just physically, though the gods knew it had done that. There was something else too. Everybody seemed mentally exhausted and, unsettlingly, a pall of anxiety seemed to be hanging over the whole army. It had started with the disquiet at Vesontio and the rumours sweeping the camp about just how big, ferocious and ungodly their new German enemies were. The level of alarm had been such that Caesar himself was forced to call together every single centurion in an attempt to restore some semblance of order and pride. Atticus didn't know what had been said at that meeting, but Plautius had been even more focussed than usual on ensuring that the century looked the part on the march that followed the next day. That had been seven days ago and they had marched every day since. Until today. Not having to break camp had been a big relief, but the mood amongst the men was still subdued. That hadn't been helped by last night's incident, when sentries from the XIth had panicked at the sight of some of the native auxiliaries who had joined the legions to provide cavalry support. The subsequent fight had resulted in a number of dead and wounded on both sides. Rather more amongst the legionaries, it had been noticed, and, aside from souring relations, the whole episode had prompted talk of ill omens and warnings from the gods. Atticus was pleased to have the opportunity to think about something else. He had no idea if the rumours about the Germans were true, but he was very sure he would rather be doing something, anything, whilst he waited to find out. Whatever that might actually turn out to be.

Relieved to have escaped the endless ropes and narrow confines of the tents that he and his comrades called home, Atticus quickened his pace and turned into the wide avenue leading to the command tent. Now paying rather less attention than previously, he almost ran straight into Plautius. He quickly stiffened to attention.

"Sorry, sir."

"And where might you be heading off in such a hurry, Legionary Capito?"

"Rescius said that a request had been made for volunteers

with riding experience. He wasn't sure why, but I grew up with horses and—"

Plautius cut him short.

"And thought you would volunteer without having the slightest idea what for? Honestly, lad, I thought you had more brains than that! What happened to keeping a low profile?"

Atticus lowered his head to avoid Plautius' steely gaze.

"I hoped that it might get me out of camp for a while, sir. Maybe get to see the enemy and what we are up against from a distance."

Plautius shook his head.

"Oh, you'll get to see the enemy all right. Just not from any distance."

Atticus was immediately intrigued.

"You know what they want the volunteers to do?"

Plautius nodded.

"Not the detail. But at the briefing this morning, the legate mentioned that Caesar had agreed to a conference with Ariovistus. Damned if I know why. We've been chasing the bastard all over Gaul looking for a fight and now he wants to talk to him. But I'm sure the general knows what he's doing…"

Atticus looked puzzled. "But what's that got to do with the request for riders?"

"Well, as I understand it, Caesar has agreed to Ariovistus' request that they be accompanied by cavalry escorts only, and the general wants Romans with him. I don't blame him for wanting legionaries at his back, but these auxiliaries seem to know how to handle themselves and their horses. It's why they're here, after all. I can't imagine it's going to sit well with them when they find out they're being replaced."

Atticus joined the queue of legionaries waiting to secure horses from the auxiliary troops. He was glad that after their conversation, Plautius hadn't tried to prevent him getting involved. He had been right about the reaction of the Gauls, though; they weren't happy.

Reluctant to hand over their mounts, tempers had frayed. On more than one occasion, the auxiliaries' leader had been forced to intervene as arguments threatened to escalate into something altogether more violent. Atticus did feel a little uncomfortable watching these men having to surrender their horses, but he wasn't going to turn down the opportunity to escape the tedium of recent weeks. And it was his turn next. Summoned by the centurion overseeing the process, Atticus was directed towards a magnificent grey animal standing passively, but alertly, with its dismounted rider on the fringes of the crowd. He had ridden some fine horses back home but nothing quite like this. Lost in thought, he was startled when the man addressed him in Latin.

"He is a special horse, soldier, and very dear to me. A gift from my sister. You would do well to return him to me unscathed."

Surprised, Atticus turned to find himself face-to-face with the auxiliaries' leader. About the same age, perhaps a couple of years older, the warrior looked very similar to him in terms of both build and appearance. Atticus was glad Titus and the others weren't around to see.

"He is, and I will. Your Latin is very good."

The man shrugged.

"We are not all savages, Roman, despite what you may have heard. Besides, is it not useful to understand Rome as well as we do our friends?"

Atticus was confused.

"But you fight with us?"

The auxiliary shot him an angry look.

"We wanted to. Ariovistus has cast a shadow across our lands. We chose to join Rome in the fight to drive him out. My men have sworn an oath to battle beside you, to spill blood, theirs if necessary. But that is not enough for your general. His lack of trust dishonours us. I hope it is not a sign of things to come."

The auxiliary gestured to the group as he offered Atticus a helping hand into the saddle.

"And he wants to replace us with this… 'rabble'. I think some of these men would fall off a whore if the ride got too fast."

Slightly spooked by the commotion and the unfamiliar feel of his new rider, the auxiliary's horse jinked violently to the left, almost catching Atticus by surprise. Allowing the stallion to have his head, Atticus dug in his knees and took hold of his mane. Gradually bringing his mount under control, he leant forward, stroking the animal's neck and offering some reassuring words in his ear.

The auxiliary gave Atticus an approving nod.

"At least it looks as if you know how to ride, Roman. But I still expect him to be delivered back safely."

Atticus turned to respond but the warrior had already gone. Atticus watched him stalk across the square to rejoin his disgruntled comrades, before pulling gently on the reins and easing his mount forward.

*

It had been several days since the conference. He had been on the periphery of Caesar's escort, but riding with him had still been an honour. It had never occurred to him when he joined the legion that he might find himself one day playing the part of an Equestrian. Caesar had acknowledged him too, recognising him from Bibracte. It was only a fleeting smile but still, he felt proud. Things hadn't gone well, though, and now they were preparing for war. Today, for him and the rest of the tent party, that meant foraging, or more precisely harvesting wheat. Not at all what he wanted to be doing in this heat.

He looked up as Julius gave him a shout.

"Hey, noble Atticus, haven't you forgotten your horse?"

"Fuck off," he replied with a smile.

Titus shook his head.

"Language, Equestrian. You don't want those fancy officers at headquarters thinking we are a bad influence on you."

"To be honest, I'm surprised that he's willing to be seen with us at all," said Maximus.

"Enough," cried Atticus.

It had been like this since they had left the camp earlier that morning. He had expected it from Julius and Titus, but now even Maximus, by far the quietest member of the tent party, was joining in.

"I told you before, I didn't know when I volunteered that the duty would involve riding alongside Caesar."

Titus gave him a nudge.

"And there was us thinking he'd asked for you personally."

Julius laughed.

"I bet he won't be volunteering again though. He came home without a phalera this time."

Atticus gave up and turned his attention back to scything the wheat. The morning mist had long since burned off and, without a cloud in the sky, the temperature was rising quickly. It was going to be another warm day, too warm for foraging. He drew his hand across his brow and wiped away the sweat. He was glad that Plautius had given them permission to march without their woollen tunics, and it had been a blessed relief to stow their weapons and armour. But the heat and the physical activity had left his cotton shirt clinging uncomfortably to his body and he knew he would be glad when they were done. Atticus bent, gathered up the cut grain and walked slowly towards the wagon where Rescius was supervising its collection. As he approached, he saw Plautius, still bedecked in full armour, returning from what had presumably been another tour of the perimeter. He was being especially watchful today, though Atticus wasn't complaining, as he didn't feel truly comfortable being away from camp with the enemy so close nearby.

Rescius looked up from his wax tablet.

"Lads giving you a hard time?"

Atticus gave him a resigned smile.

"Of course, but nothing I didn't expect."

"Don't let them get to you. It will blow over soon enough, probably helps take their minds off being out here."

"That's Aquila's doing," said Plautius as he arrived at the wagon and joined the conversation.

"Have you not noticed how as a century we get more guard duty, more work in the stables, than anybody else? And who was it sent to help the vanguard manhandle the baggage train across the ford? Us. Now this. You think it's an accident that half the century is sent out here foraging, just a couple of days after Capito here rides with Caesar and reminds Aquila just why he has it in for us in the first place? And the shame of it all is that the bloody conference turned out to be a complete waste of time anyway! Isn't that right, lad?"

Atticus nodded.

"Yes. Then again, Ariovistus did start by taunting Caesar. He said he'd received offers of rewards from the nobility back in Rome to kill him. So, I guess it was never going to go well. Not that they were ever going to agree. The general just kept repeating that Rome wouldn't desert her allies when their lands were being forcibly seized and raiding parties were crossing the Rhine."

"And Ariovistus?" asked Rescius.

"He wanted to know why Rome hadn't supported her allies previously. And why, having been declared a 'Friend of Rome',

Caesar was now prepared to fight, rather than support him."

"He was an ally too?" Rescius spluttered.

"Apparently. Turns out it was Caesar himself who granted him the honour. Just last year. If you think about it, the whole thing does seem odd."

Plautius laughed.

"In my experience, lad, it pays not to think too much about anything, other than the task at hand. Anything else is a recipe for getting yourself hurt. Leave the politics and diplomacy to the nobles. Is that how things finished up?"

"No. That was when Ariovistus' cavalry started harassing the flanks of our escort."

Rescius shook his head.

"Bastard. Was there any trouble?"

"No, I think the general knew they were only trying to provoke us. He ordered us not to draw our weapons. Not that I would have wanted to. It's true what they've been saying. They were bloody big bastards, all of them."

Plautius smiled.

"Don't you think that might have been deliberate, lad? I'm sure he handpicked the biggest brutes he could find! But just in case, best not go sharing that detail too widely, eh!"

He slapped Atticus on the shoulder.

"Though remember, big or small, they go down just as quickly with six inches of sharp steel inside them."

Rescius shrugged.

"Well, I guess with the talks having failed, we will get the chance to see for ourselves soon enough. Must be why the enemy moved their camp yesterday. How far away are they now, do you think? Five, six miles?"

Plautius scowled angrily.

"Yes, which is why this is low even for Aquila! The bastard knows the enemy will have scouts on patrol and yet he still puts us out here, in danger. Rescius, hurry them along. I don't want to be here any longer than necessary. Capito, tell the lads to look sharp. I have a bad feeling about this."

Atticus wasn't sure how long they had been working, but the sun had long since passed directly overhead. He hoped they would be finished soon. He'd wanted a rest from all the marching to ease the blisters on his feet, only to find he was now developing them on his hands. But it was the monotony that was really getting to him. He thought about the slaves on his family's estate, feeling more than a little ashamed that he hadn't previously given any thought to how they must have felt, undertaking such repetitive and backbreaking work, day after day. Just as he found himself beginning to think about home for the first time in many weeks, Julius interrupted his thoughts.

"Atticus... Atticus! Get your head out of your arse! Or Caesar's! Rescius is calling us."

Atticus turned, ready to return the insult, but Julius was already heading back towards the wagon, which had become a hive of activity as the men streamed back from all directions and began jostling for space to don their armour. This couldn't be good. Atticus grabbed his scythe. Trouble or not, he wasn't going to allow the quartermaster the satisfaction of docking his pay for leaving it behind. He ran to join his comrades. As he did so, he saw one of the pickets hurrying away, presumably to retake his position on the perimeter. Atticus realised that it must have been something significant for the sentry to leave his post, and he picked up his pace to cover the last few yards as quickly as he could. Joining the scrum of men from the two tent parties working that wagon, he could see a similar picture at the far end of the field and guessed that it was being repeated at the two wagons stationed in the next field. With help from Julius, he slid on his mail cuirass, heavy and warm despite sitting under the shade of his shield. He was grateful for the first time that day for his albeit now very wet tunic and the small degree of comfort it would offer beneath his armour. He quickly fastened his scabbard and retrieved his helmet and shield from the side of the wagon.

"Quiet!" yelled Rescius.

Although the men were not normally known for the immediacy with which they arrived at silence, the uncertainty of the situation and the unusually brusque nature of Rescius' approach meant that he had no need to repeat his order.

"The pickets have reported sight of enemy scouts, two or three of the bastards on horseback. He's not sure if they saw us, but Plautius doesn't want us to wait around to find out. He's ordered all the wagons to converge here and then we'll head back to camp, collecting up the pickets as we go. I want two lines either side of the wagons. Be ready to move as soon as they arrive."

After what seemed like an age, Atticus saw the two ox-driven carts from the neighbouring fields lumber into view and begin the gentle climb onto the track, where he and his comrades were impatiently waiting. Berated all the way by Plautius but limited by the speed of the oxen, which never seemed to vary much beyond a gentle walk, it was going to be a much longer journey back to camp than they would have wished. He watched as Plautius stalked past and joined Rescius at the head of the column. After a brief conversation, he hurried back down the line, presumably to offer whatever encouragement he thought necessary at the rear. Atticus smiled to himself; he had experienced some of that "encouragement" on marches in the past, when the cohort hadn't quite matched the pace that Plautius wanted. Spurred on by the very real sense of danger, he doubted that would be an issue today. Or at least it wouldn't have been but for the oxen. Of course, if they had been spotted by the scouts, which seemed likely, it wouldn't matter much either way.

"Move out!" ordered Rescius. "Keep tight. And stay alert."

As if mirroring the uncertainty Atticus was feeling about how things might unfold, the column lurched hesitantly into action and their return journey began.

7

Vosges Valley

Marching at the head of the column, Atticus was pleased to be escaping the worst of the dust thrown up by the wagons as they ground their way back along the sun-baked track. They had just cleared the treeline that surrounded the edge of the fields when the wagon came to a sudden halt. Atticus was about to suggest to the auxiliary driving the oxen that stopping would only incur Plautius' wrath, when his attention was drawn to the man's outstretched hand. Switching his gaze towards the front of the wagon, Atticus saw what had captured the man's attention. There in the distance, rising from the plains and extending far above the Roman camp, was an absolutely enormous dust cloud.

"What the fuck have we stopped for?" demanded Rescius, before he too caught sight of the reason for the delay. Moments later, they were joined by Plautius.

"Any chance it's moving away?" he asked hopefully.

"Afraid not. Must be their whole bloody army on the move again," replied Rescius.

"I'll wager the bastard is going to try and cut us off from our supply lines. And we'll be caught in his way if we don't get a shift on," said Plautius.

"And there was me thinking it was just Aquila we'd pissed off. Seems Fortuna wants a piece of us too," said Rescius. Plautius laughed.

"Indeed, brother, but hopefully they won't be moving much faster than us. We might still disappoint her if we can avoid their vanguard and those bloody scouts. Right. Get them moving again. As quickly as possible."

"And you…" he said, turning to the driver, "there's a cup of wine in it for you, if you can get these beasts to do passable impressions of a mule!"

They had perhaps travelled half a mile when Julius called to Atticus.

"Look," he said, pointing to the left of the column, "over there."

At first, Atticus couldn't see anything other than the heat haze shimmering over the parched landscape, but then he caught sight of the unmistakeable silhouette of riders, three of them. Any thoughts that they might not yet have been seen were dispelled immediately as one of the riders peeled off and began heading in their direction. Rescius had seen them too.

"Don't worry about them. I think we can cope with two or three of the bastards." The column crawled on, the offer of free wine seemingly adding little to the ability of the auxiliary to coax an increase in pace from the oxen.

Although visible on the horizon, the camp didn't seem to be getting any closer, unlike the scout, who was now tracking the column a little more than twenty to thirty paces away. He shouted something at them in his guttural mother tongue, turned abruptly away and trotted back to his waiting comrades. Atticus watched them come together, before one of them spurred his horse into a canter and disappeared back towards the dust cloud, which appeared to have advanced faster towards them than they had to the camp. The two remaining scouts slowly trotted forward and began to follow the column.

After a short while, one of the riders ventured in a little closer. Large, red-haired and naked from the waist up, he was a fearsome sight, especially brandishing the long spear that he waved angrily at the column. Each time he rode in, Rescius was forced to halt the column and give the order for shields to be raised. If he ordered an advance, the rider simply retreated beyond the point Rescius was happy to allow the men to stray from the column. Atticus knew the scout didn't pose any real danger, but his continued harassment meant their progress was painfully slow. After warrior's third or fourth advance, Rescius had had enough. He turned to seek out Maximus.

"Legionary Syrus, do you have your sling with you?"

"Yes, sir, always," he replied.

"Then get up there on the wagon and make sure that bastard keeps his distance."

With the wagon still moving, Maximus passed his shield to Atticus and hurried to clamber aboard. Atticus had always been impressed by Maximus' skill with a sling, something he had learnt protecting the flocks in the Apennine Mountains, which surrounded his home in Piacenza. As Maximus took aim, the warrior recognised the danger but was much too close to escape. Maximus' first shot struck him a glancing but obviously painful blow on the shoulder. As he turned to shout a curse, the second shot struck him directly on the knee. Howling in pain and grasping his leg, he slumped forward in the saddle, saving him from further injury as the third shot whistled directly over his head. As the warrior's comrade rode in to steer him to safety, Rescius called a halt to the attack.

"That's enough, lad. Well done. I don't think they'll bother us again in a hurry."

With no further interruptions, the column was able to continue its slow but steady progress. For the first time, Atticus was able to pick out the familiar features of the camp, with its watch towers rising from each corner and standards flying proudly above the main gate. They weren't close enough for him to be able to make out the sentries patrolling the wall but he knew that they would be there. Surely, they would now be able to see the column approaching, though any complacency about making it back was quickly quashed by the backdrop of the ever-expanding dust cloud, still moving inexorably in their direction. As he continued to scan the horizon, Atticus became aware of a smaller dust cloud to their left. Still some way away, it was closing rapidly with the column. Riders! Plautius had obviously seen them too and joined Rescius at the head of the column.

"Too much to hope it's ours returning back from patrol, I suppose?" he said ruefully.

Rescius smiled.

"We can hope, brother, but with our luck I wouldn't be taking that wager."

He gestured to the camp.

"Only good thing is that we are close enough now to expect a little support if things get hairy."

"True enough. But let's not take any chances this close to home," replied Plautius.

Turning away, he walked a short way down the column before bellowing, "Form square. Wagons in the centre. On me…!"

With an ease born of countless hours of practice, the men of the column quickly formed a rough square, leaving just enough space on one side for the wagons to be driven through and stowed in the centre, before that line too was quickly closed. Atticus felt his heart racing and nervously ran his tongue over his parched lips. The riders had closed in quickly and were now circling them, kicking up dust as they shouted and gestured angrily at Atticus and his comrades, who could only stoically look on. He might not have understood the snarled insults but the hand gestures were clear enough. The dizzying frequency with which the riders were circling made it hard to estimate their numbers but Atticus guessed it was between thirty-five and forty. More than enough to take out the column should they attempt to resume their journey. Probably enough to tackle them now if they really wanted to, despite their defensive formation. So far, however, they had shown no inclination to do so. At least not collectively. There had been the odd sally forward to discharge spears but Atticus hadn't heard any obvious sounds of distress and he realised that the impact was largely mental, sapping the confidence of the weary soldiers, who were unable to channel their fear into any form of response. On one occasion, a warrior had leapt off his moving horse and advanced menacingly towards the square, heavy sword in hand, taunting them to leave the line and engage him.

"Bastard!" said Julius, shifting uncomfortably from foot to foot as if itching to take up the challenge. Atticus could see that he was not the only one.

"Hold!" said Rescius firmly. "I'll skewer the first man that moves and save that hairy bastard the trouble!"

Realising that he was not going to succeed in drawing anybody out to face him, the warrior retreated. Instead of rejoining his comrades, he stopped, pulled down his pants and proceeded to piss in a wide arc in front of them, presumably passing his judgement on their masculinity and courage. To Atticus' left, Titus called out a response.

"You should know that Romans laugh at the smallest things, Barbarian."

A clever retort under the circumstances, it prompted some amusement and helped to ease the tension. Atticus wasn't sure but he thought he'd even caught a glimpse of a smile on Plautius' face. Oblivious, the warrior mounted his horse and rejoined his colleagues as they continued their relentless encirclement.

"Why don't they attack?" asked Atticus.

Rescius gestured to the dust cloud that now towered over the Roman camp and could not have been more than a mile from their location.

"No need, lad. Keep us here a little longer and their whole bloody army can roll right over us."

Atticus shook his head.

"Surely the camp can see us. Why haven't they sent help?"

"I don't know but I'm damn sure Plautius will find out. If… when we get back to camp," Rescius replied angrily.

"Find out what?" asked Plautius.

"Why nobody from that shower on the wall has reported our position and summoned help!"

"My thoughts exactly, brother, but we can't leave it any longer if we want to stay alive long enough to find out. We won't make it back with the wagons. Let's leave those but we'll remain in formation as we move. It won't be pretty but it's our only hope. Be ready if they look like making a charge. Otherwise, we stop for nothing. Nothing! Understand?"

"Yes, sir," replied Rescius.

"May Fortuna smile over you, brother."

"You too," nodded Rescius.

"What did he mean, we stop for nothing?" asked Atticus.

"Best you don't get injured, lad, that way you need never find out."

*

Plautius had just completed his march around the square when Rescius drew his attention to the camp.

"The gates are opening."

Atticus watched as the main gate slowly swung open and a stream of cavalry rode out onto the plain.

"About bloody time. Now, let's see if these Barbarian whoresons are quite so brave faced with somebody who can fight back," said Plautius.

Despite frantic warnings from some of their number, the majority of warriors remained focussed on the captive Roman column and were totally unprepared when the relieving cavalry streamed past on either side of the square, trapping the Germans between the two Roman lines. The noise was deafening. Shielding his face from the choking dust thrown up by the skirmishing warriors and their mounts, Atticus tried to make sense of what was happening. Everywhere he looked, men were locked in desperate hand-to-hand combat. To his surprise, the riders who had come to their aid were not Roman but the auxiliaries. One or two of them had fallen but the speed of their attack left a swathe of Germans dead in their wake and across the square the remainder were trying to disengage and break free. Fighting bravely but outnumbered and with limited room for manoeuvre, still more of them fell before the intensity of the fighting inevitably began to wane and a few individuals managed to slip through the press of men and horses and gallop to safety. As the dust began to settle, Atticus recognised the leader of the relieving cavalry as the auxiliary who had given up his horse to him for the conference. He was pleased to see that both horse and rider appeared unscathed.

Plautius left the square to greet their rescuers.

"My thanks, friend."

The auxiliary nodded and exchanged a smile with Atticus.

"Perhaps your general will think we are good enough now,

Roman! Meantime, I think it best we get back to camp. I suspect the next group may be too large even for us to chase off."

Plautius smiled.

"True. No need to tempt fate any further. Rescius, get them moving!"

Unimpeded by further attack and now on the flat ground of the plain, the column, wagons included, quickly completed its journey. As they passed through the camp's main gate, Atticus gave thanks to Fortuna. He hoped she would be willing to overlook the fact that he hadn't yet made the offering he had promised previously. *I will*, he thought, *I will*. The column halted as Plautius reported to the centurion commanding the watch. Atticus couldn't hear the conversation but it was certainly animated and Plautius returned shaking his head.

"What was the weasel's excuse?" asked Rescius bluntly.

"No excuse needed. Seems he reported our position to Aquila as soon as the lads on the wall spotted us…"

"And…?" enquired Rescius.

"The bastard sent a message back, saying that he wasn't clear what was being asked and requesting further information."

He gestured to the watch commander.

"Gallus, there, swears his report of the situation and the request to send assistance was perfectly clear. I'm inclined to believe him. Meaning—"

"Meaning that Aquila deliberately put us in danger by delaying his response. I can't believe it," said Rescius incredulously.

"Me neither. Fortunately, Gallus has been around almost as long as us, and he wasn't happy. He took it upon himself to have the auxiliaries readied for action whilst he reported directly to Aquila. Bastard had no choice but to act then."

"Then it seems we did Gallus a disservice and owe him a debt of thanks, as well as these lads," said Rescius, gesturing to the auxiliaries, who were still milling around, tending to their injured and celebrating their victory.

"We do. I…"

Whatever Plautius was about to say was lost as he looked up and saw Aquila approaching. He bellowed at his exhausted legionaries.

"Attention!"

Immediately ceasing their idle conversations and the good-natured exchanges they had been sharing with the auxiliaries, now they were safe again within the confines of the camp, the men hurried to comply.

"Centurion, so good to see you back safely and with such a fine haul too. I'm sure Gallus has explained that I sent aid just as soon as I was sure what the situation was."

"Gallus has explained, sir. We were grateful for the assistance. When it came."

Aquila gave Plautius a sly smile.

"Well, you know the types of delay that can occur in the communication of orders, Centurion. They can sometimes look like failures of command."

Plautius bristled at this clear reference to the incident at Bibracte but nevertheless held his tongue.

"Sir."

"I would like your report by evening watch, Centurion," demanded Aquila as he turned to leave. "In the meantime, I shall go and report your successful haul."

"No thanks to you," Atticus heard Plautius whisper under his breath. "Rescius, have the grain taken to the store and send one or two of the lads along just to make sure it all gets there. I have a bloody report to write."

Dismissed with the rest of the column, who had successfully avoided escorting the wagons, Atticus quickly joined Julius on top of the turf-covered rampart surrounding the camp. Looking over the wooden stakes that topped the wall, Atticus could see the reason for Julius' urgent summons. Streaming past in the valley below, a host of men, horses and wagons that stretched for as far as the eye could see.

"Gods above! That is some sight. Seems we made it back just in time," said Atticus.

"We did, although I expect we'll be facing them again soon enough, don't you?" Julius replied.

"If Plautius is right about them trying to cut off our supply lines, we won't have any choice. I will just be glad to have a few more of the legion at my back when we do, brother," said Atticus.

"And maybe some more of their cavalry," replied Julius, gesturing towards the auxiliaries' leader, who was now climbing the rampart to join them. Atticus nodded and turned to greet the man as he arrived.

"You have our thanks. Without your timely arrival, I think that lot would have trampled us underfoot without breaking stride."

The auxiliary shook his head.

"I don't know about 'timely'. Personally, I would not have waited so long to send aid. It seems your leader – Aquila, isn't it? – has no more love for you soldiers than your general does for his auxiliaries." He laughed. "Maybe you would like to join your fellow outcasts for a drink this evening?"

Julius looked forlorn.

"We would love to but we expect battle to be joined tomorrow."

"Surely all the more reason to enjoy a drink tonight?" responded the auxiliary with a smile.

"Not if you knew our centurion. It's Plautius we fight for, not Aquila," explained Atticus, seeing the blank look on the face of the auxiliary.

The man nodded.

"He seems like the kind of soldier you would want to follow, but he's not the one who controls your fate. I would keep my friends close as long as that man is Aquila."

Julius laughed and gave Atticus a nudge.

"But not too close. Things have a habit of getting hairy whenever you are around."

"Until we meet again then," said the auxiliary, turning to leave.

"Wait!" said Atticus. "We don't even know your name. I am Atticus Volteius Capito and this is Julius Valerius Naso, both of the Second century, First cohort of the XII Legion. And you are?"

"I am Allerix," replied the auxiliary, "son of Albiorix, King of the Aduatuci."

8

SEPTEMBER, 58 BC

Vosges Valley

The morning alarm call woke Atticus with a start. If he had been dreaming, he couldn't recall what about. But he had been warm, comfortable and very much asleep. With a resigned groan, he slowly sat up and pulled the thin woollen blanket off his legs. With the exception of Titus, who somehow was still snoring away, the tent was a hive of activity as his comrades joined him and the thousands of others across camp rising to greet the new day. Quickly pulling on and lacing up his boots, Atticus paused as he went to duck out of the tent. Smiling to himself, he retraced his steps, bent down, retrieved one of the boots that Titus had left strewn in the middle of the floor, took aim and deftly tossed it. It landed with a satisfying thud, eliciting a torrent of abuse from Titus, who was still slowly coming around. Atticus hastily left the tent and joined Julius and Maximus warming their porridge on the fire. It looked like it was going to be another fine day. The mist which had brought the chill last night was already beginning to burn off as the sun began to climb into the sky. Ordinarily, Atticus loved the early mornings, the hubbub as the camp slowly came to life, the opportunity to eat, even if it was just porridge – again – and to pass some time with his friends before the rigours of the day began, but there had been a dreary sense of anti-climax about their routine over the last few days, which had left him with a heavy feeling he couldn't shake. For the last five days, the entire army had marched out and formed up opposite Ariovistus' camp, hoping to entice him to battle. And for five days, that is where they had stood, for hours, until, having failed to draw Ariovistus out, the order was given to return to camp. In between these futile excursions there had been the inevitable round of cleaning, maintenance and guard duties. There was only so much cleaning and polishing to be done, however, even in the Roman army. It came to something when he was actually looking forward to the time spent patrolling the wall. At least, there, he was doing something meaningful. It also gave him the opportunity to observe the afternoon cavalry skirmishes, which had become another feature of daily life. These had been relatively short but fierce affairs. The German cavalry seemed to lack any structure or discipline but they were brave and skilful, and there were far more of them than the men led by Allerix. Despite this, the auxiliaries had more than held their own and Atticus had been impressed by the manner in which Allerix led his warriors. Once again, he was grateful that they were fighting with the Romans rather than against them. Not that his duties had left him any opportunity to tell Allerix this. Or indeed enjoy the drink which had been offered.

"Morning," said Maximus quietly, offering Atticus a bowl of porridge, which he eagerly accepted. Julius nodded a greeting but seemed as subdued as Atticus and unusually for them they ate in silence. Or at least until Titus arrived. He gave Atticus a friendly shove as he sat down.

"Well, I can see you're all here, so I know no one has died. What's up?"

"Nothing," replied Julius grumpily.

"Nothing is about right, brother," said Atticus. "Five days of nothing! And how many days chasing around before that? Not that I have any desire to face them again but this can only end in battle, and I'd prefer it if that was sooner rather than later."

Titus smiled.

"My old centurion used to say another day bored is another day alive. But I know what you mean, lad. Trouble is, I can't see them fighting anytime soon. Not unless we do something different. It's our supply lines that are restricted, not theirs. Now, more importantly, any more porridge in that bowl of yours, young Maximus?"

"So much for restricted supplies!" laughed Julius as the call to parade sounded and they hurried to make themselves suitably presentable.

"It will be quicker if you put the porridge down, Titus," Maximus laughed, as his friend struggled to get his armour on.

Julius shook his head.

"It's all the porridge he's eaten already that's the problem, not the one he's holding." Atticus smiled at Julius as they ducked beneath the porridge-laden spoon that came flying in their direction.

"No better with a spoon than he is a javelin."

"But okay with this," growled Titus, easing his sword from its scabbard.

"Now get going before I shove this where the sun doesn't shine."

Maximus pushed past Titus to join Atticus and Julius.

"You'll have to catch us first, old man!"

The three of them set off for the parade ground, with Titus in pursuit. With the mood temporarily lifted, Atticus was eager to see what the day held. Hopefully, something different to what had gone before.

*

Atticus looked up as he passed beneath the gantry of the twin towers guarding the main gate. It was something he'd done on every occasion he'd left the camp, and he wondered if it hadn't become an involuntary habit in case he didn't return. This time was different, though. The XIIth Legion would not be returning to camp. From their position towards the rear of the column, he could see the huge body of men and cavalry snaking out onto the plain. It was an impressive sight and went some way to quelling the sense of nervous anticipation he was feeling. Today, they marched not to parade but to build a second camp directly behind that of the Germans. Plautius had explained that this was a bid to turn the tables by restricting the flow of the enemy's supplies, hopefully forcing them into battle. Echoing Titus' thoughts that a change in tactics was necessary to force the hand of the enemy, he had been quick to claim his wasted promise when the plan to do something different was announced. The wave of insults and hoots of derision that followed ended abruptly when they discovered that once complete, the much smaller camp would be their new home. Together with the Xth Legion and the auxiliaries (or his "local friends" as Julius now insisted on referring to them), they would form the garrison tasked with holding the new position. If that wasn't bad enough, he and his friends were also going to be part of the defensive line deployed to protect those building the camp. He swallowed nervously and wondered if he might need to be more careful about just what he wished for. The look of apprehension on Maximus' face suggested he wasn't alone.

"You know we're going to be right at the sharp end out here if things do kick off?"

"Bloody thing has to be built first," replied Titus, still clearly sulking about the lack of respect for his self-proclaimed leadership acumen.

Julius gestured to the sprawling expanse of the German camp as they marched past.

"Better than having to try and hold that lot back."

"I've seen your attempts at camp construction, Naso," barked Plautius. "We're all better off with you out front. Now quieten down and listen out for the signal."

They had marched another 300 paces when the sounds of the buccina began to ring out. Almost at once, the inner of the three lines in which the legions had been marching began to peel off towards the site chosen for the second camp. The outer two lines continued marching until they had encircled those tasked with constructing the camp, establishing a defensive screen between them and the Germans. Their arrival on the plain had provoked the enemy into action, and the auxiliaries had been busy protecting the flanks of the marching legions. Atticus had seen several groups of enemy cavalry beaten back and forced to retreat after failing to affect a breakthrough. Now, as they turned to face the enemy camp, he could see hundreds of riders spilling from the gates. It looked as if the Germans were coming again, and this time in force. Splitting into several groups, the riders swept forward. Behind them, the gates remained open. It wasn't long before he could see why. The infantry was coming too. Atticus wiped his clammy hands on his tunic as a vast swarm of warriors came tumbling out of the camp. Julius sucked in his breath.

"By the gods… there are thousands of them."

Rescius tapped him on the shoulder.

"And there are thousands of us too, lad. We knew they'd come. Remember your training, and everything else will take care of itself."

Atticus wasn't sure how Rescius managed to seem so calm. He didn't think there were as many of the enemy as at Bibracte, but this time the XIIth would be fighting, not watching. Their first engagement. Fearing that he may have exhausted Fortuna's patience, he fumbled for his pendant.

"Jupiter, good and great, please don't let me dishonour my family or my legion."

Julius sighed.

"You do know that bloody thing isn't Jupiter, don't you?"

"Piss off!" replied Atticus, though in truth he wasn't entirely sure who it was supposed to be. His father hadn't said when he'd given it to him on the eve of his departure. He felt a pang of remorse about the manner of his leaving. It had left little opportunity for discussion. Still, the pendant had been in his family for as long as he could remember and, whilst it was certainly unusual in its design, it bore enough similarity to Jupiter to satisfy him. Especially now. Besides, hadn't he and Fortuna always answered his prayers...? So far at least.

"Well, I'm not stopping now, if that's what you want."

Julius shook his head.

"You carry on, brother. Say one for me. I think we're going to need all the help we can get. Wherever it comes from."

*

The ground shook as the Germans began their charge. Atticus felt his stomach tighten and tried to control his breathing as his heartbeat quickened. Careering across the plain, the horde of warriors resembled a huge wave. One that would surely sweep them away as it broke upon the Roman line. Those in the front rank shifted uneasily as they watched the enemy approach. Atticus slid his right foot slightly further back behind him and twisted it in the dirt, seeking the slightest additional purchase. He could feel the reassuring presence of the men behind him but knew it was those in the front row that were going to bear the brunt of the charge. He exchanged glances with Julius and Titus. There was no need for words. Their lives were now entirely dependent on each other and the strength of their training. The enemy were almost upon them. Close enough now for him to make out the characteristics of individual warriors, though the huge array of different clothes, weapons and shields meant there was no discernible pattern to their appearance. The one constant was the look of hostility on their faces. And the noise. The whole Roman line seemed enveloped by battle cries as the warriors approached. It was almost enough to drown out Plautius' bellowed command. Almost.

"Front rank. Draw swords!"

As one, those in the front line eased their blades free. Encouraged by Rescius, they began to make some noise of their own, banging their swords rhythmically against their shields. Plautius grunted his approval before issuing the order for javelins to be raised.

"Now, let's see about slowing these bastards down. Rear rank. Release!"

A flight of javelins arced towards the Germans before disappearing into the mass of warriors. At once, the momentum slowed, men vanishing as if spirited away by the gods. Others injured or slowed to a walk by the weight of javelins lodged in their shields.

"Second volley!" cried Plautius.

Again, the sky was filled with iron-tipped missiles. Slamming into the packed ranks, slowed by the carnage of the first flight, the second volley wreaked even greater havoc, those who had escaped injury trying desperately to extricate themselves from the mass of dead and wounded before they were trampled by those from behind. But still they came, clattering into the shield wall in small and isolated groups that were quickly despatched by the waiting legionaries. It was a temporary reprieve. The second wave arrived as one. Atticus felt the air being driven from his lungs as the weight of the collision shook his body to the core.

He leant into his shield and scrambled desperately to hold his position. It was no use. The force was just too great and he could feel the Roman line being driven inexorably back.

But the line held.

They had survived the charge.

As the intensity of the enemy attack subsided, the clash became an attritional battle for supremacy. Fought in an almost eerie silence, save for the rasp of laboured breathing and occasional cries of pain as a blade found its target. His senses heightened, the foul-smelling odour of the enemy filled Atticus' nostrils and he fought the urge to gag as the two sides struggled to wrest some sort of advantage from the scrummage. Frustrated by their failed attempt to overrun the Romans, some of the warriors had begun trying to drag individual legionaries from the line. Following suit, the broad and bearded warrior opposite him suddenly lunged forward, grabbing the top of Atticus' shield. Lips curled in a nasty snarl, the German began to pull. Atticus dug in his heels and clenched his fist as tightly as he could around the handle of his shield, but he could feel himself beginning to move forward. Desperate to avoid being pulled from the relative safety of the line, Atticus raised his sword and chopped it down against his shield, severing several of the warrior's fingers and sending them spinning into the air. As the German howled and looked plaintively at his maimed hand, Atticus slid his shield aside and punched his sword into the warrior's stomach. Hemmed in by the sheer weight of numbers, he might have died where he stood if he hadn't been pulled unceremoniously aside by another warrior, impatient to reach the Roman line. The German pushing himself forward was older and wirier than the first. A wry smile ran across the warrior's scarred face. Atticus hoped this was merely an act of bravado, but he suspected the air of confidence was borne of experience. Hoping his own inexperience wasn't equally obvious, Atticus thrust out his sword. The warrior parried the blow and quickly slid forward. Raising his sword high above his head, he swung it towards Atticus, who met the blow with the edge of his hurriedly raised shield. The shock of the blow stung his arm and he fought to stifle a cry of pain. Encouraged, the German moved forward, this time changing the angle of his attack to try and reach beyond Atticus' shield. Atticus leant away from the blade and chopped down his sword, forcing the warrior to drag back his arm. But he was quick, and before Atticus could regain his composure, the warrior's sword came sweeping in again. The blade caught him a glancing blow on the shoulder. His armour saved him from injury but the blow numbed his arm and he cried out in pain as he fought to retain hold of his sword. The warrior roared and lunged forward, slashing his sword at Atticus' head. Grimacing with pain, Atticus threw up his shield, intercepting the blow and momentarily throwing the warrior off balance. As he tried to recover, Titus drove his sword into the German, giving the blade a savage twist. The warrior snapped his head around and tried desperately to reach Titus. But his life was ebbing away. He dropped his sword and slumped forward, pinning Atticus behind his shield. Unable to shake the warrior free, Atticus dropped his knee to the ground and rolled the man into the space ahead of his comrades in the second line, where he was promptly sent to join his ancestors. Leaping quickly to his feet, Atticus was surprised to see the Germans backing slowly away, leaving a bloody pile of corpses before them. Amongst the dead, he could see a small number clad in the familiar red of the legions. His legion. Maybe even men he knew. He shivered. Had known. Plautius took advantage of the unexpected respite to order a rotation of the two lines. Those who had not already been required to fill a space in the line created by a Roman casualty stepped forward to relieve their comrades. Rescius gestured towards the pile of torn and twisted bodies lying before them.

"Make sure the bastards are dead! And be ready. They will be back."

Atticus tapped Maximus on the shoulder as they exchanged places.

"Be safe, brother."

Maximus barely seemed to notice, fixated on the carnage that had greeted him and the sight of the enormous German horde backing slowly and angrily away. Atticus gratefully took a drink from the skin Julius had offered. He wondered if he wore the same dead-eyed stare as his friend. He'd known what to expect but nothing could have prepared him for the reality of what had just happened and he bent forward to retch. Julius leant across and patted him reassuringly on the back.

"You and me both, brother."

His arm was covered in blood.

"It's okay," he said, seeing Atticus' look of concern.

"It's not mine. Titus, however, does seem to have acquired some evidence of the fight."

Atticus looked to his left, where Titus was grudgingly allowing one of the medical orderlies to tend to a very nasty gash on his face.

"You okay?"

"He'll live," the frustrated orderly replied.

"Though I'll stick him myself if he doesn't stand still."

"Go on, I'll do it," said Atticus, stepping forward to take the dressing from the clearly relieved soldier, who wasn't about to argue.

"Thank you," said Atticus as he tried to dress the wound. "The one you took care of for me..." he added, seeing Titus' blank expression.

"That's okay, lad. You'd have done the same for me."

"Does it get any easier?" Atticus asked quietly.

Titus thought for a moment.

"In a way. The fear never leaves you. But that's good. It's what keeps you alive. If you try not to think about those at the end of your sword, the aftermath gets easier too."

A pained expression flashed across his face.

"As long as your friends are all standing, that is…"

Catching sight of Atticus' inquisitive look, he smiled.

"Of course, if you really want to know, you'll have to ask someone who wasn't always taking care of donkeys!"

The three of them broke into a laugh. As Julius and Titus began to exchange their customary insults, Atticus reflected on how quickly some semblance of normality returned to life, despite the bloodshed.

"You did well!" said Rescius as he and Plautius made their way along the line.

"Did we lose many?" asked Julius.

"Some…" replied Rescius solemnly. "But they lost more. And the line held. So… first blood to us."

*

The second attack wasn't long in coming. This time, cavalry. Gathering in the distance, too many to count, the Germans spread across the plain and slowly began their advance. Breaking from a walk to a trot and then a full canter, they came thundering towards the Roman lines. Atticus could feel the ground shaking beneath his feet before the noise reached them, a low and ominous rumble that grew louder and louder as the Germans approached. Knowing that it was intended to scare them into running didn't make it any easier to remain rooted to the spot, and doing so felt very, very uncomfortable. He exchanged a nervous glance with Julius before joining the large number of his comrades looking back for direction from their officers. Plautius stepped forward.

"Eyes front! They won't risk charging a shield wall, so let's give them one. Front rank. Kneel! Shields locked! Second rank. Raise shields!"

In a move that was repeated along the line, Atticus stepped forward to angle his shield out and over the man in front, helping to create a solid-looking barrier some five or six feet tall. He hoped it would look sufficiently formidable to dissuade the charge, though he wasn't as confident as Plautius. He swallowed nervously and peered anxiously over the top of his shield, drawing Rescius' ire in the process.

"Capito! Get your bloody head down."

Complying quickly, Atticus shifted uncomfortably on the spot as the noise of the onrushing cavalry grew louder and louder. He closed his eyes and gritted his teeth as the effort of holding his shield in position began to tell. Just as he was sure the horses must come crashing through the line, the noise of the charge was replaced by a heavy rain of missiles clattering into their shields. He crouched a little lower and pulled his shield towards him as tightly as he could. He could hear the angry cries of the enemy warriors as they rode along the line, circling their horses and repeating their attacks, probing for any weakness in the Roman line. His arm began to shake and he cursed the weight of his shield, but he had never been more grateful for its protection. Finally, weapons and vitriol spent, the Germans grew tired of their unsuccessful attempts to break through and withdrew. Atticus breathed a huge sigh of relief and stretched his aching body. He cast a look along the line as he tried to shake some feeling back into his shield arm. The enemy spears had taken some toll but the line appeared largely unscathed. The wall had done its job. And Plautius had been right. Atticus gave him a nod as he arrived to join Rescius.

"How did you know?"

Plautius smiled.

"I didn't, lad. I didn't."

9

Vosges Valley

"How long do you think they'll be?" asked Atticus as he and Julius took advantage of a rare moment of quiet to assess how the construction of the camp was going.

Julius shrugged.

"They seem to be getting on with it well enough. It looks as if they just have the palisades and the gates to do. Shouldn't be more than a couple of hours now."

Atticus sighed.

"Long enough for them to try again."

"Do you think they will?" Julius asked.

"I would, if I was them. They won't want us finishing the camp."

It had been a while since the last attack and a more relaxed air had slowly settled over the Roman line. Rescius had even allowed them to fetch some sour wine and hard tack biscuits from one of the supply wagons. But he felt edgy, and he wasn't alone. Plautius had continued to stalk back and forth, ensuring that their guard was never properly dropped. And it was Plautius who recognised the danger, even before the buccina rang out signalling the alarm. Another wave of warriors had begun pouring forth from the German camp. Julius gave Atticus a resigned look as the two of them slid back into position. With Plautius and Rescius encouraging and cajoling the men in equal measure, the defensive lines were quickly reformed. Atticus gave Maximus a nod as he lined up behind him once again. His friend gave him a smile and gestured towards the legionaries labouring to build the camp behind them.

"It's a bit harder protecting that flock than the ones back home. The wolves didn't hunt in quite such big packs back there."

Atticus forced a smile and returned his gaze to the plain. Some way taller than Maximus, he had a clear view of the rapidly approaching German horde. It was a chilling sight. It hardly seemed possible but it looked as if there were even more of them in this attack than the last. He tried to take solace in the fact that he had survived their first assault. But knowing what was to come wasn't making him feel any better. Fiddling nervously with his armour, he watched the enemy warriors drawing ever closer. Maybe it was their chastening defeat first time around? Perhaps the fervour of their leaders? He didn't know. But as the Germans began their final charge, faces contorted with rage and battle cries filling the air, they appeared even more savage than before.

And then they hit the line.

Atticus was almost knocked off his feet as Maximus was driven back into his shield. He scrambled desperately to retain his footing on the dry and dusty soil as the weight of the German charge forced them to concede ground. Knowing that their lives depended on stalling the momentum of the charge, Atticus leant into his shield and pushed. Straining with every sinew, beads of sweat dropped from his brow as he fought with his comrades to slow the forward progress of the enemy warriors. His legs began to burn as the physical exertion began to take its toll. But the enemy must have been beginning to tire too and he was finally able to dig in his heels as the pressure on the Roman line started to ease. He gratefully straightened up and sucked in a deep breath of air, not that there was anything fresh about it. The fetid stench of so many closely packed bodies was an assault to the senses. But he didn't care. They had survived the charge. Now, heavily outnumbered, they had to survive the inevitably fierce fighting that would follow.

Atticus ran his tongue quickly over his parched lips and rolled his shoulders to try and ease some of the tension he was feeling. Being this close to the fighting but being unable to do anything to assist his comrades was a new experience, and not one that he liked. Not that Maximus appeared to be in any need of assistance. With a series of short thrusting stabs wielded deftly from behind his shield, he had sent the first warrior to reach him reeling away with a gaping wound to his side. Howling in pain, the German staggered to one side as he tried in vain to stem the flow of blood rapidly soaking through his tunic. A burly warrior dragged him aside and with an angry snarl stepped forward to challenge Maximus. As the two clashed, Atticus quickly scanned the enemy line. His attention was drawn to a young and sinewy-looking warrior immediately behind the German battling Maximus. He appeared to be one of a small number of warriors carrying spears. Atticus frowned; they wouldn't be much use at such close range. Unless... they were going to use them as stabbing weapons... He watched with mounting horror as the young man struggled to free his arms amidst the tight press of men, lowering the spear until it was pointing directly at Maximus. Preoccupied with the fierce struggle with which he was engaged, Maximus had no inclination of the impending danger. Time seemed to stand still as the warrior forced the spear down with all the power he could muster. Atticus lunged forward, desperate to try and deflect the spear with his sword. He shouted out a warning.

"Maximus!"

But he was too late. The point of the spear found the unprotected nape of Maximus' neck, creating a deep and visceral wound. As his assailant roughly pulled the spear clear, Maximus spun around, surprise and pain etched across his face. Dropping his shield, he reached out plaintively to clasp Atticus, pulling him close. He tried to speak but all Atticus could hear were his friend's tortured final breaths as he slowly choked to death on his own blood. No longer able to support his own weight, Maximus sank to his knees and slumped to the floor. Atticus looked up with a start as a warrior burst through the gap in the line, howling in delight. The German's joy was short-lived as he spun around and realised that the line had closed behind him. He was alone. Seemingly resigned to the inevitability of his fate, the warrior defiantly stood his ground and angrily began to taunt the startled legionaries, trying to provoke an attack. Filled with a rage he had never experienced before, Atticus was determined that the first attack would be his. Stepping to the side to free himself from Maximus' prostrate body, he wheeled around and swung his sword wildly at the warrior. The German laughed as he parried the swing with some ease, taunting Atticus to try again. Angered even further, Atticus threw himself at the German, raining down blow after blow until the physical effort of his unsophisticated and wholly ineffective assault began to take its toll on his stamina. Sensing his opportunity and with a smile playing across his face, the warrior advanced towards Atticus. At that moment, a sword point burst suddenly and savagely through the warrior's chest. Rescius had seen enough. The warrior looked helplessly from the mortal wound to Atticus and back again. He tried to turn and face his hidden assailant but he no longer had the strength. His eyes rolled and he pitched forward, crashing to the ground.

Rescius wiped his sword unceremoniously on the sleeve of his tunic and returned it to its scabbard. Reaching out, he grabbed Atticus by the shoulders and dragged him closer.

"I know you're angry, lad, but you can't bring him back. And you won't honour his memory by dying like a drunk in an alley fight. He deserves better than that. You honour him by making sure that we hold this line and that he didn't die in vain. Do you understand?"

Atticus wanted to say something about the loss of his friend and the hurt and anger that consumed his thoughts. But no words would come. He nodded.

"Good. Then get back in line. This isn't over yet."

The sheer weight of German numbers was beginning to take its toll. Despite suffering huge losses, they just kept coming and, in several places, the Roman line looked so thin that Atticus wondered if they would be able to hold out much longer. He pushed such thoughts to the back of his mind as the legionary in front of him let out an agonised cry and crashed to the floor, his helmet bearing the mark of the blow that had knocked him senseless. It didn't look fatal but the warrior that had struck him down was advancing menacingly towards his prone body, determined that the next blow would be. Atticus jumped over his stricken comrade and thrust out his shield just as the German was about to strike. The man cursed as his blow was deflected harmlessly away, and he turned to swing again. But not fast enough. Atticus slid forward and drove his sword deep into the warrior's chest. He sank to his knees, staring helplessly at the flow of crimson pooling quickly in his lap. Atticus twisted his blade free. The warrior took one last rasping breath before pitching face down into the bloody soil. Atticus stepped over him with barely a glance. That was for Maximus. Locking shields with Julius, he was surprised to see the Germans backing away from the line once more. He shuddered wearily. Probably only to allow fresh warriors to come forward. Would this never end? But nobody was advancing and, to his surprise, he could see individual warriors beginning to cast anxious glances over their shoulders. Cries of alarm began to spread amongst the retreating horde, and, as the unrest took hold, warriors started to turn and run towards their camp. Then he saw what it was that had so clearly unnerved the German warriors. Cavalry. A sizeable force, judging by the dust cloud being thrown up. More and more warriors began to flee as the cavalry made directly for the rear of the German lines. It was Allerix and his men. Closing quickly, the resolve of the enemy warriors broke and the horde that had moments earlier threatened to overrun the Roman line began flooding away in a frenzied and disorganised rush. Atticus let out a sigh of relief and steadied himself with his shield as the physical and emotional toll of the day hit him for the first time. Free from the adrenaline of battle, every bone in his body ached and he longed to rest. He quickly cuffed away a tear as Julius nodded towards the wholly unexpected events unfolding before them.

"Payback," he whispered.

Very few of the retreating warriors had reached safety before the auxiliaries arrived. Stretched out across the plain, the enemy horde presented an inviting target. Those not cut down where they stood were helplessly trampled underfoot or sent cartwheeling to their deaths as the auxiliaries cut a deep and merciless swathe through them. Allerix and his men turned and swept back amongst the warriors. Atticus could see small groups of men, perhaps possessed of greater bravery or experience, banding together behind hastily contrived shield walls to try and offer some form of resistance. But with thoughts of escape rather than defence uppermost in their minds, the majority of those fleeing were slaughtered. In a mass of flailing and shattered limbs, hundreds more warriors were sent tumbling to their deaths, before a body of German cavalry, considerably larger than the auxiliary detachment, burst from their camp. Intent on providing a screen for their beleaguered comrades and extracting vengeance for those who had fallen, it was now the auxiliaries who suddenly found themselves in trouble. All over the plain, groups of men from the respective bodies of cavalry were engaged in desperate and bloody battles for supremacy. Atticus watched aghast as a short way from the Roman line three of the auxiliaries, pinned in position by seven or eight German warriors, found themselves fighting for their lives. Exceptionally skilled, they bravely held their own and, despite repeated attacks, the Germans struggled to assert their numerical advantage. Eventually, though, they found an opening and Atticus grimaced as one of the auxiliaries slid from his horse, struck from behind by a fearsome blow across the neck. Just as it seemed certain that the surviving auxiliaries would be quickly overcome, Atticus saw three new horsemen rapidly approaching the fierce struggle. He recognised the horse before the rider. It was Allerix. Sweeping in unseen, three of the Germans were cut down almost immediately. Panicked by the sudden and savage shift in odds, two more took flight and raced back towards their camp. The remaining Germans threw themselves into battle but, brave as they were, it was over quickly. The auxiliaries possessed lighter and faster mounts, but it was their innate skill with horse and weapon that left Atticus in awe. He watched as Allerix administered the final blow. Deftly parrying his opponent's strike, he released his reins and, turning quickly in the saddle, smashed his shield down onto the still-outstretched arm of his adversary. Dropping his sword, the warrior was defenceless as Allerix swung up his own blade and thrust it deep into the man's chest. He remained upright just long enough for Allerix to remove his sword before slumping to one side and pitching headlong to the ground. His unnerved mount bolted into the distance. Allerix's two comrades dismounted to recover the body of the fallen auxiliary. Hauling him up onto one of the riderless horses that were skittishly milling about nearby, they set off back towards the main body of the auxiliary cavalry. But the battle appeared to be on the verge of breaking up as weary men and horses began to disengage and regroup, warily facing off across a widening divide. After a short standoff, both sides began a cautious withdrawal, seemingly satisfied that honour had been done. It wasn't long before the plain in front of Atticus was empty, save for the bodies of the fallen, already being picked over by the birds. Julius' hand on his shoulder made him jump.

"It's ready."

"Sorry?" said Atticus.

"The camp. It's finished, brother. Look."

Atticus turned as the buccina rang out to signal for the legions to reform. The battle was over. The camp looked identical to every one that he had come across before, but he had never seen one as welcoming as this.

"Come on," said Julius, seemingly mirroring his own desire to escape.

"Let's go."

Taking one last look across the plain, Atticus turned and followed Julius as he hurried towards Plautius, busy organising the cohort. Fewer in number, fatigued by the rigours of the day and many, like Titus, sporting the scars of battle, Atticus knew that they must have looked quite a sight. But there was something else. Honed by the battle, a feeling that they had now earned the right to fight alongside the veteran legions. Exhausted and mourning the loss of his friend, he was nonetheless filled with an immense sense of pride and belonging that he allowed to wash over him as they marched towards their new home.

*

Atticus pulled his cloak tightly around his shoulders. Typical military issue, the material was cheap and coarse but it felt oddly comforting tonight. They'd been so busy following their arrival in camp that he hadn't noticed the fading light or the cooling of the evening air until he was about to head off for his turn on watch. That had been about three hours ago and he was glad to be nearly done. He was tired and so hungry that he was actually looking forward to some of the vegetable stew that Titus had been preparing. If there was any left, he thought wryly. Dusk had long since retreated but the flames of the funeral pyres continued to illuminate the night sky, filling the plain between the two camps with a myriad of ghostly shadows. He shivered and tried to think about something other than the restless spirits of all those who had fallen that day. But that was easier said than done. He knew that the light of the pyres reduced the risk of further attack and, however hard he tried to focus on scanning the plain for danger, he just kept replaying the bloody images of the battle in his mind as he stared into the night. He knew that he couldn't have done anything more to save Maximus, but that did little to ease the pain of his loss. It was actually only a year since they had been thrust together in basic training, but they had been through so much together that it felt like so much longer. For all their differences, he, Julius, Maximus and Titus had formed a strong bond, and the loss of his friend had hit him harder than he could possibly have imagined. If they ever finished here on the wall, he and Julius would look to send their friend on his way with a drink, telling tales of their misdemeanours during training. He would rope Titus in too. He'd taken Maximus under his wing from the very beginning. Despite his gruff assurances to the contrary, Atticus felt sure that Titus would be feeling the loss of their friend every bit as much as him. The sound of cornets resounded through the night air, signalling the end of their watch.

"About time!"

He stretched and fidgeted impatiently as he watched those on the next watch approaching along the wall. He exchanged passwords with the legionary taking his place, a grizzled veteran from the Xth who nodded to the plain behind Atticus.

"All quiet, son?"

Atticus nodded.

"Yes. I don't think they have the appetite for more bloodshed today."

"I don't think anybody does," replied the veteran.

"No," said Atticus dolefully.

"You were out there?"

"Yes. You?"

"No, I was here, working on the ditch. You lads did well out there today. That was… tough."

"Thank you," Atticus replied.

"Of course, if it had been the Xth, we'd have had it wrapped up much sooner…"

Atticus tensed and turned to confront the soldier. Today was not the day to challenge the bravery of the XIIth. Then he saw the smile play out across the older man's heavily lined face.

"Easy, lad. We don't waste our time challenging those that haven't earned it."

Atticus returned the smile. Acceptance. Tapping Atticus on the shoulder, the veteran turned and moved off to begin his vigil on watch. Julius made way for him as he returned from his position a little further along the wall and hurried over to join Atticus.

"I'm glad that's over, I need a piss. And then I need a drink. I don't care what it is as long as it's not more watered wine. Bloody stuff is great for quenching a thirst but it won't do tonight."

Direct as always, thought Atticus with a smile.

"I think we will be hard pushed to find anything beyond the usual, brother."

"What about your local friends?"

Atticus smiled. He had already been thinking about seeking out Allerix. He wondered if any of them would still be here if he and his men hadn't arrived, and he wanted to thank him.

"Good idea. Let's get back to the tent. I need food and we can collect Titus. Old bugger won't admit it but he needs to drown his sorrows as well. Then we can find Allerix."

Julius slapped him on the back and together they set off towards their tent.

*

In the end, Titus hadn't taken much persuading and the three of them were soon making their way through the packed tents en route to the stable area, where Atticus felt confident they would find Allerix and his men.

"They won't stray too far from their horses. I wouldn't if they were mine."

Julius gave him a push.

"What is it with you and those big, stinking beasts? Bloody things have minds of their own and a nasty habit of biting."

"I don't recall you being quite so vocal when those 'stinking beasts' helped us out of trouble."

"Mmm," muttered Julius, wholly unconvinced.

"I seem to remember that it was bloody cavalry we needed rescuing from first time around. But I can't pretend that I haven't been glad to see your friends arrive when they have. Careful, though, any more talk of horses and you'll start sounding like Titus and his Spanish donkeys."

"Oi!" said Titus, aiming a punch at Julius. "Not the bloody

donkeys again, will that never grow old? You know it wasn't always livestock I was responsible for, I had…"

He looked away as his voice tailed off.

"Had what?" asked Atticus, his curiosity pricked.

"It doesn't matter, lad. It was another time," Titus replied with a weak smile.

Atticus might have ignored the clear inference to let the matter drop and probed a little deeper, but Titus had already moved away.

"Isn't that the auxiliaries over there?" he asked, arm outstretched.

They had emerged into a narrow lane between a row of tents and a line of tethered horses. At the end of the lane, Atticus could see a sizeable group of auxiliaries gathered around a large and inviting-looking fire. He couldn't tell if Allerix was amongst them but they wouldn't find out standing there. He gave Titus a nod and they set off, both enjoying Julius' obvious discomfort as they squeezed carefully past the horses.

"Best be careful, brother. They can sense fear, you know…"

"And Romans apparently," Julius retorted angrily as he only just managed to avoid a stray kick from one of the more easily spooked animals.

As they approached, a stony silence fell across the gathering and the three friends were confronted with a sea of disdainful-looking faces. From the midst of the group, a lone voice barked out a warning: "Piss off! You're not welcome here, Romans."

The man's accent and drink-induced slur did little to aid the delivery of his message but the meaning was clear enough. Atticus nudged Julius and gestured that they should go. Just as they were turning to leave, another voice spoke.

"Hold."

This time, the Latin was clear and the voice full of authority.

As Atticus looked up, he saw a member of the group stand and begin to address the others in their native tongue. It was Allerix. Atticus had no idea what was being said but the respect Allerix commanded was clear, and there were no dissenting voices when he beckoned them to join him by the fire.

"I have explained that you are friends and therefore welcome amongst us."

Atticus acknowledged the kind gesture with a smile.

"Thank you. We are grateful."

Allerix invited them to sit and nodded towards the warrior who had spoken initially.

"You must forgive Cabrus. He lost his brother today. We couldn't reach him in time, though we did avenge his death."

Atticus nodded.

"We saw. I'm sorry, Cabrus. Your brother fought bravely and with honour. You all did and we owe you a debt of gratitude."

The warrior nodded and took another drink. Allerix smiled at Atticus.

"My men might not have ridden to your aid so freely if you hadn't displayed courage of your own. We have heard talk of the discipline of Rome's armies. Today, we saw for ourselves. Many lines would have been broken, but yours held, despite the odds."

"We did but not without cost," said Atticus.

"You lost comrades?"

"Yes. And a friend."

"Who also died bravely and with honour," Julius added.

"Then you will share a drink with us tonight?" asked Allerix.

Atticus nodded.

"Yes. We would be honoured."

Cabrus jabbed a finger at Titus.

"Your face. From today?"

His scar still weeping and now sporting a nasty black eye, Titus nodded.

"Yes. But I look a lot better than the bastard that did it to me," he said defiantly.

Cabrus smiled and handed Titus the ornate drinking horn he had been nursing since their arrival. Titus raised it to his lips and drank deeply. He was still trailing behind Julius, who had gratefully accepted the offer of a wineskin from the auxiliary sitting next to him. Allerix took a long sup from the drinking horn he had been passed, before offering it to Atticus. The warm and sweet drink had overtones of honey but there was no mistaking the punch of the brew. He coughed but took another swig. Allerix laughed.

"You are not worried about Plautius?" he asked, with a hint of a smile.

"We are always worried about Plautius," replied Atticus. "But tonight, we will drink anyway."

10

Aduatuca

Pausing for a moment as she stepped into the sun outside of the stable, Epona closed her eyes and gratefully allowed the warmth to wash over her. She had forgotten just how cold it could get at this time of year before the sun climbed high enough to bathe the landscape. And today's ride had been especially early. She hadn't intended to venture out at all today but she had slept fitfully and her thoughts had turned inevitably to her brother's wellbeing and what the future might hold. She knew what it was. Allerix's messenger had arrived a couple of days ago to update her father. At the point of his departure, the fighting had been confined to a series of cavalry skirmishes. Thankfully, these seemed to have gone well, with Allerix and his men leading from the front, much to the pride of her father. However, more worryingly, Allerix had reported that he was certain battle would come and that, when it did, it would be fearsome. She had hoped that the ride would help take her mind off things. It hadn't. She had enjoyed it, as she always did; able to rely almost entirely on instinct, she never felt freer than when riding. Today, though, that freedom had simply meant more time to think about how the conflict was unfolding. She smiled; Allerix had at least been careful to include word that Isarno was fine. He had apparently joked that she would be more interested in that news than word that he too was safe. The messenger had been wrong, of course; she loved her brother but it was a relief to know that Isarno was well. She couldn't explain why, but, from the moment she had rescued him as a foal, she had believed Isarno was destined to play a role in shaping her and her brother's futures. It was the same feeling that years later had compelled her to give him to Allerix as a gift. It had hurt to part with him but there was an undeniable connection between the horse and Allerix, and she did not feel it was her place to question the will of the gods. Allerix was blissfully unaware of any of this, of course. It wouldn't hurt to continue the pretence, however, and she asked that on his return the messenger let Allerix know that she expected Isarno to remain unscathed. Or he had best not return.

Rubbing her hands together vigorously in an attempt to return some feeling to her chilled fingers, she headed for the hall. With luck, the fire would still be burning and she might be able to get a warming drink. She quickly picked her way through the settlement and ducked into the dark but welcoming room. She hurried over to the fire and helped herself to a beaker of mulled wine. Unusually for the time of day, the hall was a hive of activity. She had almost forgotten. She took a sip of the warming wine and tried to stay out of the way as all about her people busied themselves with preparations. There had been so much fuss ahead of her father's meeting with the Nervii that she would be glad when it was all over. It wasn't that she didn't have an interest in the affairs of the tribe. She had always been encouraged to know enough to exercise her own mind, which she had, participating in decision-making, despite the obvious misgivings of many of the male tribal elders. The trouble was, she had no patience for the seemingly endless debates that characterised these gatherings. That was something Allerix was all together more comfortable with. He had the tact and sensitivity necessary to deal with people of influence and power, whereas she had always struggled to treat such people with the reverence they thought they deserved. She had always preferred to make that assessment herself, based on what they said and did, irrespective of status. As her mother had told her on more than one occasion, diplomacy might not be her strength. She smiled; if that was the case, she was happy to leave it to others. She knew her strengths and feared that they would be needed very soon. In his message, Allerix had expressed concerns about the intentions of the Romans. He apparently believed that they were making plans to stay amongst the Belgae, even if Ariovistus was defeated and despite the fact that there would still be plenty of time for them to complete their march home ahead of the worst of the winter weather. Her father had sent word to the other tribes. A settled Roman presence in the area would be troubling and was presumably why the Nervii had responded so quickly to the invitation to meet. They would arrive today. She set her beaker down on the table, stretched one more time in front of the fire and set off to find Epomedius. Now was not the time to miss a training session. If conflict was coming, she would be ready.

*

Albiorix extended his hand in greeting and smiled at Boduognatus. He had aged quite noticeably since they had last met, some five years previously. Doubtless his guest was thinking exactly the same about him. Boduognatus still looked the part, however; resplendent in a fine blue cloak and dripping with jewellery, he looked every inch the ruler he was.

"Boduognatus, welcome! It is good to see you again."

Boduognatus nodded curtly. "Likewise, Albiorix. I am grateful to you for agreeing to meet with me ahead of the gathering of elders. I have some proposals that I thought wise to discuss with you first."

Albiorix smiled, always the politician. He gestured for Boduognatus to join him beside the parapet.

"Of course. And I thought we might enjoy some privacy up here on the wall. How many years is it since you were last here?"

"I do not believe that I have been here since the death of your father. It seems to have changed little. Although I assume that is no hindrance, given your limited aspirations as a nation." Boduognatus sniffed dismissively.

Albiorix gripped the edges of his tunic tightly and forced himself to remember that Boduognatus was here as his guest, however insufferable he was. His features might have mellowed with age but he had lost none of his arrogance. Boduognatus had been leader of the Nervii for almost as long as Albiorix had led the Aduatuci and it was true that the two tribes couldn't be more different. As far as Albiorix was concerned, that was neither a source of disappointment nor a reason for any sense of inferiority. The Nervii were the largest, and traditionally the most warlike, tribe in the region, with a fearsome reputation that had been well earned. They were proud of their territorial conquests and of the hold they exercised over many smaller tribes beholden to them for survival. In contrast, he had elected to use force only when he must, to protect his borders and not to increase them. Whilst he knew that men like Boduognatus thought this made him weak, it was a tactic that had brought many years of stability and peace, during which time his tribe had flourished. Admittedly, not to the extent of the Nervii, but they had become a nation of some significance nonetheless, despite their traumatic and difficult beginnings, and he was proud. Entirely oblivious to any afront that he might have caused, Boduognatus continued.

"The content of your message was troubling. Is the information reliable?"

Albiorix nodded.

"Allerix rides with Caesar's cavalry. He commands one wing. The other is led by Egus and Roucillus of the Allobroges, sons of King Abducillus."

Boduognatus snorted.

"The Allobroges sold their souls to align with Rome long ago!"

"It was for money and power that they sold their souls," said Albiorix. "I think Caesar is merely the one whom they believe will deliver this for them. We would be wise to take note. The problem for Caesar is that he seems to trust Egus and Roucillus with his plans and they have proven to be somewhat less than discreet when enjoying a drink, which I am led to believe is a common occurrence. It was relatively easy for Allerix to gain at least some understanding of Caesar's intentions."

"And Allerix believes they intend to stay?"

"He does. Caesar has political aspirations in Rome and needs both fame and fortune to advance his claims. He will get plenty of the first if he beats Ariovistus but I doubt much of the latter. I imagine he will look for the pretence to secure his financial gains elsewhere, which will likely bring him into conflict with us."

Boduognatus nodded.

"I agree, which is why I believe we should be preparing to take action now. We cannot allow this Roman to remain in our lands unchallenged. Since he is a threat to us all, I believe that we should respond as one, forming an alliance of all the tribes of the Belgae."

"With you in command?" asked Albiorix before he could stop himself.

"That is a matter for the Tribal Council to agree but I believe it would be entirely fitting, given the numbers the Nervii would commit and our obvious skill in battle," responded Boduognatus rather grandly.

You had to hand it to him. No airs or graces, no political subtleties, just an unshakeable belief in his right to lead. Albiorix hoped it wasn't misplaced. If an alliance was agreed, the Council would most likely appoint Boduognatus or Galba as general and they could ill afford any mistakes on that front if it did come to war with the Romans. Right now, it was more important to understand what any alliance might look like.

"You will bring the Viromandui and Atrebates with you, I know, but what about the Bellovaci and the Suessiones?"

Boduognatus sneered.

"I have talked with King Correus and King Galba, both loathsome men. Their hatred and mistrust of each other is obvious, but I believe that, and a desire to gain bragging rights, can be used to secure significant forces from each, if the Tribal Council asks."

Albiorix nodded.

"And the Morini?"

"They keep themselves to themselves but I am sure they can be persuaded."

Albiorix was sure he knew why the Morini kept their distance and hoped that the need for persuasion would be unnecessary. For the Nervii, this usually involved the pointed end of a spear.

"Have you had any word from the Remi?"

Boduognatus shook his head.

"I am due to meet with King Iccius but I do not believe he will want war with Rome. He and his kind have become lazy and fat from the spoils of their land and I fear he would rather trade than fight his way to prominence."

"He will surely not choose to fight with Caesar against his kin?" Albiorix asked.

"I don't believe so but he might offer supplies and safe passage through his lands as a way of furthering his ends."

Albiorix would have preferred any alliance to have included the Remi but even so, if they could muster the forces of the remaining tribes it would still be a formidable army. And according to Allerix's assessment of Caesar's strength, it would need to be. Something he hoped Boduognatus wasn't going to overlook.

"Allerix suggests that the Romans may prove to be a formidable force. We would outnumber them, it is true, but so did the Helvetii. The Romans crushed them and now take on Ariovistus, whose warriors have already conquered some of the biggest tribes of the south. It will be no easy task."

"That is true," replied Boduognatus, "but there will be no better time to challenge them. Despite their victories, I understand their legions comprise many new and inexperienced soldiers. They will also be weakened from the demands of tackling Ariovistus. Any victory will be hard fought and must come at some cost to them in terms of numbers lost."

One of whom might be my son, thought Albiorix, though if Boduognatus had recognised this, he showed no sign of acknowledging it.

"And we have one other advantage – cavalry."

Here it comes, thought Albiorix. The Nervii had never favoured cavalry to any great extent, being renowned for their long marches to battle. It was what set the Nervii apart, that and the strict regime of their warrior clan, eschewing any form of comfort and luxury, which they believed weakened the body and dulled the senses of a fighting man. Doubtless they would all sleep outside tonight and as usual refuse the alcohol offered by way of hospitality. He felt sure that he would be reminded about this when members of his own tribe eagerly enjoyed the wine and mead on offer. He didn't care; he'd always considered it better to remind his men what it was they were fighting to protect. And why march when you could ride? He had long believed that the lack of a tangible cavalry force hindered the Nervii tactically, and Boduognatus was astute enough to know that he would need the support of the Aduatuci's famed cavalry and warriors, like his son, to lead them if he was to persuade the nations to unite against Rome. Certainly, if he wanted to lead that alliance.

Boduognatus flashed him a smile.

"Any alliance could muster a reasonable force of cavalry, enough to challenge the resources available to the Romans. But with the addition of your horse guard, that advantage is increased significantly – not just numerically but also in terms of skills and experience."

Albiorix acknowledged the unexpected compliment; however, Boduognatus was not done.

"Your spears will count for little either way in the grand scheme of things—"

And straight back to the pompous arse of old, thought Albiorix. He interrupted angrily. "We would field twenty thousand spears with the Menapi. Warriors who I would trust to outdo many more than that number!"

Boduognatus raised his hand.

"Apologies. I meant no offence. I was simply trying to highlight the unique contribution the Aduatuci would bring to any alliance. The Tribal Council will know that collectively we can field huge numbers of infantry, but they will also be aware, as you yourself observed earlier, that such resources did not help the Helvetii. It is our cavalry forces that would swing the balance. I believe that is what will sway the Council. I should like to know that I can rely on your support. Will you join me?"

From the moment Allerix's message arrived, Albiorix had known that the tribes of the Belgae would each find themselves having to determine how to respond should the Romans elect to stay. He had wrestled with the options repeatedly. Aware that the very nature of his tribe's future might depend on the outcome of this one decision.

"Yes," he said gravely. "I will support your proposal."

Boduognatus nodded his head in thanks.

"Excellent. I am grateful. Now, if you might indulge me a little longer, I have one further proposal that I should like to share with you."

Before he could begin, a voice from behind them made them both start: "You have been up here for some time, my Lords. I thought you might welcome a little refreshment."

Deep in conversation, neither of them had noticed Olluna approaching with a tray bearing water, wine and a small plate of bread, meat and cheese. Albiorix had forgotten just how hungry he was and he gave Olluna a warm smile. But before he could gratefully avail himself of the simple but very welcome offering, Boduognatus pulled him aside.

"I wonder if we might conclude our business first? Perhaps just the two of us? I think it might be easier, given what I would like to discuss."

Albiorix turned back to Olluna and rolled his eyes.

"Thank you. We will finish our business first and rejoin you shortly."

Taking the hint, Olluna smiled and, inclining her head respectfully, she withdrew.

Albiorix knew that, although she would understand, Olluna was unlikely to let him forget her annoyance at playing the role of dutiful wife. He would pay for that later. Silently, he cursed Boduognatus. Forcing himself to smile, he turned back to his visitor.

"So?" he asked. "This proposal of yours, I am intrigued."

*

Epona hurried to swing up her sword and parry Epomedius' strike. It was the same drill they had practised hundreds of times before but today she was struggling, and Epomedius was forced to check his follow-up swing for fear of catching her. He cursed.

"Concentrate! If you focussed more of your attention on my sword and less on our visitors, you would fare better," he scolded.

"I'm sorry. I was wondering who that was with Father," Epona replied.

"I'm sure you were. I'm guessing he passes for attractive?"

Epona felt herself blush.

"I… I… I meant both of them," she stammered, although it was true her primary focus had been on the younger of the two men engaged in conversation with her father. The three of them were now walking slowly towards the training square where she and Epomedius had been working hard for the last few hours.

"The older man is Boduognatus, King of the Nervii. I imagine the other might be his son, Boduogenus, though I have never met him. Now, let's go again. And given that we have an audience this time, you might care to concentrate."

As they completed the full drill, this time without incident, Epona noticed that the younger man had made his way over to the edge of the square, where he was now loitering, awaiting an opportunity to join them. Closer now, she could see that he had a broad and powerful physique, though she didn't much care for his beard. Epomedius strode over and offered the young man his hand.

"I am Epomedius, retainer of King Albiorix and commander of his Royal Guard."

The man nodded.

"Your reputation precedes you. I am Boduogenus, son of Boduognatus, King of the Nervii."

Epomedius bowed low.

"My Lord."

Boduogenus paused for a moment as if expecting Epona to offer her hand in greeting. When it wasn't forthcoming, he smiled and dipped his head towards her in greeting.

"And you must be Epona."

Epona nodded just enough to respect the status of her visitor.

"I am not sure that I must be, but I am."

Boduogenus picked up a couple of the dulled practice blades to gauge their weight.

"Good. I have heard much about your prowess under arms. Perhaps you would allow me to witness them firsthand."

Epona followed Epomedius' gaze as he looked towards her father. Seeing his nod of consent, she picked up her practice blade once more and invited Boduogenus into the square.

"I would be honoured."

Epona watched as Boduogenus removed his tunic and took a series of slow and deliberate warm-up swings with his wooden blade. She knew this was designed to highlight his muscular frame and intimidate her. She had seen it all before. But he was a powerful-looking man and she would need to keep her wits about her. Bored with his posturing and satisfied that he should now be ready, Epona leapt forward, sword outstretched. As Boduognatus thrust up a hurried defensive block, she slid quickly to her right and aimed a swinging blow at his head. She thought Boduognatus did well to maintain his balance as he was forced to duck quickly beneath her sword. She wondered if the smile that flitted across his face was relief at remaining upright or realisation that the contest might not be as easy as he had imagined. Either way, she knew enough to expect a response and it came quickly. Sliding forward and taking advantage of his superior height, Boduogenus launched a series of blows about her head. With the skill and timing borne of countless hours of training, she moved quickly to defend the attack, but it carried significant power and she was forced to concede ground. As she watchfully backed up, eyes locked on those of Boduogenus, her foot slipped on a divot of turf presumably thrown up during her earlier practice drills and she lost her balance. She swore; not now! Sensing an opening, Boduognatus jumped forward and her careful retreat lost all of its previous poise as she scrabbled desperately to evade his attack and regain her composure. Epona caught sight of a sneering smile on Boduogenus' face, this time not quite so fleeting, he clearly now believed he had the upper hand.

"My father values the cavalry of your nation. I hope your men ride better than they fight if you are one of their best warriors. Though I will concede you do well for a woman."

Epona tensed. Arrogant shit. She had stumbled; that was all. This was not over.

"I fight as well as any man. And in case you hadn't noticed, you haven't beaten me yet!"

She crouched a little lower and gritted her teeth. He was good, she had to admit it, but he knew it, and his overconfidence was a weakness. She didn't think he was quite as quick or as agile as he might be either, his technique overly reliant on his power and size. Something she would now use to her advantage. Steeling herself, she swept into a sustained attack designed to get Boduogenus moving around the square. Pushing herself to the edge of exhaustion, she swung again and again, constantly switching the point of her attack and their direction of travel. It was a brutal assault and, as she had hoped, Boduogenus began to tire. She could feel her own muscles beginning to protest and every fibre of her being ached with the effort of her attack, but Boduogenus' breathing was becoming increasingly laboured and his sword strokes progressively ragged. He began to concede ground. Too tired herself to press home the advantage, she was relieved when Epomedius intervened, barking out a call for them to stop.

"Rest! I think your fathers have seen enough. Honour is satisfied."

Epona watched as Boduogenus gulped down a beaker of water from the pail she and Epomedius had taken out with them earlier. He gave her a smile.

"The women of our nation do not fight. There is no need when our men are possessed of such skill. I could make no exception even for one as competent as you. No wife of mine will ever be permitted to bear weapons."

Epona took a long drink of her own, the water warm but still very welcome.

"Then it's as well there is no chance I will ever be your wife."

Boduogenus turned and stalked off to retrieve his tunic before making the short walk to rejoin his father. Epomedius gave her a nod.

"You fought well. It is what happens when you concentrate."

"I had reason to concentrate. I was not about to let that man beat me," replied Epona, returning the smile of her father, who had now joined them. "I hope that I haven't done anything to damage diplomatic relations."

Her father shrugged.

"Oh, I'm sure there will be some bruised egos. But knowing those two as I do, I can't imagine the effects will prove to be long-lasting. You had best go and get ready for the feast. Let your mother know I will be there shortly."

Epona ran over to retrieve her cloak. Throwing it over her shoulder, she set off for the hall. As she reached the edge of the square, her father called after her.

"Tell me, what did you think of Boduogenus?"

Without breaking step, she called back.

"If I never see him again after tonight, I will be quite happy."

*

Albiorix slapped Epomedius on the shoulder as they watched Epona head off.

"Well, that was interesting. I really wasn't sure how it would go. It seems you have trained her well, old friend."

Epomedius laughed.

"She will be beating me soon too, Lord."

He gestured towards Boduognatus and Boduogenus as they headed back towards the hall.

"I assume they are here to discuss how we respond if Allerix is correct and the Romans elect to stay."

"Yes. Boduognatus intends to propose to the Tribal Council that the tribes of the Belgae enter into an alliance."

"Led by him, no doubt!" quipped Epomedius.

Albiorix laughed.

"Of course, although he offers us a place at the leadership table in return for my support at the Council."

"Epomedius nodded. "Are you minded to agree?"

"I am. Would you do otherwise?"

"No, my Lord, I would not. We cannot allow the Romans to settle in our lands. I can't say that I welcome the thought of being led by Boduognatus. He is arrogant and headstrong, but with you to temper his leadership, I would be more confident."

He paused.

"An alliance of all the tribes would be some sight to behold, I think…"

Albiorix placed his hand on Epomedius' shoulder. He wondered if that might be the most he had ever heard him utter.

"Thank you, my friend. I agree. Hopefully, it will be enough to persuade the Romans to leave peacefully."

"Do you think they will?" Epomedius asked.

"No," replied Albiorix solemnly. "I do not. I fear that the

peace we have long enjoyed will soon come to an end. But I know we had to fight to secure it in the first place and I take comfort from that, should we need to do so again."

"We will be ready, Lord."

Albiorix smiled.

"In truth, I am more troubled by the second proposal Boduognatus wished to discuss with me."

"Lord?" asked Epomedius, intrigued.

"He proposes a marriage to cement the alliance between our tribes."

Epomedius tried but failed to stifle a laugh.

"Epona and Boduogenus, I assume?" he spluttered, barely able to contain his mirth.

Albiorix rolled his eyes and nodded.

"What did you tell them?" asked Epomedius.

"The truth. That she is a free spirit and has her own way of measuring the worth of potential suitors."

"So that was a test?" laughed Epomedius.

"Yes," Albiorix replied. "Of sorts."

"And one that didn't go well?" said Epomedius.

"No. It would seem not. I think the alliance might have to be cemented some other way. Epona has always been a free spirit. I know someone will make an impact on her but I'm damn sure I don't know who or how."

Epomedius gave him a nudge.

"There could still be a wedding. It's about time Allerix settled down, after all."

Albiorix shook his head.

"I'm afraid not. Boduognatus has no daughters, though if there must be a hostage exchange instead, we could do worse than have Allerix riding with the Nervii."

"I assume that Boduognatus would be looking to secure our cavalry as well as our spears," said Epomedius.

"Oh, he wasn't bothered about our spears. But the alliance needs our cavalry and he knows it. Even if it pained the arrogant prick to admit it. A trait that seemingly runs in the family if Epona is any kind of judge."

"Like father, like son, my Lord. It is always the case," said Epomedius, nodding respectfully. "And I assume we would wish the cavalry to be led by Allerix."

Albiorix nodded.

"I imagine there will some pressure from the Bellovaci and the Suessiones but I have been clear that I will not accept our cavalry being led by anybody other than Allerix. He is the only one I would trust to ensure that it is used correctly."

"Then offering Boduognatus Allerix as a hostage would seem ideal," said Epomedius. "Allerix gets an early opportunity to sit at the leadership table and they secure somebody who understands cavalry."

Albiorix smiled; it was not a wedding but it would fulfil their royal commitment.

"It is a good idea. I will broach it with Boduognatus later."

He laughed.

"It will also be a whole lot easier to sell that option to Allerix than having to try and persuade Epona and Olluna of the alternative."

Epomedius smiled.

"That is not a task I would wish on anybody."

"Of course," said Albiorix wistfully. "I have to have him home to do that."

"He will be fine," Epomedius replied reassuringly. "He is a good leader. He is with fine men and the reports from the messenger bode well."

"I know but it feels wrong not to be at his side at such a time."

"It is his time," replied Epomedius. "It will do him no harm to gain experience of leading men in combat and for the men to see him doing so. None of us are getting any younger."

Albiorix gave him a shove.

"Especially you, you old dog! I know other leaders, not too far from here, who might punish a man for addressing their king in such a manner," he said, laughing. "It is true enough, though. I just can't help wishing I was there with him."

"Because battle is simpler than having to deal with people like Boduognatus?" asked Epomedius astutely.

Albiorix smiled.

"Yes. I believe it is."

"Well, unfortunately your place is here and his is there – wherever 'there' is. It is Taranis who must watch over him now," said Epomedius.

Albiorix reached involuntarily for his pendant, stopping himself as he remembered that he had given it to Allerix. It had been with him all his life and he missed its comforting presence, but he was pleased his son would be able to draw on the god's protection. He hoped he was wrong but he felt sure battle awaited Allerix, and there was no one better than Taranis to call upon during a time of war.

"Yes, you're right," he said. "Let's get going. I must focus on my guests. An altogether different struggle!"

11

Vosges Valley

Atticus peeled off his armour and set it down on the floor. Holding his head in his hands, he sank slowly onto his cot. Tired, thirsty and with a headache that would rival the kick of a mule, he felt terrible. His mood hadn't been helped by the early call to arms that morning. Just as before, they had been summoned to march out and join the other legions parading in front of Ariovistus' camp. Despite all their efforts yesterday, there had been no respite from the attempts to goad Ariovistus into battle. Yet the result had been the same. As always, Ariovistus failed to take the bait. After several painful hours on the plain, they had given up their resolute but entirely pointless vigil and marched slowly back to camp. In truth, it wasn't the rigours of yesterday's battle so much as the after-effects of the drinking session with the auxiliaries that had left him feeling so out of sorts. He couldn't recall drinking that much but, then again, he didn't recall much of anything. It had been quite some brew. He groaned as Julius ducked into the tent, whistling more loudly and (if it was possible) even more wildly out of tune than normal.

"Can't you give it a rest?"

Julius smiled but showed no sign of complying as he continued to clatter around the tent, quite deliberately, Atticus was sure. He closed his eyes and pulled his blanket over his head. Annoyingly, Allerix had seemed just as cheerful when they had seen him in the main square with his men, watching the legions return. Looking the picture of health, he had been sharing a joke about the Romans' love of parading rather than fighting their enemies. He suspected that it was not meant entirely in jest. But for once he didn't mind. He at least was glad there would be no battle today.

*

Atticus woke with a start as Titus gave him a shove. He had only meant to close his eyes for a moment but that was the last thing he could remember.

"How long have I been asleep?" he asked.

"Not long, lad. But I didn't think you'd want to miss out on the food."

Atticus smiled; he was right.

"Thank you."

"You haven't tasted it yet," laughed Titus as he slipped back out of the tent.

Atticus dragged himself slowly to his feet and trudged out into the sun. Titus shook his head with a smile and handed him a bowl of what looked suspiciously like reheated vegetable stew. Atticus gave him a nod and wandered over to join Julius, who was sitting in the shade. He eased himself down and began to tuck in. It was simple fare and had clearly seen better days, but it was warm and filling and at that moment he couldn't recall anything ever tasting so good.

"Better?" asked Julius with a smile.

"A little," Atticus replied. "How are you doing?"

Julius laughed.

"Better than you!"

Atticus smiled. It had always been the same; Julius seemed to have an innate ability to handle his drink. Mind you, his mother and father did own a tavern so that was probably no surprise. Atticus' father had been wary of his son's friendship with the son of a merchant, especially when that merchant was the purveyor of drink and other sources of entertainment. He knew that he'd never really lived up to the expectations of his position as the son of a prominent estate owner. In truth, he had never truly felt comfortable in that role and his friendship with Julius had grown despite his father's reticence, and the two of them had become brothers in all but name. That wasn't to say that his father's concerns had been misplaced, however. The tavern had been the source of many a misadventure and had certainly opened his eyes to life outside of the estate, though somehow those times already felt a lifetime away. He scooped up the last of his stew and reached out for Julius' bowl, intending to give them both a rinse, but his friend was staring in the direction of the German camp with an anxious look on his face.

"Can you hear that?"

Atticus turned his head. His heart raced. He could. There was no mistaking the low and distant rumble. Horses, lots of them. Before he could respond, the air was filled with a cacophony of trumpets and cornets sounding out in unison across the camp. They were being called to the wall. Across the camp, all those fortunate enough to have been enjoying a rare moment of quiet between duties were now anxiously rushing to make themselves ready for battle. Still unsure what had prompted the call to arms but resigned to the fact that it couldn't be good, he cursed. So much for escaping the need to fight today. Struggling into his armour, he snatched up his shield and set off after Julius and

Titus. Spilling into the open area that separated the rows of tents from the camp wall, a sense of ordered confusion reigned as men scurried off in all directions to report to their positions on the rampart. He quickened his pace to catch his friends, and the three of them hurried off to join their comrades assembling to the right of the main gate.

"Nice of you to join us," said Rescius tersely as they arrived. Atticus and Julius shared a quick glance but wasted no time in taking up their positions. The scene that greeted Atticus as he looked over the palisade explained a lot about Rescius' brusque demeanour. Spilling onto the plain between the two camps and rapidly filling the gap were thousands and thousands of warriors, screened from the main Roman camp by a huge mass of cavalry. So that was what they had heard earlier. It was a chilling sight. Transfixed, he watched the horde advance towards them, gathering pace until, with a deafening roar, they arrived, sweeping either side of the Roman defences and encircling the camp. Vaguely aware that Julius was endeavouring to say something to him but unable to hear what it was, he nodded purposefully in the hope that this was an appropriate response. And one that he hoped also conveyed a degree of confidence, which he was definitely not feeling. Surrounded and hugely outnumbered, he felt almost as vulnerable as he had during yesterday's battle, despite the camp's fortifications. Still, they had made the Germans pay dearly for their attacks yesterday and they would do so again today. How dearly they were about to discover as the first wave of warriors charged into the ditch and began to clamber up the embankment, screaming and snarling at the Romans waiting to meet them. He tugged nervously on the string of his pendant and drew his sword.

The wooden palisade shook as the first warriors to arrive hurled themselves against the narrow barrier separating them from their quarry. Many of the early arrivals were swiftly sent tumbling back into the ditch, impeding the path of those yet to climb. But it was only a temporary respite and the solidity of the palisade was soon being severely tested. Atticus could hear the levels of exertion as the warriors frantically tried to dislodge the wooden stakes and create a gap through which they might flood. He could also hear the cries of pain as, from behind their shields, he and his comrades slashed and stabbed at unprotected limbs, sending countless warriors reeling away from the fight. But the Germans were inflicting casualties of their own and, as each of his comrades fell, the intensity of the fighting seemed to increase. He drew his hand across his face to wipe away the sweat and stabbed out his sword at the burly and bearded warrior who had arrived in front of him. The warrior hurriedly stepped aside and thrust his sword over the palisade towards Atticus' head. Raising his shield to block the strike, Atticus was temporarily unsighted as the adjacent warrior swung his axe. He never saw the blow coming and was fortunate that the handle of the warrior's axe struck the rim of his shield before the blade reached his head. Its momentum slowed; the blow dented rather than pierced his helmet but its shuddering impact sent a searing pain coursing through his head. An explosion of light clouded his vision and he fought to remain upright. He felt sick and, as he regained his sight, everything seemed to be spinning chaotically before him. His legs buckled and he dropped onto one knee before leaning forward and violently throwing up the remains of the hurried meal he had only just enjoyed. The edges of his vision began to darken and he passed out, slumping to the floor in an ungainly heap. He came around almost immediately. Disorientated, but aware that somewhere above him the battle was continuing, he tried to regain his feet. The ringing in his ears was almost unbearable. He lurched unsteadily to one side and threw up again before sinking once more to his knees. He was relieved to feel Decimus' reassuring hand on his shoulder and allowed himself to be eased to his feet and led away from the palisade. Decimus set him down a few feet away, propping him up against another legionary, who was cradling what looked like a badly broken arm. As Decimus headed back, Atticus screwed up his eyes and tried to make out what was happening on the wall. His vision was still swimming but he could see Titus battling with the axe-wielding warrior who he presumed had inflicted his injuries. As the German took aim again, Titus thrust out his shield and using all of his strength barged the man back. Thrown off balance, his unprotected torso presented an inviting target for Julius, who drove his sword deep into his body. Clutching his wound, the warrior fell below the palisade and out of Atticus' eyeline. He wasn't sorry to see him go. Atticus dropped his head and fumbled with the fastener on his helmet. Finally easing it free, he slid it carefully off his head and dropped it to the floor. It had a distinctly lopsided look. Tentatively reaching for the side of his head, he flinched as his fingers ran over a sizeable lump and a fresh wave of pain washed over him. He lurched forward and retched once again. Dragging his hand across his face, he could see Decimus striding towards him. Along the wall, his comrades were grounding their shields. The fighting was over. For now. He gritted his teeth and tried to drag himself to his knees. He swayed wildly and reached out for Decimus. And then his vision darkened once again.

*

Atticus took a deep and very welcome breath of fresh air as he slipped out of the medical tent. Although a relatively large structure, it had filled steadily in the time since his arrival and he had been desperate to escape the noise and fetid heat as battles of a different sort were fought for men's lives. It had been a chastening experience and one he very much hoped never to repeat. The camp surgeon had ordered him to rest, but the orderlies had been far too busy to notice him leave. They probably wouldn't have stopped him if they had; there were men in far greater need of their assistance than him. Besides, he wanted to return to the palisade and his friends. In truth, he was still very unclear about what had led him to be there, or indeed how he had arrived. He remembered being called to the wall, the horde of warriors and fighting with the first of the attackers to arrive, but had been unable to conjure any recollection of events beyond that. Maybe it was for the best. All he knew was that his vision had returned to normal and he no longer felt like he was about to fall over. That was enough. His head hurt, his ears were still ringing and he felt extremely tired, but he couldn't remain there whilst his comrades were fighting and dying on the wall. He carefully slid on the helmet he had surreptitiously taken from the legionary in the bed next to him. He had heard the orderlies saying that the man was unlikely to survive the day. Clutching his pendant, he offered thanks that the gods had not seen fit to take him as well. He smiled. Or not yet anyway. He set off for the wall with as much swagger as he could muster. Skirting around the camp, he quickly reached the gate and clambered up the embankment. He slid into line beside Titus just as the warriors engaged in the latest attack were falling back towards the plain.

Titus gave Julius a nudge.

"Look who's back."

The strain of battle was etched on Julius' face but he welcomed Atticus with a warm smile.

"Good to have you back, brother. You gave us quite a scare."

"I scared myself," Atticus replied, "but I can't recall a bloody thing!"

Titus and Julius quickly recounted what had occurred up to the point when Decimus led him to the medical tent and returned with news of his injury.

"That's when we knew you'd be okay," laughed Julius. "Your head's too thick for any real damage to be done."

"Thanks," Atticus replied, touching his helmet. "It seemed real enough to me. I feel worse than I did this morning, and that's saying something."

"No benefits of the night before either," joked Julius.

"No. But at least I knew what was coming with the drink, unlike the axe," Atticus replied with a grimace.

Titus gave him a big grin.

"Fortunately for us, he got to fight a real soldier next. He's down there in the ditch and, unlike you, he won't be returning to the fight."

"I think you'll find it was me that put him there," said Julius.

"Yes, but only after I did all the hard work to set him up for you," Titus replied determinedly.

Julius rolled his eyes and shared a knowing look with Atticus before giving Titus a friendly shove. It was this camaraderie that had pulled him inexorably back to the wall, and, whatever lay in store, he was pleased to be amongst friends again.

"Stay alert, the bastards will be back!" Plautius shouted as he marched along the palisade. Anxious not to catch his centurion's attention, Atticus busied himself, surveying the scene below. The Germans had shown no sign of retreating any further than the foot of the rampart and he knew that Plautius would surely be right. Despite the mass of corpses littering the blood-slickened ditch, it didn't seem as if their numbers had been diminished, which made the visible thinning in their own lines suddenly feel even more concerning. His attempts to escape Plautius' eye had evidently failed and he swallowed nervously as the centurion paused at his side.

"I wasn't expecting you back, lad. Decimus said that you'd been ordered to rest. Did the camp surgeon clear you to return?"

"I'm feeling fine," Atticus lied, but none too convincingly if Plautius' face was anything to go by.

"That's not what I asked you," he said firmly.

"No, he didn't," replied Atticus guiltily, "but if we don't hold them on the wall, I'll be fighting them anyway, so it might as well be here."

Plautius gave him an appraising stare and for a moment Atticus thought he was going to order him back to the medical tent.

"As you wish, lad," he said, tapping Atticus on the shoulder, "but I'll be watching..."

Atticus let out a sigh of relief.

"How many attacks so far?" he asked.

"That was the third," Plautius replied. "And they can use fresh men each time, unlike us. The bastards are trying to wear us down."

Atticus swallowed nervously.

"From what I've seen, I think it might be working."

Plautius smiled.

"Yes, lad, but they're still on that side of the wall."

Their conversation was suddenly interrupted by an agonised cry. Atticus swung his head around quickly, instantly regretting it as a fresh wave of nausea left him fighting the urge to retch. His battle to avoid doing so wasn't helped by the sight of the legionary who had called out, his right eye lost amidst the now visible mess of shattered bone and torn flesh as he span away from the palisade. The stricken soldier dropped his sword and clamped his hands to his wounded face. Pale and unsteady, he fell to his knees and tumbled forward to lie bleeding and unconscious at the feet of his comrades. Howls of pain and cries of alarm began to erupt along the wall. Unsettled, Atticus felt something whistle over his shoulder as Plautius bellowed the order to raise shields. Complying immediately, Atticus flinched as he felt the clatter of not one but two missiles clearly meant for him.

"Bastards are using slingers," Plautius said as he ducked quickly behind Atticus' shield.

Atticus looked puzzled.

"They surely can't hope to drive us off the wall that way."

Plautius shook his head.

"No, lad. But that's not the problem. It's why they want us to keep our bloody heads down that bothers me."

*

Atticus leant into his shield and pushed it tight to the palisade, taking some of the weight off his arm. He was feeling the strain much more than usual today and the respite was welcome. The initial barrage had ended some time ago, but any attempts to snatch a view beyond the wall were met with a fresh wave of missiles and they remained frustratingly pinned down. A fresh volley clattered menacingly into the massed ranks of shields and Baculus stalked purposefully towards them from his position on the gatehouse. As he steadfastly refused to crouch, the horsehair plume on his helmet stood proudly above the shield wall, attracting both the ire and the projectiles of the Germans below. Plautius greeted him with a smile.

"That's one privilege of rank I wouldn't miss," he said, straightening up and almost immediately increasing the ferocity of the attack as the Germans were presented with two temptingly static but frustratingly unattainable targets.

Baculus smiled.

"Me neither, friend. But it won't hurt for them to see us moving about on the wall."

Atticus wondered if he was referring to him and his comrades as much as the Germans. Being so close to the enemy but almost completely unsighted was disconcerting, and the calm demeanour of the two officers was certainly a comfort.

Baculus gestured towards the gate.

"It seems that lot out there have been busy collecting material to fill the ditch. I haven't seen any ladders yet but I'll wager they have them. They're massing for an attack at the gate. It's the same story at each of the others. And we both know how this finishes up if the bastards do manage to force their way in that way."

Plautius nodded grimly.

"So, we hold at all costs."

"We hold at all costs, brother," echoed Baculus determinedly. "Trebonius wants a reserve unit at each gate, drawn from the men on the wall. In case they do succeed in breaking through."

"Trebonius is in charge?" exclaimed Plautius.

Baculus smiled.

"Yes. Don't tell me you're disappointed?"

"Of course not. We've been on the wrong end of whatever passes for Aquila's idea of leadership more than once. I just can't imagine him handing over control of the legion to anybody, let alone Trebonius."

"He isn't here. He left for the larger camp just before the attack."

"To do what?" spluttered Plautius.

"Buggered if I know, brother. Some bullshit about important matters to discuss at headquarters, although I suspect it had more to do with our position out here! I can't imagine he was planning to hurry back, even before the attack."

Plautius shrugged.

"Well, maybe it's no bad thing. Trebonius seems to know what he's doing. How many men does he want for the reserve?"

"One man in ten from the wall, to be divided between the four gates. I want you to take command of the unit here. Leave

Rescius in charge and get your men formed up below. I'll have the rest sent to join you."

Plautius nodded and saluted.

"Good fortune, brother."

"See you on the other side," said Baculus, returning the salute.

Atticus watched as Baculus made his way quickly along the palisade, passing on his orders and directing men towards their positions. He didn't notice Plautius returning from his brief conversation with Rescius, the tap on his shoulder catching him unawares.

"Care to join me, Capito? I think Rescius is going to have his hands full enough without having to look out for you."

On another day, Atticus might have protested about being held in reserve, for anything, but today was not that day. He was relieved to have a little more time to try and clear the fog still filling his head. He shared a brief farewell with Julius and Titus.

"Take care, brothers."

"You too. You won't have us to fight the big ones for you this time," replied Titus with a smile.

"Oh, and brother," Julius said with a smirk as Atticus was turning to leave, "don't forget to have your god ask Jupiter for his assistance."

Unable to conjure anything remotely suitable as a response, Atticus gave him a shove and set off after the small number of other men from the cohort heading down their side of the bank to the assembly point behind the gate. Plautius was already there, cajoling men into position as they arrived. As Atticus took his place at the front of the square, he saw Allerix and his men heading towards them. Allerix smiled as he recognised Plautius.

"Greetings, Centurion. It is good to see you again, although it seems you find yourself surrounded once again."

"We are becoming more familiar with that than I would like,"

Plautius replied with a resigned smile, "although we've brought a few more with us this time."

Allerix nodded.

"True, but I assume you would have no objection to my men and I joining your group. There will be no call for cavalry here today and we grow restless to join the fight."

"It would be an honour. You're amongst friends," Plautius said as he gestured towards Atticus. He smiled.

"Besides, I've seen what you and your men can do and so have the Germans."

Allerix inclined his head.

"Thank you. We will take our lead from you."

He shared a brief smile and a nod of greeting with Atticus and left to rejoin his men.

Atticus knew that it would be a bad sign if any of the reserve units were pressed into battle and he hoped that he wouldn't get to see Allerix and his men in action again. Or not today at least. But he wasn't confident. He drew his sword as the sound of battle horns rang out from beyond the walls. He would find out soon enough. The attack had begun.

12

Vosges Valley

Atticus fidgeted uncomfortably and looked away from the wall. He felt wretched. It wasn't just the after-effects of his injury; there was something else. Guilt. He knew that he might be called into action at any moment but it was incredibly hard standing and watching his comrades fighting... and dying on the wall. He was worried about his friends too. The fighting would surely be as heavy there. If he could only see.

"Eyes front, Capito! You have a job to do here," Plautius barked.

Atticus returned his gaze to the gatehouse. With the advantage of support from the gantry above, the defenders seemed to be holding their own. To either side, however, it was a different story and casualties appeared to be mounting. Even as he watched, a young legionary collapsed to the floor, blood gushing from a gaping wound to his neck. One hand helplessly clamped to the wound, he held out the other, desperately seeking help. None was forthcoming. Atticus swallowed nervously as the man bled out at the feet of his comrades. Baculus hurriedly stepped into the line and was immediately forced to thrust out his shield as another German appeared at the top of one of the makeshift ladders being thrown up against the palisade. The powerful blow dislodged the man from the ladder and he disappeared from view. Ducking under the wild retaliatory swing of the next warrior to appear, Baculus thrust his sword deep into the man's chest before heaving him and the ladder off the wall. Content that the immediate danger had been averted, Baculus hurried off towards the corner of the palisade where the defenders could effectively be assailed from two sides. And the Germans certainly appeared to be exploiting that advantage. A number of legionaries already lay slumped against the wall. Most were unmoving but one, his left arm hanging lifeless by his side, was desperately struggling to pull himself to his feet. He had just managed to haul himself unsteadily upright when a warrior appeared above the palisade. Impeded by his injury, the legionary bravely thrust out his sword to deflect the scything blow the German aimed at his head. Without his shield, however, he was powerless to block the strike of the warrior's comrade who had arrived at the top of his own ladder. The sword plunged deep into his chest and he fell to the floor once more. This time, for good. The two warriors quickly completed their climb and clambered into the camp. Atticus wanted to scream out a warning to the fallen legionary's comrades. Busy fighting their own battles, they were completely unaware of the danger now lurking behind them. He watched in horror as first one and then another legionary was caught unawares, looks of pain and surprise etched on their faces, before the alarm was finally raised and the Germans were confronted. But the defenders were now fighting on the back foot and conceding ground. Recognising the threat, Baculus increased his pace and charged headlong into the confused press of men. His sudden arrival sent one of the Germans sprawling down the internal slope of the embankment.

He rose quickly to his feet but had advanced no more than two or three paces before a spear tip burst through his chest. He looked plaintively at the auxiliary who had advanced to throw the weapon and crumpled to the floor. On the palisade, Baculus' intervention had bought the defenders some time and for a moment it looked as if they might just be able to repel the attack. But it was too late. Encouraged by the calls of their kinsmen and the absence of Romans on the wall, more and more Germans were clambering unopposed into the camp. Atticus lost sight of Baculus and his small group as they were overwhelmed by sheer weight of numbers and driven back against the palisade. Plautius ordered them forward. The wall had been breached.

Bolstered by the auxiliaries, Atticus and his comrades fanned out to form a skirmish line between the Germans and the gate. He took a nervous glance along the line. It seemed a painfully thin barrier but it would have to do. If they failed, the gates would be thrown open and the camp lost. He took a deep breath and braced himself as the first of the baying and shrieking Germans swept towards them, determined to break through the Romans' last line of defence. Atticus quickly thrust out his sword as a short, stocky warrior took aim at him with his shield, intent on barging him over. Alert to the danger, the warrior slowed his run and swept his shield across to parry the strike, but his focus on the sword meant Atticus was able to lean back and swing up his own shield unseen. The metal edge sliced into the warrior's face and snapped back his head. Sprays of blood erupted from his nose and he let out an anguished cry. Bellowing a curse, he stepped forward to renew his attack. Fuelled by anger, his first swing flew wildly above Atticus' head as he ducked beneath the blade. As the warrior drew back to swing again, Atticus sprang forward, driving his sword over the man's shield and into his neck, killing him instantly. Atticus steadied himself behind his shield as another warrior advanced menacingly towards him. Naked from the waist up, the man's heavily muscled torso was slick with blood. None of it obviously his. Wielding his huge sword as if it were a piece of kindling, the warrior roared belligerently at Atticus and leapt forward. Aiming to cleave him in two, the blow crashed through the top of his hurriedly raised shield, sending shockwaves reverberating through his arm and up into the base of his skull. Atticus cried out as the pain in his head exploded once more. His vision clouded, and, swaying unsteadily on his feet, it was all he could do to remain upright as the warrior fought desperately to free his sword, now embedded deep in Atticus' shield. As Atticus began to regain his senses, the warrior gave up the struggle to free his sword and pulled a vicious-looking dagger from his belt. As he lunged forward, Atticus leant around his now useless shield and drove out his sword with as much force as he could muster. His blade sliced deep into the warrior's side. He let out a pained and angry cry but continued forward, ignoring the blood pouring from his stricken body. With his arm outstretched, he clamped a huge hand around Atticus' neck. The pressure was immense. Gasping for air, Atticus desperately swung up his sword. The warrior spat in his face and he felt a sudden and intense pain in his armpit. Clamping his mouth shut, Atticus completed the swing and brought his sword down on the warrior's arm, mutilating it at the elbow and sending him spinning to the floor. Atticus gratefully sucked in several deep breaths of air. Casting aside his shield, he stepped forward and thrust his sword into the warrior's chest. As he straightened up, he was hit with another searing jolt of pain. He ran the back of his sword hand under his arm. It felt damp to the touch. As he pulled it out, several drops of blood fell to the floor and there was more smeared over the back of his hand. He had been stabbed. Gritting his teeth, he quickly scooped up the fallen warrior's shield. Much lighter than he was used to, it felt very strange but it would have to do. He winced as he flexed his arm and tried to roll his shoulder. He seemed to have a full range of movement despite the pain. That he would just have to deal with. As he stepped back into line, Atticus bent quickly to retrieve the ornate dagger resting in the now open hand of the warrior lying dead at his feet. He tucked it safely in his belt. It would be something to share later. He cast his eyes along the line and took a deep breath. If there was a later.

The bodies of dead and injured men littered the floor. The defensive line was looking a little ragged but it had not yet been breached. But Plautius was in trouble. Fighting to retain control of the line, he was being targeted by a small group of warriors, all desperate to bring him down in order to weaken the resolve of the defenders. Atticus had never seen Plautius fight before and was impressed that he hadn't allowed his years as an officer to dull his skills with a blade. Even so, the odds looked stacked against him. He looked at the man to his right. He knew him by sight if not by name. He looked pale and drawn and he was bleeding heavily from a nasty gash to his arm, but he nodded with a grim smile as Atticus gestured that he was going to Plautius' aid. As he hurried over, a lone warrior more vigilant than the rest peeled off to meet the threat. Blade outstretched, Atticus feigned to go low before lunging at the man's chest. Not taken in, the warrior easily parried the blow and let out a snort of derision as he adeptly swung down his own sword, forcing Atticus to scramble quickly away. Following up quickly, the warrior jumped forward, his raised sword targeting Atticus' head. As the blow landed on his shield, Atticus flashed out his sword, raking it across the man's legs. The warrior howled in pain and tried to land a retaliatory blow but Atticus had already slid away, determined to launch another attack before the warrior could retreat out of range. As Atticus pressed forward, the warrior gave ground before stumbling slightly and losing his balance. Seizing his opportunity, Atticus slid forward and stabbed his sword into the man's groin. The warrior bellowed an agonised cry and sank slowly to his knees, trying in vain to stem the flow of blood pulsing from the deep wound. He spat a curse at Atticus and pitched forward into the dirt. Breathing heavily, Atticus pressed on.

With the Germans' attention focussed solely on Plautius, he was able to approach the melee unseen. Singling out one of the warriors, Atticus drove his sword into the man's back, dropping him to the ground. The sudden disappearance of his kinsman momentarily distracted Plautius' opponent and the centurion took full advantage, shattering the man's jaw with his shield. The stunned warrior barely had time to register the pain before Plautius slashed him across the throat, launching a fresh spray of blood into the air. Plautius kicked the man's still upright body to the floor and gave Atticus a grateful nod of thanks. Their failure to punch through the Roman lines seemed to have rattled the Germans and, with their momentum stalled, Plautius began to press cautiously forward. With the defenders on the wall seeming to have regained some control, the influx of warriors joining the attack had been slowed almost completely. With the exit for those already present now in danger of being lost, panic spread along the line and the Germans began to retreat. With Plautius quickening the pace as they pressed forward, Atticus struggled to catch his breath. He could feel his tunic sticking to his chest as it became matted with the blood seeping from his wound. He hadn't noticed the pain whilst he'd been fighting but he couldn't ignore it now. He winced as he ran his hand instinctively under his arm. He forced himself to take shallow breaths but even that was an effort. He felt and sounded like he did at the end of a long march and it scared him. He tried to reassure himself that surely he would already have succumbed if he had a serious injury and forced himself to focus on the scene unfolding before him. A lone warrior stood defiantly imploring those fleeing to fight on. He had succeeded in rallying a small number to his cause when Allerix led his men forward. He was conceding height and reach to his opponent but he was faster and his sword strokes more economical. The warrior's strikes became increasingly ragged as Allerix turned defence into attack, forcing him to concede ground. Blocking an arcing blow on his shield, Allerix span quickly away from the blade and raked his sword across the back of the warrior's legs, severing his hamstrings. He collapsed to the floor with an agonised cry. Allerix stepped forward and ended the man's suffering with a sword thrust to the nape of his neck. The remaining warriors turned and fled. As they desperately sought any route to safety over the palisade, Plautius broke into a run, leading Allerix and a handful of others quickly up the slope to join forces with the defenders on the wall. Feeling utterly exhausted and a little unsteady on his feet, Atticus watched them go. As the last of the Germans scrambled over the palisade or died trying, he let out a sigh of relief. They had contained the breach. He set off slowly to rejoin his comrades on the wall.

*

Allerix sheathed his sword and ran his sleeve across his face. Ariovistus' warriors were streaming away, in far fewer numbers than they had arrived. The Roman camp had survived, although there had been moments during the battle when he hadn't been sure it would. He spat into the dirt and ran his eyes across the blood-soaked corner of the camp they had been defending. The victory had not been secured cheaply and some of his own men lay amongst the many dead and injured. He watched as Valis, his trusted lieutenant, began organising help for the wounded and the recovery of their fallen brothers. They would honour them tonight and ensure that they were avenged when the time came. His men had helped turn the tide of battle today, not for the first time, and he hoped Caesar appreciated the value of his father's support. He wasn't hopeful. If Egus and Roucillus were to be believed, the Roman had no intention of returning home should he defeat Ariovistus. Replacing one foreign invader with another was scant reward for the lives of his men, although it was exactly what his father had feared might happen. He shook his head. That was a concern for another day. The men who had fought and died alongside his warriors were men of honour, and he would not allow his doubts about Caesar to colour his view of all Romans. Spotting Plautius on the wall, he headed up the embankment. The centurion was watching another senior officer being hurriedly stretchered away. The Roman acknowledged his greeting and the two men clasped hands.

"Your comrade looks in a bad way. I hope he makes it."

"Me too, lad. That's our first spear and the only real leadership at the head of this legion."

The two men shared a knowing look and Plautius placed his hand on Allerix's shoulder.

"Give my thanks to your men. That could easily have gone the other way."

"It is our fight too, my friend," said Allerix.

"True, but I'm still grateful to have had you with us."

Allerix nodded and gestured towards Rescius as he hurriedly approached. Plautius sighed.

"This will be the first report on casualties. I doubt it's going to be a pretty picture."

Allerix frowned.

"It never gets any easier, does it? I will leave you to your discussions."

Plautius shook his head.

"It doesn't. I did wonder this time whether I was going to end up as one of the names on the list. I might have too, if it wasn't for Atticus. If you see him, let me know. I need to thank him as well."

*

Atticus gave Allerix a weary-looking smile as he slid into line beside him. Allerix nodded and clapped his friend on the back.

"It is good to see you, my friend. I don't think my men will ever grow accustomed to fighting on foot but they will have a tale to tell tonight."

Atticus nodded.

"I should like to hear those."

Allerix smiled as Atticus eased his arm free from the German shield he seemed to have acquired during the battle. He gave him a gentle nudge.

"I see you have adopted a less Roman look. We may make a Gaul of you yet!"

Allerix looked up as Plautius returned, giving Atticus a nod.

"He will be staying in the legion!"

Allerix raised his hands in mock surrender.

"I'm sure he will."

He gave the centurion a smile.

"Although, if my men help out the XIIth any more, we might have to consider adopting you all!"

Plautius laughed.

"Aquila would love that! Although if it's all the same to you, I'll stick to fighting on foot, thanks. Speaking of which…" He turned to Atticus. "I need to thank you for what you did today, lad. I'm grateful… Capito?"

Staring into the distance, Atticus seemed totally unaware that Plautius was trying to talk to him. He looked pale and Allerix thought he seemed a little unsteady on his feet. Was that blood on his hand?

Plautius flashed the young Roman a look of concern and took hold of his shoulder.

"You okay, lad? I'm trying to thank you, but you seem miles away."

Atticus turned slowly towards the centurion, a plaintive look on his face as he studied the bloody hand he had just drawn across his chest. Plautius leapt forward as Atticus' legs buckled and he slumped towards the floor. With Allerix's help, the centurion succeeded in easing Atticus to the ground. Julius and Titus anxiously hurried over as Plautius carefully lifted Atticus' arm.

"There's a wound. It looks nasty too. He's losing a lot of blood. Hang on, lad. Help's coming."

Atticus' eyes shut and his body went limp.

Plautius beckoned for Titus and Julius to lift their friend.

"Quickly, get him to the surgeon."

The centurion sighed as he and Allerix watched them hurry away.

"One more for the list. Let's hope I wasn't premature about him staying in the legion."

13

Vosges Valley

Allerix ducked into the muggy and humid hospital tent. It had been several hours since the battle had finished. Night had set in, bringing a noticeable chill to the plain. Not that you would notice that in here. Removing his cloak, he paused to allow his eyes to adjust to the flickering light of the oil lamps. The tent was larger than he expected. Testament to the cost of war. He had lost men in the brutal struggle to hold the camp but the Romans' sacrifice had been far greater. He hoped it wouldn't be in vain. He watched the orderlies flitting between the beds, pausing to administer treatment or offer a drink. His own people had healers, practised in the medicinal properties of plants and herbs, but nothing quite like this. He didn't know whether to be impressed at the ingenuity and organisation or concerned at how the practised ease to treat such numbers had been acquired. Either way, it raised the threshold of Rome's ability to sustain casualties in battle and that worried him. He was about to ask for assistance in locating Atticus when he saw Plautius picking his way carefully through the beds as he made for the exit. They exchanged greetings.

"You're here to see Atticus, I assume?"

Allerix nodded and Plautius gestured towards the corner of the tent.

"He's over there with a number of others from the cohort. Julius is with him."

"Your losses were heavy today?" Allerix asked.

Plautius sighed.

"Less than I feared after that bloodbath but worse than most. I am just on my way to give details of the butcher's bill to Aquila."

"He has returned?"

Plautius looked surprised.

"I wasn't aware people knew he had gone."

Allerix shrugged.

"You know how men talk, Centurion. And they don't miss where their leaders chose to be when it comes to a fight."

"No, I suppose not. And he's managed to get out of leading us into battle tomorrow as well. Caesar has asked him to lead the cavalry with Crassus."

Allerix raised his eyes.

"Caesar expects the Germans to take the bait tomorrow?"

"No. But it appears the Germans have been resisting battle because the portents for their victory are not good. At least not until after the full moon has passed."

Allerix looked quizzically at Plautius.

"Sorry, lad. It seems that some of the prisoners we took have been 'encouraged' to talk."

The two men shared a knowing look. They both knew what form that encouragement was likely to have taken.

Plautius shook his head.

"I'm not sure what to make of such things but Caesar isn't going to wait around until the new moon to find out. We attack tomorrow!"

Allerix nodded.

"We take such omens very seriously, Centurion. It would explain much about Ariovistus' approach, and pushing for battle whilst his warriors know their gods seek a more favourable time would be wise. But we both know victory will be hard-earned and that it will not be the gods doing the fighting! Take care tomorrow."

Plautius placed his hand on Allerix's shoulder.

"You too, friend. Crassus is a good man. He's young but he cares about his men and they respect him. Aquila hasn't set foot outside his tent since he arrived back. I doubt he will be interested in the details of our casualties. All he cares about is the 'glory' of our defensive stand and how well it will reflect on the legion and those at its head. I wouldn't trust him to value the lives of you or your men as highly as he should."

Allerix nodded.

"You may rest assured that I do not hold Aquila in any greater esteem than you, my friend, but I am grateful for your words of caution."

"Then I wish you well tomorrow. I have other tasks to attend to and I wanted to return later. I fear that some of those here will add to our losses before the night is out."

Allerix raised his eyebrows.

"And Atticus?"

"I don't know, lad. They say the wound was shallow and small, which is good, but they worry about his breathing, and he lost a lot of blood. They've cleaned and packed the wound and he's had whatever pain relief they can get into him. It's in the lap of the gods now. He's young and strong but if he gets a fever it will be touch and go."

Allerix nodded and the two men clasped hands.

"May your gods watch over you tomorrow, Centurion."

"And yours over you, lad. Let's hope the omens were right."

*

Allerix picked his way carefully through the crowded jumble of beds. Navigation wasn't easy but he'd recognised Julius talking with an orderly as he headed towards the far corner of the tent where Plautius had indicated he would find Atticus. He returned Julius' smile of greeting as he arrived.

"You are well?"

"I am, which is more than can be said for our sleeping friend here."

Allerix recognised Julius' attempt at humour for what it was. He had grown more accustomed than he would like lately to masking his own concerns in much the same way.

"I heard what happened. It seems you had quite a time of it," said Julius.

Allerix nodded.

"I would not care to repeat it. And your time on the wall?"

"Tough! And just enough time to rest before doing it all again tomorrow."

Allerix caught the pained expression on Julius' face and placed a reassuring arm on his shoulder.

"I heard. Hopefully, it will be enough to bring an end to all of this."

The orderly tutted as they cast a shadow over his attempts to redress Atticus' wound and he shooed them out of the way.

"He will need to rest undisturbed after I have finished here."

The two men nodded and watched as the orderly went about his work.

"That is dried aloe, is it not?" asked Allerix.

"It is," replied the surprised orderly. "You are familiar with medicinal herbs?"

"A little," said Allerix, who was thinking about all the times he had observed his sister tending to her horses.

"It will help with the bleeding, I think, but that?" he said, wrinkling his nose and pointing to the foul-smelling paste the orderly was now busy making.

"Henbane seeds and lanolin. It will ease his pain and seal the wound."

The orderly applied the paste and set it down on the wooden tray at the end of Atticus' bed.

"What's that?" Julius asked as he saw the small knife on the tray.

"I think he had it with him when he arrived. The surgeon believes it might have been the weapon that inflicted his wound."

"Can I see?" asked Julius.

The orderly muttered something under his breath but handed Julius the knife before returning to his work. Allerix watched Julius sizing up the knife.

"It is a fine blade and one unlikely to have been given up freely in life. If that is the weapon that injured him, I suspect its previous owner lies dead somewhere out there at Atticus' hand."

Julius smiled.

"I hope you're right. Tell me, who is this on the handle?"

"That is Taranis, God of Thunder. Why do you ask?"

"I was intrigued. I have seen one like it before and I wondered who it was."

"Well, now you know!" said the orderly curtly. "I will have that back, please, and then you two must be on your way. These men need peace and quiet!"

His stern look made it clear he would broach no argument and Allerix followed Julius quickly out of the tent.

"It is late, my friend. I must return to my men. Gods willing, we shall meet again soon."

Julius nodded and gave Allerix a thin smile.

"Indeed, though I fear the gods will be busy tomorrow."

Allerix watched Julius disappear between the tents. He felt sure that the Roman was right. He reached for his pendant, hoping that Taranis would be kinder to him than the warrior slain by Atticus. Hopefully, Atticus' gods would not wish to busy themselves with him just yet either. He took a deep breath and stared up at the stars carpeting the clear night sky. He knew that neither of them would have to wait long to find out.

14

Vosges Valley

Allerix pulled his cloak a little tighter about his shoulders. It was just after dawn and the slowly rising sun brought the promise of another fine day. It was not yet accompanied by any warmth, however, and a chill mist blanketed the plain. It lent an eerie feel to proceedings as a steady stream of soldiers emerged from the gloom and marched purposefully towards Ariovistus' camp. It was an impressive sight. He had come to admire the results of Roman discipline and training. They were tough and resilient. Few forces could have withstood the attacks of yesterday. Fewer still would retain the confidence, arrogance perhaps, to launch their own assault today. It made them good allies but dangerous enemies, as the Germans had discovered. But, other than the small group of soldiers he had come to know, he hadn't warmed to them as a people. He didn't trust their leaders to do what was right or honourable and he was concerned that their plans might yet bring them into conflict with his own people. It was not a thought to warm a man on a morning such as this, and he took a deep breath to clear his head.

Best get this over with.

Shaking Isarno's reins to nudge him forward, he trotted towards the small group of horsemen who would be leading the cavalry. Silhouetted against the sun, he had to shield his eyes as he tried to pick out those present. He recognised Aquila, who looked slightly more martial in the saddle than he did on foot… though that was not difficult. The other officer was presumably Crassus, who by contrast looked every inch the young warrior. They were supported by several decurions, from what little cavalry forces the Romans possessed. Roucillus and Egus were there and the group was completed by a couple of nobles that he recognised as Aedui but whom he didn't know. He slowly eased Isarno into the gathering and exchanged greetings. There was a palpable air of tension that presumably owed its origins to a distinct frostiness in the relationship between the two Roman officers. Although courteous, they did little to hide their antipathy for each other. Aquila's face was a picture as Crassus gestured to the troops forming up on the plain and began the briefing.

"Gentlemen, as you can see, our forces are to be drawn up before the enemy camp. It is Caesar's intention that we advance until the Germans are forced to respond and battle is joined. The bulk of our cavalry, together with that of the Allobroges, will support the infantry attack. I have been asked to lead this force. The remaining cavalry, which is to be led by Lucius, will remain here in reserve."

Aquila was clearly unhappy playing a subordinate role and Allerix watched him struggling to control his discomfort as Crassus continued.

"Caesar hopes that we will have no need to call on the support of Lucius' forces. Should we need to do so, the presence of you and your men is welcome, Allerix. I have heard only good things about the bravery and skill of the Aduatuci. You at least have nothing to prove."

Allerix was sure Crassus hadn't missed the barely disguised look of hostility on Aquila's face, but the young Roman carried on regardless.

"If all goes according to plan and the enemy forces are broken, Lucius is to ensure that no warriors are allowed to escape the field." Crassus paused to take stock of the preparations below. "Now, the hour of our attack draws near. If you will excuse me, I will take up my position before the opportunity to do so is lost."

Roucillus, Egus and one of the two decurions peeled away and headed back across the plain, taking their lead from Crassus. Aquila was clearly not sorry to see them go.

"Now that my young and naïve associate has left, let me be clear about our orders, for Crassus has applied a somewhat... noble veneer to Caesar's expectations. If the enemy breaks, and they will, we are to pursue and kill all those who flee, not just the warriors. I trust that I can rely upon you to ensure that these orders are appropriately relayed to your men."

Blinded by their hatred for Ariovistus, there was barely a moment's hesitation before the Aedui were enthusiastically confirming their understanding. Their positivity made Allerix blanche. He felt Aquila's gaze upon him.

"And you, Gaul? You are clear what is expected?"

"You leave little room for doubt, Roman," Allerix replied, irritated by Aquila's pompous manner.

"Good. Then we have an understanding. Let us hope that we are not denied our opportunity for sport."

With a smile, Aquila gestured for the two Aeduean nobles to rejoin their men.

Allerix watched them leave.

"I said that I was clear what you required, not that I would comply. Caesar cannot intend for innocent women and children to be killed."

"There is no such thing as an innocent German, Gaul. Any that we allow to live today will simply return to fight in the future or breed those who will. Caesar intends to rid our lands of this scourge once and for all."

"Your lands?"

"The lands of our allies. It is the same thing."

"As long as those allies serve the interests of Rome…"

"What?" sneered Aquila.

"It did not serve Rome to offer assistance to the Aedui when Ariovistus first arrived but now it does. It did not suit Rome to challenge Ariovistus. In fact, he was made a friend of Rome, only for he and his kin to be hunted now like dogs. I wonder whether it is more dangerous to be an enemy or a friend of Rome."

"You would do well to follow orders, Gaul, and have no cause to find out!"

"I do not take orders from you," snapped Allerix, his hands balling tightly around Isarno's reins.

Clearly unused to having to explain himself, Aquila's flushed face and raised voice betrayed his own rising anger.

"I speak on behalf of Caesar and you will do as your general instructs."

"Unlike you, Roman, I do not blindly serve Caesar. I came at the request of my father, to ride in support of your general. To help him defeat Ariovistus and his warriors. I will honour that commitment, but my men will take no part in the killing of women or children."

Aquila pulled angrily on the reins of his horse as he began to wheel away.

"Then you had best stay out of the way of those with the stomach to do what is required!"

Allerix turned Isarno and headed back towards his men. Staying out of Aquila's way was one order with which he would be very happy to comply.

*

Isarno pawed impatiently at the ground. Unused to being saddled and stationary, he tried again to pull himself forward, shaking his head at the continued control being exercised on his reins. Allerix leant forward to stroke his ears. He shared Isarno's frustration. He and his men were warriors, and watching rather than fighting a battle did not sit well with any of them. It did at least mean that the Romans had the upper hand, with no need to call on their reserves. Their determined approach had succeeded in forcing the Germans from their camp as planned. In fact, the two sides had come together so quickly, there had been no time for the Romans to launch their javelins before the hand-to-hand fighting had begun. The initial clashes had been fierce and evenly matched, with neither side gaining ground, and he wondered how Plautius and his men were faring amidst the turmoil. The Germans had emerged for battle in tribal groups, however, meaning that their numbers had not been evenly distributed across the plain. Their left flank had been visibly weaker and, as the casualties on both sides began to mount, Crassus' cavalry had started to make inroads. The resolve of the warriors had begun to weaken and they had started to fall back before the Roman advance. The fighting on the right flank had been heavier and bloodier. With greater numbers on that side, the Germans had briefly threatened to overpower the Romans. Fortunately, just as at Bibracte, Crassus had recognised the threat and redirected troops to relieve the pressure and wrest back the initiative. The Germans had fought bravely but the additional Roman numbers were taking their toll. Under pressure and with their left flank exposed, it would surely only be a matter of time before he and his men were pressed into action. Not that there was much honour in pursuing those who had already been defeated. It was necessary, he knew. He had no qualms about putting such men to the sword; they had condemned themselves by their actions. But even so, it was not a role he would have wished for him and his men. He grimaced. It seemed honour would be in short supply today. Nothing could ever persuade him that it was right to kill fleeing women and children, and the willingness of the Romans to do so was greatly troubling him. Was there no end to their ruthlessness? No ends to which they wouldn't go to eliminate a threat, whatever the implications? He shook his head. His men understood where their focus lay in any pursuit. He didn't think it had crossed the mind of a single one that they might be asked to chase down anyone other than fleeing warriors. And he was sure now that they would flee. The German line had begun to buckle under the strain of the Roman advance, and, in places, warriors were already beginning to turn and run.

And then the dam broke.

The trickle became a flood as all semblance of resistance crumbled and whole swathes of the enemy army began to retreat. A huge cheer rumbled across the plain as the packed ranks of legionaries realised that the Germans were flooding away and the battle was won. The Romans pushed forward. Allerix knew that many of the soldiers would be keen to avenge fallen comrades or secure some of the spoils of war, but the advance was steady and disciplined. It was all the more ruthless and efficient for that. There was nothing ordered or disciplined about the scene unfolding on the other side of the plain. Amidst the chaotic scramble to escape, men were literally falling over themselves as they sought out the quickest routes back to camp. Shields and even weapons were being discarded. Injured colleagues were cruelly left to their fates, and, on the edges of the camp, men were fighting one another for possession of any horses not already being used to hasten escapes. It was a sad and sorry sight and he could summon no feelings of joy, for all that he welcomed the crushing blow being delivered to Ariovistus. As he watched, small groups of people began to emerge from the rear of the German camp and hurry away. Soon, a seething mass of men, women, children and animals had surged onto the plain as the camp was emptied of all things living. The exodus had begun. Scattering to the four winds, the majority were resolutely heading north, towards the Rhine, home and safety. And, unbeknown to them, straight towards Aquila, Allerix and the rest of the waiting cavalry.

*

Allerix urged Isarno forward and set off after the warrior who had brought him the news. They had been sweeping the countryside for hours. Many of those fleeing hadn't made it off the plain, cut down by the cavalry forces thrown quickly around the camp by Aquila. But the cordon couldn't contain them all, and large numbers had slipped through to seek safety in the wilderness beyond. The rolling hills and stretches of woodland reminded him of home, but he had been far too preoccupied to truly appreciate his surroundings. The natural geography also made it harder to locate those on the run. Harder, but not impossible, and for miles around, the fields and hedges were littered with the bodies of those whose bid for freedom had ended at the point of a sword. If they were lucky, it had been administered quickly. Better that than the fate of some of the unfortunates he and his men had stumbled across. Cornered by the Romans and their allies, rape and torture would be the last memories many would have taken to meet their gods. And Rome had the nerve to call *them* "Barbarians"! It was some salve to his conscience that his men had been responsible only for the death of warriors. Consumed by fear and a desperate desire for escape, many of these had simply been cut down in flight. Some had sought to redeem their honour, making a stand and choosing to die with a weapon in their hand. But this sounded like something altogether different and he was intrigued to see precisely what it was that had compelled his men to seek him out. The shade beneath the trees was welcome as they followed the gently sweeping path through the woods. It appeared to run parallel to a small and shallow river that they had crossed several times already that day as it meandered through the landscape. It would have been a pleasant spot... on another day. As the treeline ended, they entered a small meadow that appeared to form one bank of the river. He could see the bulk of his warriors, dismounted and milling around. But Valis and a small number of others had crossed the narrow stretch of water to occupy the far bank, which they had evidently had to take by force, if the bodies lying prostrate in the soil were anything to go by. He fought back stabs of anger as he realised with dismay that several of the dead were his own. A sizeable group of women and children were huddled together a little further up the bank. As he drew closer, he could see a young woman standing a little ahead of the others, defiantly wielding a sword. The manner with which she struggled to hold it aloft and the opulent nature of her appearance suggested that she might be more used to receiving rather than offering protection. His respect for her grew as a consequence. He coaxed Isarno carefully into the river and they splashed quickly across. Everything about the woman's attire suggested nobility, albeit that her royal veneer was somewhat tarnished by the rigours of her flight. Judging by their appearance and the loss of his men, the warriors had been hardened and capable fighters too. They did not seem the sort to run, unless they were guarding something, or someone.

Her?

The woman instinctively pointed her sword at Allerix as he drew his own blade, but he had done so only to pass it to Valis. Hands outstretched, palms open, he cautiously approached the tired and frightened-looking group of refugees.

"I mean you no harm."

"You would be dead if I believed you did," the woman replied haughtily. "Though maybe I should kill you anyway. It would be a fitting end for one suckling at the teat of Rome."

"I am no lover of Rome, lady. Nor any invader who seeks to steal our lands."

A look of anger flashed across the woman's face.

"We have a greater right to the land than the Romans."

"And neither of you have a greater claim than the people whose home it was."

"People who begged my father for his assistance."

Allerix smiled. He had been right, though he had not expected royalty.

"You are Ariovistus' daughter?"

The woman nodded.

"I am Allia, his youngest."

"I do not blame your father for his presence here. Others must bear that responsibility. His mistake was choosing to stay, believing that he had a mandate to rule. A privilege that was neither earned, nor his by right."

"My father won his right to rule on the battlefield."

"And today he lost it in the same way. I wonder, was it worth it?"

Allia lowered her head.

"You mean to return us to Caesar?"

"My lady, Caesar is expecting nobody to be returned to him. His orders are for all those fleeing to be killed."

Allia's eyes flashed angrily and she brandished the sword in his direction once more.

"You said that you wished us no harm."

"I don't. You are alive because my men will have no part in the pursuit of those orders. But there are many out there who will have no such qualms about taking the lives of you and your flock."

"And I am no shepherd," said Allia quietly, lowering her sword.

"No, my lady, you are not. But I have seen more than enough innocent blood spilled today to send you on your way unaccompanied. I will have my men see you safely to the Rhine."

"And to whose word do I entrust our lives?"

"I am Allerix. Son of Albiorix, King of the Aduatuci."

Allia grounded her sword.

"My father did not believe his enemies to have any honour. It seems that he was mistaken. About some of them at least."

Allerix turned quickly as he heard water being kicked up by a horse moving at pace. It was one of his scouts. The man reined in his mount and bowed his head in greeting.

"My Lord. Roman cavalry approaching quickly from the west."

Allerix nodded and turned to Valis.

"Tell Cabrus he is to remain here with me. Have him select four others to accompany us. Take the rest of the men and see these people safely to the Rhine. I ask you to see that my commitment to protect them is honoured. And then return home. We are done here."

Valis looked pained.

"My Lord, I do not feel comfortable leaving you with so few men."

Allerix put his arm on Valis' shoulder.

"My friend, I am grateful for your concern but I will be fine. I do not intend to remain very long, but the disappearance of us all would arouse suspicion. I must secure you enough time to escape. Now hurry. It does not sound as if we have long."

Allerix turned to Allia.

"Please tell your people what is happening and have them ready to move quickly. Valis is a good man. He will get you home."

Allia nodded.

"Thank you."

Allerix climbed back aboard Isarno as the first of his men began to cross the river. He watched them splashing across, acknowledging Valis as he manoeuvred alongside.

"Avoid contact if you can, but do whatever is necessary to get them back and then you and the men home."

Valis nodded.

"You too. I would rather not have to explain your absence to Epomedius."

Allerix laughed.

"We will drink together soon, my friend, I promise. Travel swiftly and be safe."

The two men clasped arms and Valis trotted off to hurry along the ungainly process of getting each of the refugees onto a horse with one of his men.

Cabrus gave Allerix a smile as he reined in beside him.

"I must have done something to anger the gods. That can be the only reason I am condemned to remain here."

Allerix gave him a gentle shove.

"I suspect there is much for the gods to choose from, but Valis will rely on guile as well as muscle if he is to succeed, my friend, and you are blessed with much more of one than the other."

If Cabrus was minded to respond, his opportunity to do so was lost as the still calm of the afternoon was shattered by the dull sound of trumpet calls reverberating through the air. Allerix recognised it immediately. It was the rallying signal used by the men of the Roman cavalry. And it was close. They had arrived far faster than he expected.

"Cabrus, take the others and get back down the path! Try and slow them down."

He urged Isarno towards the few remaining refugees. Alerted to the imminent arrival of the Romans, Valis had ordered those already mounted to head for the stretch of trees that bordered the meadow on that side of the river. As Allerix approached, he saw Allia help one of the warriors pull a young boy up onto his horse. Allia beckoned for the boy to lean down and she whispered something in his ear. Then she passed the warrior her sword and gestured that it was for the boy. The warrior tucked it alongside his shield and set off after his comrades. Allia turned and walked purposefully towards Allerix. As she passed Valis, she signalled that he and the last of his men should leave.

"What are you doing?" Allerix shouted.

"You said it yourself. We must buy time for them to escape. What better way than with me? How else will you explain the bodies of six dead royal bodyguards? It is the only way!"

Allerix wanted to protest but he knew she was right. With Valis' help, he pulled Allia up onto Isarno and nodded for him to go. He and Allia watched the line of horses snaking towards the trees. Valis had just disappeared from view when the Roman cavalry burst into the meadow. Already anxious about how things might unfold, Allerix's heart sank as he recognised the figure at the head of the column.

Aquila.

He eased his sword a few inches from its scabbard.

"You are expecting trouble?" asked Allia.

"Yes. I'm just not sure how much," Allerix replied apprehensively.

He was pleased to see Cabrus and the others returning with the Romans. Aquila halted the column, which Allerix guessed was some twenty men strong, and led the two Romans accompanying him across the river.

"You again!" he snapped as he recognised Allerix.

"Greetings to you too, Roman," Allerix replied through gritted teeth.

"What happened here? And who is that?" Aquila demanded, pointing his sword at Allia.

Allerix noted the blood-covered tip. He gestured to the fallen warriors as Cabrus led the small contingent of his men back across the river.

"Those were members of Ariovistus' Royal Guard, discovered and killed by my men. And this is who they were guarding. His daughter, Allia."

"And why is she not dead too, Gaul?"

Allia jumped in before Allerix could reply.

"Because this man knows I will be of greater value to Caesar alive than dead, Roman."

Aquila's face flushed. He leant forward and jabbed his sword menacingly at Allia.

"Shut your mouth, woman! I did not ask for your opinion. The only value you and your people have is in adding to the numbers of dead we have enjoyed collecting today. And I mean 'enjoyed.'"

Allerix felt Allia ball her hands in his tunic. He tightened the grip on his sword. He hadn't doubted Aquila's willingness to follow orders but the zeal with which he had seemingly set about his task left him feeling decidedly uneasy. Aquila glanced towards the bank where his men were taking the opportunity to water their horses and share some refreshment. He was quiet for a moment as he turned his attention back to Allerix, as if weighing up his options.

"The rest of your men, where are they now?"

The hint of menace with which Aquila laced the question was not lost on Allerix. He nodded to Cabrus to be ready with his sword and pointed to the woods, which just minutes before had swallowed up the last of his men.

"I had them complete a detailed search of the woodland over there. When they found nothing, I sent them east. Where she was heading before we found her."

"Then I suggest that you give the woman to me and go after them."

"No. I will see her delivered safely back to camp."

Aquila glared at Allerix.

"Do not try my patience, Barbarian. Give her to me now!"

Allerix felt himself tense as he fought to control the feelings of rage coursing through his body.

"Watch your mouth, Roman. The lady stays with me."

Aquila's eyes narrowed and a mirthless smile ran across his face.

"So few of you... escorting a fleeing noble... your deaths an easy mistake to make in all the confusion of the day... Don't make me take her!"

Allerix set his shoulders determinedly.

"I should like to see you try, Roman!"

With a contemptuous sneer, Aquila swept his arm across the vista of the meadow, emphasising the number of men at his disposal. Allerix smiled.

"But you are on this side of the river. Are you willing to bet your life that they can get to you before we can?"

The two Romans drew their swords. Behind him, he heard Cabrus and the others do likewise. On the opposite bank, he could see the startled and confused looks on the faces of the resting cavalry contingent as they struggled to make sense of exactly what was playing out in front of them. A couple had hurriedly remounted but there had been no attempt to cross the river and, for the moment at least, they offered no threat. Aquila lowered his sword and gestured for his compatriots to do the same. He fixed Allerix with a cold stare, his lips curled in a nasty snarl.

"I will not fight you for her, Gaul. She isn't worth it. You may keep your prize, though I hardly think she is worthy of the name. I doubt Caesar will consider her anything other than a burden. Taking her back to camp would be nothing but a nuisance, given there is much more sport to be had today."

Allerix felt Allia tense; he could almost feel the hatred projected in Aquila's direction. But he breathed a little more calmly. Aquila was an odious man and he would like nothing more than to fight him, but a tense situation had been overcome and now was definitely not the time. He returned his sword to its scabbard and ordered his men to stand down. Aquila spoke quickly with one of the Romans, a decurion, who immediately turned his horse and crossed the river.

"I have asked him to select a number of men to escort you."

Allerix feigned a smile.

"That will not be necessary. I have protection enough."

"I insist. I must ensure that you all make it back to camp," Aquila sneered.

Resigned to losing his freedom to do anything other than return to camp, Allerix shrugged.

"Your choice, Roman, but we leave now."

He urged Isarno forward. As they splashed back across the water, Aquila drew alongside and leant across to close the gap between them.

"I will not forget this, Gaul. If our paths ever cross again, you will pay for your insolence."

Allerix took a firmer hold on Isarno's reins as he fought the impulse to bring the day of reckoning forward.

"If you mean to extract that payment man-to-man, the coming together of our paths would be most welcome, Roman. It is perhaps fortunate for you that such an event is unlikely."

Aquila laughed and locked eyes with Allerix.

"Unlikely? You think that we intend to leave these lands? No.

We will be staying. There will be opportunity enough for our paths to cross. If they do, know that I will be seeking retribution at the head of a legion, not a cavalry party."

He spurred his horse forward to cross the stream, leaving Allerix to reflect on his chill warning. Allia squeezed his arm.

"These men have no honour. They do only what is right for them. Rome cares not whether it is friend or foe that suffers, just so long as they can take what they want."

Allerix wasn't sure that Ariovistus' reign had been any different but the sentiment was true enough. The sooner he got home, the better. He led his men up the bank. Six of the Roman column stood passively waiting their arrival. *Presumably "the escort"*. The sullen looks on their faces were a clear indication of precisely how they felt about being assigned that duty. The remainder of the Roman riders were clustered around Aquila. He addressed them for a few moments and then, sword-waving, he led them off at a gallop. Allerix smiled. They were heading east. His men and their cargo were safe. At least for now. And with any luck he would never have to see Aquila again.

*

The first torches of the evening were being lit around the camp as Allerix emerged into the gloom. In keeping with the darkening skies, he felt strangely subdued. The journey back to camp had been tense and entirely lacking in any of the light-hearted conversation that might usually accompany such a trip. But then neither they nor their escort had been entirely comfortable with the arrangement. He had been relieved when they had finally entered the camp and could free themselves of their Roman shadows. Of course, that was when he had also had to say goodbye to Allia. He had heard Plautius speak highly of Trebonius and, hoping that he might be somebody who could be relied upon to ensure Allia was treated with some respect, he had made a point of seeking him out when they arrived. The Roman had been surprised when Allerix arrived with Allia, but he had quickly made arrangements to make her comfortable. More importantly, he had assured Allerix that she would come to no harm. It was a pity that others in the Roman hierarchy did not share his approach. He had still found saying goodbye to her surprisingly difficult. She had been the only bright spark on the journey back. Understandably nervous about the uncertainty of her future, she had been reflective but not at all morose, and he had found himself warming to her as they talked. He told himself that his heavy heart was the result of a natural concern for her wellbeing rather than any form of personal loss. But he wasn't convinced. Cabrus hadn't been either, and he had sent him off with the others to collect supplies when it became clear that the comments about his "new-found love for the Germans" were not going to end anytime soon. He smiled. He hoped Cabrus' ears were still ringing from the slap with which he had sent him on his way. He tied on his cloak and stepped into the main avenue. A light shower had started and men were hurrying to get off the street. He was not disappointed; it would make his progress easier. He had never felt entirely comfortable within the confines of the Roman camp but now he positively ached to be on his way. The events of today had filled him with a deep sense of foreboding and he was anxious to distance himself from its source as quickly as possible. But not before he had done this one last thing. He turned the corner at the end of the avenue and headed for the hospital tent. He would see Atticus and hopefully say goodbye. The rain was falling harder now and he broke into a run. Head down, he might have bumped into the tall and stocky figure leaving the tent if he hadn't called out.

"Steady, lad. The battle's over."

Allerix straightened up. It was Plautius. He smiled, pleased to see a friendly face.

"My apologies, Centurion."

"That's okay, lad, but if it's Atticus you've come to see, I can save you the time."

Allerix's face must have betrayed his concern. Plautius put a reassuring hand on his shoulder.

"He is still with us. Barely. But in no fit state to recognise anybody. They're going to send him back to Vesontio tomorrow. It's his best chance, if he survives the journey. But let's get out of this rain. I was heading back to my tent for a drink. Join me; we can talk there."

With the damp already beginning to soak uncomfortably through his cloak, Allerix was happy to agree.

"Thank you."

Plautius nodded and led them off through the forest of tents housed on that side of the camp. Most of them were occupied now and, as they carefully navigated the narrow pathways between the canvas homes, he tried to make sense of the snatches of daily life playing out before them. He cursed as he slipped on the now slick turf and caught his ankle on one of the wooden tent pegs.

"Nearly there, lad," Plautius called out as they turned into an area with slightly more room between the tents. Allerix could see the command tent at the end of the row. He winced. Hopefully, Aquila was yet to make it back. Plautius stopped outside one of the tents and shook off his cloak. He ducked inside, beckoning for Allerix to follow him.

"I've found a stray, Tullius."

Allerix acknowledged Rescius with a smile as he entered the tent.

"Greetings. It is good to see that you are both well."

Plautius gestured for him to take a seat on one of the cots.

"You too, lad. Hungry?"

He was. Extremely. He gratefully accepted the plate of dried meat and flatbread offered by Rescius. Plautius poured him a beaker of wine.

"Best if you drink that with the food. It's not a vintage to savour."

Allerix smiled.

"Thank you. Tell me, I saw the battle. Did fortune favour you with a place on the left flank?"

Plautius nodded.

"Yes. It seems that for once we were in the right place. They broke early and, after that, it was largely about containment and making sure nobody got carried away. It meant we escaped pretty much unscathed. The legion lost a few men but only injuries for us and nothing too serious, it would seem. I'd been checking when I ran into you."

Allerix took a sip of his wine. He grimaced. Plautius had not been wrong.

"I think you and your men have earned that good fortune. And Atticus?"

"He's developed a fever. I think the surgeon is more worried about that than the original injury. You know how these things go. His battle is with the gods now."

Allerix nodded.

"Then let us hope that your gods are as merciful as they are numerous."

Rescius leant forward to top up Allerix's beaker.

"I'll drink to that! And what of your day, friend?"

Against his better judgement, Allerix took a deep drink and tried to collect his thoughts. It had not been the kind of day easy to recount. However, he did his best. Plautius and Rescius listened with rapt attention as he outlined the events of the day and his intention to leave.

Plautius let out a low whistle when he had finished.

"Bugger me, lad. I never thought we'd have an easier day than you. I'm sorry for the loss of your men but fair play to you for sticking up to Aquila like that. Little shit! Can't say I'm surprised that you're looking to be on your way. Are you sure we can't find a home for you and your men until the morning?"

"Thank you, my friend, but I fear for the outcome should Aquila and I run into each other again. Besides, I have been away long enough. It will be good to get home. For you too, I'm sure?"

Plautius sighed.

"That it would, lad, but I don't think we are destined to be heading that way anytime yet. We have a command meeting with Aquila tomorrow but when the surgeon was telling me about the plans to transfer the wounded back to Vesontio he let slip that we may be preparing to winter in Sequani territory, though I've no idea why."

Allerix hung his head. He suddenly felt very weary.

"You okay?" Plautius asked.

"No. I fear this means that we may fight next as enemies rather than allies. It is a relief to have rid ourselves of Ariovistus, but any gratitude will be short-lived if Caesar thinks we will accept another master."

"I'm a soldier, not a politician, lad, but I can't believe that's his intention. I'm sure he doesn't want to provoke trouble."

"We are a proud people, Centurion, and, for many, Rome's continued presence will be trouble enough. It does not bode well. You are brave and honest men. Those you lead likewise. But I have seen another side to Rome and some of her leaders, one where honour is routinely sacrificed at the altar of expediency. I am not comfortable trusting my fate to such men, and doubt others will be either."

"Well, I hope you are wrong. I have no desire to spill the blood of those our cohort would call 'friends.'"

"Me neither. Let us hope that is not how it comes to pass," Allerix replied.

He raised himself slowly from the cot and stretched.

"But now I must bid you farewell. Thank you for your hospitality."

He exchanged his farewells with the two Romans and ducked quickly out of the tent. He set off for the stable block, where he hoped Cabrus and the others would be waiting. The rain had stopped but there was a damp chill in the air and he shivered as he pulled his cloak tightly about his shoulders. It offered some protection from the elements, but even his warm thoughts of home couldn't shake the cold sense of unease he felt inside. He hoped his discomfort wasn't a portent of things to come.

15

EARLY SPRING, 57 BC
Aduatuca

Epona kicked open the door and squelched quickly down the
path. She'd only gone a few paces but she could already feel the
cold water soaking into her boots. So much for trying to stay
dry. Here and there, patches of ice still lay in wait for the unwary,
and banks of snow lingered stubbornly around some of the huts
and under the wall, a reminder of the harsh winter that had just
passed. But the thaw had set in now and it was good to get out.
The grass always seemed a more vivid shade of green after the
snow. At least where it hadn't already been churned into a muddy
brown morass as people began to go about their business. It was
the same every year, the town's inhabitants emerging from their
enforced hibernations to reclaim their lives from the gods of
winter. But there was a greater sense of urgency this year. And
little of the positivity and joy that usually signalled the arrival
of spring. War was coming and everybody knew it. She sighed
and set out across the square. It was still early but the town was
already a hive of activity. Heads down against the biting wind as
they went about their business, the townsfolk seemed to have the

cares of the world on their shoulders. The dank, grey skies only added to the sense of gloom and foreboding. She paused to allow a gaggle of women and children to pass en route to the main gate. Foragers, one of the many working groups established to ensure the settlement was ready when the Romans arrived. She would take her turn soon enough but this morning she was on her way to the Great Hall. With his departure for the Tribal Council looming, her father had decided today was the day Cottabus and Ambilo would be sworn into the Royal Guard. She suspected it was also a good opportunity for him to take a rest from digging out the ditches and repairing the walls. Epona had always admired her father's desire to lead by example, but she knew such labours took their toll on him far more than they used to. It was the first time she'd really thought about the passage of time and his getting older, though doubtless her worries also had something to do with the threat of war. Forcing a smile, she returned the nods of acknowledgement from the passing women. Wrapped head to toe in a combination of blankets and furs and struggling with an array of baskets, they looked far less enamoured with the task than the children, who giggled and chatted excitedly amongst themselves as they followed along behind. She gave them a wave as they passed, eliciting a fresh outbreak of animated conversation. The innocence of youth! She watched the group disappear from view amongst the huts and hurried towards the hall. She would enjoy the sense of occasion but the ceremony always stirred mixed emotions, and, with war on the horizon, she felt particularly troubled. Her father would have need of a strong bodyguard, and she was pleased that Epomedius could now call on Cottabus and Ambilo for support. They were good fighters. But not so good that she couldn't beat them. She had. Many of the others too, and she'd always felt herself worthy of a place in the Guard. But it was not to be. Tradition wouldn't allow it. There were limits, even for her father, who was unusual amongst the tribal leaders, simply encouraging her to train as he did. Understanding all of that made it no easier to accept her fate and it hurt that she would never get to fight by her father's side. But she would fight. She was a warrior and she wouldn't wait passively at home with the other women, the young and the old. If that must be amongst the rank and file rather than in defence of her father, so be it.

Epona splashed along the path, doing her best to ignore the ripe smells that assailed her nose as she passed by the tightly packed animal enclosures, the plaintive but short-lived squeals coming from the surrounding huts an indication of the fate awaiting those still left in the pens. The butchers were busy. The blacksmiths too. Her father had drafted in additional labour to support the forges and they were being run day and night to try and meet the demand for weapons and tack. The blast of heat was welcome but she was pleased to escape the noise. Rounding the corner onto the main path, she caught sight of Allerix a little way ahead. It was good to have him home again. His time with the Romans sounded difficult as well as dangerous. And, knowing Allerix, she was sure he hadn't told her half of what had really happened. It had been enough, though, to convince her that the Romans must be stopped. She just wished Allerix wasn't having to leave again as a consequence. And this time, at least in part, it was her fault. She called out to him.

"Allerix, hold up!"

He paused and gave her a smile. She broke into a run to close the short gap between them. She gave him a hug. It was out of character and she had no idea where the impulse to do so had originated, but it felt right.

"I'm sorry."

"For what?" Allerix responded hesitantly, clearly startled by her wholly unexpected approach.

"For upsetting Boduognatus' plan that I marry Boduogenus and for compelling Father to agree to you riding with the Nervii instead."

Allerix smiled.

"From what Father tells me, the two of you were more likely to start a war between us than you were to bring the tribes together."

"That's true. But I would still rather have you at Father's side than Boduognatus.'"

Allerix shrugged.

"It is how it must be. I have grown accustomed to riding with strange allies, have I not? In any event, I believe that Father will be well protected. Perhaps better now than ever. Speaking of which, we shouldn't delay getting to the hall. Come on."

*

Watching from the edges of the hall, she had found the ceremony as moving as always, despite her inner turmoil. Wearing their polished mail and finest cloaks, her father and the members of the Royal Guard looked resplendent as they stood, swords drawn, in a wide arc around Cottabus and Ambilo. She knew the sacred oath by heart and had recited it as each of them was called forward by Epomedius to kneel and swear allegiance to her father. They had then run the dagger he offered across their palms and sealed their oath in blood. Failure to honour that oath would bring forth punishment from the gods, although she doubted any member of the Guard would see fit to delegate that task if one of their number failed to do their duty. Usually, the ceremony would be followed with a period of feasting but this time that would have to wait. Preparations were being made for her father's departure tomorrow. No doubt a beaker or two of ale would be taken in lieu of the feast but she would leave them to it. Epomedius' voice boomed out as she tried, unsuccessfully, to sneak away.

"Epona! Stop skulking in the shadows. The king requires your presence."

Slightly surprised by the formality of the reference to her father, she turned and made her way across the hall. Her father, Allerix and Epomedius came forward to meet her, leaving the rest of the Guard, now supplemented by its two new members, in situ. She inclined her head deferentially.

"Father."

He gave her a smile but it was Epomedius who addressed her.

"Your father knows that if war is declared, you would commit to fighting in the ranks. He would expect nothing less. None of us would. But he cannot allow it. It would be inappropriate."

She struggled to make sense of what she was hearing. Surely her father wouldn't deny her that right? He couldn't. She looked at him plaintively but he remained stony-faced and unmoved. Her mind was filled with a multitude of angry questions. They hadn't formed any sort of coherent argument but that wasn't going to stop her protesting. She took a step forward. As if he had been anticipating her response, Epomedius raised his hand, his stern look a warning that she should stave off any outburst. Dejected but conscious of the many others in the room, she bit her lip and stepped back. She could feel her hands gripping the edges of her tunic but she kept her gaze fixed defiantly on Epomedius.

"It would be inappropriate because you do not best serve your king in that way. I would gladly welcome any other warrior possessing your level of skill and bravery into the Guard, as would your father. The king rides to Samarobriva tomorrow and the full Guard will accompany him. Only the Guard is not yet full."

Filled with a rising sense of excitement and hope, she looked quizzically at her father.

"Father? What is he saying?"

He smiled.

"That we have one more oath of allegiance left to swear, if you would wish it so?"

Of course she would wish it so! She couldn't ever recall feeling so happy. Or so proud. All she wanted to do was shout her acceptance but, overwhelmed, she simply smiled and nodded her head. Allerix laughed.

"Well. That's a first. I never thought anything would render you speechless."

She quickly recovered her composure.

"Bastard! Did you know?"

He smiled.

"Of course. And a little more respect, please, for another member of the Guard."

"She is not yet a member," Epomedius interjected.

Her father nodded and gestured that Allerix and Epomedius should return to their places. She reached for her father's arm.

"Are you sure? Won't the elders be displeased that you have broken with tradition?"

Her father shrugged.

"Some of them, but I have spoken with enough. Besides, it's my Guard. Why would I not have the most able in my service? That is the tradition we should uphold, I think. I am sure. Now, go."

He set off to retake his position at the centre of the hall. Still scarcely able to believe what was happening, she hurried over to join Epomedius.

"You know the oath."

"I do."

"Then kneel and swear fealty to your king."

Trembling slightly, she lowered her knee to the ground. She closed her eyes and took a deep breath.

"In the presence of my kin and before Taranis, I offer this sacred oath to faithfully serve my king, to never desert his service and give my life for his protection. This much I swear."

Rising to her feet, she took the dagger from Epomedius, flinching as she ran the blade across her palm. But the pain was nothing compared to the sense of pride and honour that she was now feeling. She watched her blood trickle from her upturned hand onto the dagger. It was done. She was a member of the Guard. She had some unexpected arrangements to make for their departure tomorrow but perhaps she would stay for that ale after all.

*

SAMAROBRIVA

Allerix stifled a yawn and straightened his tunic for the umpteenth time. He turned and headed back across the small plateau on which the meeting hall was situated. The walk wasted no more time than the countless occasions he'd done it already that afternoon. He hated waiting. But the tribal chiefs were still locked in discussion, so wait he must. The two guards securing the entrance to the hall were doubtless as bored as he was, but all attempts to engage them in meaningful conversation had failed. He let out a sigh and returned his gaze to the now familiar view below. Samarobriva. Home of the Ambiani. Situated on a vast plain, its growth had been constrained by neither geological features nor walls. From his vantage point, he could see a huge and jumbled array of structures stretching into the distance. It had a disorderly air about it but there was no mistaking the affluence of the place. The Ambiani had done well for themselves by taxing the many trade routes that crossed their territories and from the sale of livestock and surplus produce made possible by the fertile nature of their lands. The influx of the tribal leaders and their entourages had been an unexpected boost for the local traders too. The settlement was much busier than usual at this time of year, and enterprising tavern and brothel owners had been quick to push up prices. But the coins kept coming and business had been brisk. Of course, the availability of alcohol and the proximity of so many different tribal groups had left the Ambiani busy breaking up fights or separating quarrelling factions for much of the last three days. Too many old scores or idle boasts of superiority to be settled. It was always the same. Whenever the tribal groups came together, there was some kind of trouble. But this time was different. They were hoping to build an alliance. No, they had to build an alliance. It was the only way they could defeat the Romans. If they were to have any chance of success, their leaders would need to put their pride and vanity behind them, along with all of their historical differences, however bright these burned in the memory. It was why his father had arranged for him to address the council. He wanted them left with no illusions about the strength of the enemy and why they had to act together. He would do his best. It had been reassuring as he travelled about the settlement to hear the fierce determination of those present to defend their lands against the Romans. But there was an air of misplaced bravado present that suggested they had no real sense of the challenges awaiting them. He didn't blame them. It was hard to understand just how ruthlessly disciplined and efficient the Roman army was if you hadn't seen it for yourself. As he had. As he still did some nights when he couldn't sleep. It would not be hard for him to convey the very real anxiety he felt about his people being the next to stand before the armies of Rome.

That was if he ever got into the meeting hall. The discussions were well into their second day now. At this rate, they would last longer than it had taken them to journey to Samarobriva in the first place. Three days in the saddle would usually have felt like a chore but it was nothing compared to all this waiting. Besides, it had been good to escape the confines of home and to have the chance to get Isarno galloping again. Not that they had pushed the pace. In common with almost all of the Guard, he had to admit that both horse and rider were carrying a little extra winter weight and the journey had been more measured than it might otherwise have been. He didn't mind. It had given him time to talk with his father, who appeared to be in good spirits despite the enormity of the situation confronting them. It seemed he had come to terms with his decision to commit the nation to war as well. Not that he could really do anything else. The Romans' decision to stay ensconced deep within their lands had effectively forced that choice upon him. Upon all of them. Worse still, word had begun to spread amongst the tribes of news that the Romans were attempting to recruit additional legions. These were not the acts of an ally or friend but of a nation and a leader intent on extending their power and influence at any cost. Even if that cost was war. Which he felt increasingly sure was exactly what Caesar had intended when he made his decision to stay. And so, they would fight. In what numbers and under whose command was still to be determined. Given the choice, he would far rather follow his father, but the Aduatuci were one of the smaller nations and their more measured approach to the use of conflict counted against them at such times, although it was precisely the kind of calm and calculated leadership that would be required and which he feared might prove a challenge for either of the more likely leaders. Boduognatus of the Nervii had alienated many of his peers with his innate sense of superiority, but he had been the architect of the planned alliance. He could also draw on the single biggest group of warriors and those with the most fearsome reputation. Galba of the Suessiones could commit larger numbers of men through his existing tribal alliances, which probably meant he could call on greater support in the hall, even if that loyalty was driven as much by fear as respect. Of course, as part of the alliance agreed between his father and Boduognatus, he would be riding with the Nervii either way. The outcome wouldn't change that. He smiled. But it would have a very real impact on how positive the experience might prove to be.

Allerix watched the pale winter sun sink quickly below the horizon, taking with it the last of the gentle warmth that had offered the only modicum of comfort whilst he waited impatiently outside the hall. He sighed and was about to set off on his well-trodden walk one more time, when the hall door slowly began to open. Finally! He turned to see his father emerging from the hall. He looked tired.

"How is it in there?"

His father's pained expression said it all.

"As you would expect. Too many long, self-important speeches and lots of posturing, especially from Boduognatus and Galba. There is nothing subtle about their bids to lead any alliance."

"But there will be an alliance?" Allerix asked anxiously.

His father nodded.

"The lines of division between the nations are never far from the surface, as you know, but I believe there will be, yes. I hope your experiences will be enough to persuade those chiefs who remain unconvinced. It might also help instil some calm amongst those who seem to believe that the simple deployment of our numbers will be enough to assure victory. But I doubt it. We shall see. Come."

His father beckoned for him to follow and turned back

towards the hall. Allerix nodded to the guards as they closed the huge wooden door behind him. It shut with a dull but very loud thud, interrupting the murmured conversation and drawing the eyes of the room towards him and his father. It was a temporary interruption and King Cernos of the Ambiani had to bang his goblet down on the table to secure silence. It was one of many gold and silver drinking vessels on show, a visible display of wealth and status that was in marked contrast to the plain wooden hall that surrounded them. It was smaller than he had expected and decorated simply, with furs, shields and an array of trophies from successful hunts of old. The antlers of a huge stag took pride of place over the large hearth at the end of the room, from which an array of servants were busy drawing the fire to light the torches, chasing the darkness that had accompanied the setting sun back into the shadowy recesses of the room. It gave the hall an air of comfort and warmth that he suspected might not be matched by the conversations. Cernos gestured for him to take a vacant seat in the middle of the table. It placed him opposite his father and Boduognatus. He nodded to them as he pulled out his chair. Galba had positioned himself next to Cernos at the head of the table. He didn't know any of what he supposed were the delegation of German tribes who had joined the conference but he recognised many of the others present. Albeit that it had been some time since he had seen any of them. His father smiled at him as Cernos addressed the room.

"Friends, we welcome to the table Allerix, son of Albiorix of the Aduatuci. He has ridden with the Romans. His father believes we will find his experiences helpful."

Clearly, this was not a universal view, and Cernos was forced to raise his hand as a fresh wave of whispered conversations broke out.

"He is right. We talk of battle but know nothing of our enemy. It would serve us well to listen to what Allerix has to say."

Cernos gestured for Allerix to begin. He took a deep breath and tried to recount just what he had witnessed from the sheer bloody-mindedness of the Roman pursuit of Ariovistus, to the final confrontation when he had been forced to fight. His account of the manner in which Ariovistus' army had finally been routed had brought loud cheers around the hall. The response had been a little more chastened as he told of the subsequent hunt for the survivors trying to flee the scene of the defeat.

"The battle was won. Ariovistus' army had been destroyed. But that was not enough. The Romans wanted to send a message, to punish those who had dared stand against them. And thousands of women and children were slaughtered as a result."

From the end of the hall, Galba interrupted.

"Then it is just as well that he will now be fighting men, Allerix."

Allerix pursed his lips and waited patiently for the raucous cheers of support to subside.

"There were warriors aplenty amongst those that fell, Galba. And don't forget that those warriors occupied land this side of the Rhine because they were victorious in battle. The Helvetii too had a reputation for being fearless. It didn't help them. Defeated and scattered by an army far smaller in size. We will be a larger force but so will the Romans, if these rumours of additional legions are to be believed."

This time, it was Boduognatus who felt the need to comment.

"Let them bring fresh legion! When we beat them – and we will – our victory will be all the greater!"

More cheers echoed around the hall, although Allerix noted that Galba and those loyal to him remained steadfastly silent. Again, he waited for the noise to die down.

"They can be beaten, yes. But it will take control and patience as well as bravery and skill. Coordinated attacks, not chaotic charges. They are the most disciplined army I have ever seen.

They fight as one from behind their shield wall and they are ruthless. Everything is planned or part of some routine that they have practised over and over again. They all know their place in that plan and the leaders that fight with the men are experienced and capable."

Trusted and respected too, if Plautius was anything to go by.

"And they are brave. Every one of them has armour but they do not hide behind it. I saw many acts of courage. This will be no easy fight. Even allowing for our advantage in numbers."

The room fell silent. Perhaps predictably it was Galba who picked up the mantle.

"It sounds as if you admire them, Allerix. Or is it perhaps fear?"

Allerix clenched his jaw and gripped his seat firmly with both hands as he fought the impulse to respond to the implied slur. He exchanged glances with his father. His face gave nothing away but he held up his hand to stifle any response from Allerix.

"I do not recall my son bringing news of Suessione warriors battling Ariovistus, Galba."

Ignoring the angry retorts from the end of the table, he signalled that Allerix should continue. Allerix paused, acutely aware of how any delay might appear but anxious to organise his thoughts.

"I have no love for Rome or her generals. Few display any honour and most serve only their own interests. But I do respect the legions, their organisation, their resilience and their effectiveness. How could I not? And you would do well to do likewise. I saw what they did. The Helvetii and the Suebi put their faith in numbers and died ruing that mistake. Am I scared of them? No. They die just as easily as the next man, and our warriors have more than enough courage and skill to beat them on the battlefield. But only if we are patient and choose our moments. I fear for the outcome if we do not."

As Cernos raised his hand to silence the chatter, Galba slowly pushed back his chair and stood up.

"We have done enough talking. It is time to act. I pledge the support of my nation to an alliance. One that I propose be led by me. I do not share Allerix's fear of the outcome of any conflict and nor do my people. This is why you need the Suessiones at the head of any alliance."

The room erupted into a cauldron of noise as the shouts and cheers of supporters did battle with the howls of protest from the less enthusiastic. Boduognatus leapt to his feet. Shouting to make himself heard, he pointedly ignored Galba as he addressed the room.

"Our friend is late to the realisation that an alliance is necessary. That is no surprise. The Suessiones have always followed in the stead of the Nervii, as they surely should now in battle. The Nervii will be the largest nation in the alliance and will provide its best warriors. It is only fitting that the alliance be led by the Nervii. By me."

Once again, the room descended into chaos. As Cernos tried desperately to restore calm, Allerix looked to his father. He wore a resigned look that suggested he knew this was going to be a long and difficult evening. He gestured that Allerix should take his leave. Relieved to be doing so, Allerix slid back his chair and made for the door. He took a brief look back as he swung it open. He did not envy his father. Leaving the guards to close the door after him, he walked quickly across the small chamber. This time with no intention of staying. He needed a drink.

*

Allerix ducked off the street and into the tavern. If Cabrus was right, this was where he would find Epomedius and Epona. The wave of warm air that hit him as he entered was welcome.

It was a cold evening. He paused at the top of the stairs. Even in a crowded room, he favoured his chances of spotting Epona and her shock of white hair. Especially when, as tonight, she was accompanied by what would invariably be the largest man present. As it was, the tavern was relatively quiet. The wine was supposedly very good and the food excellent but that came at a cost, and Cabrus had muttered something about high prices as he made his excuses and headed off elsewhere. Allerix smiled. It was equally likely to be the absence of working girls that had discouraged his friend and others. Epona gave him a wave as he headed over to the small table she and Epomedius had secured on one side of the fireplace. He pulled up a chair and gratefully accepted the beaker of wine that Epomedius slid across the table. It was good, just what he needed to help ease the tension of the afternoon. Epona smiled and pushed over the platter of chicken she and Epomedius had clearly been enjoying prior to his arrival. Tucking in, he helped himself to several pieces. He was famished.

"You were gone sometime, brother. We thought we'd lost you."

"If I'd had to wait any longer to get in, you might have. Although, by the end, I was very grateful to get out!"

Epomedius laughed.

"I'm not surprised. Your father said it had been tough going. Did you get any sense that they were making progress?"

With Epomedius keeping his beaker topped up, Allerix talked them through his time with the chiefs.

"I believe the council will support an alliance but I've no idea who they will agree to lead it. As I left, Boduognatus and Galba had only just started trading insults."

Epomedius frowned.

"It is what your father feared would happen. It does not bode well. They will need to find a way to work together. We all will, if we are to hold any alliance together."

Allerix sighed and reached for another piece of chicken. As he did so, Epona gave him a prod with her elbow and nodded towards the door. It was Boduogenus and he did not look happy. He picked them out at their table and strode purposefully toward them. Nothing about his demeanour suggested this was a social visit. He stood stiffly beside Epomedius, declining Allerix's offer of a chair.

"I will not be staying. Alcohol dulls the senses and weakens the body. We do not partake. It is one of the reasons the skills of the Nervian warriors surpass all others."

He glanced at Epona, a barely concealed look of contempt on his face.

"It is perhaps also why we do not have to resort to allowing women to join our Royal Guard."

Before Epona could react, Epomedius reached out to take a firm grip of her arm.

"Let it go."

Allerix watched Epona struggling to comply. He shared her frustration but Epomedius was right. It wasn't worth making a scene. Epomedius smiled at Boduogenus.

"How can we be of assistance... Lord?"

If Boduogenus had noticed the way Epomedius practically spat out the formal greeting, he didn't let it show.

"I bring a message for Allerix. We leave at dawn. My father expects you to join us."

Unable to summon any enthusiasm at the prospect of leaving so early but aware of his responsibilities, Allerix nodded grimly.

"I will be there."

Without even a nod of his head, Boduogenus turned to leave. As he did so, Allerix saw Epona quickly stretch out her leg. With no time to react, Boduogenus was sent sprawling face down onto the floor of the tavern. He leapt to his feet and spun around to seek out Epona, who was already standing. His face like thunder,

Boduogenus advanced towards her. Allerix noted with concern the grasp he had taken of his sword.

Epona raised her hands and bowed her head in deference.

"My apologies, Lord, we women are so clumsy. Let me help you dust yourself off."

Boduogenus waved her away.

"Leave me, woman! You would do well to be more careful in future. I will not be as tolerant again."

He jabbed a finger at Epomedius.

"And you would do well to have your king be more discerning when choosing his Guard!"

He spun on his heels and marched haughtily out, almost barging over an unfortunate servant. Epomedius raised his eyebrows.

"I'd say the king chose well. Although we might need to work on the subtlety of the approach."

Allerix smiled and gave Epona a shove as she returned to the table.

"Thanks. That's bound to make my life easier."

"Arrogant arse. He got what was coming to him. Besides, he's okay. The only thing wounded was his pride. Anyway, you'll be all right. He has no reason to look down on you. You know there isn't a warrior amongst them who can ride as well as you, and you can hold your own in combat. It might not be too bad."

She smiled.

"You'll be a refreshing change for the women in court too, I would imagine. There might be a Nervian noblewoman suitable for my brother. It's about time you settled down!"

She braced herself for the shove she expected to accompany the usual bluff rebuttal. But it never came. Instead, she caught him looking wistfully into the distance.

"There is a woman already? Tell me!"

Allerix shook his head.

"Fate dictates that there is nothing to tell."

As if intuitively recognising that now was not the right time to probe any further, she gave him a smile and topped up his wine. He nodded, grateful for the opportunity not to have to try and explain his feelings for Allia. He wasn't sure he could. Although, knowing Epona, the reprise was only temporary. This was something she would want to return to at some point. It was going to be some time before that opportunity would arise, however, if it did at all. The summer would bring war and nothing would ever be the same again. Their lives were destined to change. It was only how that remained uncertain. He was shaken from his thoughts by Epomedius noisily sliding back his chair and rising to his feet.

"Lord."

Allerix followed his gaze. It was his father. He pulled out the vacant chair and waited for his father to make himself comfortable. He looked exhausted.

"Are you done? Is it settled?"

His father took a long drink from the beaker Epomedius had filled for him.

"Yes, it is done. There will be an alliance. All of the nations have committed. It will be quite an army that takes to the field."

Allerix shared Epomedius and Epona's obvious relief but one nagging question remained.

"And the leader?"

His father took another drink.

"The council chose Galba." Allerix frowned.

"And Boduognatus?"

"Angry and sullen as you would expect. But he has sworn to honour the council's decision."

"Well that would explain Boduogenus' behaviour earlier," said Epomedius.

"What's that?" asked Albiorix.

"Oh, nothing. Just a little misunderstanding between friends. Things fell into place in the end," replied Epomedius.

Allerix joined in the laughter. He would explain what had happened to his father later.

"And what now?"

"The chiefs will depart to gather their warriors and arrange the exchange of hostages as agreed. We are to meet north of Bibrax at the next full moon."

Allerix raised his beaker.

"Then that is where we shall meet again. May the gods watch over you until then!"

His father reached out to put his hand on Allerix's arm.

"Be careful, my son. Boduognatus is a proud and stubborn man. I fear he may do something rash."

He reached inside his tunic and pulled out his pendant.

"I should like you to take this again. It brought you back from Vesontio. May it do likewise now!"

Allerix shook his head.

"Thank you but I think you should keep it. The whole nation rides to war. Our king needs the gods to watch over them all."

He smiled. Doubtless when conflict came, the Romans would be making similar calls to their gods. He knew those amongst them that he called friends would certainly be doing so. He wished them no ill, but if battle was to be joined in the heavens as well as on earth, he hoped that Taranis would emerge triumphant. That battle, he couldn't influence. The one in this realm was all that he could concern himself with. But that was for another time. Tonight, he would toast his family and try to forget what lay ahead.

16

North-west Gaul

Julius threw down his helmet angrily as they returned to the tent.

"Well, that's just great. I knew it couldn't be good when Plautius held the cohort back after parade. But really. Labouring for the engineers tomorrow? That's just taking the piss. How did we end up getting stuck with that fucking task?"

Titus slapped him on the back.

"You heard Plautius, brother. We were 'volunteered', all special, like."

Julius slumped onto his cot.

"Special my arse! It must have been Aquila."

Titus raised his eyes and smiled at Atticus.

"Of course it was, you daft bugger. The bastard has been riding the lad for months, ever since winter quarters. Double rations, light duties... Aquila hated all of that. And he's been making up for it ever since."

Atticus struggled out of his armour. It was true. Extra maintenance and cleaning duties, work in the stables, double guard duty, he'd done it all. Fuck, he'd even dug latrines with those on punishment duty. If there was a shitty job that needed doing, chances are he'd be right there doing it. All "simply to help with Atticus' physical reconditioning", Aquila had informed Plautius. The man really was a prick. But Atticus had promised himself that he wouldn't let it get to him. He'd cheated death and, scar aside, carried no lasting effects of his recent injury. He ached everywhere, was still struggling more than he'd like at the end of a day's march, and wondered if he'd ever get used to the annoying bite of his scar tissue when he extended his arm, but he'd been lucky. So many others hadn't. His time in hospital had been a sobering experience and he was determined to make the most of his reprieve, however hard that weasel Aquila tried to test him. As he was now. He would know full well that being assigned to the engineers meant an even earlier start than for the rest of the legion. Followed by a forced march to whatever location had been chosen for tomorrow's camp. Just so they could get construction moving before the rest of the legions arrived. It would be heavy work, most likely felling and clearing trees, and he understood his friends' frustration. He hated it when they ended up having to suffer alongside him at Aquila's hands. He smiled, grateful that they hadn't held any of it against him. Or not yet anyway. They knew who was to blame and, if anything, the shared sense of grievance had helped to cement their friendship, rather than undermine it. He levered himself slowly up from his cot.

"I'll get the soup on."

*

Allerix pulled off his tunic as he headed down the riverbank towards one of the larger rocks at the water's edge. Easing off his boots and trousers, he stood naked in the early evening sun. He took a deep breath and allowed the gentle warmth to play across his body. That would only make this harder. He picked a spot and dived into the crystal-clear waters. The cold, crystal-clear waters! The shock drove the air from his lungs and brought him quickly to the surface. Shaking uncontrollably, he fought to regain control of his short and ragged breathing. Now he understood why this wasn't something that he did every day, although he knew he would feel better for it. His whole body ached and he wondered if Isarno didn't smell better than him. The rigours of a life spent entirely under the stars had certainly taken some getting used to. The swim was also a welcome distraction from all the command meetings, which had grown increasingly fraught over recent weeks. With his breathing slowly returning to normal, he pushed off and languidly pulled himself into the middle of the river. He suspected that it might flow with some force in spring but now, as it meandered through the gently rolling hills to either side, the current was slow and the river calm. Little more than waist-deep even at its height, he could see the rock-strewn riverbed as he swam slowly downstream. With the cold beginning to numb his limbs, he turned back, catching sight of Boduognatus and Boduogenus at the top of the hill. Striding out purposefully, they were headed in his direction. This couldn't be good. He'd thought last night that Boduognatus was beginning to show the strain of the setbacks that had befallen their campaign. It had started well enough. All of the tribes had honoured their commitment and the number of warriors that had come together was simply staggering. They had even agreed a strategy to draw the Romans into battle. Unfortunately, they hadn't taken the bait. The subsequent attack on the rear of the Roman camp had been Galba's idea. He wanted to sever their supply routes and restrict their opportunities to forage. It was a sound strategy. In theory. But attacking a defensive position, even such a small one, when it was so close to the main Roman camp, was fraught with difficulty. He had opposed the plan. So had Boduognatus. Unfortunately, the latter's intervention had just served to reinforce Galba's commitment to taking action. The battle had been savage but the warriors leading the attack had almost succeeded in breaking through. Almost. They'd faltered when Roman reinforcements arrived and in the retreat that followed, their losses had been heavy. It had been a struggle to maintain the alliance after that. The relationship between Galba and Boduognatus, already tense, was strained to breaking point and they were finding it hard to maintain the sheer volume of supplies needed to keep such a huge army in the field. When they received word that Caesar had tasked his allies, the Aedui, with ravaging the undefended lands of the Bellovaci, they had left and the alliance had quickly folded. Caesar's repeated willingness to sacrifice non-combatants to achieve his aims sickened him. But as a tactic it had worked. The tribes had all left with a standing commitment to come to the aid of any nation threatened by Rome, but he had never believed that was a meaningful commitment. It had been hard enough getting them to act together when they were threatened collectively. He doubted any one nation would have the appetite to come to the aid of another, especially if they were likely to be targeted next. In any event, the Romans had simply moved too quickly to allow those commitments to be tested, arriving unexpectedly quickly in the territories of the Suessiones and then the Bellovaci. Both of whom had promptly surrendered, much to Boduognatus' annoyance. Allerix had felt for the courier bringing news of Galba's capitulation. Such was the volume of the vitriol-laden curses aimed in his direction that Galba probably had no need to await his messenger's return. That had been several days ago and the Nervii and their allies had continued their journey north. Heading home in the hope that familiarity with the local terrain might aide their endeavours. They had camped that night in the wooded heights of the hills through which the river ran. The Sabis.

He waded onto the bank and quickly shook off the worst of the water before hurriedly throwing on his clothes. He slipped on his boots and climbed to his feet just as father and son arrived. Neither of them raised a smile as the three of them exchanged greetings. As if surveying the hills beyond the river, Boduognatus stared past him into the distance as he spoke.

"Messengers bring news that Cernos has surrendered the Ambiani into the protection of Rome. So much for all his brave words at the council meeting. Maggot! First, Galba scuttles off like the vermin he is and then Correus joins him, bending the knee before Caesar, both sucking his cock, no doubt, whilst they're down there. Well, the dishonour ends here. We will meet the Romans in battle and we will defeat them."

Boduogenus smiled.

"It is fitting, Father, that the gods chose to present this task to the rightful leader of our peoples' armies."

Allerix wondered if the gods had also identified how this victory might be achieved, his moment of reflection misconstrued as reticence by Boduogenus.

"You doubt the wisdom of taking the fight to Rome?"

"No. I think it is best that we strike whilst we maintain the advantage of numbers and local knowledge. But it must be on our terms. I would also far rather have the support of my father and the rest of the Aduatuci. Their arrival will bolster our numbers, our cavalry and the morale of the warriors already here."

"Do you have any word on when we might expect them to arrive?" Boduognatus asked.

"I sent word of our location last night. I do not imagine they will be any more than one or two days away."

Boduognatus nodded gravely.

"Then I fear they will be too late. The Romans are camped less than one day's march from here. The messengers had to evade their scouts on their route here this evening."

Allerix's heart sank.

"Do you think they know we are here?"

"It is hard to draw a veil of secrecy over an army such as this. There will doubtless be a local, a mercenary, even a deserter, keen to line their pockets with silver. If Caesar does not yet know our location, I have no doubt he will soon enough. But we have received deserters of our own. Brothers amongst the Sequani and the Atrebates who no longer wish to ride under the yolk of Rome. We can use the information they bring to our advantage."

Allerix was intrigued.

"What did you have in mind?"

"We know from what you have told us that the Romans will send forward units to identify a suitable location for their camp. Our new comrades bring details of how the Romans march with the baggage train of each legion following behind them, creating a gap between them and the next. The presence of so many wagons will prevent reinforcements arriving quickly, if we attack the legion at the head of the march. The terrain will also render cavalry support almost impossible."

"You mean to effect an ambush?"

"Yes. We will marshal our forces in the woods here opposite the site they choose for their camp. The appearance of the baggage train at the rear of the first legion will be the signal to attack. They will be caught unawares and in the open. When the other legions finally arrive, we will be gone and they will find only the heaped bodies of their former comrades."

Allerix nodded. The plan certainly had merit. The Romans were nothing if not creatures of habit. They would surely have one of their more battle-hardened legions in the vanguard: experienced men who might be expected to respond quickly to the attack. But even so, with the element of surprise and superior numbers they would surely prevail. The absence of his father and the rest of the Aduatuci would be felt much less keenly this way too.

"They are most vulnerable when they cannot present a united front. Taking advantage of that weakness gives us our best hope of victory. They adapt their tactics quickly, though. I doubt they will present us with another opportunity."

Boduognatus nodded.

"I am hopeful that the loss of a legion will give Caesar cause to reflect on his continued presence in our lands."

Boduogenus turned to his father.

"I will rally the chieftains. They will welcome news of our plan. It is the chance to act that we have all been waiting for. Let us show Caesar and his men what real warriors can do. They will leave our lands or suffer the same fate as the legion that has the grave misfortune to arrive here first."

Boduognatus smiled.

"Go. I will head to the clearing. Have the chiefs assemble there. Allerix, you will join us."

Allerix nodded and watched the two of them head back up the hill. It was good to have a plan and it seemed auspicious that the gods would have the two forces collide on terms that seemed so favourable to them. If things played out as they hoped, they would secure an important victory, one that might rally other warriors to their cause or even signal an end to the hostilities. If Caesar could be forced to reconsider his strategy. He set off after Boduognatus. He would gather something to eat on the way. It might help take his mind off the recurring thought that, so far at least, nothing had played out quite as they had hoped.

*

Atticus leant forward and added a few more sticks to the fire. The meal had been warming and the evening pleasant enough, even without the fire, but he had always found the dancing flicker of a flame and the ever-changing light and colour it cast comforting.

He was enjoying the opportunity to talk with his friends, even if, by now, they really should have followed the lead of most of their comrades in trying to get some sleep ahead of tomorrow's early start. And another long march. Titus passed him a drink, the demands of tomorrow clearly playing on his mind too.

"I swear we haven't done anything this campaign but march and build camps, and tomorrow we're taking the lead on both."

Atticus remembered well enough. He felt sure they'd marched almost every day that first month out of winter camp. It had been quite some test and that had been before the rain. At some point each day the heavens had opened, leaving them soaked through and struggling along tracks that resembled roughly ploughed fields. It had been a thoroughly miserable experience, especially when it was their turn at the rear of the column, following in the deep and cloying footsteps of the thousands who had gone before. There had been some respite when they arrived in the territories of the Senones, but only for a few days, just long enough to collect supplies before they were off again. Heading further north still. In search of the armies of the Belgian tribes allied against them. And they hadn't stopped until they found them. It had been relentless, if ultimately anticlimactic, though he wasn't sure that had been a bad thing.

"Do you remember when we saw the fires of the Belgae camp for the first time? How far was it Plautius said they extended, eight miles?"

Julius nodded.

"I'll never forget, brother. Can you imagine how many men that must have been?"

"I'm just glad we never had to find out," said Titus quickly.

Atticus smiled. With eight legions in the field, he'd felt confident they could overcome anything. And then they'd seen the enemy camp and his confidence had quickly waned. Their numbers had looked even more daunting the next morning, when the two sides had lined up for battle. It would have been a savage fight and Atticus still wasn't convinced it would have gone their way. If it hadn't been for the strip of marshland deterring either army from striking first, they might have had to find out. As it was, both sides had returned to camp after a long stand off, leaving them wondering if it was going to be like Vesontio all over again. And then the Belgae had attacked the fort guarding the river crossing at the rear of the Roman camp. The XIIth had been too far away to witness any action but they'd seen how many men Caesar had thrown at the defence of the bridge. He must have been seriously worried about them breaking through. But they hadn't and, after being beaten back, the Belgae had begun to disperse. Almost immediately, the legions were back on the march again.

"Do you think the remaining tribes will fight?"

Julius shook his head.

"We've chased after three of them and they've all surrendered. I thought the Suessiones were going to resist, stuck behind that bloody big wall of theirs, but they gave up as soon as they saw the siege towers. And we didn't even have to threaten the Bellovaci or the Ambiani before they were looking to parlay. The only injuries we got were the blisters from all the tramping around."

Titus slapped Julius on the back as he slowly pulled himself to his feet. He stretched and grimaced.

"I'd best rest these weary bones before we are at it again."

Atticus gave him a nod and topped up Julius' beaker.

"I'm not so sure. I think they might have surrendered by now if they were going to. They're out there somewhere and Plautius seemed fairly sure we should be expecting a fight. He didn't much like the idea of us marching off when we have no idea where they might be waiting for us."

Julius shrugged.

"I know these Nervii are supposed to be fearless but I just can't see them being any different. I don't think they will bother us, even if they are anywhere near this 'River Sabis' when we get there tomorrow. But I guess we will find out soon enough, brother. It's us who will be marching out first."

Julius drained his beaker and climbed to his feet.

"I'm away to bed. You'd best not be long. If we aren't asleep before Titus starts snoring, we might as well stay up!"

Atticus smiled. That was true enough, although he didn't much feel like sleeping at the moment. He took another sip of wine. At least the campaign had been notable for something other than all the marching. They had been joined by two legions of new recruits. The XIIth had gained a good deal of respect for their part in the victory over Ariovistus but they had still been the new boys. Not anymore. And, just as they had done at Bibracte, it was the new legions who had been left to guard the baggage whilst the XIIth had marched out with the senior legions to confront the Belgae. He smiled. Had it only been a year? So much had happened in that short time that it felt like so much longer. He might not have been in such a hurry to experience combat if he knew then what he did now. He gave the fire one last stoke and watched the disturbed embers spiralling into the night sky. He hoped Julius was right about tomorrow.

*

Atticus followed the huge auxiliary into the water. Unencumbered with armour or a shield, the crossing was considerably easier for him than it was for Atticus, who was desperately trying not to lose his footing. The water felt pleasantly cool on his legs, however, and he wished he could soak the rest of his achy and grime-covered body. After a long and extremely arduous morning, the very last thing he had wanted to do was don his armour once again. The enemy scout on the bank opposite had remained stubbornly watchful, however. With the engineers hard at work marking out the camp, their tribune had ordered Plautius to conduct a sweep of the treeline on the other side of the river. It was hot, he was tired, and he had amassed a fine collection of blisters, bruises and cuts, now painfully aggravated with every movement of his shield. The only saving grace was that the physical torture of hauling logs was finally over. Hopefully, the patrol would be uneventful. The scout had sunk back into the forest as soon as they had splashed out of the river, and the tribune had been dismissive about the likelihood of encountering any larger enemy forces. He had nevertheless directed one of the Remi auxiliaries, Garmanos, to accompany Plautius on patrol. Apparently, he was an expert hunter and tracker. Atticus found that hard to believe as he watched the hulking figure lumber up the slope towards the point where the scout had disappeared. But having watched him wield his axe to devastating effect earlier in the day, he would be keeping such thoughts very much to himself. Garmanos paused as he reached the treeline. Plautius called out to them as they waited.

"Spread out! I know it's dark in there but there's no need for you to be holding each other's hands. Regular intervals. And keep each other and Garmanos in sight."

He slid into line next to Atticus. Satisfied that the path was clear, Garmanos disappeared into the trees. Taking his lead, Atticus and the others followed suit. It took a few moments for his eyes to adjust to the shadow beneath the thick canopy of trees, but escaping the heat of the sun was a pleasant relief. He picked his way carefully up the slope, keeping a watchful eye on Plautius and Titus to either side. The forest had grown steadily denser as they climbed, making it difficult to maintain a straight course. The ferns and grasses carpeting the forest floor didn't help with climbing either and once or twice he had lost his footing or been forced to use his shield to help lever him over a hidden tree root or hollow. Still, thus far at least, there had been no sightings of the enemy. Atticus was glad of the opportunity to catch his breath as they reached a narrow ridge cutting across the hill. They hadn't travelled that far but already the river and any sign of the camp had been lost from view. The hill looked a little steeper up ahead but he could see the plateau and the sun breaking through the curtain of trees that crested the top of the hill. The ridge had clearly been adopted as a useful path through the forest, and a well-defined track, flat and devoid of any vegetation, stretched away into the distance on both sides. At least it would have, if what seemed like tangled masses of hedges hadn't cut across the path at various points. They looked decidedly out of place. He watched as Garmanos returned from the nearest of these obstacles, paying close attention to a piece of the hedge he had broken off. He approached Plautius, who advanced a couple of paces to meet him.

"I'm guessing that's not a good sign."

Garmanos shook his head. His Latin was rough but he was able to make himself understood well enough.

"The Nervii fight on foot. They use these to deter the raids of neighbouring tribes who might have greater cavalry forces. We do the same. It is not a surprise to find them but this one is fresh."

Plautius looked concerned.

"How fresh?"

"No more than one or two days. And the tribes they might usually wish to deter are riding with them. You should stay here whilst I go on ahead."

Plautius nodded and gestured towards Atticus.

"Take the lad with you."

Garmanos looked Atticus up and down and shrugged.

"As you wish."

He turned and set off to restart his climb.

"Get after him then, lad. Leave your shield and lose the armour too. Victor, get over here and help Capito! The rest of you, get off the path. Keep your eyes open and stay quiet."

Free of his armour, Atticus set off up the slope after Garmanos. Surprisingly nimble for one so large, he was already approaching the top of the climb. Determined to close the gap, Atticus gritted his teeth and pushed on. It was hard going and he was dripping with sweat and breathing heavily as he reached Garmanos, who was by now lying prostrate on the forest floor. He signalled for Atticus to do likewise and together they inched forward until they were able to peer cautiously over the ridge. Screwing up his eyes against the glare of the sun, Atticus could see that the ridge was topped with a grass-covered hollow. It was quite narrow but extended for some distance along the ridge. Garmanos nudged Atticus and gestured toward the remains of a fire in the centre of the open space. It didn't look like it had long been extinguished. He could see the signs of several more at either end of the hollow. By the looks of it, a sizeable group had camped here and very recently too. He felt decidedly uneasy. Garmanos took one last look around and jumped to his feet. Atticus followed him down the bank and watched as he quickly surveyed the ground. He wasn't sure how Garmanos had determined which of the paths to follow but he seemed confident enough.

"This way. But quietly. There are men and horses on this side of the hill."

Leaving that thought hanging he set off down the path. If anything, the hill was steeper on this side but the path wound its way down the slope in a series of wide arcs sweeping between the trees and they were able to make good progress. As they rounded one of the bends, Atticus could see that the path dropped abruptly into a ditch running parallel to a wider track cutting across their own. He followed Garmanos into the ditch and was about to climb out when he felt a tug to his sleeve. Garmanos signalled for him to be quiet and pointed to a moss-covered tree trunk that had long since fallen into the ditch. Atticus wasn't sure what was happening but he followed Garmanos as he hurriedly edged towards the tree and squeezed into the space between the upturned roots and the wall of the ditch. Garmanos pointed towards the right of the track.

"Riders. Two of them."

Atticus hadn't seen or heard anything but he wrapped his arms tightly around his legs and tried to make himself as small as possible. He pulled some of the larger ferns across the gap and tried to control his breathing. For a while, Atticus wondered if Garmanos had been mistaken. Then he heard the sound of hooves on the road. He swallowed nervously; they were tucked well into the bank but he still felt horribly exposed. And he would have walked right into their path if it hadn't been for Garmanos. Perhaps he had misjudged his prowess as a guide after all. Hardly daring to move, he peered towards the path from the corner of his eye. The two riders trotted slowly into view. Warriors. They were talking animatedly as they rode but gave no indication that they had seen anything untoward. Relieved, Atticus let out a deep breath. As the riders reached the intersection of the two paths, they paused. After what seemed like a heated discussion, they set off again, continuing along the wider track, passing directly above them as they did. Atticus could hear them laughing. Garmanos waited for a few moments and quietly crawled back into the ditch. Atticus followed him out from under the roots, keeping a careful watch on the track.

"What was that all about?"

"They are looking for you and your friends. The scout must have alerted them to our presence in the forest."

"What were they arguing about?"

"Whether they should explore the smaller path."

"Why didn't they?"

"The wider track was easier and…"

Garmanos paused. Atticus felt a pang of concern.

"And what?"

"They said it wouldn't matter since you would all be dead soon enough anyway."

Atticus' blood ran cold. He had to warn Plautius but what about? He didn't know how many warriors there were. He needed to know more. Fighting the impulse to head back immediately, he gestured in the direction from which the warriors had approached.

"Can we follow the track a little further?"

Garmanos seemed a little surprised at this but he shrugged and nodded his head. Remaining in the ditch for safety, they carefully moved forward. They hadn't gone far when the path started to dip and the treeline began to thin, revealing what looked like a narrow valley nestling between the hills. It might have been a pleasant sight if the lush green fields hadn't been filled by a huge camp. Stretching as far as the eye could see, the valley was filled with tents, wagons, horses and a growing number of enemy warriors. Those already on the plain were being jostled slowly forward as more and more spilled out from the woods on either side. Atticus was filled with a sudden sense of dread. The first of the legions would surely be arriving soon.

They were walking into a trap.

He had to get back. He nodded to Garmanos and they hurriedly set about retracing their steps. Atticus desperately wanted to break cover and use the track but he knew it increased the risk of them being spotted. He was growing ever more anxious, however, as they finally arrived back at the path they had originally followed. Inching up the bank, he craned his neck to see if he could detect any sign of the warriors behind them. Nothing. Yet. They might still have time. Garmanos dragged himself up the bank and with one final look he set off back up the hill. Atticus followed suit. Running for his life and those of his unsuspecting comrades on the opposite side of the hill.

*

Atticus wiped away another bead of sweat as it trickled down his forehead. His tunic clung uncomfortably to his body beneath his armour and he was desperate for a drink. Despite his best attempts to rid himself of the dirt he had collected about his person whilst on patrol, he knew that he wouldn't pass muster on parade. There was nothing he could do about that now and it didn't matter.

What was important was his news. He had to warn the legate and quickly. If only he could be allowed to see him. Much of the dirt had been from the falls he had taken on the way back. Several times, he had been sent sprawling to the ground as he tripped over tree roots or simply lost his footing as he pushed himself on as fast as he could. He had been grateful when they reached Plautius. As soon as he had recovered his breath sufficiently to talk, he had explained what he had seen. Plautius wasted no time in getting them back to camp, retracing their steps far more quickly than on the original journey up the slope. But to what end? The tribune had been sceptical about what Atticus had seen and was now talking to the legate. And Aquila seemed in no hurry to see him. Atticus fidgeted nervously; this was madness. He took several steps towards the cluster of senior officers a short distance away. Plautius grasped his shoulder.

"Steady, lad. Don't give him any more reason to come after you."

Atticus let out an exasperated sigh.

"He won't have the chance if he doesn't do something soon. Those bloody warriors will be right. We'll all be dead!"

Atticus looked anxiously back towards the hill once more. Several scouts had reappeared to resume their watch but otherwise everything was still.

For now.

On their side of the river, camp construction continued. The XIIth had arrived in the vanguard with the VIIth following close behind. Somebody had said that the VIIIth and the XIth were close by and presumably the IXth and the Xth would arrive soon after. For some reason, Caesar had decided to reorganise the whole column today and move the baggage trains to the rear. To be guarded by the newly recruited XIIIth and XIVth. With no baggage to occupy their attention, a far greater number of men than usual had been directed to construction activity, and the hillside was a hive of activity. But they were still totally unprepared and blissfully unaware of what was about to befall them. He turned to Plautius.

"I'm sorry. We have to act now before it's too late."

He marched quickly up to the senior officers. Aquila was holding forth and it sounded as if the focus of the conversation was on his exploits chasing Ariovistus' shattered nation rather than their present predicament. They didn't have time for this. The heads of the four officers whipped around as he snapped to attention and saluted. Aquila looked him up and down with a barely concealed look of contempt.

"You! The tribune said one of the men on patrol had been making claims about an army on the march. I might have known it would be you, Capito. Must you always be the centre of attention?"

He smiled as Plautius arrived.

"Centurion. Have this man placed on a charge for disorderly conduct."

Perhaps sensing Atticus' rising anger, Plautius edged in front of him as he addressed Aquila.

"I will, sir. But perhaps it might be wise to have the men stand to. If what Capito says is right, the enemy army is just over that hill."

"We know they are about somewhere, Centurion. That is why we are here. I think it unlikely, however, that an army of that size could catch us unawares, don't you? Besides, none of our scouts have returned to report anything."

Atticus shot Plautius a look of concern as the centurion tried again.

"Perhaps there is a reason why none of our scouts have returned, sir. Could I recommend a picket line at the very least? That is standard practice when constructing camp."

"Do not lecture me on practice, Centurion! Caesar has not seen fit to give such an order. I will not be seen to question his judgement on the back of a wild tale about an army nobody else has seen. An army that would never dare attack eight legions in a marching camp."

"We are not yet in camp, sir. I really think—"

Aquila waved his hand dismissively as he interrupted Plautius.

"I suggest you leave strategy to those in command and return to duties more fitting of your station. And take Capito with you."

He sneered at Atticus.

"Perhaps the boy has grown nervous after his injury. I suspect this is nothing more than a warband or scouting group. Either way, they pose no threat to us. You are dismissed."

Atticus couldn't believe it. Aquila was ignoring his warning; worse, he was questioning his bravery. And after all he'd done to get the information to him in the first place. Whatever Aquila thought about him, he had a duty to the legion, to the men. He had to act. Plautius had turned to go. He knew he should do the same but he couldn't.

"This wasn't a warband or scouting group, sir. These were warriors and there were thousands of them."

Aquila fixed him with an angry stare.

"You have been dismissed, soldier. Leave. Before I see fit to increase your punishment."

He felt Plautius' hand on his shoulder. He had to get Aquila to see the danger they were in. Maybe there was another way…

"Sir. If you would just speak with Garmanos, he saw them too."

Aquila exploded.

"Enough! I will hear no more."

He turned angrily to one of the tribunes.

"Have this man detained until I am better placed to consider his fate. And you, Centurion, will find yourself returned to the ranks if you cannot instil the virtue of discipline amongst your men."

He turned and stalked away, leaving the luckless tribune to oversee his instructions.

"Your sword, soldier."

Atticus numbly complied, scarcely able to comprehend what was happening. Detained for trying to save lives! How was this possible?

"Hold while I fetch the guard. Centurion, if this man leaves that spot, I will hold you responsible."

His mind reeling, Atticus turned to Plautius.

"I was just trying to warn him."

"I know, lad, and I believe you. You may be an idiot but you're not a coward. I will warn Baculus. We can try and have the first two cohorts on alert if nothing else. After that, we take our chances."

The tribune returned with two men from the legates' guard.

"Tie this man to that wagon and watch over him until I send word for him to be delivered to the legate."

Plautius touched him gently on the arm.

"Go. I will find you later."

Still dazed and confused, Atticus tried to replay events in his mind as he was led away. He wasn't mistaken. He had seen the warriors; they were coming and his comrades were not at all ready. How many of them would pay with their lives if the camp was overrun? He wondered if his fate was destined to be something altogether grislier than a meeting with Aquila. And if that fate was what awaited them all.

*

Allerix edged cautiously down the hill towards Boduognatus. Something was wrong. From his allocated position on the hill, he had watched the first of the legions arrive with a sense of nervous anticipation. Their patrols had taken care of the enemy cavalry scouts that had strayed too far into the forest and the Romans showed no signs of having been alerted to their presence. Construction had been continuing on the camp but it was far from ready and would offer little protection to the unsuspecting legionaries when they launched their attack. And everything was ready. Throughout the forest, the warriors of three nations waited to pour forth, thousands and thousands of men anxious to turn the tables on Rome. But the baggage train had not yet appeared. Instead, the insignia of one legion after another had marched into view. With a rising sense of dread, he realised that their plan had been thwarted. They were no longer going to be faced with one legion but all of them. He scrambled down the final few yards, his hurried arrival catching Boduognatus' attention.

"We must halt the attack. This was not what we planned. There will be other opportunities."

Boduognatus gestured to the massed ranks of warriors lining the slopes.

"Why would we halt the attack? We still hold the element of surprise. Our warriors are ready and a match for the Romans. We will have our victory."

Allerix's heart sank.

Perhaps? But at what cost.

Ambushing a single legion without support was one thing; tackling the whole Roman army was quite another. The fate of the alliance, their existence as free nations, would rest on the outcome of this battle and the odds had shifted against them. Continuing was either brave or foolish. He thought he knew which. But it didn't matter. It was too late. Horns and battle cries were ringing out around the hill. The baggage train had finally arrived and the attack had begun. He snatched up his shield and followed Boduognatus out through the trees and into the sun.

17

SUMMER, 57 BC

North-west Gaul

Atticus took another glance towards the hill. Still nothing. He was beginning to doubt himself. What if they weren't coming? Suppose he'd been wrong? That would be good news for his friends at least. He was fucked either way. His fate in the hands of Aquila or those of the Nervii. He winced as the rope that bound him securely to the corner of the wagon cut into his wrists. How had it come to this? Tethered like a criminal for an act that should have been welcomed. Fucking Aquila. With a sigh, he sank slowly to the floor against one of the wheels. His two guards looked at him disdainfully, blissfully unaware of what had prompted his detention. Or what was coming. They were just grateful to have escaped any of the work usually associated with establishing camp.

"Let's hope the legate is in no hurry to deal with him. I think that's the baggage train finally arriving."

"Looks like it. I won't be sorry if we're stuck up here a little longer. I swear that prick Aquila gets more demanding each time we make camp."

Atticus forced a wry smile. It seemed he wasn't the only one with a less than positive view of their legate. The taller of the two guards gave Atticus' foot a kick.

"I wouldn't think you've got much to smile about, lad. What was it you did anyway? I know it doesn't take a lot to get Aquila angry but this is a first."

Atticus was about to try and explain when an ear-splitting roar filled the air. Echoing ominously across the valley, it drowned out the sounds of camp construction and sent a nervous shiver running down his spine. The two guards exchanged anxious glances.

"What the fuck is that?"

Atticus knew. It was the enemy and they were coming. He pulled himself quickly to his feet, flinching as the rope cut ever more deeply into his wrists. He swallowed nervously. There were so many men the entire hill seemed as if it was moving. He thought the numbers he'd seen earlier had been bad enough but this was just terrifying. Sweeping down the slope, the first of the warriors were already crossing the river, whilst still more continued to spill out of the woods. And the camp was wide open. Belatedly, horns began to sound out the alarm and he could see battle standards being hurriedly raised across the hill. He needed to free himself – to join his friends. Deep in conversation, the guards barely seemed to notice him.

"We have to go. We need to find the legate. That's the battle standard down there."

"I know but the tribune ordered us to stay here."

The taller guard shook his head.

"Fuck the tribune! It's Aquila we have to worry about. Let's go."

As he turned to leave, his comrade nodded towards Atticus. "What about him?"

"Leave him. I'm not risking a charge for letting him go. Come on."

Atticus looked anxiously towards the remaining guard as he began to back away, following after his comrade.

"You can't leave me like this. Set me free. Please!"

The man shrugged and held out his hands apologetically.

"You know I can't. I'm sorry."

Ignoring the pain, Atticus frantically tried to loosen the knot tethering him to the wagon. If he could just work it free… but it was no use… the guards had done their job too well. He bellowed after them as they headed towards the melee below.

"Set me free! You have to set me free!"

He let out an anguished cry and swung a kick at the wheel as he watched them disappear from view. He was alone.

*

Allerix fought to maintain his footing as he was almost carried along amongst the tight press of men. The silence of the forest was shattered as the warriors bellowed their war cries across the valley, channelling the anger and frustration that had been building for weeks. Thundering towards the Romans, they seemed to occupy the entire hillside. It was an awe-inspiring sight. To his right, the Atrebates and the Viromandui, their war banners held proudly aloft as they charged towards the eastern edges of the Roman position and the newly arrived legions. At the heart of the charge, the Nervii, rushing headlong towards the main body of the Roman camp. Such as it was. With no defences and no time to organise the shield walls behind which they were so brutally effective, the Romans were vulnerable. But with so many more of them than they expected, maintaining the momentum of their attack was going to be crucial.

That was not yet an issue and he was swept into and across the river before he knew it. And just as quickly pushed up the opposite bank. As they arrived amongst the panic-stricken

Romans, he could see the full extent of the disarray created by their assault. Many of those caught unawares were simply cut down where they stood, some transfixed with fear, others dying bravely but quickly, with a sword in their hand. Behind them, men fled in all directions, desperate to escape the onslaught, to find comrades – any comrades – and some form of safety in numbers. But any relief at securing sanctuary was short-lived. As quickly as small, isolated pockets of resistance formed, they were surrounded and slaughtered, overwhelmed by sheer weight of numbers. The impetus of the attack was just too great. Amidst the carnage, riders from the small Roman cavalry contingent galloped this way and that, seemingly unconcerned whether it was friend or foe they swept aside in their search for an escape. Frantic camp followers added to the mayhem as they fled before the attack or threw themselves – unsuccessfully – at the mercy of the advancing warriors.

It was chaos.

All the invitation the onrushing warriors needed to press home the attack. Picking his way through the bodies of the dead and dying, he set off in pursuit.

Weaving quickly between the many small and brutal fights raging across the hillside, Allerix joined a larger group of warriors as they rushed towards a thin and ragged-looking line of legionaries, strung quickly across the hill amidst the panic. Fresh from the construction activity they had been engaged in just moments before, many of them didn't even have helmets or shields. Allerix targeted one that had both and threw himself forward. Wide-eyed with fear, the young legionary determinedly thrust out his sword as Allerix approached. Pushing out his shield, Allerix brought his own blade arcing down towards the Roman's head. Hurriedly throwing up his shield to deflect the strike, the legionary thrust out his sword and nearly lost his arm as the warrior beside Allerix swung down his axe, forcing the soldier back behind his shield. Before he could recover his poise, Allerix swung once more, again targeting his opponent's head. It was a feint. As the soldier instinctively raised his shield, Allerix dropped to one knee and thrust his sword deep into the man's groin. The legionary let out an agonised cry and stumbled to one side. With a forlorn look at the blood already pooling at his feet, he began to back unsteadily away. Allerix advanced. The soldier waved his sword defiantly but he was struggling to maintain his balance and, with a pained expression, his legs buckled and he sank slowly to his knees. With his attention focussed on Allerix, he never saw the sword of the warrior to his left until it punched through his chest, pitching him face first into the blood-stained grass with barely a murmur. Allerix stepped over the body and glanced quickly to his left. It was over. The legionary would travel to meet his gods in the company of all those with whom he had stood. Pausing for breath, Allerix spotted Boduognatus and his guard a little further up the hill. They were amongst a horde of men heading towards a far larger group of Romans. And this group appeared ready and organised. It was certainly the first real barrier to their progress the warriors had encountered. Three lines deep and standing resolutely behind their shield wall, it was as if this group alone had been prepared for some form of attack. As he drew closer, he recognised the officers fighting bravely at either end of the line. His heart sank. It was Baculus and Plautius. Leading by example, as he would have expected. He had known this day would come, when he would be forced to face his Roman friends in battle. He had never imagined that it might be quite so directly. But they were here in lands he had sworn to protect and so protect them he would. They would expect nothing less. He steeled himself to do what must be done and attacked the line.

*

Atticus shuddered as the sounds of battle began to drift up the hill. It was all happening so quickly. The enemy were everywhere. He shuddered as he watched them swarming up the hillside, barely seeming to pause as they cut down those individuals who had the misfortune to be caught at the forefront of the attack. Even some of the small groups that had managed to throw together some form of defensive front were simply being swept aside. There were just too many warriors and they hadn't been ready. If only Aquila had listened. He gritted his teeth and tried once more to wriggle his hands through the rope binding his wrists. It was no use. He was stuck fast. Already knowing he'd fail, he made one last desperate attempt to dislodge the knot attaching him to the wagon but that too remained stubbornly fixed. He had never felt more helpless. He slid forlornly to the floor. Utterly distraught, he cursed Aquila and then the gods. What had he done to deserve this? Defenceless and chained like an animal, he could do nothing but await his fate. He reached beneath his tunic and clasped his pendant. He would try and accept death with dignity when it arrived, as it surely would. With Jupiter's help, he would also make Aquila pay. In this world – or the next. He closed his eyes and tried to shut out the noise of the slaughter below.

*

Forced ever tighter against the Roman shields by the number of warriors arriving, Allerix had pushed with every ounce of strength he had. He'd heard the grunts and laboured breathing of the legionaries as they too expended every effort to stand firm. But they couldn't. Slowly but surely, they had been forced back. The line had begun to bow, creating gaps in the shield wall through which they could strike. Legionaries had started to fall from the line as blades found their targets. As the relentless press continued, those not struck a mortal blow were ruthlessly despatched where they lay, the bodies of the fallen afforded no respect, merely obstacles to be clambered over en route to the next opponent. But unlike so many of their comrades, these Romans had shown commendable discipline. When a gap appeared in the line, it was quickly filled. And they had exacted a high price for the progress made by the warriors, so much so that their brave rear guard action had begun to have an impact, slowing if not entirely halting their advance. With the Viromandui and the Atrebates seemingly struggling to make any real progress on their side of the camp, they had to find a way to press home the attack. The Romans didn't appear to have any reserves. If they could only break through here, victory could still be theirs. He dug in his heels and leant into the shield wall once more.

*

Eyes still closed, Atticus let out a deep breath as he heard the sound of laboured breathing and clinking metal draw closer. The enemy were here. Determined not to disgrace himself, or the legion, he tried to control his shaking hands. He would do this on his feet and facing the enemy. He opened his eyes and struggled to his feet. His heart jumped. It was Julius. His friend gave him a big smile.

"Not coming to the party, brother?"

Scarcely able to believe what was happening, Atticus offered his bound hands to Julius, who carefully cut him free. Atticus gratefully clasped his hand.

"Thank you, brother! I thought I was going to die here."

Julius laughed.

"Save your thanks until later. There's still time. It's a bloody mess down there but Plautius didn't want you missing out on all the fun."

His friend handed him the sword he had used to cut him free.

"You'll need that: the bastards are everywhere. Stay close."

*

Allerix drew his hand across his sweat-covered brow and nodded his thanks to Boduogenus. He might never warm to the man but there was no denying his skill with a sword, and his intervention had been very welcome. The young prince dipped his head and gestured to the pair of legionaries lying at their feet.

"I merely evened the odds."

"You have my thanks nonetheless. I was trying to reach your father. To warn him about the Viromandui and the Atrebates. They're being pushed back."

Boduogenus nodded gravely.

"I saw. Come. We shall go together."

Allerix was beginning to feel uneasy. They had begun to gain ground as the relentless pressure of their assault started to tell and the numbers in the Roman ranks began to thin. But the Viromandui and Atrebates, who had earlier seen their attack stall, were now being driven slowly back towards the river. They had shown no sign of breaking, but not even the Nervii could hope to press home the attack on their own. As he and Boduogenus forced their way through the horde of men, Allerix caught sight of Boduognatus. He was on the move, with a sizeable contingent of his guard. Had he noticed the danger too? No. He was heading forward, around the line of Romans in front of him. What was he doing? Then Allerix saw it. The advance of the legions battling the Viromandui and the Atrebates had left the right flank of the Roman rear guard totally exposed. The attackers now had an uncontested route to the rear of the Roman lines and the centre of the camp. Allerix exchanged glances with Boduogenus and the two of them set off in pursuit of the young prince's father. If the Viromandui and the Atrebates could regain the upper hand, or at the very least keep their legions occupied, the beleaguered defenders must surely now be surrounded and destroyed. If not, that was the fate awaiting him and the Nervii. Gritting his teeth, he broke into a run and joined the charge.

*

Atticus tried to catch his breath as he followed Julius quickly along the ridge. His heart was still beating like a drum at the sheer relief of being freed. He knew just how badly the odds were stacked against them but his despair had been replaced with a renewed sense of purpose. If this were to be his last battle, he would go down fighting. And he would do so alongside his friends and comrades, if he managed to get there in time. Twice they had been forced to pause, bracing themselves to fight only to realise that the figures charging towards them were camp followers or auxiliaries trying to escape the attack. But with men of both sides scattered across the hill, there was no guarantee of safety in any direction, and corpses littered the floor. They weren't all Roman, however, and they had seen several clusters of legionaries battling bravely amongst the wagons. He hated skirting around or behind these life-and-death struggles, but their intervention probably wouldn't have influenced the outcome and they needed to reach the XIIth. As they arrived at the crest of the hill, Atticus could see the full expanse of the battlefield for the first time. The enemy had crossed the river along the entire width of the hill, forcing the Romans to engage over a huge area, stretching their defensive line, if you could even call it a line. At one end, the IXth and the Xth seemed to have got themselves reasonably organised. They would have been amongst the last to arrive and had perhaps still been in marching order when the attack came. Next to them, however, what looked like the VIIIth and the XIth were scattered along the bank with no discernible order and little cohesion. Many of the cohorts had been unable to link up with neighbouring units and were being forced to fight their own desperate and isolated battles. Ones they seemed destined to lose. It was a similar story at this end of the river with the VIIth and most of the XIIth hopelessly disorganised and in danger of being overwhelmed. It was a complete shambles. If it hadn't been for the battle lines of the XIIth's first and second cohorts, he feared they would already be facing defeat. Amidst all the chaos, they had succeeded in throwing a barrier across a significant part of the hill. They were heavily outnumbered and slowly being forced to give ground, but the line hadn't broken and the advance of the enemy was being checked. Julius followed his gaze.

"Baculus and Plautius had us ready. Thanks to you. Just as well, too, or the whole bloody lot would have made it through. Come on, we'd best get down there. It looks like they could use our help."

Atticus smiled. Perhaps his warning might yet make a difference after all. Breaking into a run, they set off down the hill.

As they passed a small cluster of bodies, Atticus gave Julius a nudge.

"Hold on. I could do with that shield. It doesn't look like he'll be needing it anytime soon."

Knowing that it paid to remain alert, even amongst those bearing the hallmarks of death, he made his way quickly through the bodies. When he reached one of the Romans, he knelt to roll him over and free the shield.

"Forgive me, brother. You deserve better. I'll…"

He paused. It was one of his guards. He slid the shield free and climbed to his feet. Bastard. He took a few paces back towards Julius and stopped. It was no good. The man might have been a bastard but he was still Roman, a legionary like him, just doing his job. He hurried back and bent to close the man's eyes. Julius gestured towards the battle as he returned.

"Look! The Xth are beginning to push them back."

They were. Slowly but surely, they were beginning to force the warriors they had been battling back towards the river. But there was a problem. With the VIII and the XI being forced back, the advance of the Xth was creating a gap in the line, a gap through which the warriors who had been held up by the XIIth were now beginning to pour. He watched in horror as they began to circle behind the XIIth's shield wall to attack them from the rear. But some of the warriors weren't stopping. They were heading up the hill towards what he realised must be all that remained of the command group a little way in front of them. It was a pitifully small group: several guards, one of the tribunes, the camp prefect and Aquila. He might have known the little prick would find a way to survive, though maybe not for long. The number of men heading in their direction was surely too large for them to fight off. He wanted to get to the XIIth. His friends and comrades were in even more trouble than they had been before and it was where he should be. But they couldn't ignore the danger facing Aquila and the others. They had to go to their aid. But why should he try and save that man's life? He hated him, now more than ever. Every man that perished was one that might have survived if he'd only listened. Why not let him join the fallen? Hadn't he asked the gods for just such an opportunity? And they had answered his prayers far more quickly than he could ever have imagined. With the warriors' attention focussed on the officers it would be possible to leave Aquila to his fate. But he was still their legate. The leader he had sworn an oath to follow. It didn't matter that he was a prick. He had to try and save him. He tapped Julius on the shoulder and nodded towards the small group of Romans.

"We have to help them."

Julius raised his eyes.

"I know, but if we live, I'll kill the little shit myself if he doesn't stop tormenting you."

Atticus clasped his hand.

"Thank you, brother, but there will be a queue. Come on."

*

The startled legionary cried out as Allerix drove his sword into the man's chest. He hadn't even seen him coming. The sudden incursion of Boduognatus and his warriors at the rear of their lines had taken the Romans completely by surprise. Their focus had been on withstanding the frontal assault and, in the midst of the panic, the Nervii had run amok. Carving a blood-laden trail across the hill. There had been no structure to the warriors' assault. Consumed by bloodlust or simply too brave for their own good, they had literally thrown themselves at the defenders, and the dead and dying of both sides lay everywhere. There was no denying that it had been effective. The wild ferocity of the attack had sent shockwaves through the camp. Men were beginning to desert their posts. The Roman cavalry, already put to flight once, had broken again. Allerix had narrowly avoided being run down by a riderless horse, evidence that not all of those seeking escape had been successful. Even the Treveri, the German auxiliaries riding with Caesar and famed for their bravery, had taken flight, adding to the desperation of those that remained as they left the camp in a frenzied cloud of dust. In the confusion, the Nervii had succeeded in driving a wedge between the Roman forces. Free to attack from both sides, they had inflicted huge numbers of casualties, whilst the few remaining officers tried desperately to reorganise the line. Allerix pushed on, ducking under the wild swing of the legionary backtracking before him, his raw and ungainly approach evidence of a lack of experience fighting away from the packed and disciplined ranks of the Roman line. But caught out of position, like so many others, he had been forced to fight alone as he desperately tried to rejoin his comrades. He was fighting bravely, however, and the last warrior who had tried to curtail his retreat lay dead at his feet. Bravery could only carry him so far though. Allerix advanced, determined to end this quickly. The legionary thrust out his sword in warning but Allerix knocked it aside with his shield and stepped forward, forcing his opponent to plant his feet and push out his own shield in response. As the legionary swung his sword again, Allerix slid back and swept his shield forward, catching the Roman's sword arm and forcing him side on. Limbs flailing, the soldier tried desperately to recover his position but Allerix had already closed the gap. Before the soldier could square up once more, Allerix forced his sword under the legionary's chain mail and high into his midriff. The legionary sucked in a huge gulp of air as the sword sliced through his stomach. He tried to grip Allerix's shield but the sword had already reached his heart. His eyes glazed over and he dropped his sword. Leaving a bloody trail on Allerix's tunic, he slid slowly to the floor. Allerix stepped over the body and headed towards the hard-pressed defensive line. A cluster of warriors were trying to reach the one senior officer still visibly standing. It wasn't Baculus. Allerix had seen him fall as they started the incursion, going down under a hail of blows as he bravely tried to stem the flow of warriors trying to encircle them. But he recognised the centurion immediately as he stepped forward to reinforce the line and tackle his would-be assailants head on.

It was Plautius.

Allerix was still worried about the Viromandui and Atrebates. The Nervii would be left horribly exposed if their allies should suffer defeat, but there was no going back. The first signs of a shield wall had started to appear as the Romans began to recover.

It was now or never. What was it Boduognatus had said to the chieftains on the eve of the attack? *Death or Glory.* He was about to find out which.

18

North-west Gaul

Spotting a gap to the left of the melee surrounding Plautius, Allerix found himself fighting besides Boduognatus. Enthusiastically setting about the defenders, he was wearing his age well. If anything, he seemed to have been energised by the opportunity to rid himself of the concerns of leadership and throw himself into the fight. His presence was certainly having a positive impact on the surrounding warriors. All keen to follow the lead of their king, they were driving a wedge through the shocked defenders. It was brave but it was also reckless, as those at the head of the surge became vulnerable to attack from all sides. With his attention fixed on the legionary slowly retreating before him, Boduognatus didn't see the soldier to his left preparing to thrust out his sword. But Allerix did. And he almost made it, but his despairing lunge could only divert not stop the strike. The blade sliced across Boduognatus' body, tearing a deep and bloody gash in his side. He threw back his head and let out a huge roar. The angry cry was pained but defiant and, in a wild frenzy of blows, Boduognatus renewed his attack. The unfortunate legionary before him stumbled and lost his footing as he was driven back. He reacted quickly, throwing up his shield to parry the first of Boduognatus' follow-up strikes but, desperately trying to regain his footing, he could do nothing about the second. The blow sank so deep into the man's neck that it almost separated his head from his body. He fell to the floor, the blood from the last beats of his heart pulsing into the soil. Boduognatus' assailant lay dead too. With his sword arm still extended and his shield planted on the wrong side, the legionary had no defence as Allerix stepped forward. Clattering his shield into the side of the man's head, the soldier crumpled to the floor in a heap. Allerix ran his sword quickly across the man's throat and joined the stream of warriors following their king through the breach he had forced in the Roman line.

Allerix hurried towards Boduognatus as he stopped suddenly at the top of the rise. His tunic was heavily matted with blood and he was clearly in pain, but his attention was directed across the hill. A large group of soldiers were heading quickly towards them. So much for taking advantage of their breakthrough. Boduognatus snarled as the Romans drew closer, raising his sword defiantly above his head. Allerix watched as he slowly lowered the blade until it was pointing towards the figure at the centre of the group. Surrounded by a clutch of guards and with his unmistakeable red cloak draped loosely about his shoulders, it could be only one man.

Caesar.

Organising his men as he marched, Caesar snatched up a shield from an injured legionary and headed directly towards Boduognatus. The challenge had been accepted. However much Allerix despised Caesar as a man, there could be no doubt about his courage. Boduognatus ordered his men to fan out across the slope and the two groups quickly converged. Allerix targeted one of the senior officers at the heart of the group. A young tribune. He was tall, lithe and resplendent in his highly polished armour. The two men sized each other up for a moment, before the Roman jumped forward, launching a series of blows at Allerix, who carefully gave ground as he absorbed the weight of the attack. The tribune was strong and evidently knew how to handle himself, but there was something ungainly about his approach. Allerix stepped deftly to his left and thrust out his sword. The tribune swung his shield clumsily back across his body and bore down with his own blade. Allerix smiled as he slid away to his right. This man was clearly unused to fighting with the shield of a common legionary, which made him vulnerable. He attacked again. The tribune dragged his shield towards the blade but Allerix's thrust was too fast and he caught the man's arm with the point of his sword, drawing blood and an angry curse. The tribune dragged his arm across his tunic and stared at Allerix, arrogantly addressing him in Latin.

"Clever. But it will take more than that to beat me, Barbarian."

Allerix looked his opponent slowly up and down.

"In all that finery, I should hope so, Roman."

The look of surprise on the tribune's face at being addressed in his mother tongue was short-lived as Allerix quickly stepped forward, closing the gap between them. The tribune swept his blade forward, forcing Allerix to thrust out his shield. The Roman glared menacingly but Allerix was already on the move, spinning to his left, sword raised to strike. Recognising the danger, the tribune hurriedly threw up his sword as Allerix's came flashing down. Their blades locked. Straining with every sinew, Allerix could feel his opponent beginning to yield. The tribune fought to resist but Allerix had the momentum and the Roman's blade was forced further and further down. In desperation, the Roman slammed his shield forward but Allerix was quicker and, as the boss of the tribune's shield struck him in the chest, his came crashing down on the Roman's outstretched arm. Catching Allerix in the ribs, the tribune's shield sent waves of pain coursing through his body, but his own had wrought far more damage. Swaying unsteadily, the tribune's arm hung helplessly by his side, blood streaming from the point at which the jagged edges of his shattered bones had pierced his skin. Hand clamped to his chest and still struggling to catch his breath, Allerix advanced towards the ashen-faced tribune. The Roman threw down his shield and painfully took up his sword in his left hand. He swung it back and forth, adjusting to its strange feel, and set himself for the next attack. In the presence of his general, there was no chance he would seek to retreat, but this was brave. Allerix threw down his own shield and walked purposefully forward. Blocking the tribune's ungainly hack with the edge of his blade, Allerix raised his arm and smashed the handle of his sword against the side of the man's head, dropping him to the floor. His helmet would have saved his life but he was out of the fight and for Allerix that was enough.

*

Picking out warriors at either end of the skirmish, Atticus and Julius edged slowly towards Aquila's beleaguered command group. When he was sure they could go no further without being seen, Atticus gave his friend a nod and they broke into a run. Head down and shield outstretched, Atticus ploughed into the man at the edge of the enemy line, sending the surprised warrior sprawling to the floor, arms and legs flailing helplessly. Swinging around as quickly as he could, Atticus kicked out at the warrior's hand as he desperately tried to regain his footing, sending him face first into the ground once more. Before the warrior could roll away, Atticus leapt forward and drove his sword into the man's back. Perhaps disconcerted by the sudden disappearance of his comrade, another warrior lay dead at the tribune's feet. Atticus smiled as he recognised the man who had detained him earlier. The tribune waved his sword ominously at the nearest warrior as Atticus circled back to join the line. Acknowledging the grateful nod of the tribune as he slid into line beside him, Atticus caught the look of surprise on the officer's face as he realised just who it was that had come to their aid. Looking quickly to his left, he was pleased to see that Julius' arrival seemed to have had a similar impact on the other side of the line. Now the fight was fairer. With the camp prefect and the four legionaries leading the way, the Romans locked shields and started to inch forward. Determined not to give ground, a burly warrior at the centre of the enemy line bellowed an angry cry and heaved his heavy axe up into the air. The prefect hastily threw up his shield as the blow arced towards his head. He howled in pain as the axe crashed through his shield, embedding itself in the splintered wood. The prefect did well to remain on his feet but the warrior wasn't done. Taking hold of the shield with both hands, he began to pull. To either side, swords were jabbed out between the shields to try and force the man back, but it was too late. With the slope aiding his endeavours, the warrior succeeded in manhandling the prefect out of the line. Dragged forward, he lost his footing and sprawled to the floor. As he struggled to his knees, the warrior drew a knife from his belt. With a triumphant roar, he threw himself forward, wrestling the Roman to the ground before driving the savage blade into the prefect's chest. The Roman's spasming corpse would be the last thing the warrior saw as one of the legionary guards stepped forward and punched his sword deep into the man's back. As the soldier sought to retrace his steps, one of the dying warrior's comrades threw himself forward, slashing his sword across the man's neck. The soldier's eyes widened in shock and, with the colour draining rapidly from his face, he turned plaintively towards the Roman line. He snapped his gaze down as the tip of the warrior's sword burst through his chest. He tried to speak but, already choking on the blood filling his lungs, he sank quietly and helplessly to his knees. The warrior kicked him aside and marched forward to confront Aquila. The defensive line was broken. Atticus swallowed nervously. The numbers were evenly matched but they had once again lost the initiative. And the warriors knew it, pushing forward quickly to square up man-to-man against the remaining Romans, their survival now inextricably linked, not just to the outcome of their own battle but those being fought by their comrades.

Circling him cautiously, Atticus' opponent appeared in no rush to engage, waiting for the perfect opportunity to strike. His calm and controlled approach lent him a detached air of confidence that Atticus found unnerving. He planted his right foot and sprang forward; he wasn't going to let the warrior dictate their fight. The warrior thrust out his shield and rolled away from danger as Atticus stabbed out his sword. They locked eyes and the warrior smiled as Atticus moved quickly to parry a thrust that had been merely a feint. Atticus cursed; he was better than that. The warrior swung again, this time in earnest, and Atticus hurriedly swept his shield forward to deflect the blow. Moving quickly to change the direction of his attack, the warrior sent his sword flashing towards Atticus' unprotected sword arm. He saw the danger just in time and thrust out his blade to parry the blow, clamping his teeth tight to stifle a cry as the force of the impact tore at his shoulder. Ignoring the pain, Atticus thrust out his shield and stepped forward. With a clear height advantage, he aimed a blow at the warrior's head. The man ducked behind his shield and Atticus pressed forward, raining down blow after blow and forcing the warrior to give ground. As the man steadied himself to receive another strike, Atticus swung his shield around and drove the metal rim into the back of the warrior's leg. He let out an agonised cry as his legs buckled and he dropped to his knees. Atticus moved quickly forward. The warrior thrust out his shield defiantly as he used his sword to help him climb unsteadily to his feet. Atticus attacked. Pain etched across his face, the warrior edged back under the barrage of blows. But he wasn't finished yet and with a howl of pain he lunged forward. Atticus managed to block the blow but the warrior's follow-up strike was a little faster than he'd expected. He cried out as the man's blade raked across his arm. A smile formed on the lips of the warrior but, clearly struggling on his injured leg, he made no move to press home his attack. Atticus sprang forward. The warrior managed to evade the blow but Atticus slid quickly to one side and swung again. As the warrior threw up his shield, Atticus thrust out his foot, crunching his hobnailed sandal into the man's injured knee, prompting fresh cries of anguish and sending him staggering back down the slope. His face wracked with pain, the warrior fought to retain his footing. He managed to steady himself but it was too late. As he looked up, Atticus thrust his sword into the man's stomach and up into his chest. The warrior gasped for air as Atticus withdrew his blood-covered sword and the man grabbed at his shield as his legs gave way beneath him. Shrugging him off, Atticus waited just long enough to see the warrior's death throes subside before switching his attention back across the hill.

*

Allerix cursed as he was almost knocked to the floor by a wounded Roman officer, driven into his path by a triumphant warrior. He clearly didn't need any help but Boduognatus did. He was still locked in combat with Caesar. Drenched in sweat and bearing the bloody scars of their clash, neither had conceded ground. They couldn't. Their fight was about much more than personal superiority. The momentum of the battle had begun to change. The Romans had started to regain some control. Caesar's desperate intervention had slowed their advance and, with Plautius bravely marshalling his men, they had regrouped, providing a focal point around which the defenders could coalesce. The Nervii were continuing to fight with their customary ferocity but they were no longer making any ground. And the standard of another legion had appeared on the edges of the camp, presumably the Roman rearguard. More soldiers they had not expected to face. Killing Caesar may now be their last hope of achieving success. But something was wrong. Boduognatus' blood-soaked tunic clung to his body as he traded blows with Caesar and he looked laboured. Caesar was gaining the upper hand. Keeping his focus on the two leaders, Allerix picked his way through the savage fighting. He was almost there. Caesar let out an angry cry as Boduognatus caught his arm with a wild swing. But he had left himself open. The Roman swept forward, bursting through Boduognatus' ragged defence and raking his sword across his chest. Boduognatus roared angrily and stepped forward to launch his own attack. He raised his sword to strike but he faltered in mid-stride and his legs buckled beneath him. He sank to his knees. Allerix threw himself forward. As Caesar swung his sword to finish Boduognatus, Allerix thrust his shield between the two leaders. The force of the blow shook his body and the tip of Caesar's sword bit agonisingly into his shoulder. The two men cried out: Allerix in pain, Caesar in frustration as his attack was thwarted by Allerix and his shield. The two squared up. The Roman didn't seem much like a warrior but clearly looks could be deceptive. Allerix steadied himself and thrust out his sword.

*

Startled by his sudden arrival, the tribune defiantly raised his sword before he realised it was Atticus. Slumped beside the corpse of his defeated opponent and cuffing away blood from his mouth, he looked in a bad way, but he waved Atticus on. Aquila, Julius and the other legionary were all still locked in battle. Aquila was fighting with a good deal more skill than Atticus might have given him credit for and Julius looked as if he was holding his own, but the legionary was in trouble. A deep gash to his leg appeared to be hindering his movement and he was clearly in some distress. That was where his presence would be of most use. He had gone no more than a couple of paces when the legionary cried out in pain. The warrior had punched through his defences once more and was moving swiftly forward to strike again as the soldier desperately tried to throw up his shield. Atticus wasn't going to make it. The warrior threw himself forward and barged the stricken soldier to the ground. Looming over him, the warrior disdainfully kicked aside the soldier's shield before burying his sword deep in the man's neck. Stepping over the legionary's still convulsing body, the warrior made straight for Aquila. Focussed on his opponent and completely unsighted, the legate had no idea of the fate about to befall him. Atticus couldn't believe it. Were the gods deliberately trying to test him? Fuck. He put down his head and charged towards Aquila. With his attention focussed on plunging his sword into Aquila's back, the warrior didn't notice Atticus until it was too late. He tried to react but, caught unawares and thrown off balance, he was in a hopeless position to defend himself as Atticus raised his arm to strike. With a look of abject terror on his face, the warrior could only watch as Atticus' sword sank into his chest. His anguished cry captured the attention of both Aquila and his opponent. The legate stared in surprise at the dying warrior who just moments before had been destined to end his life. Atticus pulled his sword free and the warrior's lifeless body fell to the floor, joining the legionary he had just killed, destined to share the blood-drenched hill in death, as they had in life. Angered by the death of his comrade, Aquila's opponent had renewed his attack, but it was an even contest once more and this time he was going to help his friend. Atticus exchanged a nod of greeting with Julius as he arrived and his friend smiled at his surprised opponent as he began to switch his attention anxiously between the two Romans.

"Not so much fun now, is it?"

The warrior backed cautiously away as the two friends edged forward. To his left, Atticus could see Aquila's opponent also beginning to retreat. Julius gave him a nudge.

"Let them go, brother."

Atticus had no wish to argue. He didn't know why they had chosen to leave and he didn't care. They had survived. He let out a deep breath and grounded his shield. He suddenly felt very weary. He turned quickly as the unmistakeable sound of a buccina rang out across the valley, signalling the arrival of a legion. Not one but two. It was the XIIIth and the XIVth and they were entering the camp in ever-increasing numbers. They were inexperienced and they were untested but they were heading enthusiastically down the hill to join the fight, and their arrival might be enough to swing the battle in their favour. He smiled as the retreating warriors gave up all pretence of caution and turned to run back towards the river. Beyond them, he could see the XIIth. They had somehow managed to link up with the VIIth, presenting a more formidable barrier to the enemy, but the battle still raged. He looked forlornly for his cohort. If they could just hold on...

"Only a little longer, brothers. Help is coming."

Atticus jumped as he felt a hand on his shoulder. It was Aquila.

"I owe you a debt of thanks, soldier."

Atticus turned. The smile disappeared from Aquila's face as he recognised his rescuer.

"You!"

*

He'd been right. Caesar could indeed fight and Allerix's injured shoulder was not helping his movement. Caesar had caught him with another blow early in the fight and the blood from the wound on his arm had started to pool in his already sweaty palm, making it ever more difficult to retain the grip on his sword. But Caesar hadn't escaped unscathed and the two had fought an even fight. He thought he'd even seen a grudging look of respect on the Roman's face as they battled. But that didn't change the fact he wanted Allerix dead. Just as much as he did Caesar. He swung again. The Roman blocked the blow and flashed out his sword, forcing Allerix to move to his right, deflecting the blow with his shield. As Allerix raised his sword to retaliate, several warriors threw themselves into the line, almost knocking him aside in their desperation to reach Caesar. Allerix felt a hand on his collar. Heart missing a beat, he turned, sword poised ready to strike. It was Boduogenus. The young prince held up his hand and gestured back across the river.

"Forgive me. My father lives. He asks for you."

Allerix dragged his bloody sleeve across his face and followed Boduogenus down the hill. They splashed through the river and onto the opposite bank, where Boduognatus had been set down. He lay on the floor surrounded by several of his Royal Guard. As Allerix approached, Boduognatus struggled to pull himself upright and beckoned him over. Allerix knelt beside the king. Boduognatus gripped his hand and pulled him closer, his voice frail and faltering but still defiant.

"Caesar has the luck of the gods but he is as mortal as I am. He can be beaten. Rome can be beaten. Ride to your father. Let him know the lengths to which we pushed Caesar here today. Continue the fight."

With a mournful sigh, he let go of Allerix's hand and sank

to the floor. Allerix stood and allowed Boduogenus to ease past and join his father. He turned his attention back across the river. They were losing the fight. It had been the extra legions. That and Plautius' rear guard. Why had Caesar chosen that day to change his marching order? How had Plautius known to be ready? Maybe Boduognatus was right; perhaps the Roman really did have the gods on his side, but they had pushed them to the very edge of defeat. Shown what could be done. It wasn't too late to withdraw. They could regroup. Join his father and try again. Boduogenus appeared by his side.

"He is gone. Our ancestors await his arrival. And mine. For soon I shall join them too."

Allerix turned to face him.

"You're not going back?"

"I must! My father waits in the afterlife to renew his battle with Caesar. I must try and send the Roman there myself."

Allerix shook his head.

"But that doesn't have to be today! My father is coming. We will have other opportunities. It's not too late to pull back."

Boduogenus shook his head.

"I cannot. Too many of my brothers have fallen here. We will avenge them. Or die trying. Besides, I fear the chance to withdraw is lost."

He pointed towards the top of the hill and the edge of the Roman camp. Streaming over the ridge were scores and scores of fresh legionaries. Boduogenus clasped his hand.

"Go! Find your father and have him prepare your people. Rid us of this Roman scourge forever and let all know how the Nervii died to make victory possible."

Raising his sword, Boduogenus set off to rejoin the fight, his warriors following unquestionably in his stead. Allerix watched as they splashed through the river before turning dejectedly to start the climb back into the forest.

As he reached the treeline, Allerix paused to take a last look back at the battle. He felt terrible but he knew he had to warn his father. Help him prepare for the Roman attack that would now surely come. But it still felt wrong to be leaving.

He hadn't wanted to launch the attack.

It had been foolish.

And yet they had so nearly succeeded, and brave men were still laying down their lives as he walked away. It hurt, although he had a sinking feeling that his turn would come soon enough. Bolstered by their reinforcements, the Romans had succeeded in forming a formidable shield wall that now extended in a wide arc before the Nervian warriors. They were still battling, even climbing on and over the bodies of their fallen comrades to attack the line. But it looked hopeless. He couldn't see Boduogenus but guessed he would be somewhere near Caesar, who was still fighting alongside Plautius and his cohort. A great many legionaries would owe him a debt of thanks tonight. He wondered if Atticus was amongst them. As he turned to leave, he caught sight of movement to his right. Warriors. Emerging from the trees. Atrebates and Viromandui, and they were heading back towards the river. Back towards the fight. Had they beaten off their Roman opponents? Might there still be hope? He reached for his sword. No. Something was wrong. There were too few of them. More emerged but they were heading in his direction. Away from the battle. They were fleeing. And then the first of the legionaries appeared from the forest, quickly followed by many more. It was the Romans who had been victorious. Ignoring those fleeing towards the trees, they formed a line and marched towards the camp. They were going to close in on the Nervii from behind. He dropped his head. He couldn't watch anymore.

Exhausted and with the pain of his injured arm ever more apparent now he had left the heat of battle behind, the climb was hard. He forced himself on. There would soon be many more men on the hill and Isarno would be quite the prize for those looking to make a swift escape. He finally reached the brow of the hill. Breathing deeply, he wiped away the sweat from his face, cursing at his carelessness as the movement opened up his wound. Pulling out his dagger, he hacked off a rough strip of cloth from his tunic and wound it around his arm. Taking a moment to get his bearings, he set off down the track, looking for the small copse of trees that bordered the thicket in which he had left Isarno. Picking his way through the branches, he was relieved to see his prized horse patiently awaiting his arrival. Allerix freed his reins and led Isarno back onto the path. As he mounted, he heard a low wave of sound that seemed to reverberate around the valley. Muted by distance and the dense woodland surrounding them, its origin was still immediately apparent. The Romans were celebrating victory. He nudged Isarno forward. The sacrifices of today had bought his father time but they would need it. Caesar would certainly have been unsettled by today. His legions had been badly weakened and the morale of his men must surely have been undermined by the spectre of defeat that had confronted them for so long. That at least was positive. But somehow, the Romans had wrestled victory from the jaws of defeat and Caesar would surely use this to drive his men ever onward. Provoked and very nearly chastised, he would be an even more formidable foe than before.

The Aduatuci were now all that stood between Rome and total domination. Experience had taught him that standing between Rome and anything was unlikely to end well.

19

SUMMER, 57 BC

North-west Gaul

Plautius' face broke into a big smile as he saw Baculus edging around the corner of the tent and heading gingerly towards them.

"Gods preserve us! I didn't expect to see you up and about so soon."

The two men clasped hands.

"Turns out the gods didn't want me, brother, although they thought about it for a while. I wasn't going to stay in hospital long enough for them to change their minds. Besides, after this shitstorm, the general's going to need all the officers he can get. Even the lame ones like me. Although if he wants anything more than my opinion, we're buggered! But if the camp surgeon asks, I'm fit for duty."

Plautius laughed.

"I don't think the surgeon will be asking too many questions, my friend. He was at the briefing this morning. I've never seen so many centuries represented by optios. Fuck, we even had tesserarii and signifiers. It's not much better up the line. You know we lost the prefect but none of the tribunes made it either. Shitstorm is right. It's good to have you back."

Baculus nodded towards Atticus.

"It would have been a lot worse if it wasn't for you and the lad here."

Atticus returned the nod of gratitude and then, quickly remembering himself, snapped to attention. Baculus waved away his salute.

"Relax, lad."

Atticus smiled ruefully. Relax... easy for him to say. He wasn't the one on a charge. Waiting to appear before the legate. Again. The second time in his short career that his fate had been in the hands of "that" man. The man whose life he had saved, despite all thoughts to the contrary. Not that any of that seemed to matter. Aquila had been quick to send word that the original charge would still stand. Prick! After everything that had happened, he was still going to have to defend himself. He had been lucky the last time he appeared before Aquila. Events had taken a very surprising turn and the outcome hadn't been what the legate had intended at all. Quite the opposite, in fact. Aquila would surely want to make amends for that this time. The only saving grace was that Atticus had been permitted to remain on active duty, although he knew that was by necessity rather than any gesture of goodwill. The late arriving rear guard aside, all of the legions had suffered heavy losses. They had needed every man still standing to try and restore some order to the chaos with which they had been confronted once the battle was over. And he was no exception. He had known the inevitable summons would come at some point, but he had been too busy to dwell on the potential outcome. It had been a tough few days and not just physically. First, he had been called to assist with setting up Aquila's command tent or more precisely help transfer his huge volume of baggage. Just how many things did one man need to make life bearable in the field? To make matters worse, word had spread quickly amongst Aquila's guard that Atticus was the soldier their comrades had been detaining when the attack came. It didn't matter that he hadn't been responsible for their deaths. All these men knew was that he was there and their comrades weren't. Of course, Aquila had done nothing to dispel their anger and it had been a deeply uncomfortable experience, one that he had been pleased to escape when Aquila had belatedly allowed him to rejoin his comrades labouring to complete camp. Under normal circumstances, with the enemy beaten and the men exhausted, camp construction was a task likely to draw vehement and profanity-laden complaint. Not this time. With their narrow escape fresh in the memory, the safety of the wall had been particularly welcome. The familiar routine had been a comfort too. Something to occupy their minds whilst they tried to come to terms with the loss of so many friends and comrades. The funeral pyres had been burning day and night, bigger and brighter than those that had illuminated the plain at Vesontio. He had had his fill of that miserable task too. Anxious to treat fallen comrades with respect but equally keen to speed them on their way to Elysium and escape the stench of death and decay that lingered oppressively in the heavy summer air. He had found it almost as hard at the hospital tent. There he had been helping to move the injured onto wagons, for transport to the more permanent camp back at Vesontio, a task that stirred memories of his own experience, many of which he would rather have forgotten... The fetid smell of the tent that hit you even before you entered... Inside, it was almost unbearable. The air so thick with the smell of the wounded and the medicines being used to treat them, you could almost taste it. And there had been so many wounded. Every available space had been filled with a cot; in places, they had been crammed together so tightly that the hard-pressed orderlies had almost to climb over one man to get to another. Stretched to breaking point, the medical teams were struggling to deliver anything but the most rudimentary level of care. Hence the transfer to Vesontio. He wondered how many of the pallid and stricken men would survive the journey, let alone anything beyond. He shuddered at the thought. At least his time helping with the wounded had given him an opportunity to spend time with Titus. Paired together carrying stretchers, it had been the first opportunity he'd had to catch up with his friend since they had arrived in camp. Aside from a few cuts and bruises, Titus had come through the battle unscathed. After listening to him recount his story of the enemy's attack and the cohort's part in the brave rear guard led by Plautius, Atticus still wasn't sure how. He didn't think Titus was either. Although having lost friends in other cohorts, Titus shared Atticus' anger that Aquila had known of the danger and had chosen not to act. The anger that had resulted in him now waiting to appear before the man himself, some five days later.

"You listening, lad?"

If Baculus and Plautius had been talking to him, he hadn't heard a word.

"Umm… no, sorry. I was just thinking…"

Baculus rolled his eyes.

"Well, now you need to focus! I haven't been able to speak to the legate. So, I've no idea what's on his mind. He doesn't have his tribunes to talk to either. But that might be a good thing. For you anyway."

Atticus was confused.

"Why? The tribune from the engineers knew that I tried to warn Aquila. He must have told the others."

"Exactly. And if there was any chance of that information getting out now, you would be in far more trouble than you are. As it is, anyone who knew Aquila ignored your warning is dead, so he can safely pretend it didn't happen. Which is what I suggest you do."

Atticus was livid.

"Pretend it didn't happen? He had a chance to act and chose not to! How many men died needlessly as a result? What he did was wrong!"

Atticus' outburst caught the attention of the guard outside Aquila's tent, who looked him up and down with a barely concealed look of contempt. Atticus felt Plautius' hand on his shoulder.

"Calm yourself, lad. It's the only way. Do you want him thinking he needs to be rid of you? One way or the other?"

Atticus sighed. He hadn't thought about that.

"No. But he shouldn't get away with it."

Baculus nodded.

"You're right. But unfortunately, one privilege of his position is not being subject to the same rules as the rest of us. It's not fair but that's how it is. He will still have to explain himself to the gods. And they will know. In the meantime, he is in your debt and we can use that to your advantage. Hopefully."

Atticus swallowed nervously. Aquila had never given him any cause to believe hoping for the best was helpful, but he had saved the man's life and that had to count for something. He gave Baculus a nod and turned to look out across the camp.

Atticus turned quickly as Plautius gave him a nudge. He'd been replaying the day of the attack in his mind and was grateful for the interruption. Thinking about it left him feeling numb. It could have turned out so differently. For them all. The guard had appeared from Aquila's tent and he beckoned them forward. He was about to discover just how things would turn out for him.

"The legate is ready for you."

Baculus and Plautius edged past the legionary into the tent. The soldier scowled at Atticus as he followed suit.

"I hope you get what you deserve."

Atticus sighed. He didn't think there was any danger of that. If there was, he wouldn't be here. Following Plautius' lead, he snapped to attention and saluted. Their arrival drew a disdainful wave of acknowledgement from Aquila, whose attention had already switched to Baculus as he joined him on his side of the desk. The legate accepted Baculus' salute with a good deal more respect.

"First Spear. It's good to see you up and on your feet. Although I must confess, I wasn't expecting to see you this morning. This is a matter I am quite content to manage alone, should you need to rest. Legionary Capito and I have been here before, after all."

Atticus swallowed but said nothing, fixing his gaze on the back of the tent. Baculus pulled out a chair beside Aquila and slowly eased himself down.

"It's no burden, sir. Military discipline relies on the consequences of our actions being recognised, after all…"

He paused and shot Aquila a subtle glance.

"… at all levels. I'm happy to ensure that justice is seen to be done. Given all of the circumstances."

Atticus thought he saw a momentary flash of guilt cross Aquila's face before he regained his composure, nodding curtly.

"Very well. Let's get on!"

He turned to run his eye over Plautius and Atticus.

"Centurion. I am grateful that your men fight with considerably more discipline than they display at other times. Of course, I gave no orders for your cohort to be mobilised. It is fortunate for you that Caesar is grateful for the role we played in withstanding the attack. I have received his thanks and as such we need not consider this particular matter any further."

Ignoring Plautius' indignant stare, Aquila fixed his attention on Atticus.

"However, your behaviour, soldier, cannot be overlooked. Insolence must always be punished, whatever excuse you believe you had for your actions. It is true that we were attacked after I had received your report raising that possibility. However, your warning, if you could call it that, was insufficiently detailed for me to consider it necessary to raise the alarm. At least that is how it will be recorded... if it is necessary to do so."

Atticus could feel his fingers digging into his palms as he balled his fists and tried to remain calm. Aquila flashed him a smug smile as he continued.

"Good. Regrettably, Garmanos cannot join us today to confirm what he may have seen. Unfortunate, I know, but he lost comrades in battle and I felt it only right and proper to encourage him to return home with their bodies. I imagine he will be gone some time. Ordinarily, I could have relied upon my tribunes to attest to the events of the day but, unfortunately, they all perished during the attack. The engineer was with me when the command group was attacked. But then you already know that, don't you, Capito? Just how is it that you came to be there when I know you were tied up as I had instructed?"

With Aquila staring at him intently, Atticus felt himself tense. He hadn't expected to be asked that question. His mouth suddenly felt very dry and he shuffled on the spot. What could he say that wouldn't get Plautius or Julius into trouble? Thankfully, Baculus came to his rescue.

"I sent Naso to find you, sir, and report on our situation. He ran into Capito just before they found you. He must have been able to break free in the melee when the Barbarians reached that part of camp."

Aquila didn't look at all convinced.

"Is this true, Capito?"

Atticus swallowed hard.

"Yes, sir. One of the guards killed a warrior and I was just able to reach his sword and cut myself free."

Baculus gave him a sly wink and turned to Aquila.

"It's lucky that he did, sir. Who knows what might have happened to you if Capito and Naso hadn't arrived when they did?"

Aquila sat back with a pained expression on his face. He closed his eyes and brought his hands together under his chin. For a moment, Atticus wondered if he might try to deny that he owed him his life. After all, nobody else had seen it happen. It was exactly the kind of thing he had come to expect from Aquila. Noble birth or not. Aquila opened his eyes and leant forward. Atticus had never seen anybody looking quite so uncomfortable.

"You are right, First Spear. I cannot deny that your arrival was opportune, Capito. It seems I find myself in your debt."

He fixed Atticus with a steely glare.

"A debt you may rest assured that I do not intend to have outstanding any longer than necessary. Whatever the means by which I must have the slate wiped clean…"

Atticus swallowed hard; that sounded more like a threat than an expression of gratitude. It was like Bibracte all over again! He tried to shake such thoughts from his mind as Aquila smiled smugly and turned towards Baculus.

"In the meantime, First Spear, I shall be guided by you in respect of a suitable punishment for Capito's insubordination."

Atticus was stunned. He was still going to be punished? His face had evidently revealed rather more emotion than he had intended.

"Yes, Capito, punished. Debt or no debt, you disobeyed an order and must face the consequences. First Spear, your advice?"

Baculus thought for a while.

"Well, the usual punishment would be flogging but I couldn't recommend that, sir... given subsequent events. I fear such a public display may also raise questions you might prefer remain unasked..."

Aquila shot Baculus an angry look. For a moment, Atticus thought he was going to challenge the veteran soldier but he remained tight-lipped as Baculus continued.

"I do have an idea, however, that might reinforce Capito's respect for order. Attach him to me for a few weeks. When he is not on duty with the rest of his cohort, I can use him. I might be up and about but I won't be covering the ground anything like fast enough. Capito can help take up the slack. It will be menial work, running orders mostly, but it will be during time he would have called his own and he'll have plenty of opportunity to reflect on his actions."

Atticus was still finding it hard to accept that any punishment was warranted but this didn't sound too bad. He tried not to look too hopeful as he met Aquila's gaze.

"Very well, First Spear, I shall have Capito assigned to you. Make sure he is kept busy... It would be most unfortunate, for him, if we needed to reconvene and consider other options..."

He left the threat hanging as he sat back in his chair. Atticus remained impassive, staring directly ahead and refusing to meet Aquila's eye. He wasn't going to give him the satisfaction of drawing any kind of visible response. Seemingly content that his point had been made, Aquila waved his hand towards the exit of the tent.

"That will be all. You are dismissed. First Spear, a brief word before you go."

Atticus followed Plautius out of the tent. He raised his hand to cover his eyes as they stepped out into the bright sunshine, grateful to have an excuse to avoid the gaze of the guard. Clear of the main thoroughfare, Plautius paused.

"I'll wait for Baculus. You get back to the tent and get something to eat. You'd best get used to grabbing meals when you can. You know Aquila isn't going to be happy unless Baculus has you working night and day, though there could be worse punishments. Baculus did you a favour there…"

"I know. And I am grateful, but I still end up getting punished when Aquila's the one in the wrong. I was right about the attack and he knows it. We had chance to prepare! It would have made a difference. But he didn't act. And I nearly did the same when I saw him in trouble that day. I wanted him to suffer. For all of those that we lost. But I couldn't do it. Some thanks. Maybe I should have left him."

Plautius shook his head.

"No. Going to his aid, even when you didn't want to, is what makes you a better man than him. Never forget that. But the army relies on discipline. We can't pick and choose which orders we follow or there would be chaos. Even if they appear wrong. That doesn't mean you have to follow them without thinking. There will be occasions, like this, when you need to raise concerns. The key is how you do that and with whom. Challenging your legate in public is probably not the best approach, especially if that legate is Aquila. Learn to pick your battles."

He gave Atticus a slap on the back.

"Now, get going."

Baculus joined Plautius as he watched Atticus heading back towards his tent.

"How's he taking it?"

"As you'd expect. He's grateful to you but still angry that he has ended up getting punished at all. I think a spell with you will do him good. Let him see how important following orders is for keeping a legion functioning in the field."

"It was the best I could come up with at the time. I wasn't sure if Aquila would go for it but I knew he wouldn't want anything that might raise questions. Besides, I wasn't lying about struggling to get about. I'm feeling my age, brother, and no mistake."

Plautius smiled.

"I think that has more to do with enemy swords than age, my friend. That and a stubborn disregard for medical opinion! Take advantage of Capito. He will manage the workload just fine."

Baculus nodded.

"He's a good lad. We know courage isn't an issue and he can certainly fight. He seems to have his wits about him too. Most of the time anyway. If we can just get him to channel his energy in the right way, he has potential."

"Remind you of anybody, brother?"

Baculus gave Plautius a quizzical look.

"Who?"

Plautius laughed.

"You! Now we'd best get moving. This army isn't going to organise itself. The Aduatuci might not have been here but I know Allerix was, and so does Caesar. I'd wager that's where we will be heading next. And soon."

20

LATE SUMMER, 57 BC

Aduatuca

Allerix reined Isarno in as they entered the shadowed sanctuary of the walls. They had come far enough. The Romans had called off their pursuit, anxious not to venture too close. He smiled. Word of Epona's prowess with a bow must have spread. He waved his men forward and followed them through the heavy wooden gates. They slammed shut behind him and he paused to enjoy a welcome moment of quiet in the shade of the gatehouse. The skirmish had been short but fierce and, although he and his men had secured the upper hand, he was relieved that they all appeared to have returned unscathed, which was more than could be said for the Romans. They would be returning to camp two or three riders light. Again. He couldn't summon up any enthusiasm to celebrate, however. Any joy he might have felt about inflicting yet another defeat on the Roman cavalry was tempered by the realisation that this would be the last foray he and his men would make. The Romans had almost finished their wall. As soon as Caesar's legions had arrived, Allerix and his men had begun riding out to disrupt their attempts at establishing a camp and, later, to target the foraging parties, scouts and messengers that the Romans relied upon so heavily. They had drawn out the Roman cavalry on almost every occasion and, after each skirmish, he and his men had ridden away victorious. He knew their attacks would ultimately prove little more than an annoyance, but the watching population had enjoyed seeing the Romans repeatedly being forced to down tools and scurry for cover. The success of their cavalry skirmishes had helped instil a degree of cautious optimism too – could this really be the fabled army that had defeated the Nervii and their allies?

But that was before the Romans had begun to build their wall.

Construction had started almost as soon as the Romans had finally finished building their camp. And what an undertaking. They hadn't known what to make of it when the construction began. But it became clear soon enough. Caesar was attempting to surround the settlement with a rampart and ditch. Allerix and his men had done all they could to disrupt its construction, but to no avail, and, with every day that passed, the earthworks had cast an ever larger and more ominous shadow across the plain. One that had ushered in an altogether more sombre mood amongst the population. Slowly cut adrift from the outside world and with any hope of either rescue or escape receding, the threat posed by the armies of Rome had suddenly seemed far more real. Twelve feet high, topped with a wicker palisade and wooden watch towers, the barrier truly was an awesome sight. He sighed. The wall would corral them in place, much like the animals they had penned within the town, but it was hard not to have some grudging respect for the Romans' ingenuity and determination. They always seemed to have an answer and the means to deliver it. He had continued to lead out his men but he knew this was now more about boosting morale than securing any real military advantage. His own included. The forays had been a useful means of keeping him occupied, giving him something to think about other than the defeat of the Nervii at the Sabis. He still felt guilty about leaving the scene of the failed attack, although he knew he had done more than enough to satisfy the honour of his people. Yet so had the Nervii, and even their bravery hadn't been enough. He couldn't help but wonder what might have happened if his father had been there to support the attack. Perhaps, with the additional numbers and the mobility of their cavalry, they might have been celebrating a famous victory rather than mourning the loss of the alliance that had offered the only real prospect of defeating the Romans. Now the Aduatuci had been left to face them alone and it was hard to be hopeful about the outcome. With a heavy heart, he nudged Isarno into the sun and after his men, already lost amongst the dense throng of people milling about the square. His father had ordered all of their other settlements abandoned and, with almost all of the Aduatuci now temporarily residing in Aduatuca, it was far busier than he could ever remember. It was the right decision; they couldn't hope to defend their entire territory against the advancing Romans, and Aduatuca was a natural stronghold. It had been some undertaking to relocate the population but there were plenty of supplies in store, and the value of the preparations his father had ordered earlier in the year had now been realised. Space might be at a premium but food and water were not, and the Romans would have a long wait if they were looking to force their surrender by siege.

If.

It had been impossible to miss the assault towers slowly taking shape behind the Roman lines. Caesar was clearly in no mood to delay the moment of reckoning. Regardless of the heavy price his soldiers would pay attempting any form of direct attack. Allerix paused to allow a gaggle of women, laden down with firewood, to edge across his path. He caught sight of his father, who, as usual, had been watching from the wall. He gave him a wave and acknowledged his gesture to join him. Allerix knew that carrying the nation's fate was weighing heavily upon his father. He hid it well, publicly at least, displaying the same calm air as he had that night on the road when they had been reunited and Allerix had shared news of the battle and its bloody outcome. His father had listened quietly, probing for detail but displaying no emotion. Almost at once he had begun to make plans, busying his chieftains and focussing their attention on the strengths that had brought their nation to prominence. It was surely no coincidence that they had spent each of the evenings on the journey home listening to his father and Epomedius recount stories of their ancestors. And many of their own. He never tired of listening and it had been a pleasant surprise when his father invited him to add to the history with his account of the defeat of Ariovistus at Vesontio. It was only later, after the drinking was done and the dying embers were all that remained of the fire, that his father had let his mask slip. In the company of just his children and Epomedius, he had shared his fears about the strength of the Romans and lamented the loss of the alliance. He had cursed the actions of those who had brought it to an untimely end. Galba and Correus, who had ultimately given up without a fight, for all their fine words at Samarobriva and Boduognatus, whose actions had angered and frustrated his father, mindful of what might have been had he exercised just a little more patience. The Nervii had paid a high price for Boduognatus' misplaced arrogance. A cost his father feared the Aduatuci might now be forced to share. As a nation, they had fought many times before to protect their way of life, but this was different.

There could be no going back though. Too many men had already perished to turn their back on the struggle now. And so, with a heavy heart, his father would choose to fight once more. Allerix nudged Isarno forward. He wondered who would tell their tale in the future and what kind of story their stand against the Romans would turn out to be. For now, he was simply relieved that he was able to help his father and that he would have the chance to fight at his side when the Roman attack came. Arriving at the square, he leapt down from Isarno and handed his reins to one of the young boys allocated to look after the horses. Allerix gave the lad a smile and watched him leading Isarno slowly away. He should be off playing in the sun, not caught up in a struggle that might deny him the opportunity to enjoy any more of his childhood years. He shook his head and set off to join his father.

Hurrying up the final few steps, Allerix turned on to the top of the wall. Shielding his eyes from the sun, he returned the greetings of his father and Epomedius as he joined them looking out across the plain.

"You led the men well again today, Lord."

Allerix smiled half-heartedly.

"Thank you. Although I might feel more deserving of your praise if we weren't battling an enemy that seems intent on repeating the same tactics. They have grown predictable."

Epomedius nodded.

"But recognising that weakness and taking advantage of it is what makes you a good leader."

Albiorix smiled warmly at Allerix before returning his attention to the plain.

"Epomedius is right. Besides, any fight from which you return with the same number of men as you left is a good one. However, I fear that this next battle will not be fought or won by cavalry. And I fear from what you have told us about the Romans, my son, that they are a good deal more adept on foot than in the saddle. Could any other army have survived the attack at the Sabis?"

He paused and gestured towards the Roman wall.

"And now, just a few short weeks later, here they are with enough men, knowledge and bravado to build this."

Acknowledging Epona as she arrived, Allerix nodded towards the plain.

"It's even more impressive from down there and they will have it finished by the end of the day, I'm sure."

Albiorix placed a consoling arm on his shoulder.

"And with the Romans safely behind their barrier, you will be left kicking your heels with the rest of us. Waiting to see what comes."

Allerix sighed. His father knew him so well.

"Do you think we will have to wait long?"

Albiorix shook his head.

"Not if those siege towers are any indication. The people mock them. They feel safe behind our walls and do not believe the Romans have the capacity to move such structures across the plain. It cheers them to think that way but I suspect if Caesar can build them, he will have the means to move them. And I have no doubt, the will to use them too."

Epomedius cast his eyes along the wall, busy with those on watch.

"And we will be ready, my king."

Epona nodded.

"The Romans will not find us as accommodating as the Helvetii or Suebi, Father. Defeating the Nervii as they did was impressive, but dislodging us will be another challenge altogether. The walls will run with blood. Is Caesar willing to risk that it is ours rather than theirs that flows most freely?"

Albiorix sighed.

"I believe he is, yes. And so do the elders. Some of whom talk openly of surrender."

Allerix shook his head in dismay.

"Surely not? What use is there in saving lives if we lose the right to choose how to live them? They have to see that. Must we really battle the elders as well as the Romans?"

Albiorix raised his hands.

"I agree and I believe that for now I have steadied their resolve. Though I suspect what happens next will depend on how quickly Caesar deploys those towers."

*

Julius inclined his shield towards the hive of activity on the plain below.

"That's quite some sight."

Atticus nodded.

"It is, but I don't envy them. It was hard enough building the bloody things, let alone moving them."

Julius glanced at his blistered hands.

"I know but it's the poor bastards inside the towers I feel sorry for. Can you imagine what it's like to be stuck in there, knowing what's to come?"

Atticus smiled.

"Almost makes you glad to be on watch."

Titus frowned and looked back along the rampart.

"Maybe. I'd feel better about it if we weren't stuck up here in the tower furthest from camp."

Atticus gave him a nudge.

"Furthest from the food, you mean?"

Julius laughed.

"Don't forget his cot. The old boy needs his rest."

Titus rolled his eyes.

"I just don't like being this close to town with only you two for company, that's all.

Besides, given that we have to be back here again later, there's not much chance of us getting any rest, is there? You'd think we might have earned a break but no, double duty it is."

Julius nodded towards Atticus.

"You know the legate. Always happy to send extra duties the way of his 'favourite son.'"

Atticus sighed. It certainly felt that way. Even with all the running around he'd been doing for Baculus, Aquila hadn't missed an opportunity to add to the burden. He didn't mind guard duty, though. It made a change from all the physical work they'd been doing. After the camp, it had been the siege towers and then their part of the rampart. That had been the hardest. They had all known the order for siege towers would come, but a rampart and ditch? To surround the entire town? Atticus was sure nobody but Caesar had imagined that. It had been heavy and laborious work, sapping the strength and spirit of the men, still badly shaken from the last battle. The march into the lands of the Aduatuci had been short and relatively easy. Although Caesar had pushed the pace, the weather had been kind and the terrain easy: things that might usually be expected to lift morale. But the mood had remained subdued. And that was before they had seen the formidable defences of the settlement. Defences they would have to find a way through before the long and bloody campaign could finally be concluded. With the inhabitants showing no signs of seeking surrender, the legions had laboured in the shadows of the walls and cliffs surrounding the town, knowing, even as they toiled, that far bloodier work lay ahead.

The constant attacks of the enemy cavalry hadn't helped morale either. He knew from his own experience how wearing the daily attacks had become. Seeking refuge behind their shields until the Roman cavalry arrived reminded him of Vesontio. Only this time, Allerix and his men had been the ones launching the attacks. He still found it uncomfortable to think of Allerix as an enemy rather than a friend, and he wasn't sure he'd ever understand why that was the case. He knew Caesar couldn't allow the Aduatuci to escape retribution after the attack. They had been part of the alliance, even if they hadn't been at the river. It was why they were fighting the alliance in the first place that bothered him. Especially as the very people they were now besieging had so recently been aligned with them, helping Caesar secure victory... saving their lives... more than once. Not that this would count for anything when the huge and imposing towers reached the walls of the settlement. It didn't make any sense. Not to him anyway. But it wasn't something that seemed to concern anybody else and so he put it to the back of his mind, which was easier when he was running errands for Baculus. He simply hadn't had time to think. Baculus had let him sleep once, when Aquila was away at a briefing, but, otherwise, he'd been true to his word and kept Atticus busy. It had been hard leaving his friends around the fire, or asleep in their cots whilst he staggered out of his, but, as punishments went, he knew it could have been a lot worse. He'd learnt a lot too. Including, to his surprise, just how many workarounds, favours and bribes it took to secure men, equipment and supplies for the legion. For an army that prided itself on order and regulation, who you knew – and how you knew them – seemed to be every bit as important. He supposed it had been much the same in Verona, although he had resolved to take more care in remembering the names of these contacts than he had the merchants back home. You never knew when it might come in handy...

He shivered as the sound of the buccina rang out across the plain. Having sat menacingly before the town whilst the legions assembled, the towers began their slow but inexorable journey towards the wall. For all the devastation he knew they were intended to reap, it was hard not to look upon them with some sense of awe. He could only imagine how the inhabitants of the town must be feeling as the men and machines began inching forward. Julius gave him a nudge.

"No turning back now. Let's hope it's over quickly. But taking that wall isn't going to be easy."

Titus nodded.

"It's not. We've seen what they can do in battle. This could get ugly."

Julius snapped to attention as Plautius negotiated the final rungs of the ladder and joined them in the tower.

"You're right, it could. But with luck it won't come to that. As soon as the towers appeared on the plain, the general received an envoy seeking terms for surrender. It appears the locals believed we'd need divine intervention to move them and that in doing so the gods must favour us."

Julius laughed.

"I didn't see any gods helping to build them and I know it's men moving them, though I'd be happy to play the part if it helps get this over with peacefully."

"I'm fairly sure you'd be one of the least qualified, Naso! But that won't be necessary. The envoy has already returned."

Atticus looked enquiringly at Plautius.

"And do you know if the general offered them terms?"

Plautius nodded.

"He did. They have until the towers reach the wall to decide whether or not to accept them. They've been told they have to cast their weapons over the wall as a sign of acceptance. So, keep a lookout. You'll know sooner than most whether or not they've decided to fight."

*

Albiorix held up his hands and waited for the noise to die down.

"I know. I feel the same but the elders have not yet agreed to the terms and I may yet persuade them against doing so. I will not try to do so without your support, however."

The room erupted into a cacophony of noise once more as the assembled crowd of chieftains, Royal Guard members and senior warriors made their thoughts clear.

Albiorix waited patiently again for the noise to subside.

"The elders fear the Romans. And they are right to do so. The army at our gates have defeated the Helvetii, Suebi, Atrebates, Viromandui and Nervii and forced the surrender of the Bellovaci and Suessiones. We are outnumbered and our cavalry is rendered useless by the Romans' wall. Remember, too, the savagery with which Caesar slaughtered the women and children of the Suebi after Vesontio. If we fight, we commit our families as well as our warriors to battle. I understand therefore why the elders thought it prudent to at least hear what terms might be offered. My only demand was that the elders should know your views before we decided our response. We do not have long. If we do not accept his terms before the towers reach the walls, Caesar will sack the city."

Allerix exchanged glances with Epona as the expectant faces in the crowd all focussed on their father, eagerly awaiting news of the terms that had been offered.

"Caesar demands that we pay tribute and offer hostages to secure any agreement. We would do likewise – such a demand is not unexpected. He calls too for men and horses to supplement his cavalry. He has demanded the same of all nations bending the knee to Rome. It is a clever move, strengthening his forces whilst weakening those that might stand against him. I have no wish to see our warriors riding once again for Caesar. It would pain me as a father and as your king. As both, I must ask myself, however, whether opposing such a term is worth committing those very warriors to battle."

Allerix nodded to his father, although he was beginning to feel slightly uneasy about just where he might be attempting to lead them. An unease seemingly shared by many amongst the crowd, if the anxious glances and hushed conversations were any indication.

Ignoring the murmurs of disquiet, Albiorix continued.

"Caesar has ordained that I may remain as king and that the elders may continue to exercise the rule of law. However... that law must be Roman. They demand that we kneel before Caesar and accept the rule of Rome... forever. And... we are compelled to relinquish our weapons... all of them."

Albiorix paused, clearly expecting the howls of anger and derision that spontaneously filled the room. Allerix looked plaintively at his father. Surely, he was not going to suggest that such terms were acceptable. Slowly, some semblance of calm settled across the room and Albiorix began again.

"Caesar tells us that, as a client kingdom, we will have Rome's protection; our neighbours will be commanded to respect our borders. I imagine the Aedui were told much the same when they became 'Friends of Rome'. A title that counted for little when they were left to suffer the indignities of defeat and servitude at the hands of the Suebi. And did not Caesar himself then grant Ariovistus the same honour, before the interests of Rome changed once more and the Suebi were massacred? Can we trust that Rome's interests will not change again?"

Allerix suspected that his father had intended this to be a rhetorical question but in the febrile atmosphere of the room it was met with a thunderous roar of protest, forcing Albiorix to pause once more.

"As for our neighbours, I trusted them when they pledged

to fight with us against the Romans. A pledge that counted for nothing when they scurried away to make peace, leaving others to fight and die on their behalf. I will not make that mistake again. Some of the elders feel differently, however. They believe that the towers approaching our walls are a sign that the gods fight on the side of Rome. That resistance will invite retribution and signal our demise as a nation. They would accept the terms, to spare our people."

Albiorix turned briefly to look at Allerix as he waited for the fresh wave of animated conversations to come to an end.

"I am reminded, however, of the words of a future king, wise beyond his years. Surrender may save the lives of our people but it will not protect their way of life. The demise of our nation would occur just as surely as if we had perished on the battlefield. And if the gods did help the Romans to conjure these towers, I know they didn't build them. Just as it is men who now move them across the plain. Soldiers! Flesh and blood. As mortal as you or I. And what of our ancestors? Our gods? Will they not fight beside us, if we must defend our home?

"The elders know therefore that I choose to fight. The terms offered are not those that, as your king, I believe I have any place accepting. To do so would dishonour all that we and our ancestors have accomplished as a nation. I think the time is right for Caesar to discover that we have learnt the lesson that trust cannot be taken for granted. But I am aware what I am asking of you. And so, before I attempt to persuade the elders to commit to battle, I would know that you and all those you lead are with me."

For a moment the room fell silent.

Epomedius reached for his sword and turned to face Albiorix. He knelt.

"My sword is yours, my Lord. Now, as always."

Epona nodded at Allerix as she walked forward to join Epomedius.

"Father, I don't kneel because I am compelled by my oath but because I have the freedom to do so. I would fight to protect that right."

Allerix watched as without hesitation each of the warriors knelt, adding their voice to the chorus of support echoing around the room. He turned to his father. He didn't think he had ever seen him looking quite so emotional. He smiled.

"I believe you have your answer. And you know mine."

He knelt. Albiorix tapped him quickly on the shoulder and beckoned him to stand. He waved everyone else to their feet.

"Thank you. Your loyalty and bravery do me great honour. I will be proud to fight beside you. If only I can convince the elders that we should be permitted to do so."

*

Julius sighed for the umpteenth time that morning.

"Do you think we're nearly done?"

Titus laughed.

"Now who's keen to get back to camp?"

Atticus smiled as their good-natured bickering continued behind him. He had been so engrossed in the slow but steady progress of the huge towers towards the settlement walls that he'd lost all track of time. He doubted any of the men on the plain had. He knew from experience just how unpleasant it could be standing in the full glare of the sun. And he could only imagine what it must be like for those tasked with actually moving the towers. They were getting close now, though. It wouldn't be long before they arrived at the walls and their relentless and back-breaking toil would finally be over. And then what? He had seen people on the walls, monitoring the progress of the towers, but there had been no sign of surrender. It looked as if Allerix and his people had decided to fight. Atticus glanced along the rampart, looking for any indication that their watch might be about to end. He would rather not have to watch the men, of either side, fall in battle. Nothing. He sighed and turned back towards the settlement, where the numbers on the wall were increasing quickly.

"Look! On the wall. Warriors, lots of them!"

Julius masked his eyes from the sun.

"Are you sure?"

Atticus nodded.

"I think so. They look like they have weapons anyway."

Titus frowned.

"That's it, then. They're going to defend the walls. I didn't think they would…"

Julius shook his head.

"You know Allerix and his men. Did you really think they would surrender?"

Titus shrugged and nodded to the assembled legions.

"I hoped. For their sake."

Atticus was relieved as the sounds of the buccina rolled along the palisade, finally signalling the end of their watch. He waited until he could see their comrades marching out to replace them and gave Julius a nudge.

"Come on, let's get ready to go. At least we'll be spared the need to watch."

As he turned to retrieve his shield, Julius thrust out his arm towards the wall.

"It's not just us being spared, brother. Look! They're throwing the weapons away. They're surrendering."

The three friends watched in silence as more and more warriors appeared on the wall to discard their weapons. Atticus noticed one or two of the onlooking Romans baiting the warriors from the safety of the towers, no doubt relieved not to be facing the weapons quickly filling the ditch at the foot of the wall. A few warriors defiantly replied in kind, but most seemed intent on leaving the scene as quickly as possible. He could only guess how hard this must be for them. They were warriors and fiercely proud of their nation. At least they wouldn't fall in battle now, and he wondered if too much blood had been spilled to hope that they might one day fight again as allies. Julius passed Titus his shield.

"So, what now then?"

Titus shrugged.

"Get the lads inside as a show of strength and make sure they stick to whatever terms were agreed, I guess. After that, who knows? I can't imagine anyone other than the officers are thinking much beyond how to celebrate."

Julius smiled.

"Good! I could do with a drink."

Titus gave him a shove.

"May the Gods help me. You do remember we have to be back here again later?"

Julius' smile disappeared from his face.

"Fuck. I'd forgotten."

Atticus laughed.

"Probably trying not to think about how dull it's going to be. Especially now they've surrendered."

Titus moved aside to allow the first of their replacements into the tower. The legionary offered the password and exchanged greetings as he waited for his comrades to complete the climb. They had barely straightened up before Titus, anxious to be on his way, began to update them on the events of the morning, which didn't detain him long. Surrender aside, it had been a very uneventful watch, with little prospect of any change. Collecting up the last of their equipment, Julius and Titus set off down the ladder. One of the legionaries nodded to Atticus as he waited to follow them down.

"You lads done now?"

Atticus groaned.

"I wish. We're back here again tonight."

The legionary grimaced.

"Fuck, that's rough. Who did you upset?"

Atticus shrugged.

"It's a long story."

Though he feared the tedium of another three hours on watch was going to feel a whole lot longer. He paused before disappearing from view.

"Have a drink for us at midnight. We'll be out here on third watch."

*

Epona waved away the dust as she watched the Roman column exiting the settlement. Tramping silently out through the same gates they had so loudly and triumphantly entered earlier that day. She swore an oath not to stand so idle next time she had a Roman in her sights. As the last of the legionaries disappeared from view, she gave her brother a nudge.

"Is that the last of them?"

"I think so, yes."

"Good. Then let's shut the gates before Caesar changes his mind and orders them back in."

She gestured towards a group of warriors disdainfully watching the Romans from their vantage point on the wall above the gate.

"Is that Tascus up there?"

Allerix nodded. She waved at the warrior until she caught his attention and beckoned him over. He hurried down to join them.

"Close the gates and have someone on the wall at all times. You know what creatures of habit these Romans are. If they do anything out of the ordinary, we need to know immediately. Then find Valis and join us in the hall."

As he hurried away, she smiled and called after him.

"And don't forget where you left that axe of yours!"

She tapped Allerix on the arm and they set off for the hall.

"Why do you think Caesar withdrew his men?"

Allerix shook his head.

"I don't know. He told Father he was concerned about the risk of violence and looting if he allowed them to stay. But I'm not sure I believe that."

She shot him a look of concern.

"Do you think he suspects trouble?"

"Maybe. Withdrawing his men is a sign he might. Perhaps he seeks to protect them and not us."

Epona smiled.

"Then they have not ventured anything like far enough, brother. As they will discover tonight. With luck, they will be too busy celebrating to pay any attention to the gates of the town."

As if on cue, the gates crashed shut behind them. She wasn't surprised to see this act as a signal for people to begin cautiously emerging back onto the streets. A palpable air of tension had hung over the settlement all day. The chores of daily life had been curtailed as people, anxious to avoid the Romans, sought the sanctuary of whatever refuge they could find, a few brave souls breaking cover, driven by necessity or the surreptitious search for materials. She smiled. As soon as her mother had learnt of their plan, she'd set about organising the women and children to offer assistance. And as a host of crudely fashioned wicker and hide shields, wooden ladders and faggots began to appear, the fruits of their labours became clear. A surprise to her brother, judging by the look of consternation on his face. She gave him a gentle push.

"What? Did you think that, whilst Father had us dumping weapons over the wall, Mother wouldn't have had the womenfolk doing something that might actually help us beat the Romans?"

Allerix laughed.

"We did manage to hide a few as well, you know."

She smiled.

"I know. I'm still surprised the Romans believed that collection of rusty blades, farm tools and practice swords was everything."

"I think they saw what they wanted to see. Besides, we did include most of the new ones Father ordered to be made earlier in the summer. I hear the smiths were so upset, they had to be restrained from following their hard work over the walls."

Epona shrugged.

"It's a shame the blades never got to draw Roman blood but a price worth paying if it protects the element of surprise. Better still if it sends Tascus and his fellow smiths into battle angry."

She paused as they approached the hall, watching the sun slowly dip below the wall.

How many of them would see dusk tomorrow? Perhaps it was a good thing such matters were known only to the gods. Fear of death kept a warrior alive. And she was afraid. She knew she wasn't alone but they were doing the right thing and that was all the gods could ask of them. She looked up as Allerix called out.

"You're too early to be howling at the moon, sister! Father is waiting..."

She smiled as he reacted just a little too slowly to escape her kick.

Epona stretched to try and catch sight of her father. The hall was almost full and she couldn't see him amongst the crowd, but there was no mistaking the huge frame of Epomedius. Guessing that's where she'd find her father, she began to ease her way towards the front of the hall. The sweet smell of mead hung in the air and the occasional waft of roasting pork had her licking her lips as she drew closer to the fire, but it was a sense of nervous anticipation rather than revelry that filled the room. They were ready to take the fight to Rome despite the grave dangers that lay ahead. And that was before her father had roused them for battle. He greeted her with a smile and pulled them aside.

"The Romans have gone?"

She nodded.

"They have and the gates are closed. The town is ours again."

"Good. Then preparations can begin. I have agreed with the chieftains that we will launch attacks at either end of the rampart. The fortifications look a little less formidable at these points and that way we force the Romans to split their forces. With luck, we can overcome those on the wall quickly enough to press home our attack before they summon the soldiers from the main camp. It's our best chance."

Epona was reassured to see both Epomedius and Allerix nodding their agreement. She smiled at her father.

"And when do we attack?"

He laughed.

"We'll let the Romans tell us. The call to summon those with the misfortune to be on third watch will be the signal for our attack to begin."

21

LATE SUMMER, 57 BC

Aduatuca

Julius called out the password as they approached the sentry. The bored-looking soldier responded in kind and gestured them through with a cursory wave of his hand, Julius' attempts to engage him in conversation falling on deaf ears. He shook his head.

"Miserable bastard."

Atticus shrugged.

"What do you expect? He's on duty."

"At least his watch is nearly done. He'll be back in camp soon. Unlike us," said Titus grumpily.

Julius smiled.

"Oh, come on, it could be worse. At least we're not on fourth watch."

Atticus glanced towards his friend.

"You seem in surprisingly good spirits for someone dragged away from the comforts of camp."

Julius laughed and nodded towards Titus.

"I'm not sure about comforts, brother. Did you try that monstrosity he was passing off as stew?"

Titus gave Julius a shove.

"Fuck off! You were lucky to get anything passable this late in the campaign."

Julius raised his hands.

"I know, I know. But that's it. Surely the campaign must be over now. Missing out on tonight's celebration is shit, but if we're done for the summer, I'll take that. There's talk that we might even be heading home."

Atticus had heard that too, although it was only one of many rumours circulating around camp. It was always the same. No sooner had one task been completed than speculation began about what was next. It was certainly true that they could do with a break; even the veterans were complaining about how hard they'd been pushed. He tried not to think about it too much. The gods and that bastard Aquila had a funny way of delivering exactly what you didn't want. Besides, he was still feeling anxious about the prospect of facing his father and wasn't quite as keen as Julius about the prospect of returning home. He would settle for the campaign being all but over, though. That was a comforting thought, one which made the briefing they'd just had with the duty tesserarius even more curious. Usually, watch briefings were incredibly tedious but this one had been very different. Apparently, the general was concerned that the Aduatuci might launch a surprise attack. He'd given orders for signal fires to be positioned on the rampart and reserve cohorts to be stationed in a makeshift camp close to the rampart. Atticus looked up as they passed the gates of the hurriedly built camp.

"I bet nobody in there is impressed with all this caution. Off duty and still can't enjoy a drink."

Julius nodded.

"You're telling me, brother. It all seems a waste of time to me. I mean, they've surrendered their weapons. What could possibly happen now?"

Titus shook his head.

"Don't tempt fate, lad. The general was concerned enough to act and, if he didn't trust them, neither should we. I won't be happy until we're done."

Julius shared a smile with Atticus and pointed to the moonlit plain.

"Surely even you don't think there's any chance of an attack? You'd have to be mad to try anything on a night like this."

"Or desperate," muttered Titus as he strode purposefully on.

*

As they eased through the tightly packed square and approached the gates, Allerix was reminded of his time with the Nervii. So many men and not a horse in sight. It was a strange way to wage war but one born of necessity on this occasion. He wrinkled his nose. It smelled much the same too. Sweat, fear, warriors taking a last chance to piss before the attack began. And, mixing with it all, the stink of animal fat with which they had liberally coated the hinges of the gates. He had always liked the familiar creak of the heavy wooden gates as they protested each and every move but, tonight, he hoped they had done enough for them to open without complaint. The success of their attack depended on it. That and making it across the plain unseen. He glanced skywards. The moon was slowly edging out from behind the bank of cloud that had rolled across its path, all too fleetingly casting them into shadow. Others were poised to follow in its wake but it seemed the cloak of darkness would offer only limited protection tonight. He hoped Epona was right and that, busy celebrating victory, the Romans might be a little less vigilant than usual. He greeted Epona and Epomedius as he and his father returned from their walk around the town. His father had wanted to check on the additional fires he had ordered to be burned on the walls furthest from the plain. He hoped it would lull the Romans into believing life was continuing as usual and detract attention from the fact that none of the fires on the front wall had been lit. His father had seemed in no hurry to complete the task, lingering to gaze across the rooftops of their home rather more poignantly than Allerix would have wished.

He pushed such thoughts from his mind as Epona gave him a smile and handed him one of the makeshift shields.

"I won't be there to watch over you, brother. Be careful."

He slipped the shield onto his arm and gave her a nod.

"You too. Try not to forget what I taught you."

She gave him a shove.

"If I am reliant on what you taught me, brother, I will be in trouble."

Epomedius tapped Epona on the shoulder.

"If you two are done bickering, it's time."

Allerix gave Epona a hug and watched her follow after the huge warrior as he strode purposefully toward the gates. His father gestured towards the huge body of men massing on the far side of the gatehouse: a little over half the warriors who would be joining the attack that night.

"Valis and his men await their leader. Dividing our forces is a necessary evil tonight. Our plan depends upon it. But I would not have chosen such a strategy if I did not believe there was a suitable warrior to share the burden of leadership."

His father reached for Allerix's arm and gave him a proud smile.

"Now go, my son. Let us take the fight to Rome and hope that Caesar and his gods are busy resting on their laurels."

Almost as soon as his father was lost from view amongst the throng of warriors clustered around the gates, Allerix heard the piercing blasts of the Roman horns signalling the change of watch.

The muted conversations and idle chatter of the waiting warriors quickly ceased. Now was the time to make peace with the gods and ready oneself for what was to come. Allerix offered his own silent prayer as he joined Valis on the opposite side of the gatehouse from where his father, Epona and Epomedius were waiting to lead out the men joining their attack. He returned Valis' nod of welcome and the two of them watched as the heavy oak beam barring the gate was manhandled away and quietly set down against the wall. His father waited a moment for some welcome cloud cover before giving the order for the gates to be opened. Allerix held his breath. With barely a sound, the heavy wooden gates were eased apart. One hurdle overcome. As Epomedius led the first of the warriors out onto the plain, Allerix turned his gaze towards the Roman fires he could see burning on the rampart. If anything, it looked more ominous than ever but taking it was their next hurdle and the men were waiting. He briefly clasped arms with Valis before drawing his sword and leading them into the dark.

*

With Titus grumpily leading the way, they passed quickly through the remaining checkpoints, arriving at the watch tower just as the horns signalling the change of watch began to pierce the night air. Atticus followed Titus and Julius swiftly up the ladder. He recognised the men in the tower from one of the other centuries in the cohort. They were as keen to be away as he and his friends had been earlier. And they had been just as bored too, if the handover was anything to go by. Julius smiled at Titus as he repeated what they'd heard.

"So, nothing happened at all?"

The departing legionary shook his head.

"Not a fucking thing! It's been quieter than a barrack block at Saturnalia."

Titus turned his back on Julius and stared at the walls of the town. He shook his head.

"I know they haven't got much to sing about… but have you ever known a settlement to be this quiet? I don't like it. I think the general was right to be cautious. Stay alert!"

Atticus smiled as Julius rolled his eyes but he had to admit it was eerily quiet and he couldn't help feeling slightly uneasy himself. He turned to gaze out onto the plain. Occasional shadows rolled over the landscape as scattered clouds drifted across the night sky, but he couldn't see anything else moving. Reassured that his edginess owed more to Titus' anxiety than any threat of imminent attack, he allowed his mind to wander, thinking about what might lie in store before they eventually returned home. He was dragged abruptly back to the present by Titus, frantically pulling on his arm.

"For fuck's sake, lad! I worry about you sometimes."

He relinquished his grip on Atticus' arm and pointed towards the gates.

"Have a look out there. We've lost the moon behind the clouds but I'm sure I saw something moving in the shadows."

He turned to Julius.

"And before you say it, I wasn't imagining it."

"Well, I couldn't see anything. I think you're just getting jumpy, old man."

Julius dodged Titus' attempts to cuff him on the head as they moved aside to allow Atticus the best view of the gates. Atticus shielded his eyes to block the dim but distracting light of the torches on the rampart and stared into the inky blackness. It was hopeless; he couldn't see a thing. He leant forward, allowing his eyes to adjust to the gloom.

Movement.

His heart skipped a beat.

It was only fleeting but he was sure there was something, or someone, on the plain. Surely not. He must have been mistaken. No, there it was again. And again. His heart rate quickened and his mouth suddenly felt very dry.

"Well, lad. Can you see anything?"

"Yes, I think I can... Fuck."

Titus gripped his shoulder.

"What is it?"

"The gates... they're open."

Titus slid beside him as the moon slowly began to emerge from behind the clouds.

"Are you sure? We don't want to signal the alarm and bring everybody running for nothing."

Atticus stared into the night, grateful for the watery light cast onto the plain once again. His blood ran cold. A steady stream of warriors was slipping silently out of the gates and concealing themselves in the shadows beneath the wall.

"I'm sure."

Titus gave Julius a shove.

"Jumpy old man, my arse. Get down there and start that fucking fire!"

Altogether more concerned, Julius disappeared quickly down the ladder, bellowing out a warning to the legionaries on the rampart as he went.

Atticus twisted the string of his pendant nervously as the number of warriors spilling onto the plain continued to grow. At least some of them appeared to be heading away, edging through the shadows towards the other end of the rampart. But that did little to ease his anxiety as the huge numbers that remained drew closer and closer to their position. All too familiar with the chilling battle cries that usually accompanied any advance, the eerie silence with which the warriors now approached was unsettling, and he took a deep breath to steady himself. He glanced down at the ditch and rampart, thankful that he wasn't one of those tasked with trying to take it. But, even with reinforcements so close, he wasn't sure they could hold it. There were just so many of them. This was why it didn't pay to think too much about the future. Home suddenly seemed a very long way away. He kissed the bronze figurine and slipped it beneath his tunic as Julius returned to the tower. They watched in silence as one by one the signal fires lit up along the length of the rampart. All they could do now was try to hold out long enough for help to arrive. Titus passed him a javelin and Atticus dragged his shield into position as a wave of noise rolled ominously across the plain. Alerted by the signal fires that their attack had been detected, the warriors had broken cover, all thoughts of stealth forgotten. Charging towards the rampart, their defiant roars almost drowned out the call to arms coming from the fort. As the first of the warriors arrived in the ditch beneath them, Atticus wondered whether the sound of the buccinas would be the only thing swept aside by the enemy that night.

*

Unable to communicate amidst the din, Epona waved her father on and reached for her bow. Their chaotic and noisy charge across the plain hadn't taken long but she still needed a moment to catch her breath. If she could make these arrows count, it might ease the path of the warriors tackling the fearsome climb. She'd cursed when the Roman signal fires had swept along the rampart, but now they were lighting up her targets nicely. It would be a shame not to take advantage. She pulled an arrow from the quiver slung around her waist and nocked it quickly in her bow. Steadying herself, she drew back the bowstring and sent the arrow spiralling towards the tower. Arcing unseen through the night sky, it plunged into the back of a hapless legionary who had leant just a little too far from cover in his eagerness to engage the warriors. He slid silently out of the tower and dropped to the floor, javelin still clutched firmly in his hand. She was ready with the second arrow before he had completed his fall but cursed as it slid past its intended target and thumped into the wall of the tower. The startled Roman reached quickly for his shield, but his comrade was a little slower to react and paid the price as the third of her arrows pierced his armour and sent him spinning to the floor. It probably wasn't a fatal blow but it was enough to take him out of the fight. With the surviving legionary scurrying down the ladder, there would be no further danger from that tower. Breaking into a run, she joined the mass of warriors at the foot of the imposing and already blood-soaked turf wall blocking their path.

*

Javelin poised, Atticus held his breath as the next warrior began his climb. He had already sent one man crashing back into the ditch, his still-spasming corpse unceremoniously buried by the rapidly growing pile of material deposited by the enemy to ease the path of their attack. Titus and Julius had cut short the climb of two others. But there was always another, equally determined to try and reach the defenders. He took aim again, not that he could really miss. It was almost too easy. He took no pride in killing such brave men but the rampart was all that stood between them and he had to make that advantage count. He knew the seething mass of warriors would offer him no quarter if they succeeded in breaking through. Bracing himself against the wall of the tower, he leant forward and hurled his javelin towards the warrior at the head of the climb. Plunging into his unprotected back, it sliced clean through his body and buried itself in the soft turf beneath, pinning him to the rampart like some kind of macabre offering to the gods. Two more of the scrambling warriors were sent flailing to their deaths as his friends found their targets again too. He turned as Julius tapped him on the shoulder.

"That's the last of the javelins, brother. What now?"

With no means to slow down the assault, a fresh wave of warriors would soon arrive at the top of the climb. Their comrades on the rampart were spread far too thinly to hold them off for long.

"Come on, let's go. We can't do any more here."

Titus nodded his agreement.

"Let's hope Plautius has the rest of the cohort on the move. That lot down there aren't going to forget who was dishing out the pain with the javelins."

As he waited for Julius to follow Titus down the ladder, Atticus glanced quickly to his left. Still no sign of any movement from the fort. He swallowed nervously and hurried after his friends. Landing at the foot of the ladder with a crash, he cursed and set off along the rampart. The horde of warriors looked even more fearsome from there and the first of them were about to reach the palisade.

*

Fighting for room, Epona fired off a couple of arrows at the few remaining Romans on the rampart. Already protected by their palisade and preparing for the attack behind the safety of their shields, she knew there was little chance of success but she felt so angry. With the Romans raining down missiles, the warriors leading the initial wild charge had been hopelessly exposed, and the bodies of the dead and dying formed a gruesome and wholly unwanted path for those that followed. At least the defenders seemed to have exhausted their supply of javelins, which gave some hope to the warriors now desperately trying to scale the wall. Warriors like Tascus, who she could see leading the mad scramble up the slope with several of the other smiths. All huge, they were using their strength and the fearsome axes they had adopted as their weapons of choice to propel themselves up the slope, carving out a series of ragged hand and footholds as they went. She caught her breath as one of them lost his footing and slipped a little way down the slope, sending several of those behind careering back into the ditch. It was so hard to watch them struggle but they were nearly there and, with the roars of his watching comrades encouraging him on, Tascus finally managed to reach the palisade. Hauling himself to his feet, he threw up his axe and brought it crashing down on the willow barrier separating him from the Romans. A huge swathe of the palisade crumpled beneath the blow and Tascus stepped forward to try and rip it aside. A sword flashed out from the darkness. Tascus howled in pain as the unseen Roman forced the blade deep into his chest. Tascus staggered to one side and Epona let out an angry cry as he slipped off the rampart and crashed into the ditch.

Enraged by the loss of their comrade, several of the other burly smiths hauled themselves onto the rampart. Bellowing at the Romans, one of them wrenched aside a piece of the damaged palisade and turned to call his comrades on. Waving his axe menacingly at the defenders, he disappeared from view, reappearing moments later with a pool of crimson on his tunic marking the point where a Roman blade had found its target. As he backed up, Epona could see he had tight hold of a legionary, whose blood-tipped sword had presumably been the one to inflict his wound. The soldier was desperately trying to free his arms to wield his blade once more but the powerful smith was too strong. Kicking and screaming, the legionary tried frantically to arrest their progress. With the last of his strength, the warrior let out a defiant roar and sent the pair of them cartwheeling into the ditch. If the fall hadn't killed the Roman, the posse of warriors that fell upon his body needed no encouragement to do so. Back at the top of the rampart, a legionary had hurriedly placed himself in the midst of the damaged section of palisade. Epona needed no second invitation. As the soldier turned to ward off the next warrior to complete the climb, his legs buckled beneath him as her arrow seared into his unprotected thigh. Pitched into the path of the advancing warrior, the soldier barely had time to look up before the axe sent his cleaved head spinning from his shoulders in a cascade of blood. She lowered her bow as the warrior stepped over the body and through the palisade. Several others followed him through. Epona waited anxiously but the gap in the palisade remained open and the number of warriors disappearing from view continued to grow. She could see her father and Epomedius in the midst of those still climbing. Discarding her bow, she pushed forward to begin the climb herself. They had secured a breach in the wall.

*

Atticus picked a spot and planted his shield. This would have to do. He seemed a long way from either of the two sentries he had positioned himself between but, with so few defenders on the rampart, they had little choice but to spread out and cover as much ground as they dared. He'd left Julius beneath the tower with one of the sentries and Titus was a little further to his left with two more. They'd done their best but the line was pitifully thin. He twisted his feet nervously in the dirt and braced himself for the attack. It arrived almost immediately as a tall, bare-chested warrior appeared before him. Dripping with sweat and breathing heavily from the exertion of his climb, he snarled at Atticus and stepped forward. He carried no shield but that didn't deter his advance and Atticus hurriedly thrust out his sword. It slid past the warrior as he deftly moved aside and Atticus had to hurriedly throw up his shield as the man hacked at his arm. He was forced to move even more quickly as the warrior swung again, this time at his head. But the man had overreached and, ducking beneath the blow, Atticus jabbed out his sword, sending it raking across the warrior's shoulder. With an angry cry, the man threw himself forward but Atticus met his strike and, leaning into his shield, he forced the warrior back. Off balance, he swung wildly at Atticus, who parried the blow and sent his sword plunging towards the warrior's chest. Atticus saw the look of abject terror in the man's eyes as he drove his sword home. The warrior let out a muffled cry and sank slowly to his knees. As Atticus wrenched his blade free, the man looked forlornly at his wound before closing his eyes and slumping to the floor.

Atticus wiped the warrior's blood from his hand and moved towards the edge of the rampart. Three more warriors had begun the climb beneath him. There were even greater numbers massing below Titus. Shit. They would never hold them off. He looked anxiously to his right and his heart sank as he saw the lifeless Roman body lying against the palisade, blood spilling into the dirt from the gaping neck wound that had killed him. For a moment, he thought it was Julius, but his friend was still battling away. So much so that he was oblivious to the danger behind him as a warrior eased himself through a gap in the palisade and stepped over the fallen legionary. Over the noise of battle, Atticus had no way of alerting Julius to the danger. He took a quick glance down at the warriors who were still struggling up the climb and broke into a run. Busy with his opponent, Julius still hadn't seen the warrior bearing down on him from behind. With one final effort, Atticus threw himself forward, barging into the startled warrior and sending them both cartwheeling to the floor. Arms and legs flailing, he scrambled to extricate himself from the damaged palisade and regain his footing ahead of the warrior. But the man remained prostrate, head twisted savagely to one side, his neck broken by the fall. Surprised by Atticus' sudden arrival at his feet, Julius had to react quickly to avoid an opportunistic swing from his opponent. It would be his last attack. Forced to switch his attention between two Romans, the warrior blocked Atticus' thrust but was powerless to avoid Julius' sword as it sliced through his stomach. The man backed away from the palisade and disappeared from view as he fell from the rampart. As another warrior approached the palisade, Atticus grabbed Julius' arm and pointed back along the rampart. Several warriors had almost hacked their way through the palisade and one of the sentries lay dead at Titus' feet as he and the surviving legionary desperately tried to hold off the attack.

"Leave him, brother. It's hopeless. We have to get back to Titus. It's the only chance we have of holding them off."

Julius nodded and the two of them set off, the howls of abuse from Julius' erstwhile opponent ringing in their ears. As they raced back along the rampart, he saw another Roman body hit the floor. It was Titus. He let out an angry cry, pushing himself on even harder, determined to get to those responsible and make them pay. But Titus was struggling unsteadily to his feet. He was alive. For now, at least. That wasn't the only good news. The door to the fort was open and he could see the cohort's battle standard advancing along the rampart. Help was coming and, with the number of warriors on the rampart growing ominously quickly, not a moment too soon.

*

Hauling herself over the edge of the rampart, Epona climbed slowly to her feet. She dragged her hand across her face and stooped to pick up the battered shield of a fallen warrior. One of many. Evidence of the gruesome cost paid to secure the breach. She had passed the bodies of Cottabus and Ambilo on the climb, both lying broken and contorted where they had fallen, their cold and soulless eyes cast heavenwards, as if in search of the ancestors they would now be joining. She would remember them with the happy countenance they'd worn on the day they joined the Royal Guard. But that would have to wait. Now she must focus on avenging their deaths. Drawing her sword, she hurried towards the centre of the rampart, where an older, thickset legionary was wielding his sword to some effect, leaving one warrior bleeding at his feet and creating a degree of hesitancy in the minds of the men now facing him. Epona pushed her way to the front and stepped forward. A faint smile ran across the Roman's face as he realised with surprise that his next opponent was a woman. Epona smiled. That was his first mistake. Trying to rely solely on his power and strength to overpower her was his second. She had experienced it all before and knew he would tire as she deftly drew him on. He was a big man and withstanding his attack took every ounce of her strength, but his last swing had been by far his least powerful and his breathing had become noticeably shorter. Now it was her turn. Sliding to her right to evade the legionary's latest wild swing, she thrust out her sword. Parrying the strike just in time, he took aim at her with his shield but she was already on the move, changing the point of her attack. Darting forward, she jabbed her sword at the soldier's chest, forcing him to hurriedly drop his guard and block the blow. Their swords locked. Thinking that he now had the edge, the legionary began to swing his shield towards her. That was his final mistake. Spinning quickly away, Epona freed her sword and sent it flashing in a wide arc towards the Roman's head. His eyes snapped open as her blade sliced through his neck and buried itself in his spine. He dropped to the floor wearing much the same surprised expression he had worn when the fight started.

She tugged her sword free with a satisfied smile. That was what happened when you underestimated a woman.

With the last of the Romans overwhelmed by the melee of warriors fighting beside her father and Epomedius, the short and brutal fight was over. They held the rampart, although a large contingent of Roman reinforcements was already on its way. Would they never stop? She cursed. Of course they wouldn't. They knew as well as she did that taking the rampart wasn't enough. The success of the attack depended on them holding it and pushing quickly on. These men were simply the first of many that would be thrown forward in an attempt to dislodge them. And there were so many more of them than she had expected to face. The night was going to get much bloodier yet. She rolled her shoulders to ease some of the tension and smiled as her father's impromptu speech to the men massing on the rampart ended in a huge roar and the defiant clatter of weapons and shields. If they were destined to fail, it would be for want of neither bravery nor heart. As her father returned the warriors' cheers, she noticed a dark crimson stain on his tunic. He tried to hide his grimace as he turned back to face the rapidly approaching Romans, but she saw it.

"You're hurt."

Her father placed his hand gently on her shoulder.

"It's nothing. A flesh wound I would have avoided when I was once as quick as you were today."

He saw Epomedius' raised eyebrows and smiled.

"If I ever was."

As the Roman column halted and began to form up before them, her father took hold of Epomedius' arm.

"It has been my honour to call you friend."

The two men embraced.

Her father watched Epomedius take his position at the head of the waiting group of warriors and turned to Epona.

"As your king, I fight for our nation that we may live in peace, and I am grateful to have such a fine warrior at my side. As your father, I fight for you and your brother. I am proud to do this for a daughter such as you."

He raised his sword.

"Now, let us test the resolve of these Romans."

Waving his men forward, her father let out a huge roar and broke into a run. Choking back emotion, she added her own voice to the wall of noise and joined the charge.

*

Allerix stepped forward and drove his sword into the body of the young legionary. His brave resistance would delay them no longer. As the soldier's legs began to buckle, Allerix took hold of his shoulder, pushing his blade in and searching out the man's heart. He had earned the right not to die a lingering and painful death. The legionary's eyes rolled and Allerix felt the bloody mist of the soldier's final breath on his face as he slowly withdrew his sword. He barely had time to look up before a badly injured legionary staggered into him as he tried to follow his few remaining comrades back along the rampart. Allerix brought his sorry retreat to an end and turned quickly as another figure approached. He lowered his sword; it was Valis. He greeted Allerix with a nod.

"The rampart is ours, Lord."

Allerix smiled. Valis gestured towards the small and beleaguered group of legionaries retreating back along the rampart. Supporting a clearly injured comrade and harassed at every step by a pursuing band of warriors, they were making slow progress. But they were maintaining their discipline and he could see the bodies of several warriors lying dead or dying in the wake of their brave retreat. It was hard to be sure but the tall legionary at the centre of the group reminded him of Atticus.

"Shall I send men to finish them?"

Allerix shook his head. His attention had been drawn to a far larger body of men emerging from the makeshift fort the Romans had clearly constructed to house reinforcements. He cursed.

"No. We have a bigger problem to deal with."

So, Caesar hadn't trusted them after all. He'd been right not to, of course, but what choice had he given them? They had to fight. Just as they now had no alternative but to continue the attack, despite the surprisingly large Roman presence. He and his men still had the advantage of numbers. The problem was going to be making that advantage count on the narrow rampart. Taking it had been costly enough but, with so few defenders, weight of numbers had inevitably told. Reinforced and fighting from behind their beloved shield wall, it would be a wholly different story. Allerix watched as the relief column swept past the retreating group of legionaries, brushing aside the warriors who hadn't been alert to the danger. He tapped Valis on the arm.

"Ready the men. We will attack in waves. If we can't punch through, we'll wear them down. It's the only way to take advantage of our numbers. And have some of the groups attack from the ditch. Let's try and keep them busy on two fronts."

Valis nodded and hurried off, bellowing orders as he went. Allerix turned as the relief column came to a halt before them. A ripple ran through the massed ranks of the relief column as the men parted to allow their centurion to stride purposefully through to the front rank. Plautius. Stepping into the midst of danger, just as he had at the Sabis River. Allerix had been grateful when they hadn't crossed swords that day but it seemed the gods were determined that the two of them should fight. Very well. He would give them what they wanted. Nodding to Valis, he raised his sword and launched the attack.

22

Aduatuca

Epona ducked beneath the blade and thrust her sword towards the Roman's chest. He swung his shield across his body and flashed his sword towards her head. She flinched as the strike caught the edge of her hastily raised shield, almost wrenching it from her hand. He was good, but sliding his shield that far across had presented an opening and she sprang forward. The soldier desperately dragged back his shield but not fast enough, catching Epona's arm rather than her sword. The stinging blow made her gasp with pain but it was nothing to the agonised cry of the legionary as Epona's sword sliced through the back of his arm, carving a path to the bone of his elbow and leaving the mutilated limb hanging uselessly at his side. The ashen-faced soldier relinquished the grip on his shield and jabbed out his sword forlornly as Epona advanced. Swatting it aside with her shield, Epona slashed her blade across the legionary's throat. Gasping for air that would no longer come, he slumped to the floor. Epona stepped over his body, anxious to reach the fierce fighting that lay ahead. Somewhere at the heart of the carnage was her father. With her mind focussed on reaching him, she barely had time to react as an injured warrior staggered across her path, blood flowing freely from a deep wound to his stomach. Stepping around her stricken comrade, she found herself face-to-face with a tall and wiry-looking soldier who sank back behind his shield as she turned to face him.

Isolated and precariously backed up against the edge of the rampart, the Roman and his two remaining comrades had little room for manoeuvre and even less chance of escape. But that made their dogged resistance all the more impressive. These were clearly brave and capable men, whose grim battle for survival had to be ended. She gritted her teeth. Her father would have to wait and the legionary would pay for that. Her overeager first swing sailed harmlessly above the ducking legionary's head and she chastised herself. She was going to have to be a good deal more measured than that. She slid quickly to one side as the soldier jabbed out his sword in response and chopped down a strike that raked across his arm as he hurriedly tried to withdraw behind his shield. He cursed and shook off the blood but his eyes never left her sword. As she swung again, he stepped forward, blocking the strike with his shield and forcing her to give ground. She snapped back her head as he violently pulled up the shield but the metal edge caught her a glancing blow on the temple. For a moment, the night was filled with light, before pain kicked in and her blurred opponent swam back into view. She hurriedly thrust out her sword as the legionary looked to advance. Her ears were ringing and she could feel blood trickling down her face as the two of them traded blows, but she could see more clearly again now. As the legionary drew back his sword once more, she slid forward. Punching her sword towards the soldier's chest, he dragged his shield across his body, inching back as Epona attacked again, forcing him back towards the very edge of the rampart. Before he could set himself, she threw herself forward, barging into his shield with every ounce of strength she could muster, intent on sending him crashing down the slope. Time seemed to stand still as he fought desperately to retain his balance, but she had driven him just far enough. With a look of terror in his eyes, his foot came to rest on the downward slope of the rampart. There was no way back. As gravity took hold, the soldier dropped his shield and thrust out his arm, grabbing hold of Epona's tunic. His fingers closed tightly around the fabric and she felt herself being dragged forward. With an icy dread filling her heart, she realised she was about to follow him down the slope and into the shadowy recesses that lay beyond.

*

Atticus watched the enemy backing slowly away and spat the blood from his mouth. Julius gave him a nod.

"You okay?"

Atticus grounded his shield and reached gingerly for his jaw. He was going to feel that blow later.

"I think so. I'm just grateful it wasn't a proper shield he had with him. It still fucking hurts though."

Julius laughed.

"Well, he was a big bugger. But he left looking a lot worse than you. I know the ladies love a scar but his face was a mess. I doubt he'll be back tonight."

Atticus hoped he was right. The trouble was, there were plenty more to take his place and, despite their heavy losses, the enemy's ferocious attacks kept coming. He was exhausted and he hadn't even expected to be fighting again after they'd survived the first attack. Plautius had ordered them back to the fort as he'd marched past with reinforcements. Atticus had never been so happy to see the rest of the cohort. Caesar had been right to be cautious.

Titus had been right. They might never hear the end of it, if he recovered. At least he had a chance once they'd made it back along the rampart. Atticus hadn't been sure they would. Their little group had become a beacon of hope for any man left standing, swelling their numbers as they retreated along the rampart. But they remained hopelessly outnumbered and, with injured colleagues to convey, their progress had been painfully slow. When one of their comrades had been dragged from the front line, he'd set Titus down and steeled himself for what he feared would be their last stand. Somehow, they'd managed to close ranks and hold off the band of warriors just long enough for the relief column to arrive. Sweeping past, they'd engaged the main body of the enemy almost before he and Julius had manhandled Titus to his feet. With the sounds of battle ringing in their ears, they'd trudged back along the rampart, arriving in the makeshift fort just as Titus had finally collapsed to the floor. Atticus knew what it was like to nurse a head injury and, judging from the damage to his helmet, Titus had caught quite some blow. He'd done well to stay on his feet as long as he had, and it had been a huge relief when the medical orderlies arrived to take charge of their friend.

Grateful for a moment of respite, he and Julius had slumped beside the gate, though neither of them had felt particularly comfortable watching the battle from the safety of the fort. When they'd spotted the first of the walking wounded heading in their direction, they'd dusted themselves off, collected their shields and set off back along the rampart. If they hadn't, they might have missed the front ranks of the column being shattered by the enemy's attack and Plautius' desperate attempts to hold the line together. He had succeeded. Just. But Atticus and Julius had arrived to find the cohort badly depleted and Plautius on his way back to the fort with a badly injured arm. He'd been in too much pain to raise any questions about their arrival and Rescius hadn't complained, slotting them straight into the midst of the column. Since then, the enemy had attacked repeatedly and, as the number of dead or injured had begun to mount, they'd been forced to give ground. But they hadn't broken through, and, with Plautius back once more in the front rank, they had withstood yet another assault. The centurion gave them a thin smile as he and Julius took their places alongside him at the head of the column. Atticus could see blood running down Plautius' arm from beneath his bandage. The centurion irritably shook it off as he watched the enemy begin massing for another attack. In the moment of quiet, Rescius barked out an order.

"Stand to! Looks like the bastards want another taste of Roman steel. Make sure you oblige them."

From behind his shield, Atticus watched in dismay as the warriors' leader waved them forward.

It was Allerix.

*

Allerix pulled the ragged piece of cloth tightly around his friend's head and quickly knotted the ends. He was never going to be mistaken for a healer but it would do for now. He'd hardly recognised Valis when he first appeared, his face covered in blood from the deep gash that would almost certainly cost him an eye. Valis nodded his thanks and, with a grimace, dragged what remained of his tunic sleeve across his face. He gestured towards the fighting.

"They do well to withstand our attacks."

Allerix nodded. He wasn't surprised. The Romans were nothing if not resilient. And every time their attacks had threatened to shatter the resistance of the column, Plautius had bravely rallied those around him to hold the line. Twice already that night, the two of them had clashed. He was slower than Allerix but experienced, and with all thoughts of friendship and respect cast aside – however grudgingly – the two of them had been well matched. He'd succeeded in driving the Roman away from the front ranks after their last clash, temporarily at least, forcing him to seek assistance for a badly cut arm. Yet he was at the forefront of the fighting again now, however, bloodied and bandaged. A brave and stubborn thorn in their side. One that he must try once more to dislodge. He sighed and took hold of Valis' arm.

"I'll lead the next attack. Have your men ready to follow. But you head back home."

Valis wiped away the blood seeping through his makeshift bandage and shook his head.

"Do you think Catiola will welcome me to her bed looking like this, if I leave you to fight alone?"

Allerix smiled as Valis stalked away to address his men. Gathering together his own, he turned towards the Romans and broke into a run.

*

The air was driven from Epona's lungs as she landed face down on the turf. Pitched forward, she tumbled towards the foot of the slope, arms and legs flailing as she tried, unsuccessfully, to arrest her descent. She slid to a halt, gazing up at the night sky. Shaking her head, she struggled to her knees. Everything hurt but she seemed to be in one piece. But where was the Roman? And where was her sword? Head spinning and breathing still ragged, she forced herself to her feet. Casting off the tattered remnants of her shield and trying to make sense of the gloomy surroundings, her heart jumped as she saw the glimmer of light on metal. Her sword. Wincing as she bent hurriedly to retrieve her weapon, she heard the unmistakeable sound of footsteps gathering pace behind her. He was alive. She snatched up her sword but the Roman was already upon her, charging out of the dark and driving her to the ground. Landing in a heap, her elbow struck the floor and she felt her sword slipping agonisingly from her grasp. Pinned beneath the legionary, she thrashed and kicked in a desperate attempt to break free. It was no use. She steeled herself for the fatal blow but it didn't come. The soldier was fumbling for his dagger; he'd lost his sword too. There was still hope. She balled her fist and swung up her arm, catching him square on the jaw. His head snapped back and he lurched to the side but she couldn't shake him off. Wrenching his dagger free, the legionary thrust it towards her chest with a snarl. She threw up her arm to block the blow, her other hand frantically sweeping the turf in a desperate attempt to locate her sword. Was that leather? Her quiver! And there were still arrows in it. She fumbled for the opening, hooking her fingers around one of the feathered flights. She began to slide it free.

With a look of grim determination, the soldier leant forward. Beads of sweat gathered on her face as the pressure on her arm began to increase as it was slowly, haltingly, forced back towards her chest.

If she could just reach the arrow's shaft…

The legionary grunted and pushed again. His face so close she could feel the heat from his short, laboured breath. The stale odour of his sweat-soiled tunic filled her nostrils. The blade pierced her tunic.

Got it.

Just as the dagger began to draw blood, she wrenched the arrow free and drove the metal tip into the soldier's neck. She felt his whole body tense, and all pressure on the dagger ceased. Epona turned her head as the legionary's blood began to spill onto her face and tunic. He pawed half-heartedly at the arrow before his eyes rolled and he slumped forward. Scrambling to free herself, Epona lay shaking as she struggled to catch her breath. She rolled slowly to one side and vomited into the grass. She had never come quite so close to death before. Dragging the back of her hand across her face, Epona climbed unsteadily to her feet. Above, the battle raged on, her comrades so close, yet, in the moments of her desperate struggle for life, so far away. Taking a deep breath, she began her climb back up the rampart.

*

Allerix swung his sword towards Plautius' head. Unflustered, the experienced Roman slid back, raised his shield to block the blow and thrust out his sword. Allerix span to his right and watched the centurion's blade pass harmlessly by. He chopped his sword at the Roman's hand. Plautius dropped his arm and Allerix's sword continued its downward trajectory, throwing him off balance as the centurion thrust out his shield. Forced back, Allerix had to react quickly as Plautius advanced. The Roman blocked his wild swing and attacked again. Allerix threw up his shield but could only deflect the blow and the Roman's sword raked agonisingly across his chest. Trying to ignore the pain searing through his body, Allerix scrambled to his left as the centurion swung again. As Plautius turned after him, Allerix stepped forward, determined to prise the initiative away from the Roman. Forced to check his stride, Plautius jabbed out his sword as Allerix closed the gap between them. Skirting around the blade, Allerix swept his sword forward, slashing the centurion's arm for the second time that night. Plautius threw back his head and roared in pain, hurriedly thrusting out his shield as Allerix attacked again. The centurion bravely weathered his energy-sapping assault but Allerix could see that the Roman's defensive efforts were beginning to take their toll. Losing blood heavily, Plautius could barely manage a strike in anger. As Allerix pressed forward, the centurion staggered, his face racked with pain. The Roman grounded his shield, taking a firm hold of its edge as he desperately tried to steady himself. Allerix advanced. With a grimace, Plautius pulled himself upright and defiantly beckoned him on. Killing him was a necessary evil but that wouldn't make it any easier. As he swatted Plautius' wavering sword arm aside, the centurion swayed unsteadily before his legs buckled and he sank to the floor in a crumpled heap beside his shield. Standing over the stricken Roman, Allerix raised his sword. He met the Roman's gaze. Cursing the gods for the demands they made of men, he reluctantly drove down his sword. Allerix recoiled in shock as another blade struck his, painfully deflecting it away from the stricken centurion. Turning quickly, he hurriedly raised his shield and locked eyes with the soldier responsible.

Atticus.

*

The startled warrior lowered his sword as he recognised the diminutive figure emerging from the gloom. Epona reached gratefully for his outstretched hand and scrambled back onto the rampart. Despite the rapidly rising number of casualties, neither side appeared to have made much headway. If anything, the Romans looked to have consolidated their position. Time was running out and they were losing too many warriors. She would be no help standing there. Wiping away the blood from her face, she broke into a run. As she approached the tight press of men, Epomedius emerged from the scrimmage carrying an injured warrior. The huge warrior turned and her heart sank as she caught sight of the blood-soaked face beneath her father's distinctive and now badly damaged helmet. Fighting back her tears, she reached out to touch his face. He stirred but, barely conscious, there was no hint of recognition in his glazed and distant eyes. Gently laying her father down, Epomedius beckoned across another warrior, before giving her shoulder a squeeze.

"We must get him home. He is strong. You must be too."

He nodded towards her blood-soaked tunic.

"You are hurt?"

She shook her head.

"No. It belongs to the Roman who prevented me being at Father's side."

Epomedius took hold of her face.

"Then he paid appropriately and you could have done nothing to avert the blow. None of us could. But you can make a difference now. Let the men see that you live. Rally them to fight on whilst there is still hope. However small."

She nodded and he relaxed his grip, giving her a reassuring smile.

"Here, you will need this."

As he eased his battered shield onto her arm, she took one final look at her father and angrily began to try and push her way towards the front of the fighting. It was bad enough that the Romans had seized their lands; had they now stolen her father from her too? Recognising one of the huge warriors ahead of her, she grabbed his arm.

"Ebrus, you big ox! Must I really wait for the Romans to reach me?"

With the smiling warrior taking the lead, she bumped and bored her way through the crowded press of men. She thought she sensed a renewed enthusiasm as she passed through their ranks, lifting the spirits of the weary warriors. Having a member of the royal family fighting alongside was always good for morale, even if it wasn't their king. She hoped her reputation as a warrior was helpful too. When the fighting was this savage, even the slightest edge could make all the difference. And as they arrived at the heart of the fighting, the full scale of the carnage became clear. Slick with the blood and guts of the dead and dying, the rampart was littered with bodies, slowly being trampled into the ground as men of both sides fought on or over their fallen comrades, desperate to reach those still living. A desperation she shared. One of these men had injured her father and, for that, they would all pay. Easing herself between the warriors in the front line, she glared at the Roman standing before her. He nervously jabbed out his sword. Raising her shield, she smiled and threw herself forward.

*

Atticus cursed as Allerix's sword thudded painfully into his shoulder. Grateful for the protection of his armour, he still had to fight to retain the grip on his sword as waves of pain ran through his arm. Desperate to shake some life into it, he slid back warily behind his shield. Allerix swung again. Hurriedly pulling his shield across to block the blow, Atticus grimaced as the clash numbed his fingers once more. He instinctively thrust out his sword as Allerix looked to follow up and had to lean back quickly to escape the swing of Allerix's shield as it whistled past his chest. Enough. He wasn't going to let Allerix dictate the fight any longer. Gritting his teeth, he leapt forward, driving Allerix back beneath a cascade of blows. As he neared the edge of the rampart, Allerix threw out his sword and scrambled to escape the drop. Closing on him quickly, Atticus swept Allerix's blade aside and thrust out his sword. It punched through the wicker shield, drawing an angry cry from Allerix as the blade gashed his arm and then his chest as it plunged forward. Allerix dragged his shield back, almost wrenching the sword from Atticus' hand. Breathing heavily and with blood from his wound rapidly colouring his tunic, Allerix began to back up. Anxious to draw breath himself, Atticus was equally grateful for a pause in hostilities and the two men cautiously circled one another. Atticus had no idea how long the battle had been raging. He only knew he was tired and that he probably looked every bit as dreadful as Allerix. But he had already defeated Plautius, and, if Allerix shared any of Atticus' qualms about fighting somebody he had regarded as a friend, it wasn't holding him back. He couldn't expect anything else. He had no idea why they had decided to attack but, having done so, victory was the only way they could avoid the consequences of breaking the peace. He shuddered to think what those might be. Atticus sighed. This was no place for personal sentiment. A view clearly shared by Allerix as he suddenly sprang forward, sword aloft. Atticus threw up his shield, deflecting the blade harmlessly aside, and swung at Allerix's head. Allerix ducked beneath the blade and brought down his sword. Atticus met it with his and the power behind the blow almost dragged him off his feet. As Allerix slid his sword free, he drove his shield towards Atticus' chest. The wooden shield splintered as it crashed into his body and Atticus gasped as he desperately and painfully fought for air. He sought sanctuary behind his shield.

Beyond the fort, at the other end of the rampart, Atticus could see that the second breach appeared to have been contained, although at some cost, judging by the depleted ranks holding the Roman line. And finally help was on its way! A whole legion, from the main camp. He hoped whoever was leading the warriors at that end was smart enough to recognise this was a fight they couldn't win. There was still time for them to save themselves and withdraw. There had been enough slaughter for one night. But, if anything, the bleak situation at the other end of the rampart seemed only to strengthen Allerix's resolve and he pressed forward once more. Atticus slid back and dragged his shield across his body as Allerix thrust out his sword. Stepping to his right to avoid Allerix's follow-up strike, Atticus sprang forward, forcing the warrior to hurriedly throw up his shield. Pushing forward, Atticus swung again. As Allerix was driven back, he trod on the upturned shield of a dead legionary. Thrown off balance, he stumbled, catching his foot on the legionary's body. Pitched back, he threw up his hands in a desperate attempt to retain his footing but it was no use. With a look of dread on his face, Allerix crashed to the floor.

*

Epona stepped over the body of the hapless young legionary as a stocky and grizzled-looking soldier moved to fill the gap she had created in the Roman line. They were wearing the Romans down. Slowly. Too slowly. The veteran soldier slowly looked her up and down. Clearly unimpressed, he slid forward and jabbed out his sword. Easing to her right, she parried the strike with her shield and slashed at his arm. He threw up his shield and the two of them exchanged blows as they each probed for a weakness. He fought with a confidence born of experience, but his style was ragged and, like most of the Romans, limited in scope. That was her chance. Pressing forward, she hacked down at his head, forcing him to hurriedly raise his shield. He thrust out his sword as she moved quickly to her left but she swept it aside, opening up the chance to strike again. He dragged his shield across just in time to block the blow and stepped back as she raised her sword high into the air once more. The legionary threw up his shield as she leapt forward. As he did, she dropped to one knee and drove her sword into his groin. The soldier let out an agonised shriek and dropped his sword. Staggering to one side, he looked helplessly at the blood pooling at his feet before his legs buckled and he collapsed to the floor. Epona ran her sword across the Roman's throat and cast her eyes across the rampart. The Romans had begun to back slowly away, chased enthusiastically by Ebrus, whose cleaving of a young legionary almost in two might have been instrumental in temporarily weakening the Romans' resolve. She wiped the sweat from her brow. They were only withdrawing to regroup, however, and she called him back. He grudgingly returned to the line, kicking aside the body of the veteran soldier she had killed. For the first time that night she was grateful that Allerix was fighting elsewhere. Had he seen her use the signature move he had delighted in showing her as they grew up, she would never live it down. In the relative quiet of the moment, she allowed herself a little smile.

The moment was short-lived. The Romans were on the move again. Calling the men together, Epona thought she heard the sound of a signal horn cutting through the night. She must have been mistaken. No. There it was again. Taking a deep breath, she tilted her head. Above the noise of the marching Romans and the restless warriors at her side, it was hard to hear anything, but this time she was sure. And it sounded as if it was coming from behind. With a rising sense of panic, she thrust a warrior into the front rank beside Ebrus and began to force her way towards the rear of the crowd. A palpable sense of unease had begun to spread through the horde of warriors and she could see more and more of those in the rear ranks craning their necks behind them. Pushing through the last of them and out onto the clear rampart, her worst fears were confirmed. A large relief column was snaking along the rampart, presumably from the main Roman camp. Her heart sank. One force of Romans they could defeat, but two? Her men were brave and she knew that they would willingly fight and die by her side if that was what she ordered. But death would surely now come. For them all. There were just too many of them. Every fibre of her being yearned to stay and fight. She had no desire to live under the heel of Rome, and how much worse might that be now they had tried to make a fool of Caesar? Yet running from the Romans would dishonour her nation. No. That dishonour lay with those who had chosen to cower behind their walls and not fight at all. And they could only drive the Romans from their lands if they lived. So she could honour her vow tonight, taking as many Romans with her as possible to the afterlife but in the knowledge enough of them would survive to cast a permanent shadow across their lands. Or she could choose to live and nurture her hatred of Caesar and his legions through whatever came next, waiting for the opportunity to rise up and strike once more. Her father had once told her that being brave was not merely about being willing to fight; sometimes the hardest thing was taking an alternative path for the greater good. He wouldn't needlessly sacrifice men and neither would she. She kicked the ground in frustration and let out an angry cry. With a sigh, she turned and gave the order to return to the settlement. It was over. Tonight. But she would never forget this moment. Her battle with Rome had only just begun.

*

Atticus leapt forward as Allerix scrambled to get to his feet. The warrior made it to his knees before Atticus drove him back down to the ground with a swing of his shield. Allerix looked up at him forlornly and closed his eyes. Atticus raised his sword. From the corner of his eye, he caught sight of movement on the plains below. The warriors from the far end of the rampart were flooding back towards the town. He didn't know if he could actually have killed Allerix but now he might not have to find out. He cautiously picked up Allerix's sword and gave the warrior a kick. Allerix's eyes snapped open and Atticus gestured for him to climb to his feet. Seeing the look of confusion on Allerix's face, he pointed to the exodus of warriors on the plain below. Allerix looked warily behind him and his shoulders dropped. He turned back to Atticus and a look of surprise ran across his face as Atticus offered him his sword.

"We have fought as enemies tonight but I cannot forget that you have ridden to my aid as an ally, as a friend. Go. Take your men with you. There is no need for further blood to be spilled tonight."

Allerix took the sword from his hand and Atticus returned the nod of gratitude as he stepped carefully away. Allerix turned and called across the rampart to his men. Slowly, the warriors began to disengage, funnelling back down the rampart and onto the plain. It was over. Atticus reached for his pendant, offering a silent prayer to the gods. Below the horizon, the soft light of the dawn sun heralded the start of another day. Atticus shuddered. His whole body ached and he suddenly felt very, very tired. He watched Allerix following the last of his men back into the settlement as the gates shut. He sighed, wondering how those inside must be feeling and what fate the new day would bring. He dragged up his shield and wearily trudged back towards the Roman lines. He looked up as Rescius called out his name.

"Capito! Are you trying to make my life difficult? You know our legate believes the only good Barbarian is a dead one. How am I supposed to explain this?"

Atticus looked down at the floor.

"I... I know... but it's different with him..."

Rescius reached for his shoulder and gave him a smile.

"I know, lad. You're not the only one who owes him a debt. Just as well I saw the two of you fighting right up until the moment the enemy was driven back."

He gave Atticus a wink.

"Best not make a habit of it, though, lad. And let's not tell Plautius until he's feeling better!"

23

Aduatuca

Epona hurried down the steps from the wall above the gates. Allerix had shepherded the last of his battered and bloodied warriors into the settlement and she needed to get him to their father. She waited impatiently at the foot of the tower as the lines of men trooped dejectedly past, their morose expressions and slumped shoulders mirroring those she had led back shortly before. She watched them head towards the square, where family members had gathered anxiously awaiting the return of their loved ones. For many, the wait would be in vain, and anguished cries began to punctuate the night air as word of the fallen began to spread. Even the celebrations of those fortunate enough to be reunited seemed strangely muted. How could it be otherwise, when so many of their kin lay dead? And with the Romans battered but not broken, all those that lived faced an uncertain future. Allerix sank to his haunches as the gates slammed shut. Epona hurried over to join him. He looked drained but he returned her smile as she arrived, and climbed wearily to his feet. He was as blood-covered as she was, but, unlike her, much of it appeared to be his own. They shared an embrace.

"It is good to see you, brother, but you are hurt."

He grimaced.

"I have been better, sister, but I will live."

He pointed to the deep crimson hue of her tunic.

"Roman."

She touched the bruise forming above her black and closing eye.

"This, however, is mine. A reminder from the gods that the line between life and death is narrow. I'm fine. But Father is hurt and it doesn't look good. He's with Mother and Senila, the healer. Come, we need to go."

Their journey across the crowded square took time, as they stopped repeatedly to acknowledge those who had returned and to commiserate with the families of those who had not. And there were so many more of the latter. It was hard not to feel as if some of the vibrant heart of the nation had died along with the fallen. Despite the inner turmoil she was sure he must be experiencing, Allerix somehow managed to remain positive. A calm and reassuring presence amidst the tumult of emotion. He looked every inch the king she feared he might soon have to become. They had so nearly lost him as well. She had seen his tussle with the legionary as she headed back across the plain, almost not daring to watch as the fierce fight unfolded. She had wanted to run and help but knew that would have been a futile gesture. And then he had fallen. Horrified but unwilling to dishonour her brother by tearing her eyes away, she had steeled herself for what she knew must come. In utter disbelief, she had watched the legionary spare her brother and save her the pain of losing him. As they finally left the square, she was determined to find out why.

"I saw you fall on the rampart. Why did the Roman let you live?"

"I fought with him at Vesontio. Our paths crossed both on the battlefield and off. Under different circumstances, I think you'd like him. He is a good man, a friend."

Epona shook her head.

"I'm grateful to have you here, brother, and must accept I owe this man a debt for making it so, but he is still Roman."

Allerix shrugged.

"They are not all bad. Some of them have no more desire to fight us than we do them. It is their leaders' and Caesar's thirst for power that bring us to this."

He sighed and for a while they walked on in silence. Away from the square, it was unnervingly quiet, the usually bustling homes shuttered and devoid of any of the usual signs of life. The people were afraid, worried about what was to come. It was a concern she shared.

"Do you believe the Romans will be lenient?"

Allerix took a moment to gather his thoughts.

"Caesar wishes the world to see him as wise and just. He did offer clemency to the Suessiones and Bellovaci, although they chose not to fight, and I have seen the other side of the man. Someone who condones the killing of his foes long after the battle is won and slaughters men, women and children because it serves his purpose. He may take account of our support for him at Vesontio but there will be others seeking to influence him who are not disposed to think of us so favourably."

Epona could see the first signs of dawn beginning to break as they reached the hall. They would not have to wait long to discover their fate. She pulled open the door and ducked inside. News of their father's fate would come much sooner.

Shadows danced around the walls as the draft from the door excited the last remnants of the fire burning unattended in the centre of the room. Ordinarily, she would have found the warm welcome of the hall comforting, but tonight the waning intensity of the flames matched her sombre mood. Aside from Epomedius and the small group of warriors he was directing to join the watch on the walls, the hall was empty. He looked every one of his advancing years now that the emotion of battle had ebbed away, although he had clearly been busy, keeping the men occupied, organising the defence of the city, and she knew they were lucky to have him. Her father had chosen his hand well. He sent the warriors on their way and hurried over, greeting them with a bow of his head and a thin smile.

"Come, I will take you to your father."

He turned and led them quickly across the hall. Something about his countenance troubled Allerix.

"It is bad?"

Epomedius nodded gravely.

"It is a nasty head wound, Lord. I am no healer but I have seen enough men with such injuries lose their fight for life. I fear the worst."

Epona exchanged an anxious glance with Allerix as they followed Epomedius into the corridor leading to their parents' chamber.

"How did it happen?"

"At the head of the fighting, as you would expect of your father. We were surrounded. We managed to break free but during our escape he was hit. I'm sorry."

Epona reached for his arm. She knew he would be suffering almost as much as them.

"He is with Senila. If anybody can keep him in this world, it is her, and he owes that chance to you."

He dipped his head.

"Thank you. I just wish we hadn't lost so many others."

She nodded.

"Do we know how many?"

"Not yet but I would think around about half."

Her heart sank… 4,000 men, in just one night… She knew their deaths would be weighing as heavily on her brother and Epomedius as they were her.

"We have paid a high price but the Romans will be licking their wounds too, and you know the men would rather have fought and died than live with the dishonour of not having fought at all."

Epomedius flashed her a brief smile as he nudged open the door of her parents' chamber and slipped inside. She reached for her brother's arm.

"And when Caesar comes knocking tomorrow to extract a further price for our defeat, he will know the bravery of our people and their leader, and that must count for something."

Allerix smiled.

"It will count for something, sister, I am sure, but whether it is to our benefit or not, only Caesar and the gods will know."

The door opened and Senila followed Epomedius into the hallway. She looked pained.

"Your father asks for you. I have done everything I can but I fear that the pull of our ancestors is too strong for him to resist."

She gestured towards Epomedius.

"If you need me, I will be nearby, looking after my husband, who thinks he can hide his injuries from me. I have left something for your mother in case she needs it. Be strong for each other."

The room felt warm as they entered. Epona thought she could smell elder and marigold amidst the heady mix of scents that floated on the heavy air. Wisps of smoke swirled about their heads, transported by the oil burners and candles filling the room. Her father lay beneath a pile of furs on his low wooden bed, his head covered with a fresh poultice. The evidence of previous unsuccessful attempts to stem the bleeding lay piled in the corner. He looked peaceful but very pale and his breathing was shallow. Her mother was perched on the edge of the bed, gently stroking her father's hand. She wiped away a tear and rose to give them both a hug.

"I was afraid that you might have been lost too."

Allerix gave Epona a look, willing her to keep his brush with death to herself. Epona squeezed her mother's hand.

"We wear no scars that will not heal. What of Father?"

Olluna stifled a sob.

"He drifts in and out of sleep, each time awake shorter than the last. I am scared that he will soon sleep for the final time."

Allerix reached for their mother's hand and gestured towards their father.

"Not yet."

Olluna hurried over to deter their father from continuing his laboured efforts to raise himself. He wisely gave up on the struggle and waved them over. He gratefully took a drink from the beaker offered by Olluna. He beckoned her forward and whispered in her ear. She relinquished her grip on his hand and reached into the folds of her dress, pulling out Albiorix's pendant. Olluna beckoned Allerix forward and slowly pressed the bronze figurine into his hand.

"He wants you to have this. Keep it safe, a link with your father and the gods."

Albiorix weakly raised his hand as Allerix started to protest.

"It is yours, son. We both know that I will soon have no further need for its protection."

Epona choked back a sob; he sounded so quiet and frail.

Albiorix closed his eyes, resting for a moment before gratefully taking another drink and continuing.

"It witnessed the rise of our nation. It need not see its demise. Do what you must to protect our people. Settlements may be lost but a nation can never truly fall as long as its people live."

He laid back his head, clearly battling to keep his eyes open. He smiled at Epona.

"Remember what I said on the rampart. Look after your brother."

He looked up at Olluna and gave her hand a squeeze. She gave him a long and lingering kiss. His hand slipped from hers and he was gone. Her mother straightened up and, searching for Albiorix's hand once more, began to weep. Epona felt tears slowly running down her own face as she walked over to console her mother. Allerix embraced them both before kneeling to close their father's eyes. Tears streaming down her face, Olluna reached for her husband's sword, propped up against the end of the bed. She offered it to Allerix.

"This belongs to the king."

Acknowledging Allerix's hesitance to accept the blade, Olluna curled his fingers around the hilt and kissed him on the cheek.

"I am so very proud of you."

She waved Epona over and the three embraced.

"Now. I should like a few moments alone with your father."

Allerix nodded and headed towards the door. As Epona turned to follow, Olluna called her back. She slipped her silver horse brooch into Epona's hand.

"Mother?"

"A gift from your father but I have memories enough. Take it; may it watch over you as it did me!"

She pulled Epona close.

"Holding the sword is one thing but it is nothing without the wisdom to accept wise counsel. Your father knew that and Allerix does too. He will need it now more than ever. I'm glad that you will be there for him. He is lucky to have you. We were lucky to have you. Always remember that.

She kissed Epona and returned to sit beside Albiorix.

"Goodbye, my daughter."

Wiping away a tear, Epona quickly left the room, closing the door behind her.

Epona stood for a moment with her back to the door, allowing her mind to settle. She could hear her mother crying and talking quietly to her father. They had been together for so long and ruled so well together; she could only imagine how hard it must be for her now. With the Romans sure to exert their power, it was going to be difficult adjusting to life without him. For all of them, not least Allerix. He was stood a little way down the corridor, leaning against the wall, still staring at the sword as if he might somehow spirit it away and undo all that had just happened. He looked exhausted and his tunic was even more matted with blood than earlier as his wounds continued to weep.

"You had best get Senila to have a look at you when she is done with Epomedius, if you don't want to suffer later."

He nodded; she thought she saw him shiver as he slowly straightened up. He was being typically stoic and she might have put it down to the relative cool of the corridor, if his red and bloodshot eyes didn't suggest otherwise. She put her arms around him. He smiled.

"Let's go and find Senila and Epomedius."

They set off back towards the hall.

"What did Mother say to you?"

She gave him a gentle push.

"Nothing that I care to share with you! But I'm worried for her…"

She paused. Her mind was racing and so was her heart. Why had her mother bid her farewell so finally? What had Senila left her? Allerix looked at her quizzically.

"What is it?"

Epona turned back.

"She said goodbye."

As she started towards the door, she heard the sound of breaking glass from within the room. Afraid her worst fears were about to be confirmed, she cried out.

"Mother!"

Practically knocking the door off its hinges as she barged through, she faltered and sank to her knees as she saw the remaining contents of the broken bottle at her mother's feet, spilling slowly onto the floor. Perched on the bed, her head resting on Albiorix's chest and her arms draped over his body, her mother could almost be asleep. A tear ran down Epona's face and dropped onto her tunic. She wiped away another and looked up at Allerix as she felt his hand on her shoulder. He squeezed it gently and she climbed slowly to her feet. She would take comfort from the fact that her mother had chosen when and how she would leave this world and that her parents would soon be reunited once more. Destined to be together in life, they would fittingly also now accompany each other on the journey to join their ancestors. She turned as Epomedius burst into the room.

"I heard a cry!"

Quickly surveying the scene, he dropped his head.

"I am sorry."

Allerix placed his hand on Epomedius' shoulder.

"They go safe in the knowledge that there are trusted friends left behind to watch over us."

Epomedius raised his head.

"Thank you, Lord. I will…"

He stopped himself and slowly lowered himself to one knee.

"Forgive me."

He freed his sword and laid it at Allerix's feet.

"My sword is your sword, my King."

Following suit, Epona knelt and offered Allerix her sword too. He gestured for them both to rise.

"Do not get a taste for it, brother. I am still older and wiser than you."

Allerix returned her smile.

"With the Romans at the gate, I doubt there will be any need for you to get used to it, sister. I do not think my reign will be anything other than very short-lived."

She took hold of his hand.

"I don't know what the future holds but I am sure our battles with Caesar do not end here. Remember what Father said: our nation lives as long as our people do. I believe you were saved for a reason, brother. What better reason could there be than helping ensure our people survive and our nation continues? Starting tomorrow.

*

Epomedius nodded that all was ready, and Allerix gave the order for the gates to be opened. He raised his hand to shield his eyes as the early morning sun spilled through the slowly opening gap before him. It had been a long and difficult night and the warmth of the sun was comforting. Unlike the view. Aligned on the plain before him, he could see the full might of Caesar's legions. They had arrived just after dawn. A show of strength, no doubt intended to deter any further attacks and reinforce Rome's superiority. But the siege towers were conspicuous by their absence, suggesting that Caesar was at least willing to consider ending this without further mass bloodshed. Allerix had confirmed his willingness to talk when he'd sent his envoy to Caesar earlier that morning. And so here they were. Epomedius, Epona and the few surviving members of his Royal Guard, about to join him on the ride to surrender to Caesar. Not the first act any king would wish to endure. But endure it he must and with some success too, if he was to save his people. *If.* He felt more apprehensive now than he had last night, when they had slipped out of these very same gates to battle the Romans. When, even outnumbered and fighting on the enemy's terms, they had taken the fight to Rome. Then he had retained some level of control over the course of events. This would be very different. Now it was Caesar who exercised control and they both knew it. How he would choose to exercise his advantage was now all that mattered. Allerix had briefed all those with him that he was prepared to lay down his own life, if that would appease Caesar and deter him from wreaking bloody havoc on the rest of the population. They had grudgingly sworn not to resist should that eventuality come to pass. Of course, after their earlier deceit, it was entirely possible that Caesar might slaughter them all as soon as they arrived. There was only one way to find out. He nudged Isarno forward and they edged out onto the plain.

Allerix wrestled to rein Isarno in as they approached the Roman delegation. His mount had not enjoyed his enforced confinement any more than the people, and, desperate to run free, he had almost pulled Allerix's arms from their sockets as he fought to control their progress. He would like nothing better than to meet Caesar at the gallop and maybe one day they might, but for now he was intent on trying to maintain an image of dignity and composure. Much like that cultivated by Caesar. Sitting astride his white horse, bedecked in his gold armour and flanked by a retinue of highly polished officers, he looked more like a king than a general. A reflection of his future aspirations, perhaps? Would their defeat really mark the end of his campaign of conquest? Or was he intent on ruling all of Gaul, maybe even Rome herself? And how many nations would face subjugation to advance his aspirations? He sighed, painfully aware that he was about to add the peoples of the Aduatuci to that growing list of nations. He nudged Isarno forward and came to a halt directly opposite Caesar. He ran his eyes quickly along the line of officers. Most he didn't recognise but he knew the two men flanking Caesar: Trebonius and Aquila, the latter sporting a self-satisfied and contemptuous smile, doubtless thinking back to their last encounter and his threat to meet Allerix with a legion at his back. He'd been right, of course, although they offered him no protection here, and he was sorely tempted to try and wipe the sneer off his face permanently. Isarno jinked his head and Allerix realised that he had been bunching his hands ever tighter about his reins. He relaxed his grip and returned his attention to Caesar.

"I am Allerix, newly crowned King of the Aduatuci."

Caesar nodded and ran an appraising eye over him, as if trying to place a vaguely familiar face.

"And who put you in charge of these people?"

Allerix tightened his grip on Isarno's reins once more.

"You did. When your legions killed my father."

Caesar sniffed.

"Your father killed himself when he dishonoured the terms of our truce."

"The terms of the truce dishonoured us. We rode as your allies. We had no quarrel with Rome until you chose to attack our lands and our way of life. Would you have bent the knee so readily, if asked to do so on the terms you required of us?"

Aquila leant forward and jabbed his finger at Allerix.

"It would pay you to show some respect, Barbarian! Why are you not already kneeling before your ruler?" Allerix glared at Aquila.

"I kneel to no one until our business is concluded and I know the fate of my people. And you would do well not to test my patience again, Roman."

Caesar raised his hands.

"Enough."

He looked Allerix up and down once more.

"You rode with me at Vesontio. I thought I recognised you."

Allerix nodded.

"And against you at the river."

Caesar smiled.

"I remember. And bravely too from what I recall... both times."

He nodded towards Epona.

"And I assume this must be the white-haired she-wolf my men talk so animatedly about in camp this morning?"

Allerix had asked that he alone address the Romans but he had learnt a long time ago not to speak for his sister and he gave her an encouraging smile.

"I am Epona, warrior and princess of the Aduatuci, sister of Allerix. Given the origins of your city, I will take comparison with a wolf as a compliment."

Caesar nodded respectfully.

"I believe it was intended as such. It takes a lot to unnerve soldiers of the legion."

He turned back to Allerix.

"It was a mistake to attack us but you know that already. We were prepared for you and held all the advantages of position. Yet you came anyway and thousands died needlessly as a result. But were our roles reversed, I too may have fought. Your people showed great courage and character, traits that I value and admire above all others. They do your nation great credit. I am almost inclined to overlook the fact that you reneged on the terms of an agreed surrender to launch your attack. But we both know that I cannot do that. What message would that send to those nations who have submitted themselves compliantly into Rome's protection?"

He paused to gesture to his delegation.

"My officers are divided on the course of action they believe

I should adopt. Some favour clemency. Others, that we raze your home to the ground and kill all that reside within. A lesson to those who have yet to be convinced of the power of Rome."

Allerix imagined at which end of the spectrum Aquila had cast his vote. He gestured towards the settlement, suddenly very grateful that he had arranged for a large number of the inhabitants to be armed and positioned on the walls, in the hope that it might convey a misleading impression about the remaining strength of his warrior caste.

"You have referred to the bravery of my people. How much greater will that be if my men are tasked with protecting the walls of our home? You will ultimately succeed in taking the settlement, I am sure. I am more familiar than most with the capabilities of Rome but it will come at great cost to your legions, as you already know. I am willing to lay down my own life if blood must be spilled to satisfy the honour of Rome. But I have no wish for further bloodshed and I do not believe that you do either. Besides, great power is not defeating those over whom you hold superiority. That is the way of tyrants. Great leaders create a legacy by having the power to act but choosing not to."

Caesar stared at Allerix for a moment and then slowly nodded.

"I am content that honour would permit me to extract full retribution for the deceptions perpetrated by your people. But you advocate well on their behalf and I am not minded to condemn any more here to death. I cannot permit your people to escape punishment but I can allow them to live. But that is up to you. I will stand down my legions on the condition that your people are delivered to me, for sale into slavery. If I must order my men forward, it will be with the instruction that all those who shelter within your walls perish. Do we understand one another?"

Allerix nodded gravely. His warriors may prefer death to

a life of servitude, but giving them that chance would subject the rest of his people, the women and children, to the kind of atrocities he had witnessed at Vesontio. He would do whatever he must to spare his people such a terrible fate. He shifted in his saddle and began to ease himself to the ground.

Caesar held up his hand.

"Your word is enough."

Denied the opportunity to see Allerix kneel before him, Aquila's face was a picture.

"I accept your terms. I surrender my people to you."

Caesar nodded.

"I will grant you four hours to prepare your people. I need not reiterate what the consequences will be if they do not come willingly."

Allerix smiled.

"Your men would do well to treat them with respect if they wish to avoid trouble. But they will not seek confrontation."

It was Caesar's turn to smile.

"I think my men will be wary enough after last night, but you have my word that your people will receive no ill treatment from the soldiers of Rome."

Allerix nodded and stifled a smile as he caught sight of the look of indignation on Aquila's face. Caesar turned his horse.

"Very well. Then we are agreed. I will have my legates arrange the details ahead of the appointed hour."

Trebonius and Aquila joined Allerix as he watched Caesar return to camp. Trebonius greeted him with a nod of respect and a smile.

"Well played. The plea to his vanity was an especially nice touch. I really thought he would look to sack the city."

A view clearly shared by Aquila, who was practically foaming at the mouth.

"Your weasel words may land like honey in Caesar's ears but

they do not wash with me! Death, not slavery, is the fate your people deserved."

Allerix leant forward.

"Hunting the women and children as you did at Vesontio, Roman? It is funny… I do not recall seeing you on the battlefield when it was warriors you might expect to encounter."

Aquila lunged at Allerix. He leant back in the saddle and allowed the blow to pass harmlessly. Aquila turned as Trebonius took a firm hold of his arm, to prevent his trying again.

"Lucius, remember the men are watching. We have an agreement. Do you think Caesar will take kindly to you breaking the terms already?"

Aquila shook his hand free and jabbed it animatedly at Allerix.

"Do not think we are done yet, Barbarian! It matters not whether I was or wasn't on the battlefield. My legion was and they led the resistance to your attack. They have earned much credit for that, credit that I will now use to claim you and your witch of a sister for my own."

"Then you would do well to watch your back, Roman. I do not think keeping your enemies close would be a good strategy for you to adopt."

Aquila laughed.

"I have no use for your worthless hides but my brother-in-law seems to get through slaves very quickly on his estate."

He looked menacingly at Epona.

"He will especially enjoy looking after her. I could not persuade Gaius to rid himself of the woman you returned at Vesontio, but this one will serve as adequate compensation."

Allerix nudged Isarno in front of Epona's horse as she moved forward to challenge Aquila. She glared at the Roman.

"He'd best not touch me with anything he isn't prepared to lose."

Aquila smirked.

"Fine words, vixen, but you will find such spirit serves only to encourage Quintus."

He locked eyes with Allerix.

"And you, 'your majesty', will work like you have never laboured before. You will learn the meaning of respect for Rome. Or you will die. Personally, I am not bothered which. And of course, you will have no need of such a fine mount where you are going. He will make a fine addition to my stable. Enjoy your last ride."

Epona reached for Allerix's arm as Aquila rode away.

"And I thought I was the one who struggled with people!"

Trebonius laughed.

"He and your brother have history but I know of few people who do not struggle with Aquila, myself included. In truth, he is an odious little shit but he is useful to Caesar, who appreciates the value of his wealth and political connections. I have no doubt he will persuade Caesar to support his claim for the two of you, despite the fact he never left camp. I am sorry it has come to this."

He nodded to Epona and extended his arm to Allerix.

"Farewell."

As he turned to leave, Trebonius looked back over his shoulder.

"You should know, Allia is safe. I couldn't keep her from slavery but she resides with a friend of mine in Piacenza. A neighbouring estate to the one where you are headed. She is well treated. Far better than I fear will be the case for either of you. Be careful."

Allerix wondered whether the gods were taunting him or offering him another reason to live. He would choose to believe the latter and hope the gods were inclined to look favourably upon him. He had unfinished business with Rome, and mention of Allia had sparked an unexpected desire to see her again. That was reason enough to endure. He felt for his father's pendant... his pendant. The spectre of what was to come loomed large but Piacenza need not be the end of their story. And the indignity of slavery need not signal the end of the Aduatuci either. Caesar could strip them of their home and their possessions but, as long as his people lived, the essence of their nation would survive. Carried in the hearts of the displaced to burn brightly in whatever corner of the Roman world they eventually found themselves. Alongside the fires of resistance forged by an abiding memory of this day.

He turned to Epona.

"Come, sister. We have news to break and spirits to try and lift. Rome will regret the day it scattered the Aduatuci!"

24

AUTUMN, 57 BC

Journey to Tours, north-west Gaul

Epona waved away Valis' protests and wrapped her blanket around his shoulders. It had been another mild day but the temperature was beginning to fall away in the evenings and despite his protestations, she knew he was suffering. The journey was taking its toll on all of them, especially those, like Valis, carrying injuries from the battle. She grimaced as he shivered and moved a little closer to the meagre fire. He was running a fever. The landscape through which they had been passing was rich with plants and herbs that could have helped, but, chained together and forced to keep pace with the legions, there had been nothing she could do. With a sigh, she sat back and tried to ease her own aching limbs. It had only been ten or eleven days since their surrender; the relentless pace and the mind-numbing monotony of the march made it hard to keep track, but it already seemed a world away. And how life had changed! Forced from their home and stripped of all their possessions, they had been rounded up by the gangs working for the myriad slave traders that seemingly followed the legions, eagerly awaiting the opportunity to exploit Rome's victories. She shook her head. There was no honour in such a profession. But there was money; the traders were scarcely able to believe their luck at the sheer scale of the bounty with which they had been presented. Aquila had been true to his word and she and Allerix had been exempted from the sales, pre-purchased by the Roman, along with the remaining members of the Royal Guard. The bastard had made sure they were forced to watch the heart-breaking auctions, however: her people being bartered like common cattle, many of them split from family and friends, even children, probably never to be reunited. He'd made certain that they hadn't escaped any of the other indignities of life as a slave either. And so, chained and tethered, they had joined the long column of slave wagons heading south. One small part of the huge baggage train following the army to Tours, where she'd heard the legions would be spending the winter. There would be no rest for her or her fellow captives, of course; they would be moved on again quickly to whichever destinations they had been committed. She knew nothing of Piacenza but it didn't bode well that Aquila could barely conceal his glee at the daunting life awaiting them. As Allerix had predicted, the Roman had come to see them off, gloating at them from atop his horse as they began their march. He'd promised to return but, so far, they'd been spared that humiliation. She smiled ruefully, grateful for small mercies. They needed no reminders from Aquila of their new lowly status in life. She flexed her wrists gently, careful not to aggravate the areas of skin rubbed raw by the heavy iron manacles that had become such an uncomfortable feature of life since they'd left home. They received some measure of respite from the cruel demands of wearing them when they were temporarily released from the tethers that joined them together on the march. Unfortunately, this was when the harsh rigours of another day on the road kicked in and everything else began to hurt. Still, she had to be alive to feel pain, and, thanks to Allerix, they all were. She glanced up cautiously and surreptitiously felt for her mother's silver horse, pinned inside her tunic to avoid detection. Staying alive long enough to inflict the same kind of pain on Rome was what was keeping her going.

Lost in thought, Epona jumped as she felt a hand on her shoulder. Spoiling for a fight, she balled her fists and jumped to her feet before realising it was Allerix.

She shuffled along the log to allow him space to join her beside the fire.

"Sorry, brother. I thought it was him again."

She had been on the receiving end of some very unwanted attention from several of the slave traders since their journey began, but one of them, Magnus, a Gaul of all things, had left her feeling particularly anxious. A big bull of a man, he was fond of his drink and quick to anger. The lead trader and his henchman were the dominant members of the group, but Magnus clearly held some sway over the rest and already he'd tried to take advantage, posting a lookout whilst he tried to drag her away from camp. She had resisted long enough to wake Allerix and Epomedius and his intentions had been thwarted, but she knew he would try again and that next time she might not be so lucky. As it was, clearly accustomed to getting his own way, Magnus inflicted quite a beating upon her the next day for her temerity in standing up to his advances. Set free, she would give the brute a taste of his own medicine, but, manacled and weak from the exertions of the march, she felt vulnerable. Allerix squeezed her arm and offered her a piece of bread. She took it gratefully. It would be as stale and as tasteless as always but she was beyond caring. Their meagre rations were barely enough to keep them alive and the pangs of hunger had become a constant companion. Hard enough for her, she could see the impact this was having on Allerix and the rest of the warriors, who were weary, irritable and all wearing their belts much tighter than before. Epona broke the bread in two and gave one piece back to Allerix.

"You need to eat too, brother."

He shook his head but she pressed the pathetically small offering into his hand anyway. He gave her a thin smile.

"I feared any ill treatment would be dished out by the Romans, not some of our own."

She nodded.

"These men are pigs, brother, and with luck we shall meet them again. Without these…"

She waved her manacled hands and immediately regretted it, kicking the floor in frustration as the stabbing pain radiated through her arms.

"It is down to you that we do not have to contend with the Romans as well. Caesar has kept his word and his men leave us alone."

Allerix shrugged.

"I wish I could've been persuasive enough to avoid all of this happening in the first place."

She shook her head.

"We both know that was never going to happen, brother. If it wasn't this, it would have been war, and all of our people would most likely now be dead. They survive because you impressed Caesar."

She gave him a gentle push.

"And it seems they are not the only ones who owe you their lives. I saw your reaction to the news that Allia, whoever she may be, is alive and well. I think you have avoided talk of her for long enough, brother."

He smiled and she knew that he had accepted defeat.

*

Atticus mopped up the last pieces of stew with his bread and set down his bowl. He hadn't eaten properly since breakfast and that had hit the spot. He wasn't sure he wanted to know how Titus had managed to bag some meat to grace the pot but he was very grateful. Julius gave him a smile.

"Good?"

Atticus nodded.

"Surprisingly so."

Titus shot him a dark look as he emerged from their tent, his black eye and broken nose painful evidence of his altercation with a warrior's shield that night on the rampart.

"I heard that!"

Atticus raised his hands.

"I meant it was an unexpected surprise to have something other than vegetables for once."

Titus looked at him dubiously for a moment and then tossed his empty beaker at him.

"I know what you meant."

Atticus retrieved the beaker and returned it to Titus with a smile as his friend joined them by the fire.

"It was good, thank you. My stomach was beginning to think my throat had been cut after missing out when we stopped earlier."

Julius added a few more sticks to the fire.

"Yes, where did you get to?"

"I made the mistake of running into Baculus on the way back from having a piss. I think he's forgotten I was only supposed to be running his errands for a few weeks. He had messages for the cohort centurions and wasn't going to pass up the opportunity of having somebody else find them all. By the time I'd finished, we were ready to move off again. I did see Allerix, though, and some of his people, from afar."

Titus offered him a jug of watered wine.

"How did they look?"

"Not good. They still carry themselves well enough but they're suffering. That much is clear. I wouldn't want to be in their shoes."

Julius snorted.

"Perhaps they should've thought about that when they attacked us, instead of honouring the terms they'd agreed."

Atticus nodded. It had been a reckless act, one that explained why they'd fought so fiercely. They knew the implications of failure but something had obviously driven them to take such drastic action.

"True enough, brother, but do you think Allerix and his people would have chosen death over life under our sovereignty if we hadn't pushed them to it?"

His friend smiled and gave him a nudge.

"I think... you think too much."

Titus laughed and refilled their beakers.

"Well, he is the educated one, though I'm not sure it makes a great deal of difference what any of us think. It doesn't matter whether we follow the trouble or trouble follows us, we end up fighting either way. All I know is that the campaign is over and we've earned a rest. And that's worth celebrating."

Julius nodded and held his beaker aloft.

"I'll drink to that."

Atticus smiled. It had been a long and tough campaign and they'd all had their share of good fortune, him especially. Many hadn't been so lucky. Maybe that was enough. He raised his beaker.

"To Maximus, fallen comrades and a well-earned rest. Wherever that may be."

Julius downed his drink in one and dragged the back of his hand across his lips. He refilled their beakers.

"And here's to the taverns and brothels of Tours and the fine ladies that will hopefully delay the start of that rest."

Atticus smiled.

"I doubt there will be many fine ladies where you'll be looking, brother."

Julius slapped Titus on the back.

"Exactly! And they'll be so pleased to see the men of the legion that even this poor disfigured soul will find a warm welcome somewhere."

Titus gave him a shove.

"Don't you worry about me. I'll be fine. It's you young pups who should be concerned. I'm not sure you could handle a real woman, especially if all the women of Gaul are like this 'she-wolf' we keep hearing about."

Atticus allowed himself a little smile.

"I think I saw her this afternoon. She was with Allerix in the slave column."

Julius looked interested.

"Is she as fearsome as they say?"

"Not manacled like that, brother. But there is something about her. She stood up to one of the traders when he wouldn't give them water. He wasn't impressed and she took a bit of a beating but she got it for them. She has spirit and it's a shame to see it chained."

Julius laughed.

"Ahh… so now we know why it took you so long to deliver Baculus' messages!"

Atticus felt his cheeks beginning to colour.

It was true he'd spent longer on that part of the road than he had any need or reason to, but something about her had intrigued him and he'd found it hard to tear himself away. He nodded to the others as he saw Plautius stride into view. Ordinarily, his imminent arrival at their tent would be cause for mild alarm. Tonight, he was grateful for the distraction.

Plautius gave them a smile and gestured for them to return to their seats.

"It's good to see Rescius has been keeping you on your toes whilst I've been laid up, but I'm only here to see how you and the rest of the cohort are doing."

He looked pale and he grimaced as he carefully tried to adjust the sling holding his injured arm tightly across his chest. He was clearly still experiencing a good deal of discomfort. Atticus could relate to that.

"How is it?"

Plautius gave him a grateful nod.

"I'll live. Thanks to you, lad. I'm going to be stuck like this for a while but they were struggling to control the bleeding so it could have been a whole lot worse. I'm supposed to be taking it easy but Aquila has called the centurions to a meeting tonight and, as everyone's assuming it's about where the legion is headed next, I was buggered if I was going to miss out."

Plautius gestured towards Titus.

"Looks like I'm not the only one carrying a reminder from that night."

Titus ran his hand tentatively across his face.

"I don't remember much about it, to be honest, though I damn well know about it now."

Julius laughed.

"You should be thanking them, improving your looks like that. They did you a favour."

Plautius stepped back quickly as Julius scrambled to escape Titus' attempted swipe.

"I'll take that as evidence Naso is fit and well. How about the rest of the tent?"

Atticus shrugged.

"Flavius has been with the medics since the battle. He has a nasty leg wound, which doesn't seem to be healing, but the rest of us are only carrying cuts and bruises. Better than most, judging by the numbers on the march."

Plautius nodded.

"It was a tough night for the legion, especially those of us in the fort. But we did well. If we hadn't held them up for as long as we did, they'd have been in amongst us before the other legions arrived. We'd have lost a lot more then."

Julius gave Titus a push as he returned to his seat.

"Well, let's hope Aquila recognises that and we get to go home as a reward. Or, failing that, earn a nice, long rest in Tours."

Plautius raised his hand.

"There's no doubt he recognises it. Baculus says he's been dining out on the bravery of 'his legion' ever since, though nobody can recall seeing him lift a sword in anger. Whether we benefit from that recognition is quite another matter. You know our legate better than most!"

Titus sprang to his feet.

"Speak of the devil."

Atticus cursed. What was he doing here? With a weary sigh, he pulled himself to his feet before joining the others at attention. Aquila would need little reason to find fault, even though they weren't on duty. The legate half-heartedly acknowledged their salutes and looked them up and down dismissively.

"Good evening, Centurion. I thought I saw you heading this way. It's good to see you on your feet again, though I can't say that your recovery has improved your choice of company."

Atticus caught his breath as he saw Plautius tense, but he should have known the centurion was far too experienced to allow a jibe like that to draw a reaction. Instead, Plautius merely smiled and gestured to the surrounding tents.

"I was visiting the cohort on my way to your briefing, sir. I know you've been keen to celebrate the legion's part in the battle and I was just telling the lads I was sure it would only be a matter of time before you stopped by to acknowledge their part in holding the rampart."

Momentarily lost for words, Aquila looked furious, and Atticus quickly dropped his eyes, afraid he might lose the fight to suppress a smile. He needn't have worried; Aquila had fixed his glare firmly on Plautius.

"I believe I am yet to receive your report from that night, Centurion; my thanks for reminding me. I will expect it in the morning. I cannot deny that you and your men acquitted yourselves well, however, and for that you have my thanks."

He paused.

"More than you know."

Atticus shot Julius a quick glance. Had Aquila volunteered praise? It was not what he'd been expecting or what they had grown accustomed to. And then he saw the sly smile run across the legate's face. There was something else. It had been too good to be true.

With a flourish, Aquila waved the scroll he had been carrying in his hand.

"I was saving this news until the meeting but it seems a shame not to share it early. As a reward for defending the rampart, Caesar has requested that the senior officers of the legion ride with him when we return to Verona."

Julius let out a yelp.

"The legion is going home?"

Aquila laughed.

"Oh, I'm sorry, you misunderstand. When I said 'we', I didn't mean the legion, just the senior officers. You men have an altogether different reward to look forward to."

Clearly now enjoying himself, Aquila paused for effect. Atticus had a bad feeling about where this was heading. He shifted anxiously as Aquila eagerly scanned their faces before continuing.

"Apparently there is trouble brewing in Gallia Transalpina, some of the locals looking to exert more influence on the flow of trade than Rome would like. Caesar intends to send a legion to hold open the pass at Octodora. He thought the XIIth might welcome a break but I was able to reassure him that this was just the kind of opportunity a young but battle-hardened legion like ours would relish. Fortunately, he agreed. I'm just so disappointed that I will be unable to join you. In my absence, Legate Galba will lead the expedition."

Atticus tucked his arms behind his back for fear that his balled fists would be visible. Were there really no levels to which this man wouldn't stoop? Aquila smiled and stepped a little closer to Atticus.

"A small number of slave wagons will be joining you, those heading to Piacenza via the pass. Including the one destined for my brother-in-law's estate. Make sure they arrive at the pass in one piece or I will hold you personally responsible, Capito. Oh, and do be careful yourself. It's a long march and winter in the pass will be tough, much like the locals, I imagine. And we don't expect they will take kindly to our appearance."

He prodded Atticus in the chest with the scroll.

"It's just what you need after lazing around winter quarters last year, but I'd hate for anything to happen to you and for me to be freed so unfortunately from my debt before it could be repaid."

He laughed.

"I do hope that was the kind of acknowledgement you were after, gentlemen. Enjoy the rest of your evening."

With a smile, he turned away.

"Come, Centurion, let's go and break the news to your comrades."

As the two officers disappeared amongst the tents, Julius sank to the floor.

"Cock-sucking bastard! Can he even do that?"

Titus passed him what was left of the wine.

"Of course he can, brother. It's how the world works. People like him take the credit and we get the pain. How far is it to the pass anyway?"

Julius shook his head.

"Fuck knows. It's what we find when we get there that I'm worried about."

Atticus shook his head. He shared Julius' concerns but he couldn't help wondering if the greatest risk to their safety wasn't someone a lot closer to home.

25

Journey to Vienne, south-east Gaul

A drop of water ran slowly down Epona's face and fell onto her mud-covered boots. She shivered and inched a little closer to the fire. It had finally stopped raining, but, huddled uncomfortably beneath her soggy blanket, she could feel the chill beginning to seep through her bones and desperately needed some warmth. They had left Tours in the sun, bound for Vienne, home of the Allobroge. It would be their last stop this side of the mountains that for so long had marked the boundary of Rome's territorial ambition. With far fewer soldiers and slaves joining them on this part of the journey, progress had been easier and conditions almost bearable. But then the rains had arrived. And had kept coming: heavy summer storms that seemed to run into one another with barely any respite. Soaked to the skin and with the discomfort of their chains magnified by the cold and damp, they had soon found themselves having to battle through cloying, ankle-deep mud as the paths quickly disappeared, churned beneath the feet of those ahead of them in the column. For days, they had struggled along and, with sleep rendered almost impossible by the near-constant rain, it was hardly surprising they had begun to flag. That was when the whips had come out. Valis had been the first to suffer the trader's wrath and had been a regular recipient as he fought illness and the stresses of slavery, but he wasn't alone. They had all received a taste of the lash at one point or another, with Magnus especially keen to wield the whip. That was no surprise. She had encountered his kind before; he was a bully and, as long as they remained chained, he would be dangerous. She shook her head. Life had a strange way of reminding you to be careful about what you wished for. She had wanted to escape Tours so much; it had actually been a relief when they began their journey again. It wasn't so much the conditions that bothered her, though, penned like sheep in a stockade barely big enough for the usual animal occupants and treated much the same, those were bad enough. No, it was the attitude of the locals, Magnus' people, the Turones, which she found so difficult to understand. She had defiantly returned the looks of pity on the faces of the town's inhabitants as they came to leer at the captives with the morbid curiosity of those unaccustomed to the aftermath of war. Smug with the mistaken sense of their superiority, they were under Rome's yolk just as surely as if they had also been beaten in battle. Their meek subservience to Rome and willingness to accept the enslavement of a fellow Gallic nation was sad. Worse still, they had returned as spectators when the traders, keen to encourage some sport for their amusement and that of the locals, had forced some of their exhausted and hungry group to take part in trials of strength and unarmed combat with the local warriors. Men who, bereft of experience on the battlefield, clearly needed to try and demonstrate their power in other ways. Unsurprisingly, the outcome of these uneven struggles had almost always been a victory for the warriors of the Turones, although Epomedius had succeeded in embarrassing one of the locals, defeating him in a trial of strength for which they had all been punished with reduced rations. Such as they were. It had been worth it, although the smell of pork wafting tantalisingly in their direction from the trader's fire was an unhelpful reminder of just how hungry she was, and she clamped a hand to her stomach. It had been much the same for the last week or so, her captors feasting merrily on the supplies they had procured in Tours, whilst she and the others eked out a miserable existence on dry biscuits and the occasional scrap that might be tossed their way. The supplies had seemingly included significant quantities of wine and, if the raucous laughter and bawdy singing were any indication, it had started to flow even earlier than usual tonight. The contrast with the sorry, bedraggled and utterly exhausted-looking group on their side of the camp couldn't be greater. She swallowed nervously. The flow of alcohol only increased the likelihood of her receiving yet more unwanted attention from Magnus. She looked up as Allerix gave her a nudge. Shit. He and one of the other traders were on their way over with what passed for their food. She sighed. Another opportunity for Magnus to throw his weight around in what had become a humiliating nightly ritual.

Epona kept her eyes fixed firmly on the ground as Magnus strutted along the line of captives. He was carrying a beaker of wine and a large piece of pork, which he was contemptuously waving around beneath their noses. Salivating, she watched the drops of fat falling slowly to the floor and tried to ignore the pangs of hunger biting deep within. Who would he choose to antagonise first? She felt herself tense as he paused in front of her and slipped his hand under her chin to force her gaze upwards. He flashed her a lecherous smile and turned to the thin, weaselly-looking man who had followed him over, a sack of their dry biscuits in his hand.

"She's a feisty wench, this one, but I like that in a woman."

Epona recoiled as he tried to run the back of his hand over her cheek.

He leant forward.

"And I promise you'll find out just how much, very soon."

Horrified but anxious not to give him the satisfaction of averting her gaze, she glared at him defiantly until he broke eye contact and moved on. He kicked Allerix needlessly as he passed and angrily squared up to Valis as he momentarily looked to rise in protest. Magnus struck him across the face.

"You have something you want to say, big man?"

Valis looked at him angrily but remained silent.

"Good. Then stay seated!"

A slow smile ran across Magnus' face and he waved the piece of pork in his hand slowly back and forth in front of Valis before dropping it to the floor and grinding it into the mud beneath his boot. He looked menacingly back at Valis.

"Eat it."

Valis spat at Magnus' feet.

"No."

Magnus struck him across the face once more.

"Everybody will go hungry tonight if you don't. Now eat."

Desperately hungry, a small part of her still hoped he wouldn't succumb, but she knew he would never let them suffer on his account and he slowly reached for the meat. Magnus stretched out his hand as Valis attempted to wipe off the mud on his tunic.

"As it is."

Valis locked eyes with him and for a moment she thought he was going to refuse, but he brought the filthy slice of pork hesitantly towards his mouth and began to chew. Magnus smiled as he watched him swallow the last mouthful. He turned to his companion and beckoned for some of the biscuits. He took a handful and broke them into pieces in his hand. With a flourish, he scattered them onto the floor at Valis' feet.

"And now your biscuits. This time on your knees, like the animal you are!"

She watched as Valis slowly pulled himself to his feet.

"I am no dog."

He doubled over as Magnus punched him in the stomach.

"You are no man, slave."

Valis pulled himself up defiantly to his full height.

"Why don't you remove the chains and we can find out?"

He took a step towards Magnus. As he did so, the other trader jumped forward and kicked him to his knees. Before he could struggle to his feet, Magnus took hold of his head and brought up his knee, sending it crashing into Valis' chin. His head snapped back and he fell to the floor in a heap. Epona leapt to her feet as Magnus took aim at Valis' prostrate body with his boot. He landed one sickening blow before she could block his path and, infuriated, he struck her across the face. She staggered backwards under the weight of the blow but remained on her feet and would have thrown herself forward once more if Allerix hadn't taken hold of her shoulder. Alerted by the commotion, their leader had appeared, flanked by his henchman. Older than the others, he had a rotund body, which suggested that slave trading had not been unkind to everyone. Nevertheless, his scarred and weather-beaten face pointed to an earlier life when his ability to use the heavy wooden club he was twisting menacingly in his hands might have been necessary.

"What the fuck? Haven't I told you before about damaging the merchandise? What use are they to me if we don't get to deliver them, you idiot?"

Magnus took half a step forward and then thought better of it.

"He was lame anyway."

"Well, she's certainly not, and I don't want her marked before Piacenza! Now get them fed and tethered for the night and keep your hands to yourself. Or you'll find yourself taking his place."

Satisfied that order had been restored, he stalked away,

leaving Magnus sullenly watching him head back towards the fire. He gestured for his companion to hand out the food and returned his attention to Epona. She spat at his feet as he advanced towards her.

"Go. Before your master misses his pet!"

He leant forward with a snarl.

"I am no pet, bitch, but I will enjoy taming you..."

He eased his dagger from its scabbard as Allerix moved threateningly towards him. Epona stuck out her arm to hold her brother back. Magnus smiled and turned away. She took a deep breath and looked down at her shaking hands, with an ominous sense of foreboding. This was one fight she didn't know how to win.

*

She watched Magnus pour another drink for his leader. It had been a couple of days since they had buried Valis and Magnus had kept his distance, clearly trying to restore favour. But he had kept an unnervingly close eye on them nevertheless, just as he did now, furtively running his eyes over her whilst the others laughed and joked, oblivious to his lecherous gaze. Escaping his mindless violence and arrogant taunting had been a relief, but his constant attention meant that she was always on edge and she cursed him for making her feel that way. She wrapped her blanket just a little tighter around her shoulders and tried to get comfortable. Not that sleep was coming easily at the moment. Beside her, Allerix stirred. He had taken Valis' death very badly. The warrior's spirit had slipped peacefully away during the night of Magnus' attack, lost to them before his time. The only consolation was that he had escaped his chains to join their ancestors, where he could once more drink, feast and fight like the proud warrior he had been. She'd reassured Allerix that there wasn't anything he could have done, but she knew her brother felt responsible for his loss. Losing a warrior in battle was one thing; losing a friend at the hands of a thug like Magnus, quite another. He would miss him; they all would. She stretched out her arm to squeeze her brother's shoulder and returned her gaze to the other side of the camp. Several of the men had drifted away to settle down for the night but Magnus was still holding forth, wine in hand.

Epona closed her eyes, though she knew sleep would not come easily, or remain undisturbed when it finally did arrive. It hadn't now for some time: too many dark thoughts clouding her mind. He'd seen to that and she cursed him for it. She would do so much more than that if only she wasn't chained. She shifted uncomfortably and reached for her brooch. One day...

*

Epona snapped open her eyes with a start. Her heart was racing and she felt cold beads of sweat running down her back. He had been coming for her again. She quickly cast her eyes towards the trader's fire. It was quiet but he was there, helping the leader's henchman guide their leader back to his tent. He had clearly had his fill of wine; his henchman didn't look much better and the short journey took some time as the three of them staggered back and forth before arriving at their destination. The two men helped the leader inside. As they emerged, Magnus slapped his colleague on the back and watched him head off unsteadily towards his own tent. He watched him battle with the entrance to the tent before turning and striding purposefully back towards the fire. Very purposefully. He wasn't drunk. He must have been left on guard. She felt an icy sense of dread run through her body. Who would guard her from him?

*

Epona fidgeted uncomfortably. Magnus was nowhere in sight. He'd left the fire two or three times before, dutifully walking the edges of the camp. Each time, she'd turned her head and pretended to be asleep as he passed slowly by but this was different. He had disappeared into the darkness on the far side of the camp and hadn't yet reappeared. She twisted the edge of her tunic nervously, hating how badly she had allowed this man to unsettle her. Her eyes darted back towards the fire as she saw Magnus emerge from the shadows with his weasel-faced friend. She quietly tried to wake Allerix, prodding him with her foot. He stirred but remained asleep. They were coming towards her. With a rising sense of panic, she kicked Allerix again, harder this time, not caring who saw. Both men were carrying knives. Her heart sank. This was it. She balled her hands into fists and desperately tried to scramble to her feet, almost pulling the still-half-asleep Allerix upright as she did. But the traders were upon them too quickly and Magnus kicked her to the ground, any thought of a scream stifled as he forced his knee into her chest and clamped a big hand across her mouth. She felt the point of his knife against her neck.

"I doubt anyone will hear you after all the wine I plied them with tonight, but if you do make a sound, I will kill you."

He gestured towards Allerix, on his knees and already nursing a bloody nose at the hands of Magnus' companion, who was now holding a knife threateningly across her brother's throat.

"And him!"

Magnus smiled.

"Nobody will miss you... Just another couple of slaves caught trying to escape... The master will be angry but I had to defend myself, and, thankfully, Epitus here was alerted just in time to see it all happen."

Epitus grinned and Magnus eased his knee off her chest.

"Now. Are we clear?"

Epona swallowed hard and nodded.

"Good. Then you and I are going for a little walk to pick up where we left off the other day."

He pulled her to her knees. She tried to regain control of her trembling hands as Magnus began to slice through the rope tethering her to the others. Feeling nauseous, she averted her gaze as he smiled and looked her up and down. He laughed and finished hacking through the rope. He tucked his knife into his boot and pulled her to her feet. She held out her hands, offering him the opportunity to release her manacles. He smiled.

"Oh, you'd like that, wouldn't you? But I don't think so. I get to focus all my attention on things other than your hands that way."

She spat in his eye and he slapped her across the face. Allerix began to struggle and Epitus pulled the knife from her brother's neck and smashed the handle down on his head. Allerix buckled under the blow but refused to stay down. As he slowly pulled himself back up, Epitus kicked him savagely in the back, forcing him to the ground once more. He moved quickly to take hold of Allerix's head, the point of his dagger nestling against her brother's throat once more. Magnus pulled her close.

"Don't make me do it."

Epona looked plaintively at Allerix and held out her hand.

"Enough, brother. We have already lost Valis. I will not have you taken as well."

Magnus smiled and turned to Epitus.

"If he moves again, finish him."

He grabbed her arm and gave her a shove, forcing her forwards. He was steering her towards a small hollow that separated the Roman camp from those of the traders. Clearly anxious to cover ground as quickly as possible, he forced her on, shoving her hard in the back whenever she dragged her feet. He relaxed his grip as they arrived at the edge of the hollow and took a final look around. Seemingly satisfied that the coast was clear, he led her down the slope and out of sight of their camp. Her blood ran cold; she realised there was no escape.

Epona clamped her arms across her chest as he pulled her in front of him. He reached for her shoulder and she took a step back – and another – as he tried again. He snarled and lunged forward, taking hold of her tunic. She threw up her hands, trying to break his grip, and he cried out as the edge of one of her manacles struck his arm. He relinquished his hold and punched her in the stomach, driving the air painfully from her lungs. Struggling for breath, she forced herself to straighten up, kicking out as he moved towards her again. He cursed as the blow landed but he kept coming and she swung her arms across his path, trying to use her manacles as a weapon once more. He swatted them aside and struck her across the face. She could taste the blood almost before she felt the pain and spat it at him as he grabbed hold of her hair, sweeping her legs out from under her. He wiped his hand over his face and stepped forward, looming over her. He smiled.

"I've never met a woman yet who didn't look better on her back."

He began to loosen his belt. She pulled herself onto her elbows and frantically tried to drag herself away. He followed her along the path for a few paces and discarded his belt.

She let out a scream as he threw himself to the floor, landing on top of her and pinning her to the ground. He grabbed her hands and pushed them back beyond her head, forcing them into the dirt and clamping them there with one of his hands. She bucked and kicked, frantically trying to throw him off, but he was sitting astride her hips and she couldn't dislodge his weighty frame. He began to paw at her tunic. She twisted and turned but that only seemed to spur him on and, with a self-satisfied roar, he succeeded in ripping it open, exposing her chest.

"Mmm, I wondered what you had been hiding under here, very nice."

He began to run his hands roughly over her breasts. She turned her head away and fixed her gaze on the few stars visible in the night sky, desperate to try and take her mind away from what was happening. It was no use. Nothing could drown out the sound of his increasingly heavy breathing or quell her rising sense of anger and frustration. She threw up her knee as he dragged down his trousers and eased his weight on her slightly, to try and reach hers. He cursed as the blow struck him in the back and he was momentarily thrown off balance. She tried to kick out again but it was no use; she couldn't shake him off. He grasped the braided belt of her trousers and with a snarl began to ease them down. She had known for days that it would come to this, but nothing could have prepared her for the sense of utter helplessness and dread that washed over her as she closed her eyes, desperate for it to be over. He slapped her across the face.

"Eyes open, bitch. I want you to remember this."

He leant forward until he was almost touching her face with his own. She fought the urge to gag as his fetid breath and stale musk threatened to overwhelm her senses. He sneered.

"You never know, you might enjoy it more that way too."

Overcome with anger, she let out a cry and snapped her head forward. He threw back his head and let out a howl of pain as her forehead crunched into the bridge of his nose. His blood splattered onto her tunic as he struck her across the face once again.

"Oh, you struggle, bitch. The tougher the hunt, the more enjoyable the feast. And I am going to enjoy this!"

She could feel the tears beginning to well and was bracing herself for the final act of humiliation, when she heard heavy footsteps on the path behind her. Someone was coming. It was too dark to see who it was but she didn't care. Magnus had heard them as well and had paused his assault. He looked up as she called out for help and she saw the look of panic flash across his face. He began struggling to his feet as the footsteps drew closer. She felt the presence of another body and suddenly Magnus was gone. She struggled to pull up her trousers and sat up, tucking her knees tightly into her chest. Magnus was lying on his back amidst the bushes and scrub that lined the path, pinned helplessly beneath the body of a Roman legionary. She jumped as she felt a hand on her shoulder. It was another Roman. He offered her his hand. Still shaking, she scrambled unsteadily to her feet and did what she could to pull together the tattered remains of her tunic. The soldier astride Magnus jumped up and quickly drew his sword. He took hold of Magnus' hair and began to drag him to his feet. As he struggled to escape the soldier's grip, Magnus caught her eye. Overcome with rage, she flew forward and swung a kick at him. Still on all fours, he was powerless to react and he let out an agonised cry as her boot crunched into his ribs. He sank to the floor and she took aim again before she was restrained by the other soldier.

"He deserves it and he will pay, but we have to go. Are you okay?"

Magnus spat at the soldier as he slowly climbed to his feet.

"What do you care, Roman? She is a common slave and this is nothing to do with you. Fuck off and leave us alone!"

Magnus doubled over as the legionary sank the handle of his sword into his stomach.

"Open your mouth again and I'll use the other end."

Magnus shot the Roman a hate-filled glare as he straightened up, but he remained silent.

Epona turned back to the soldier standing beside her. He was a good bit taller than the one guarding Magnus and she was forced to raise her head. He smiled reassuringly at her as their eyes met and she nodded gratefully.

"I am okay, thanks to you, but I must get back to the camp. This bastard has a friend and he holds my brother captive."

The two Romans exchanged anxious glances. The taller one drew his sword.

"I'll take care of this. You go. One of us needs to get back before we are missed."

As if about to protest, his comrade hesitated for a moment before nodding his agreement.

"Okay. But make it quick! I can only cover for so long."

He smiled.

"And no heroics either just because it's her!"

The taller legionary nodded and shoved Magnus forward. He cursed and turned as if to resist, but the Roman stepped forward quickly and held his sword threateningly to Magnus' chest.

"Move. I won't ask again."

Magnus glared at the Roman as if weighing up his chances. Something about the soldier's demeanour suggested that wouldn't be a good idea and Magnus dropped his head. He turned and set off back along the path. She quickly fell into line beside the Roman.

"What did he mean, 'because it's her'?"

She thought the soldier looked a little uncomfortable.

"Your reputation precedes you after your exploits at Aduatuca and I made the mistake of talking to my loose-lipped friend about seeing you with Allerix during our journey."

Epona looked quizzically at the soldier.

"You know Allerix?"

"Yes. We fought together at Vesontio. I doubt I would be here if it wasn't for him."

Her mind raced as the realisation suddenly dawned.

"You are the legionary that spared my brother on the rampart?"

The soldier's eyes widened.

"You are Epona, Allerix's adopted sister?"

It was her turn to be surprised. She nodded.

"Yes, he is all the family I have left now. I will kill this piece of shit and his weasel friend if anything has happened to him."

The soldier smiled.

"And I wouldn't try to stop you."

Magnus turned, a look of consternation on his face. The soldier jabbed out his sword to encourage him on and the three of them scrambled up the slope leading out of the hollow.

She could see her brother. He was alive, though still on his knees with Epitus standing over him. Epomedius had dragged himself up beside Allerix, and Epitus was waving his knife menacingly between the two of them. She quickened her pace, forcing the soldier and Magnus to do likewise. They covered the ground quickly and Epitus moved warily behind Allerix as they approached, knife once more clamped to her brother's throat. They paused and the soldier called out.

"Stand down!"

The anxiety on Epitus' face betrayed his surprise at the wholly unexpected nature of Magnus' return but he held firm.

"Why should I, Roman?"

The soldier turned Magnus side on, revealing the sword in his back. He eased the point forward, forcing Magnus to cry out.

"Leave him, Epitus. They're not worth it."

Epitus hesitated, looking forlornly between the three of them and the captives at his feet but he slowly lowered his knife. The soldier beckoned him over.

"Do they have a leader?"

Epona nodded and pointed towards the small tent on the other side of the camp.

"He's probably drunk but he'll be in there."

The soldier pushed Magnus forward and gestured for Epitus

to fall in beside him. They set off across the camp and she ran over to rejoin her brother. She dropped to her knees and ran the sleeve of her tunic carefully across his battered face. He spat the blood from his mouth and gave her a weak smile.

"I will be fine. But… I thought I'd lost you."

She took his hand.

"I'm okay, brother… thanks to the Roman."

She smiled. The irony of being saved from a fellow Gaul by those who had so recently battled and enslaved them was not lost on her. But she had been grateful for the intervention, however hard it was to admit. She dropped her head.

"But I lost Mother's brooch. It must have come off in the struggle. My last link with her gone forever."

Allerix grimaced as he raised his hands and gestured towards his chest.

"You will never lose your link with her in here; stay strong. It is what she would have wanted."

Epomedius touched her arm.

"Judging by his face, I'd say you gave him a taste of his own medicine."

She stared at her manacles.

"Not nearly enough. But if I ever see him again without these chains, he will pay."

Epona looked up as the sound of angry shouting drifted across the camp. It was the trader's leader haranguing Magnus and Epitus. The noise had drawn some of the others from their tent and they clustered protectively around the leader as he continued his angry tirade. The soldier had left them to it and was on his way back over. She stood and helped her brother climb painfully to his feet. He nodded to the Roman as he arrived.

"Atticus. It seems that I am in your debt again."

The soldier shook his head.

"We were in the right place at the right time, just as you were for us at Vesontio. If we weren't in friendly territory, we would have been stuck in camp and not patrolling the perimeter. We might never have heard anything or been able to arrive in time."

He gestured in her direction.

"As it was, we heard the struggle and your cries for help. We couldn't stand by and do nothing."

Allerix smiled.

"I know of one Roman who could, as do you."

He held up his manacled hands.

"Men who would do this. I wonder how you follow such individuals."

The soldier seemed stung by the comment.

"I fight for Rome and I follow the Eagle, not Aquila."

Epona gestured along the line of her tethered kin.

"But it is Rome that does this."

Her brother shook his head.

"No, sister. It was not Rome that took our family, our friends, our home. It was Caesar and those like Aquila who share his avarice and thirst for power."

Her brother stared at the soldier.

"I rode for Caesar as an ally, supported him to end Ariovistus' domination over the nations he had supposedly come to help. And for what? For my people to find themselves attacked and enslaved when your general decided he too preferred conquest over peace. He is no better than the tyrant we fought to remove."

The young soldier dropped his head.

"It would not have been my choice to fight, nor to have it end this way. I'm sorry."

Angry, Epona took half a step towards the Roman; his pity was no good to them now. But his remorse seemed genuine enough and she relaxed her fist as the two of them locked eyes. On the opposite side of the camp, the leader was busy barking instructions and she was grateful for the distraction as one of his men began to stride over. She watched him hurry across, feeling a little uneasy about what to expect after the events of the night.

As if sensing her concern, the soldier smiled.

"I have let the leader know where you are heading and under whose orders you travel. He is very clear about the risk to his business if anything further should happen to you en route."

She nodded and he turned to leave.

"I must get back. May your gods watch over you!"

Allerix placed his hand on her shoulder and the two of them watched the soldier stride back towards the hollow and his camp. Her brother sighed.

"And yours too, friend. At the rate Rome makes enemies, your gods may be all that are left to save you."

The Roman turned, giving them one last look before disappearing into the night.

EPILOGUE

AUTUMN, 57 BC

Vienne

Epona yawned and brushed the straw from her tunic as she slowly eased herself to her feet. One of the horses on the other side of the stable shifted warily, no doubt unaccustomed to sharing his accommodation with quite so many people. She wandered over, glad to be free of the tether, if not the manacles. The horse nuzzled her face and she closed her eyes, thinking back to the stables at Aduatuca. They had been her second home and, although those at Vienne were far smaller in comparison, she had found the familiar sounds and smells reassuring after the travails of her journey. The wooden structure was relatively warm and dry and she had slept better over the last two nights than at any point since they had left home. Last night had also been the first time since Magnus' attack that she hadn't found herself waking in a cold sweat, reliving the terrors of that night. She shuddered and ran her fingers gently through the horse's mane. His ears flicked attentively as she shared her whispered gratitude for the departures of Magnus and Epitus from the convoy. She smiled, aware that this would only serve to reinforce her brother's view that she communicated better with horses than people. But her discovery that both men had been sent back to Tours had been almost overwhelming and she didn't care with whom she shared that. She jumped as the stable door flew open and the Allobroge warrior guarding the door moved aside to allow one of the traders through. He had brought them some food. It was still basic and repetitive fare but it had arrived in larger quantities and more regularly since the night of the attack, and she supposed that she had this… what had her brother called him… Atticus… to thank for that too. She had spent more time thinking about him over the last few days than she would care to mention. And she had never been more conflicted. She detested everything that Rome and its leaders stood for and hated being beholden to a Roman for anything. But she owed this man a debt of gratitude, as did her brother. He was unlike any Roman she had encountered before and yet he marched with the very legions she had sworn to drive from their lands at the point of a sword. It was disconcerting. He was disconcerting. She hurried over to join the others in the hope that it might take her mind off things. Allerix passed her some bread and a small piece of cheese, an unexpected treat that she tucked in her tunic to savour later. How life had changed. She smiled as Epomedius and her brother shared a joke. It was nice to see some signs of the people they had been before the journey had taken its toll.

A cool breeze played across her face and she looked over to gaze beyond the trader, who was idly gossiping with the guard in the open doorway whilst he waited for them to finish eating. Behind him, people were scurrying about their business, heads down against the chill wind. It was definitely colder now. The sun was somewhere low on the horizon and the grey and heavy skies full of menace. Winter was upon them and they would be on the road again soon. They would have to be if they were going to make it through the pass before the first snows began to fall. She shivered, although whether that was in anticipation of the harsh journey to come or the uncertainty of what lay ahead when they reached their destination, she wasn't entirely sure. At that moment, the safe and comfortable lifestyle enjoyed by those in the settlement seemed quite attractive. But she didn't envy them. How could she? That lifestyle came at a cost – allegiance to Rome. The Allobroge, like the Turones, grew rich on the back of their brother nations suffering. They were no better than the Roman conqueror they served, and no freer than she was. Their continued independence merely a pretence, allowed by Rome providing they did her bidding. She'd had some dark and desperate times on the journey but at no point had she ever regretted taking the decision to defy Rome. Nor would she allow what had befallen them since to deny her quest for vengeance. Her brother interrupted her thoughts, tapping her gently on the arm. He smiled and gestured towards the door, where Atticus had seemingly just arrived. Their guard appeared reluctant to allow him to pass but the trader recognised him quickly enough and after a few quick words he was ushered through. He took a moment to locate them amongst the others and wandered over, greeting them with a smile.

"I wanted to let you know, I've heard you will be leaving tomorrow. You travel with a convoy of merchants heading for the pass at Octodura. It's seven days' march from here and a little more again from there to Piacenza. And it seems Isarno travels with you."

She was sure the look of surprise on her brother's face would be mirrored by her own.

"Julius overheard the decurion in charge of our cavalry recounting how Isarno was so unruly that Aquila had him added to the inventory for his brother-in-law's estate."

Epona's brother smiled.

"I should like to have seen that. Is that why he has been keeping his distance?"

Atticus shook his head.

"He's not here. He travels with Caesar to Verona. The comforts of home call louder than a winter campaign in the mountains, though I can't say that I am disappointed to be free of his leadership for a while."

Allerix nodded.

"Such as it is. Will the legion be marching with us?"

"No. We head to Octodura but must visit the lands of the Nantuates and the Seduni first. We march at dawn to get ahead of the convoy, although I think Aquila must have had words in our new legate's ear, as you will have a small contingent of Allobroge cavalry riding with you."

Allerix looked pensively at Atticus.

"You are expecting trouble?"

Atticus shook his head.

"There has been some unrest, disputes about trade access and the price of tolls at the pass. It's why we are here but I don't think you will have any difficulty. Judging by the way the trader's leader has been enjoying what passes for the delights of Vienne, I'd say he has more than enough coin for the toll."

He pursed his lips in thought.

"Besides, I suspect it's us rather than the trade convoys that will have to be on the lookout for trouble."

Allerix looked quizzically at the legionary.

"Will your leaders never be satisfied?"

Atticus shrugged.

"I know only that we are here to protect the trade routes. It doesn't pay to have enemies this close to our door but I hope we can avoid conflict. I have seen more than enough of that."

Epona snorted.

"Then you had best leave our lands, Roman, or conflict is all you will get."

They locked eyes and she felt a wave of emotion course through her body. The anger and hatred she recognised, the intense feelings of fascination and attraction, were altogether unexpected. She shifted self-consciously on the spot and was pleased when Atticus looked down, clearly feeling as uncomfortable and conflicted as she was. Her brother was wearing what looked suspiciously like a smirk and she returned her attention to Atticus, who was fumbling with the leather pouch on his belt. He prised it open and reached inside. He smiled at her and slowly held out his hand.

"I believe this might be yours."

Her heart leapt as she recognised the brooch she thought she'd lost forever.

"I found it on the way back to camp. I wandered off the path in the dark and would have blundered around for ages if the moon hadn't cleared the clouds to light the way. That's when I saw it. I guessed it might be yours."

With tears beginning to well in her eyes, she scooped up the small silver horse and kissed it gently.

"It is. Thank you. You don't know how much it means to me."

Atticus nodded and looked back towards the door. As he turned to leave, Epona called out.

"Wait."

She reached for her wrist and slowly removed the simple leather bracelet that she had worn since childhood. It had seen better days but it was all she had.

"Your general leaves me with precious few possessions but it is our custom to repay acts of kindness. Take it, it's yours."

Atticus closed his hand around the unexpected gift and flashed her a self-conscious smile.

"I should go. Farewell again."

He turned and headed back across the stable, nodding at the intrigued guard as he edged out of the door. She smiled at her brother and wandered over to watch Atticus quickly crossing the square.

"It seems you may have been right about our lives being linked by the gods."

She turned the brooch absent-mindedly in her hand, unsure how she felt about the prospect of her fate being entwined with that of a Roman. And there was something else, something that she didn't yet understand. A sense that the gods might not have stumbled upon this particular Roman by chance, a feeling that their paths were destined to cross again…

ACKNOWLEDGEMENTS

Thank you for buying this book. I know just how much competition there is for your reading attention and I'm grateful to you for choosing this story over the many others that you might have selected. I trust you will find the storyline suitably rewarding and, as this is the first of a trilogy, I hope that the trials and tribulations of Atticus, Epona and Allerix might entice you back for future works. Thank you also for taking the time to read these acknowledgements. I must confess that, as a reader, I haven't always paid as much attention to these as I would have done had I known then what I do now.

It has taken the best part of three years to bring this novel to life. I couldn't have done so without the support and assistance of my daughters Kitty and Abigail. They believed in me when I made the decision to begin this journey and have supported me ever since, dealing admirably with the highs and lows of living with an aspiring author. Their patient reading or re-reading of draft material and willingness to engage in what I suspect seemed like endless discussions of plot and character development, were also invaluable. I will be forever grateful to you both. Knarlies and lots of love, Papa.

I also owe a huge debt of gratitude to Lisa Harker. In addition to her general support and encouragement, Lisa devoted a considerable amount of time to helping me edit the final draft. Her willingness to take time from her busy schedule to offer thoughts on clarity and consistency, as well as helping to polish my grammar and punctuation, was very much appreciated. Most of the time!

I'm also grateful to Annie for her support, my wider family for theirs and to ex-colleagues Jess Henry and Isobel Clements, who have had to listen to me talking about the book for almost as long as I have been writing it. Thank you.

It would also be remiss of me not to mention Estelle Thistleton, who supported me from a coaching perspective throughout my executive career. Taking my career change entirely in her stride, Estelle was on hand to offer support and wise words of guidance at the outset of my venture. Thank you for believing.

Finally, and very definitely falling into the last but not least category, to the team at Matador Publishing, especially Fern Bushnell, Philippa Iliffe and Hannah Dakin, without whom none of this would have been possible. Thank you for taking a chance on my novel and for all the professional support and advice that made it a reality.